THE BRICKMAKER'S BRIDE

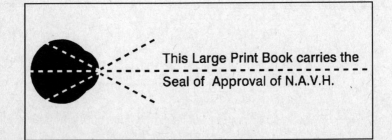

This Large Print Book carries the
Seal of Approval of N.A.V.H.

REFINED BY LOVE

THE BRICKMAKER'S BRIDE

JUDITH MILLER

THORNDIKE PRESS
A part of Gale, Cengage Learning

GALE
CENGAGE Learning·

Farmington Hills, Mich • San Francisco • New York • Waterville, Maine
Meriden, Conn • Mason, Ohio • Chicago

GALE
CENGAGE Learning®

LIBRARY OF CONGRESS CATALOGING-IN-PUBLICATION DATA

Miller, Judith, 1944–
    The brickmaker's bride : refined by love / by Judith Miller. — Large print edition.
        pages ; cm. — (Thorndike Press large print Christian fiction)
        ISBN 978-1-4104-7451-3 (hardcover) — ISBN 1-4104-7451-8 (hardcover)
    1. Brickmakers—Fiction. 2. Scots-Irish—Fiction. 3. Tygart Valley River (W. Va.)—Fiction. 4. Large type books. I. Title.
PS3613.C3858B75 2015
813'.6—dc23   2014038479

Published in 2015 by arrangement with Bethany House Publishers, a division of Baker Publishing Group

Printed in Mexico
1 2 3 4 5 6 7 19 18 17 16 15

For Jessa:
A special joy in my life.

And they said one to another, Go to, let us make brick, and burn them thoroughly. And they had brick for stone, and slime had they for morter.

Genesis 11:3 KJV

CHAPTER 1

Along the banks of the Tygart Valley River,
  West Virginia
September 1868

An unexpected rush of sentiment caught Laura Woodfield by surprise. She tightened her grip on Winston Hawkins's arm as she stepped down from the carriage. Why did entering the brickyard, even the one established by her father, provoke such an awkward show of emotion?

Winston patted her gloved hand. "You have more strength in that small hand than I would have ever imagined. Don't falter now."

"I'm sorry." Laura loosened her grasp and forced a smile. "This place holds many memories, and I haven't been down here since . . ." The final words caught in her throat.

Her father hadn't returned from the war. Still, the Tygart River continued to flow, and the seasons still changed without fail. Fall had arrived and the ancient trees that surrounded the Tygart River Valley were already bursting with color. Her father had often declared that God had given him the most beautiful place in the world to perform his labor, and Laura agreed.

While her friends had longed to move to Wheeling, Allegheny City, or Pittsburgh, Laura remained content, feeling more at home in the foothills of the Allegheny Mountains. Though she enjoyed occasional visits to the city, she was always happy to return home. Over the past week, she had wondered if her feelings about this place would change once they sold the brickyard. Surely not. Surely she would never want to leave the valley.

She removed a lace-edged handkerchief from her pocket and dabbed her eyes.

"This isn't a time for sadness. You and your mother should be delighted that someone has finally shown interest in purchasing this place." Winston's words were firm yet kind. He gestured toward the huge kilns in the distance. "It's been more than three years since the war ended. Your father would want you to ease your burdens and sell the business."

A brown curl escaped Laura's bonnet as

she tipped her head to one side. "I don't know how you can speak with such authority when even I don't know what my father would have preferred. He always spoke of this business as something that would sustain our family for the rest of our lives."

"I'm not attempting to speak for your father, Laura, but when he told you of his dreams for the future, he had no idea the country would go to war." Winston removed his black felt bowler and traced his fingers through his thick sandy-brown hair. "Where are those two Irishmen?" The corners of his lips drooped into a frown as he settled his hat back atop his ruffled hair. "I dislike tardiness. If a man can't keep on schedule, how can he expect to succeed? I've been told the Irish are prone to drinking. I do hope they're not sitting in a saloon somewhere."

"Only yesterday you told me they were excellent prospects, industrious and financially stable. Today you believe they are sitting in a saloon rather than coming here to discuss a contract?" Laura arched her eyebrows. "I wouldn't want to deal with men of ill repute, and I certainly do not wish to sell my father's business to men who won't be good employers. Father prided himself on treating his employees with respect and paying them a fair wage."

Winston straightened his shoulders and appeared to immediately grow several inches taller, his lanky frame towering over Laura's mere five foot two inches. "Forgive me. My words were spoken out of frustration, but I detest tardiness almost as much as I dislike surprises. I suppose it's the lawyer in me."

There was a strained note in his voice that deepened Laura's confusion. She wasn't sure what to expect from these prospective buyers. Were they good, industrious men who could be trusted, or were they drunken immigrants to be avoided at all costs? Surely Winston wouldn't have presented the offer to her mother if he didn't have confidence in the men.

Unable to remain still for even a moment, Winston pressed his spectacles onto the bridge of his nose. If the men didn't appear, he likely feared her mother would consider him a lack-luster representative.

Moments later he turned his head and gazed toward the road. "Ah, I believe I hear hoofbeats." He pointed toward the path leading down to the brickyard. "Here they come." Heaving a relieved sigh, Winston folded his arms across his chest. "You would think they'd urge their horses to move with a little more speed. I'm certain they can see us waiting on them."

Turning aside, Laura surveyed the vast expanse that had been her father's pride before he'd marched off to war. He'd worked so hard to create this business, determined to make it a success. And he had. Their home and financial security were a testimony to his resolve.

Even his departure had been filled with optimism. The day he and many of the local men had headed off to war, he'd spoken of the future. And his subsequent letters had revealed no fear. Instead, he wrote about the new machinery he would purchase when he returned and how he planned to expand the brickyard. Of course, none of that would happen now.

Winston placed a steadying hand on her arm. "If this is too difficult for you, please tell me. It's my intention to achieve the highest financial gain for you and your mother, but if you appear weak in front of the prospective buyers, it could hurt our chances."

She inhaled a deep breath. "I'll be fine as long as I can rely upon you to take the lead."

"Of course, my dear. That's what your mother hired me to do. I wouldn't consider anything less, but please try to appear strong — don't let them see any hint of tears."

She'd momentarily forgotten Winston was performing a duty for his client. Fortunately, he possessed no personal attachment to the brickyard and could remain firm and detached as he conducted the business at hand.

"I plan to put all of my negotiation skills to good use so that you and your mother will receive the highest possible price for the brickyard."

Laura didn't doubt his word. Winston was considered one of the finest lawyers in the area, and though there'd been no mention of fees, her mother would expect to pay Winston. The fact that he'd been courting Laura would not deter her mother. She would insist upon compensating him for his time and services.

Laura appraised the two riders as they approached. Winston had revealed the men were related, an uncle and nephew from Ireland who were in search of a fully operational brickyard — one that would turn a generous profit in a reasonable amount of time. They claimed to have had years of experience making bricks back in Ireland and believed a brickworks best suited their capabilities and would provide a sound return on their investment. Winston seemed certain the Woodfield Brickworks would meet their requirements. Laura wasn't as sure. Much depended upon what these men considered a generous profit and a reasonable amount of time.

The younger of the two men cut a fine figure, with broad shoulders and a muscular build. Laura leaned a bit closer. "The younger one looks like he's worked in a brickyard all his life."

"Either that or digging potatoes." Winston grinned and tugged on his jacket sleeves. "His physique would put most any man to shame, but I suppose he has manual labor to thank for his muscles. I do wish the buyers weren't Irish, but we've had no other offers."

The men had dismounted and were walking toward them, but Laura silently reminded herself to inquire later about Winston's dislike of the Irish. Many people still held Irish immigrants in low esteem, but she didn't realize Winston's negative feelings ran so deep.

The older man extended his hand to Winston as he neared. "Mr. Hawkins. 'Tis a fine day we have for our meeting. A wee bit of sunshine with the smell of autumn in the air." He dropped his hold on Winston's hand and nodded at Laura. " 'Tis a surprise to see a woman in the brickyard."

"Miss Woodfield is more knowledgeable about her father's brickmaking operation than I am, and it was her wish to be here." Winston turned toward Laura. "Miss Laura Woodfield, let me introduce you to Mr. Hugh Crothers and his nephew, Mr. Ewan McKay."

Laura dipped her head. "Women and children were never an unusual sight in this brickyard, Mr. Crothers. They often brought lunch to their husbands and fathers. During the summer months of my childhood, I spent as much time at my father's side as he would permit. Once I was older, I tallied the hours and pay for the workers. Of course, that was before the war."

"I might add that her mother wasn't particularly pleased," Winston put in.

Before Winston could speak any further about her mother's protestations, Laura motioned the men forward. "Shall we begin?"

Both men praised the clay deposits in the hills that surrounded the site and expressed their approval of the eight domed brick kilns, their chimneys rising to the skies. Laura escorted them past the long storage sheds constructed around the periphery of the complex, and they offered favorable smiles when Laura added that the Tygart

River gave them easy access to water for the soaking pits.

"We have access to both the railroad and the river for transporting the bricks." Laura inhaled a deep breath. "I think you'll agree it is a sound operation. The Woodfield Brickworks is well known for producing quality bricks."

"Aye, I do not doubt what you tell us, Miss Woodfield. You do have a fine brickyard. But I must be truthful with you. Ewan and I struck an agreement that we would not purchase a yard that did not have at least two VerValen machines. You have only one machine in your yard. If we're to secure the kind of contracts we want, I think we need to have the ability to produce in larger quantities."

Ewan studied the yard and then looked back at Laura. "Though I think one Ver-Valen would be enough, my uncle is firm about having two."

Laura sucked in a breath. "My father managed very well with this equipment. He paid his men a fair wage, and our family never wanted for anything. Perhaps our brickworks isn't a good fit for you gentlemen."

Winston shot her a warning look. "Please forgive Miss Woodfield. Since her father's

15

death, she has been particularly sensitive to criticism of his business." His lips curved in a sympathetic smile. "I'm sure you gentlemen understand."

"Aye." Mr. Crothers nodded, then reached into his pocket and removed a pipe. "True it is that womenfolk are better suited to tending the home fires than the kilns of a brickyard."

Angered by the condescending comment, she attempted to pull free of Winston's arm. With a quick movement, he held her hand in place and gave a slight shake of his head. She understood Winston's concern: He didn't want her to ruin the possible sale, but given the price these men had been quoted for the brickyard, they expected far too much. And they needed to be told.

She'd abide by Winston's warning and remain calm, but she didn't intend to remain silent. "If you have visited other brickyards in the area, I'm sure you've discovered there are few that have even one of the VerValen machines. I cannot imagine any brickyard owning two. It simply isn't necessary."

After a long draw on his pipe, Mr. Crothers blew several smoke rings into the air. "Fine it is this brickyard of yours, Miss Woodfield, but our Scots-Irish dreams are

16

much larger than you can imagine."

The man must be daft. Either that or he had no idea how many bricks could be molded in one day using the machine. "That one machine can mold at least fifty thousand bricks a day, Mr. Crothers. Do you believe you'll have orders that require you to surpass that quantity?"

"Is it unskilled at securing customers you think us, Miss Woodfield?" There was a lilt to his voice and a twinkle in his eye.

"Of course Miss Woodfield doesn't believe you are unskilled as brickmakers or as businessmen, do you, Laura?" There was a hint of panic in Winston's voice. He wanted to close this deal for her mother.

"No. I don't believe either of those things, but I do think their expectations are unreasonable. If they want two VerValen machines, then they'll need to purchase one themselves or look for another brickyard. They'll not secure a better yard or a better price than what we've offered."

Mr. McKay chuckled and nudged his uncle's arm. "You may have met your match, Uncle Hugh."

" 'Tis true you are as determined as any woman I have met, Miss Woodfield. But we need a contract that is a good arrangement for everyone, not just for you. Purchasing

17

an additional machine would be a huge expense."

"That's true enough, but you need not purchase a second one immediately. And certainly not until you've secured contracts that prove you have need of the additional machinery."

Mr. Crothers glanced toward the sky as a bank of gray clouds gathered. "There are some other sites we yet need to visit." He extended his hand to Winston. "We will contact you once we have made a final decision." He turned toward Laura. "If you and your mother should decide to lower your price, have your lawyer send word. My wife and her sister will be staying at the hotel in Bartlett while we continue our search."

When the two men started toward their horses, Winston stepped forward. "If it's the money to purchase machines that's holding you back from making a decision to purchase this brickyard, I believe I can be of some assistance."

The older man glanced over his shoulder. "How is that, Mr. Hawkins?"

"I'm on the board of directors at Bartlett National Bank. I think we could offer you a loan at very low interest should you wish to purchase additional equipment." Winston gestured toward the yard. "You would have more than enough collateral to secure a loan for a VerValen molding machine — even two or three, if you'd like."

Mr. McKay stopped short. "That is most kind of you, Mr. Hawkins. I believe —"

"Ewan!" Mr. Crothers glared at his nephew before tipping his hat to Laura and Winston. "Thank you for showing us the yard. When we make a decision, I will let you know."

Thunder rumbled in the distance, and Winston clasped Laura's arm as they stepped toward the carriage. "We should hurry. I don't want you to be stuck out here in a downpour."

He didn't wait for her response before grasping her elbow and urging her toward the carriage.

Once they were on their way, Laura folded her hands in her lap. "I have a feeling you're unhappy with me, but I felt compelled to speak my piece. Besides, there are no brick-yards in the area that are anywhere near the size of this one. I think Mr. Crothers is bluffing to see if we'll give in to his de-mands."

"There's nothing to say they're not look-ing elsewhere, is there? There are brickyards in many other parts of the country. They could take a train up to New York and discover many a brickyard along the Hudson River up near Haverstraw. I still hold strong hope that they'll return with an offer your mother can accept."

Laura had heard tales of the huge brick-yards on the Hudson River from her father. He had kept every news clipping and article he'd ever read about various yards and the production of bricks. She surmised Winston had learned of Haverstraw while going through her father's papers.

"They were in Pennsylvania, up near the New York border, before coming here, so I would assume they've already surveyed all of the brickyards farther north."

"You never fail to surprise me with what goes on in that head of yours." The horses, undeterred by the continuing rumbles of thunder, plodded onward.

Laura arched her brows. "I hope that doesn't mean you think women can't so much as deduce the obvious."

"Of course not. I give credit where credit is due. You're more intelligent than many of the men with whom I conduct business."

His tone was flattering, but she doubted Winston's words were entirely genuine. Few men thought women their equal when it came to business. Still, she was pleased by his compliment.

The skies continued to darken. Changing winds labored through the densely wooded hillsides, and leaves scattered to the ground in a profusion of autumn-colored confetti.

Winston's face tightened as a bolt of lightning split the sky. "We'll talk more when we get back to the house." He flicked the reins. "Come on, boys. Let's get the lady home before the rain begins."

She wondered if he hoped to convince her mother the sale was in their best interest. Would her mother agree with Winston? In any event, Laura was determined to make certain Winston understood her position. "I do hope you'll remember that the brickyard has been an important part of my life."

Winston pulled back on the reins as they came to a halt in front of the Woodfields' grand brick mansion. "I do understand, Laura, but your mother believes it's time to move forward, and I agree. This sale will give you both the freedom to do so." A groomsman scurried from the carriage house and held the reins while Winston circled the buggy to assist Laura. He tilted his head to the side and met her gaze. "I hope you don't think me unsympathetic, but I believe your mother will know what's best in this circumstance."

"We'll see. I do hope you don't plan to

21

use all of your courtroom skills in an attempt to convince her to sell." Laura extended her gloved hand and stepped down. "There are very few things I believe are worth an argument, but the brickyard is one of them. I would be extremely unhappy if the brickyard sold for less than its value."

"I think you might want to give further consideration to the burden the brickyard places on your mother and consider bowing to her wishes." Together they continued up the front steps. "The final decision belongs to your mother, so I hope you won't hold it against me when I advise her to sell to these men." Winston gave her a sideways glance. "After all, there have been no other offers."

Laura stepped into the foyer and met his gaze. "True enough, but Mother values my opinion, and I hope that after you plead your case, she'll take my advice."

CHAPTER 2

Lightning cracked open the sky, and sheets of rain spilled forth as Winston paced back and forth in front of the library fireplace. He stopped periodically and glanced in Laura's direction. His pleading looks wouldn't be enough to change her mind, but she didn't interrupt as he set forth the terms of Mr. Crothers's offer to her mother.

When he completed his final line of reasoning, he heaved a sigh and sat down opposite Laura's mother. "I hope you'll consider dropping your price somewhat to meet the expectations of these men, Mrs. Woodfield. I feel certain we'll not receive a full-price offer."

"You must forgive me if I don't immediately agree." Laura's mother refreshed her cup of tea and added a spoonful of sugar. "During our marriage, Isaiah and I made all of our important decisions together. Now that I no longer have his counsel, I feel the need to be cautious — especially with such a major decision. I'm sure Laura concurs; don't you, dear?"

"Indeed I do, Mother." From all appearances, her mother wasn't ready to sell the business. Winston had waged a good argument, but her mother wasn't going to be rushed into a hasty decision.

Winston leaned forward and rested his arms across his thighs. "I understand that your husband's death has forced you into an undesired position of responsibility. That's why I had hoped to ease your burden and handle this matter for you."

"That's most kind, Winston, but I'd prefer to spend some time in prayer and see what the Lord would have me do. I'm sure if these men are the ones who should own the business, the decision will become clear to all of us."

An hour later, Laura escorted Winston down the hallway to the massive front door hewn from black walnut trees on their own land. He'd waited for the rain to abate before taking his leave and had used a good portion of the time to urge her mother to move forward with the sale, but her mother had remained steadfast in her decision. However, when Laura returned to the library, she was surprised to see her mother pacing the same length of carpet Winston had tread only a short time earlier.

"Between you and Winston, we may need to purchase a new floor covering before year's end."

"W-what?" Her mother blinked and looked down at the black-and-gold floral-patterned carpet before lifting her gaze.

"You appear worried. Are you having second thoughts now that you've asked for additional time to make a decision?" Laura grasped her mother's hand and gently walked her to one of the leather-covered chairs her father had chosen for his library.

"Though I hate to admit it, I suppose I am. Winston did make some valid points." She lowered herself into the chair and scooted back until her feet barely touched the floor. "I never have liked these chairs. They're far too big."

"We could replace them," Laura offered. "If we removed them and repositioned the desk, we could place a settee near the window. You'd have a lovely view of the foothills and wonderful light to sit in here and read on winter days."

"You may be right. I'll think about it. We could purchase something that would match the new carpet you think we may need." Her mother grinned. "What did you think of Mr. Crothers and Mr. McKay? If I'd gone along with you to the brickyard, perhaps it would have been easier for me to make a decision. I wouldn't mind selling for a little less than the worth of the business if they are honest men and will provide jobs for our workers who were fortunate enough to return from the war."

"I wasn't particularly drawn to Mr. Crothers. He appears to be far more interested in excessive profits than in helping others. His nephew seemed to have a kinder bearing, but I believe Mr. Crothers holds the purse strings, so I think he will be the one who decides whether they will buy." Laura patted her mother's hand. "Mr. Crothers has high expectations. I don't believe he'll find any brickyard that will meet his ambitious dreams."

Her mother downed the remains of her tea and wrinkled her nose. "The tea is cold."

"Shall I ask Catherine to brew a fresh pot?" Laura reached for a bell to summon the maid.

"No. I believe I've had —" A loud knock at the front door interrupted her mother's response. "Who could that be? Do you suppose Winston forgot something and has returned?"

"I don't know what he could have forgot-

ten. I'll go to the door. Catherine is down-stairs, so I doubt she heard the knock."
Laura hurried down the hallway. As she pulled open the heavy door, her breath caught and she took a backward step.

"Good afternoon, Miss Woodfield. Sure I am that you weren't expecting to see me again today."

Laura bobbed her head. "That would be a correct assumption, Mr. McKay. What brings you to Woodfield Manor?" She made an attempt to see beyond Ewan McKay's broad shoulders.

"I'm alone, if that's what you're trying to discover, miss." He chuckled and stood to one side. "I hope you do not think me overly forward in making such a visit by myself, but I hoped to speak with you and your mother in private." He hesitated a moment. "Without your lawyer or my uncle present. Would that be possible, miss?"

"I believe it would, Mr. McKay. Why don't you step into the parlor, and I'll invite my mother to join us."

Laura hurried back to the library with a muddle of questions suddenly racing through her mind. Why would Mr. McKay return without his uncle? And why did he want to speak to them without Winston present? Did he hope to strike some far-fetched bargain and impress his uncle? If that was the case, he might as well head back to the hotel in Bartlett. She'd not be bamboozled by those twinkling eyes or that broad smile of his.

Mr. McKay was standing looking out the east windows when Laura and her mother stepped into the parlor. He turned and offered a slight bow as Laura introduced her mother. " 'Tis a true pleasure, Mrs. Woodfield. I hope you'll forgive me for arriving without a proper invitation."

The older woman glanced at her daughter. "We don't stand on a great deal of ceremony here at Woodfield Manor, Mr. McKay. My husband always preferred to have me run a more informal household." She glanced toward one of the chairs. "Do be seated. Would you like a cup of tea? Or coffee, perhaps?"

"No thank you, ma'am. This is surely a lovely home you have here. I counted at least five chimneys as I came up the path. I'm guessing the brick used to build this house was fired in your own brickyard . . . am I right?"

"Yes. My husband was involved in every step of the construction, but we chose the site and decided upon the plans together."

"And a better site you could not have

chosen. What a lovely view you have of the valley and foothills. The green of this valley reminds me of home."

Mrs. Woodfield nodded, and Laura could see the distant look in her eyes. They'd lived in a nearby smaller frame house for many years — until her mother had conceded to Mr. Woodfield's desire to build her a fine brick home. *"It isn't good business for the owner of a brickyard to live in a frame house."* That had been the argument that finally won her mother's agreement. Once she'd agreed, hired men set to work clearing the hilltop and digging the basement. Each day Laura and her mother had gone to the site and watched the house steadily rise up and take shape.

"From where in Ireland do you hail, Mr. McKay?" Mother settled on the divan and motioned Laura to join her.

"I'm from Ulster, a province in northern Ireland. Some folks in this country refer to us as Scots-Irish or Ulster-Irish. Perhaps you've heard the expression?"

"I've heard the term Scots-Irish. There are many who are known as Scots-Irish in this area, Mr. McKay." Laura settled on the divan beside her mother. "I've never understood if they were Scottish or Irish."

"I suppose it depends on who's doing the

explaining." Ewan's lips curved in a generous smile. "We're descendants of the Scotsmen who were sent to Ireland when King James I took the English throne back in 1603. The good king planned to bring the Irish under his control, so he decided to colonize northern Ireland with immigrants of the Protestant faith, mostly from Scotland, but some from England and even a few from Germany and France. The king's idea did not turn out as he planned. Instead, there has been nothing but turmoil and fighting between the north and the south." He cleared his throat. "I suppose you could liken the bloodshed of good men there to what you've suffered here in America."

Mrs. Woodfield reached for her knitting in a basket beside the divan. "The bloodshed would be the same, but our causes were different, Mr. McKay."

"Aye, 'tis true, but I fear the outcomes will prove much the same. Wounds remain open, and hatred exists for far too many years after the sword is laid aside." He inhaled a slow breath. "But that is not what I've come to discuss with you."

Mrs. Woodfield wrapped a strand of dark-blue yarn around her knitting needle. "I am sure it's the brickyard that brings you back, is it not?"

"It is. And I'm hoping I can trust you ladies to keep this matter in confidence. There would be no pacifying my uncle's anger should he discover what I'm about to say, but I consider it my duty as a man and as a Christian to speak with you."

In spite of the afternoon's warmth, Laura's skin prickled. She didn't want him to pass along clandestine comments that might anger Mr. Crothers. "So long as what you tell us will not bring trouble to our doorstep, Mr. McKay."

"I would not do such a thing, miss. I came here to tell you that my uncle is a man who looks out for himself above all else. He knows that you have a fine brickyard and that you're offering to sell at a fair price. We've looked at yards from New York to Virginia and back again. It's your brickyard and this valley that impress him. Do not be deceived by his blustering. He'll pay what you're asking if you hold your ground."

"And why have you told us this, Mr. McKay?" Mrs. Woodfield's knitting needles clicked in a steady rhythm while she spoke.

"Because I was taught to follow the teachings of the Bible. My own mother was particularly fond of sharing the passages that state we should look after widows and orphans and be honest in our dealings with others." He swiped several strands of chestnut-brown hair off his forehead. "I think because she'd been unfairly treated by our landlord after my da died."

"And has she come to West Virginia with you?" When Ewan didn't immediately answer, Mrs. Woodfield looked up from her knitting. "Your mother — is she at the hotel in Bartlett?"

"Nay. She died a year after my da. I have Da to thank for my training in the brickyards. I've never met another with such skill." Ewan cleared his throat. "My mum's been gone for five years and my da for six. We were told it was consumption that took the both of them. My sisters are still in Ireland with some distant relatives, but I hope to bring them here once my uncle makes his decision about the brickyard. My oldest sister, Rose, and I have been caring for the twins since our mum passed. The four of us had never been separated until I sailed. I miss them very much."

"And how old are your sisters, Mr. Mc-Kay?" Once again the older woman's knitting needles clacked their familiar beat.

Mr. McKay straightened and smiled. "Rose is sixteen, soon to turn seventeen. She's a real beauty, with dark hair and blue eyes. Ainslee and Adaira are twins. They'll

soon be twelve. Rose has her hands full trying to keep them out of mischief." He
chuckled. "Good little lasses they are, but
they do enjoy their pranks as much as any
lad I've ever known."

Laura smiled and glanced at her mother.
"I think my mother will agree that girls can
engage in as much mischief as boys. Isn't
that right, Mother?"

"Indeed, it was true of you, my dear.
Keeping you out of the woods and away
from the brickyard proved a fruitless endeavor." She hesitated a moment. "I'm sure
you look forward to being rejoined with
your family as soon as possible, Mr. McKay.
Is Mr. Crothers eager to bring other family
members to America, as well?"

"If you're meaning will he hurry to make
a deal on the brickyard because of his family back home, the answer would be no.
There are two things that concern Uncle
Hugh. One is holding on to his money, and
the other is keeping his wife content. Aunt
Margaret tends to be a wee bit demanding
at times." He grinned. "I'll say no more on
that matter."

"Then let us hope that Mrs. Crothers
convinces her husband they should remain
here in West Virginia."

Mr. McKay stood. "I should be on my

way. I said I was going for a ride, but I'm thinking my uncle will expect me to return soon. I'll do my best to convince him, but mind what I've told you, ladies. Hold to your price. Don't let the lawyer rush you, either. My uncle will come around."

After escorting Mr. McKay to the door, Laura returned to the parlor. "What do you think, Mother?"

The older woman continued her knitting. "I think he is a very handsome man with a good heart. I believe the Lord sent him to reveal what we should do, and I plan to heed Mr. McKay's advice."

Laura arched her brows. "But I thought you were going to pray before arriving at a final decision."

Her mother stood and grasped Laura's hand. "One need not be on her knees to seek the Lord, my dear. I was silently praying the entire time Mr. McKay was here with us."

Hoping to release the tension that clutched her midsection, Laura expelled a deep sigh. Isn't this what she wanted? A short time ago, she'd told her mother the same thing. But now fear assailed her. Could they believe anything Mr. McKay had told them? Should they trust the Irishman and his promises, or heed the advice of

Winston Hawkins, a highly respected lawyer and pillar of the community? She wasn't sure, but it seemed her mother had no doubt.

And her mother would make the final decision.

CHAPTER 3

Ewan slid his foot into the stirrup and mounted the gray gelding, one of the riding horses his uncle had purchased in Pennsylvania when they began their search for a brickyard. Because Ewan was the only one who ever rode the horse, he'd come to consider the animal his own, though his uncle would reject such a notion. After all, the bill of sale was made out to Hugh Crothers, not Ewan McKay. And unlike Ewan's father, Clive, Hugh held fast to his belongings.

Many a night Ewan had grieved for both of his parents. Uncle Hugh and Aunt Margaret were no substitute for his loving mum and da. Over the years, Ewan had often wondered how his da and uncle could have been raised by the same parents. Though the brothers bore a strong physical appearance, the resemblance stopped there. Ewan's father had been an honest, upright man — admired by those who knew him. The opposite could be said of Uncle Hugh.

That knowledge had weighed heavily upon Ewan while wrestling with his decision to sail with his relatives. However, tales of opportunities awaiting immigrants in America had eventually tipped the scales in favor of the voyage. He wanted a better life for his sisters, and coming to America seemed the path to achieving that goal. Although he'd be tied to Uncle Hugh and Aunt Margaret for a few years, the end result would be worth the sacrifice. At least that was his prayer.

The horse's hooves sucked at the mud created by the earlier cloudburst and slowed their pace. The seldom-used path leading from the road to Woodfield Manor could use a bit of attention. If it belonged to him, he'd use lammies, the bricks distorted from too much heat in the kiln, to pave the area leading from the front of the house to the road. No doubt Aunt Maggie would insist upon first-grade bricks to pave the driveway once she was settled in the manor.

He glanced over his shoulder. From a distance, the chimneys looked like sentinels perched atop the roof of Woodfield Manor. Would that fine home soon be known as Crothers Manor, or would Aunt Maggie decide upon a name reminiscent of her Irish heritage? Perhaps she'd christen it Margaret's Mansion. He chuckled. Unless someone convinced her the idea was in poor taste, naming the house after herself was certainly a possibility.

More important, where would Miss Laura Woodfield make her home? The young woman had captured his interest when they first met, and after visiting with her this afternoon, he longed to know more about her. She possessed a charm and substance that went beyond her outward appearance, and the fact that she'd actually spent time in the brickyard intrigued him.

With her small frame, she couldn't have trucked loads of clay or pushed hackbarrows of molded brick. The men who performed those jobs needed muscles the size of melons. Still, the fact that she'd acted as a timekeeper and maintained the books revealed a bit about her. Would she have been as interested if her father had owned some other business? A dry goods store or a coal mine?

"Where have ya been, Ewan? I expected you back an hour ago." Waiting outside as Ewan approached the hotel, his uncle pointed to the mud caked on the horse's hooves and fetlocks. "Is it through trenches of mud you've taken my horse? Just look at the mess you've made of him."

"I'd forgotten how much rain fell earlier in the day and went off to see a bit of the countryside. I'll see to the horse right away."

His uncle grunted and shook his head. "Take him to the livery and tell the boy to take care of him. Margaret and Kathleen have been waiting to go to supper. Thanks to you, neither of them is in good humor."

"I'll be sure to apologize. Had I known of Aunt Margaret's plans, I would have returned before now. If it will help, you can escort them to the dining room, and I'll meet you there after I wash up." With a light nudge to the horse's shanks, he turned the gelding toward the barn.

"Mark my words, there's more than arriving late for dinner you'll be answering for." His uncle's warning bore a sharp edge that created a sense of foreboding.

Other than being late, he couldn't imagine what he'd done to anger Aunt Margaret. He'd not seen her since breakfast. His thoughts raced around like the thoroughbreds Uncle Hugh used to wager on at the track back home. When Ewan finally entered the dining room a short time later, he hadn't arrived at any conclusion.

From the dour look on his aunt's face, he

wouldn't have to wait much longer. She appeared poised to attack. Hoping to appear unruffled, he stood behind his chair and smiled. "Uncle Hugh tells me you ladies were waiting for me to return. I am very sorry. I did not realize we would be eating supper so early."

Aunt Margaret waved her fan toward his chair. "Sit down, Ewan. We'd like to order our meal."

The moment he was seated, a waitress scurried to their table and announced the evening specials of roasted pork or fried chicken. After she'd stepped away from the table, Ewan's aunt leaned toward him. "When your uncle returned from the brickyard, I inquired how soon we would be moving, and what do you think he told me, Ewan?" Her lips curled in a sneer.

"I think he told you that he had not made a decision because the price was more than he wished to pay and because he wanted at least two VerValen machines." Ewan arched his brows and forced a lilt to his voice. "Is that not correct, Uncle Hugh?"

"Aye, that much is true, but I also tried my best to have the lawyer negotiate a better price from the widow Woodfield. And what did you do, my boy?"

Before Ewan could so much as pour

cream into his coffee cup, his aunt jabbed him with her elbow. "You took sides with those women against your own uncle."

"I wasn't taking sides so much as stating that believers should follow the teachings of our Lord and treat widows and orphans with kindness and generosity. I know my mother would have appreciated a touch of generosity from strangers when she was caring for all of us after Da's death."

Margaret's lips tightened in a thin line, and she glowered at Ewan. "I may not be a widow, but I've suffered my share. More than most, thanks to your uncle's bad habits."

Kathleen squirmed in her chair. Like Ewan, the topic of Aunt Margaret's suffering and Uncle Hugh's gambling created an air of discomfort.

Hugh's thin lips flicked beneath his dark, drooping mustache. "Ya need not blame all your suffering on me, Maggie. 'Twas the effects of the potato famine that nearly robbed you of your life, not me. After two generations, your family still has not recovered."

Maggie squared her shoulders. "That may be true, but your gambling has robbed me, as well, and you know that's the truth. We'd have been able to come to America long ago if you wouldn't have spent your time and

41

money at the racetrack and local pubs. I'd still be the woman you married had ya kept your money in your pocket instead of running off to the gaming tables and racetrack whenever I turned my back."

Hugh patted the pocket of his wool jacket. "You best remember that I wouldn't be sitting here with money if it weren't for my winnings at the racetrack." Hugh motioned to the waitress and lifted his coffee cup.

Ewan and Kathleen were forced to listen as the couple resumed their ongoing quarrel. While Ewan sympathized with the horrors his aunt had experienced during her lifetime, many other people had gone through worse and hadn't become greedy and demanding. Yet he couldn't deny that Uncle Hugh's behavior would be enough to set any woman on edge.

Aunt Margaret's childhood deprivations had formed her into a covetous, selfish adult, and Uncle Hugh's gambling had reinforced her fears and stinginess. She constantly harped about his gambling, but it hadn't stopped him. Instead, he was willing to take the tongue-lashings and abide her greedy nature because he'd come to believe it justified his own behavior. Unfortunately, their abhorrent conduct spread like a contagion and contaminated most folks

42

who crossed their path.

"I thought it was Ewan you had a quarrel with, but it seems you'd rather hash over the past with me."

Ewan cast a glance across the table. Though his uncle was eager to deflect his wife's ire, Ewan didn't miss the glimmer of fear lurking in the older man's eyes. Did he worry Ewan would give away his secret, or was it only this morning's meeting at the brickyard that caused him concern?

Margaret waited until after the waitress had refilled her husband's cup and stepped away from the table. "I was talking to Ewan before the conversation took an unexpected turn."

"Aye. A turn that went down a mighty crooked path. As if you planned it that way. Eh, Ewan?" Hugh cocked his left eyebrow and leaned back in his chair.

"I planned nothing, Uncle. I do not think Aunt Margaret will forget to ask me whatever it is she wants to know about this morning's dealings."

The aroma of roasted pork filled the air as the waitress set their plates in front of them. Ewan's stomach rumbled, a reminder that he hadn't eaten since morning, He nodded to his uncle. "Will you be offering thanks, or shall I?"

"I'll pray. I'm hungry and your prayers go on too long. Besides, I doubt you'll have much to be thankful for once your aunt finishes with you."

Ewan bowed his head but didn't miss the fact that his uncle had picked up his fork before he offered a one-sentence prayer.

His uncle jabbed a piece of meat. "See how short a prayer can be, Ewan? Doesn't take more than a few words to bless the food." He glanced at his wife. "Did ya have nothing more to say to Ewan about the brickyard, Maggie?"

Perhaps Ewan had misread his uncle's earlier look, for he didn't appear fearful at the moment. Instead, he seemed to relish the fact that he'd be an onlooker rather than the recipient of Aunt Maggie's attention.

Maggie buttered a piece of warm bread, then placed the knife across her plate. She was like a hawk circling its prey, waiting for the precise moment and taking pleasure in the hunt. "From what your uncle tells me, I believe you are an extremely ungrateful young man, Ewan. We paid for your passage to this country, we've supported you since we arrived, and your uncle is doing every-thing possible to help you establish a new life here. You did say that was what you wanted, didn't you?"

"Aye, you know it is. I came to be Uncle Hugh's partner in a brickmaking business and provide a better life for my sisters."

"And how is it you plan to become an owner when you thwart your uncle's negotiations? It appears you're more interested in impressing the Woodfields than in striking a deal." She wagged her head back and forth. "To think you would take sides against your own kin makes my blood run cold."

"Is it going against my kin to speak the truth, Aunt Margaret? I do not think the Crothers or McKays want to be known as liars or cheats in their new homeland. Do you not see that the best way to build a business is with honesty and fairness?" He waved toward his uncle. "Tell her, Uncle Hugh. The price they were asking was fair, was it not?"

"Aye, I suppose it was, but I'm a man who enjoys bartering and making a deal."

Ewan bit back the words he longed to speak: the secret he'd learned while crossing the sea. He'd promised to keep his lips sealed, and he would keep his word. But he would not become a party to cheating anyone.

"It's not your money that's crossing hands, is it?" Margaret speared several green

45

beans with her fork. "You owe your uncle money, and you need to do as he tells you."

Ewan inhaled a deep breath. "I do owe him money, but that does not mean I'll compromise on this point. I'm sure I could find work as a brick burner and eventually repay him."

"But you'd never earn enough to bring your sisters over here, now would ya?" Margaret glared across the table.

"We all need each other, and arguing won't settle things. There's been enough talk for tonight." Hugh nodded to his wife. "Ewan and I will settle our differences in private." He signaled to the waitress. "I could eat a piece of that apple pie."

Maggie pushed away from the table. "You enjoy your pie, Hugh. Kathleen and I are going upstairs so you and Ewan can settle your differences." She stood and rested her palm on her husband's shoulder. "Just see to it that any differences settled between the two of you don't interfere with a move into the Woodfield Manor by the end of the month."

Hugh's lips tightened and caused his mustache to droop more than usual. "You're hovering over me like a black shadow, Maggie. You need to remember that purchasing a quality brickyard is more important than any house. I haven't made a final decision to buy from Mrs. Woodfield, so don't be making plans to move into her house just yet."

Margaret squared her shoulders and squeezed his upper arm. "I'm tired of traveling, and this is where I want to settle. There's not a man alive who can strike a better bargain than you if there's no one interfering in the process." She cast a warning look at Ewan. "I just want to make certain you understand my position before I go upstairs."

Hugh glanced over his shoulder. "Aye, and now that you've said your piece, will ya let Ewan and me discuss our differences?"

"No need to speak in such a gruff tone. I said I was going upstairs." Margaret motioned to her sister. "Come along, Kathleen. Let's give the men their privacy."

The two women wove between the tables, with Kathleen following close on Margaret's heels. Hugh nodded toward them. "Ya'd never know they were sisters. O'course Kathleen is nearer your age than Maggie's, so I guess she's a wee bit afraid of Margaret. Still, the differences between the two are immense. Kathleen's quiet as a mouse while my Margaret's as loud as a yapping dog. Took me a lot of years to abide her ways,

47

but I understand she means well, and I've learned to make allowances because of her childhood. Besides, I'm not the easiest man to live with, so she has a right to complain from time to time. I wouldn't want anyone ever to cause strife between us." He leaned forward and rested his arms on the table. "You understand what I'm sayin', boy?"

Ewan stared at his uncle. Of course he understood. Because of Uncle Hugh's gambling, the couple had separated more times than he could count on one hand. A year ago he'd given his solemn oath that those days were behind him. If Aunt Margaret ever discovered that a portion of the funds to finance their voyage and to purchase the brickmaking business had been won at the racetrack and gaming tables during that year, Uncle Hugh would never hear the end of it.

And that wasn't the worst of it. When Uncle Hugh had been in his cups during their voyage, he'd confided why he'd been in such a rush to leave Coleraine, and now he spoke of it again. "It was a piece of luck that came my way that day, and I took full advantage. That fellow could afford to lose. He didn't fool me none. He was one of them wealthy Montclairs. He thought he knew how to play a game of cards, but he'd never come up against the likes of me. I know more tricks than any of those fancy fellows. I liked the idea of sitting opposite him — just the two of us — and taking his money every hand. None of the locals had enough money to wager against him."

"You did." Ewan lifted his coffee cup and downed the remaining cold liquid.

"Aye, but that's different. I'd been saving from all my gaming over the past year so I'd be ready when an opportunity came along. And thanks be to me, I say. We'd still be sitting in Coleraine if I hadn't been saving my winnings."

"And thanks be to the Lord that Lyall Montclair was a poor shot or you'd be under the ground."

"He couldn't aim that pistol any better than he could play cards." Hugh guffawed. "Glad I am that he didn't have my name and we were able to set sail two days later. He's probably still lookin' for me."

Ewan shook his head. "What you did was wrong, Uncle Hugh."

"What's the matter with you, boy? With Montclair's money and power, the law would have taken his side against me, and you know that to be true." He slapped his palm on the table. "All of that is behind us now, and I don't want you talking about it any more. There's no good that can come of telling Margaret or anyone else. Understand?"

Lying, keeping secrets, and finding excuses for his unscrupulous behavior had become a way of life for Uncle Hugh. He enjoyed this game of cat and mouse, and Ewan doubted the man would ever change. He also doubted Lyall Montclair had been dealt even one fair hand of cards.

"Well?" His uncle nudged him. "You gonna answer or keep staring at me like a dead mackerel?"

"I would never intentionally cause trouble for anyone, but I told you back then and I'm telling you now, I won't lie or cheat to keep your secrets. I never wanted to hear any of it."

"I know ya didn't." His uncle wiped his napkin across his mouth. "If I hadn't had a wee bit too much to drink, I would have kept me trap shut. Would have been better for the both of us."

"Aye, but you didn't." Ewan leaned back in his chair. Maybe this was the right time to press his uncle to sign the papers. "What about the brickyard? Aunt Margaret made it clear she's set on staying here, and I don't think we'll find a better place. I think you should pay what they're asking and sign the papers as soon as possible. We need to hire men and begin digging clay before winter sets in or we won't be able to make bricks come spring. We'll lose a year of production if we wait much longer. You and I both know it, and so does that lawyer. He's not going to budge."

"If I pay full price and this doesn't work, it's gonna be on you. If this turns out bad, there may not be a racetrack or gaming table to make up my losses. You a good enough brick man to earn my money back for me?"

"If you listen to me, you'll see more profit than you're expecting. If not, I can't promise what will happen."

Hugh's brow furrowed and he narrowed his eyes. "Can't say as I like giving you so much control."

"It's not my money at stake, but my future depends upon making the yard a success. I'm giving you my word that I'll do everything I can to make the company the best brickyard in all of the state." Ewan hiked a shoulder. "You have my word. There's nothing more I can offer."

"Make it the best brickyard in all the country, not just this state." Hugh grinned and extended his hand. "We'll go and see the lawyer in the morning and sign the

51

papers."

Ewan shook his uncle's hand, pleased to have the matter settled. No doubt, Aunt Margaret and Aunt Kathleen would be knocking on the front door of Woodfield Manor tomorrow afternoon. He hoped Margaret would extend the widow and her daughter every courtesy. Even with the help of servants, moving all of their belongings from the mansion would take time.

And Aunt Margaret wasn't known for her patience.

CHAPTER 4

Laura greeted her mother as she entered the dining room. "Sorry to keep you waiting." She touched her fingers to the soft brown curls that brushed the neckline of her lavender poplin walking dress. "My hair wouldn't cooperate this morning. I don't know who became more exasperated, me or Sally."

Her mother chuckled. "I would imagine Sally, since she was the one trying to tame those curls of yours. Unfortunately, it appears your chignon is not going to hold tight, but let's eat breakfast. Sally can attend to your hair later."

Catherine bustled into the dining room. "How would you like your eggs, Miss Laura?"

"No eggs this morning. I'm not particularly hungry, but I'll have one of your biscuits with strawberry preserves."

The maid tsked and shook her head.

"That's not a fit breakfast, Miss Laura." Catherine looked at Mrs. Woodfield for affirmation.

"Catherine's right. You need a more substantial breakfast, my dear." Mrs. Woodfield looked at the maid. "We'll both have poached eggs and sausage."

"No sausage. I'll eat an egg, but no sausage. I didn't sleep well, and I have the beginning of a headache."

Mrs. Woodfield leaned to the side and placed her palm on Laura's forehead. "You don't feel warm. I do hope you're not coming down with something."

"I didn't sleep well, that's all. I couldn't stop thinking about Mr. McKay and his advice. The entire visit seems so odd, doesn't it? I don't discount that he appeared sincere in his desire to be fair, but going behind his uncle's back doesn't seem right. I wonder if it's some sort of plan they've concocted between themselves."

"I think you're misjudging Mr. McKay, though his advice was a bit odd. Winston will be upset that I'm not taking his advice, but I've decided that if the Lord wants us to sell to Mr. Crothers, we'll receive some sort of sign. Something that will give me a feeling of certainty before I agree to sell." Her mother picked up a small china pitcher

54

and poured cream into her coffee. "This won't be the first time Winston and I have disagreed. He's a good lawyer, but a bit too pushy. If you decide he's the man you want to marry, make certain you don't let him control you overmuch."

For most of her life, Laura's mother had been easily swayed — especially by men. She had always bowed to her husband's decisions. That's what society expected. Women weren't considered bright enough to understand business or politics, and if they had an opinion regarding such matters, they were expected to keep it to themselves.

Mrs. Woodfield had held fast to those rules until the war. When her husband marched off to battle, she'd been forced to take charge. The change had proved difficult, and Laura had encouraged her mother and praised each decision. As time passed, her mother fully embraced her new role, and it appeared she wasn't prepared to relinquish her decisions to anyone except the Lord.

There was a touch of irony in her mother's cautionary remark. "We're not yet engaged, so I don't think you need to worry about marriage any time in the near future."

Mrs. Woodfield arched her brows. "I

believe Winston has already made up his mind that you're the woman he wants at his side. No doubt you can expect a marriage proposal very soon. You offer what he wants in a wife."

"And what is that, Mother?" She arched her brows. Had Winston already expressed his desire to propose? Had he spoken to her mother?

"You'd be the perfect wife to aid him in his political ambitions. You possess the poise and charm to connect with voters. And since he doesn't want —"

Laura held up one hand. "Let's not discuss this now, Mother. I fear my headache will worsen, and I'm expected at the orphanage this morning."

"I'm sorry, my dear. I didn't mean to rattle on." Her mother finished her eggs and took a final sip of coffee. "It's a beautiful morning. I thought we might sit on the porch. The fresh air might help your headache, and I could use your assistance. Our Ladies of the Union group has decided we should begin meeting again. We've met only a few times since the end of the war, and we'd like to resume regular meetings so we can serve some charitable needs in the area."

Laura followed her mother to the front porch. "I do believe it's time for a new name, as well."

Her mother lowered herself into one of the cushioned willow chairs. "Perhaps, but I don't believe you can fault us too much. There are several Southern states that haven't yet been readmitted to the Union. You'll recall that our neighbor, Virginia, is among those states."

"Of course I do, Mother, but you don't need to wait until every state is readmitted before you change the name of your organization. Since the club was initially organized to make quilts and knit socks for the soldiers, perhaps now you could turn your attention to the needs of those soldiers' widows who remain in the area. I'm sure there are many who continue to struggle. If the ladies need any further ideas, you can let them know that assistance is always needed at the orphanage."

"I know helping the orphans gives you both solace and pleasure, dear, but most of the ladies in our group don't possess the physical stamina necessary for such work."

Laura didn't miss the pity that shone in her mother's eyes as she reached forward to pat Laura's hand. "There are many things they could do that wouldn't require physical strength. I doubt it would tax the ladies to read a book to the children."

"That's true enough, but the noise and activity at the orphanage would surely prove too much for us. The younger ladies should fill that void." Her lips curved in a weak smile. "Besides, I think our organization is seeking fund-raising and sewing projects rather than volunteer work. Enid Matheson thought we should start a movement to raise money for a new state capitol building. She says that renting the Linsly School is demeaning and we need a beautiful structure that will rival those of other states."

"And what do you think about Enid's suggestion?" Laura turned her rocking chair away from the sun before sitting down. "Are you interested in organizing fund-raisers for our lawmakers?"

"Enid isn't fooling me. Her husband, Hubert, hopes to win a seat in the legislature, and she'll do anything or use anyone to make sure it happens, including our Ladies of the Union group." Her mother sniffed. "I find her behavior shameful."

"Now, Mother, you ought not jump to conclusions. I've heard others say that construction of a new capitol building would not only help beautify Wheeling, but would also provide work for men in need of employment."

"*Pshaw.* That's a lot of political puffery, if

you ask me. Just take a look around Bartlett and note the lack of able-bodied men. Our men who didn't die in the war came home injured. Most of them can't perform the jobs they had before the war."

"That may be a bit of an exaggeration, Mother, but I do understand your point. I think if you present your concerns with some actual facts and figures, the ladies will rally behind you rather than Enid." Giving a slight push with her foot, Laura set the rocking chair into motion. "Perhaps Winston could help gather some figures for you."

"I suppose, but I may be capable of doing that myself. I can go into town and speak with folks on my own. I'm sure the mayor can help."

Laura shaded her eyes and gazed toward the road. "Yes, but isn't the mayor a friend of Hubert Matheson?"

"That's true. He's probably not a good choice." Her mother twisted in her chair. "Someone's coming. It's early for a caller. I hope there isn't some sort of trouble."

"I think it's Winston." Laura squinted and stared for a moment longer. "Yes, it's him. I wonder what brings him out our way."

Mrs. Woodfield rose and stepped to the porch railing. "He must have news regarding the brickyard. No proper gentleman would call this early in the day unless it was a matter of importance."

Laura couldn't disagree with her mother's assessment. Winston was a proper gentleman. Wearing his tan cutaway tailcoat and tall black riding books of polished leather, he made a striking appearance. Up close, Winston wasn't the most attractive man she'd ever met, but he possessed a debonair charm that proved difficult to resist.

"Good morning, ladies. A fine morning for a ride, wouldn't you say?" Winston dismounted and tied the horse's reins to the cast-iron hitching post. "I do apologize for the early morning visit, but I believe you'll forgive me when you see what I have." He reached inside his breast pocket and withdrew a folded paper. Waving it toward them, he climbed the porch steps. "This, ladies, is a contract of sale for Woodfield Brickworks."

Clasping a hand to her bodice, Mrs. Woodfield lowered herself into the wicker chair. "So soon?" Her surprise was quickly replaced by a desire for information. "At what price? Did you bargain with them and lower the price without gaining my permission, Winston? If you did, I won't sign those papers."

60

"If you'll give me a moment, I'll explain." He nodded toward the door. "Shall we go inside, where you can more closely examine the contract?"

Laura leaned close to her mother's ear. "Looks as if the Lord has given you that sign you asked for."

"We'll see. I haven't read the contract," her mother said.

The three of them gathered in the parlor, and once they were seated, Winston detailed the terms of the contract. When he had finished, he leaned back in his chair and smiled. "Everything you asked for, Mrs. Woodfield. Mr. Crothers met your price and wishes to take possession as soon as possible."

"Just what was it that convinced him, Winston? When you left here yesterday, I didn't believe he would meet my price. Something must have happened. Is there something in the contract you're not telling me?"

"Of course not. I'm your lawyer, Mrs. Woodfield. It's my duty to protect your interests. While I'd like to tell you it was my negotiating skill that convinced Mr. Crothers, that wouldn't be true. I believe his nephew is the one who convinced him that they would lose a year of production if they'd waited much longer. Mr. McKay wants to take possession so they can begin digging clay."

Mrs. Woodfield extended her hand. "Let me read the contract." When Winston didn't immediately hand it to her, she waved her hand. "You don't expect me to sign without reading it, do you?"

Laura grinned. "You might as well give it to her. Arguing will only prolong things."

After a firm nod, he handed the papers to her mother. Arms folded across his chest, his gaze shifted between the clock and Laura's mother.

When she had turned to the last page, he leaned forward. "Ready to sign?"

"I believe I am. Before giving them the deed to the land and bill of sale for the equipment, make certain they've paid the full amount. Have them count it out in front of you. I don't want to be cheated."

"Rest assured that I will require payment in full from Mr. Crothers and I'll immediately deposit the payment into your account at the bank. I do hope you know that you can trust me to protect your interests, Mrs. Woodfield."

"He's right, isn't he, Laura? If we can't trust Winston, who can we trust?" Rising from her chair, Laura's mother crossed the room and sat down at the hand-carved maple writing desk. She dipped her pen into the ink, signed her name, and blotted her signature before handing the document back to Winston. "Thank you for your assistance, Winston. And do tell Mr. Crothers and Mr. McKay that if they have any questions regarding the books and paper work at the brickyard, Laura will do whatever she can to assist them."

"I'm sure they'll be capable of handling matters, but I'll pass along your offer." He smiled at Laura. "Don't feel any obligation, Laura. Irishmen can be a rough lot, especially when they're drinking. Once they take possession, any problems belong to them. I don't want you mingling with them, and there's no need for you to go near the brickyard."

Winston's cautionary command surprised her. Although he'd escorted her to several social gatherings, he obviously didn't know her as well as he believed. If so, he would have withheld his attempt to keep her from the brickyard. "Irish or not, I have no worries about Mr. Crothers and Mr. McKay." She offered him a bright smile. "I appreciate your concern, but I am confident they are honorable men."

"Of course they are. We're going to be pleased to have them as our neighbors."

Mrs. Woodfield reached across the table and patted Winston's hand. "Would you care for a cup of coffee to celebrate? I have a few questions about our Ladies of the Union group. Laura thought you might be able to furnish me with some information."

Winston folded the documents and returned them to his inner pocket. "Mr. Crothers and Mr. McKay are anxiously awaiting my return. Perhaps I can come back and discuss your questions later in the week."

"Of course. It's not urgent." Mrs. Woodfield grasped Winston's arm and walked him to the front door.

"I wouldn't be surprised if Mr. McKay were out at the brickyard digging clay before noon. The man is impatient to begin work."

"That kind of determination would certainly win my admiration. My husband had that same type of resolve. That's what made his brickyard a success. I hope it will do the same for Mr. Crothers and Mr. McKay." She stepped onto the front porch and smiled up at Winston. "I'm sure you feel the same way."

Winston muttered an inaudible reply before mounting his horse. "Good day, ladies."

Laura followed her mother inside. "I'm

sorry to rush off, Mother, but Zeke will be bringing the buggy around for me any minute now." She picked up her gloves from the table and started tugging them on. "If I don't hurry I'll be late to the orphanage, and Mrs. Tremble will think I've forgotten I'm scheduled to help this morning."

Her mother sighed. "I wouldn't want you to be late. I suppose I can sit on the porch and finish my morning coffee by myself."

Laura chuckled and patted her mother's shoulder. "Now, don't be acting so gloomy. I'll be home in time for the noonday meal. I promised the children we'd do something special today, and I don't want to disappoint them."

"I know the youngsters at the orphanage look forward to your time with them, but I believe the visits are even more important to you." A look of concern clouded her mother's eyes. "Be careful with your affections, my dear. Becoming overly attached can only lead to heartache."

Laura leaned forward and brushed a kiss on her mother's cheek. "Please don't worry about me, Mother. I'm merely doing what you've taught me: helping those in need." Laura assumed a carefree air as she took up her reticule and strode toward the door.

Mrs. Woodfield followed close on her

heels. "I hope Mrs. Tremble hasn't convinced you to take over her position when she retires. I know she thinks you'd be the perfect replacement. Volunteering to help with the children is one thing, but taking over as the administrator of the orphanage is quite another. You're a young woman who needs to be looking toward marriage and —"

"I really must be on my way, Mother. Your worries are completely unfounded."

Laura hurried out the door and down the front steps, thankful Zeke was waiting with the buggy. Though her mother meant well, Laura didn't need to be cautioned every time she departed for the Bartlett Orphanage. With her bag of supplies tucked beside her, she flicked the reins. Rather than the toddlers, she'd be helping with the older children today, and she hoped they would enjoy what she had planned for them.

Though the bleak wooden structure was a depressing sight, Laura's spirits soared when she entered the building. The interior wasn't lovely, but Mrs. Tremble had done her best to enlist help painting the walls, and she'd hung colorful curtains at the windows in an effort to create a homelike setting. But it was the children who created the genuine joy in this place. In spite of all they'd suffered in the past, most of these children remained happy and carefree.

Eddie Logan barreled toward her the minute she crossed the threshold. "What did you bring for us to do today, Miss Woodfield?" His pug nose and cheeks were layered with freckles that made him the brunt of occasional teasing, but he'd learned to ignore the remarks — most of the time. On occasion young Eddie would raise his fists in warning, but thus far he'd refrained from striking anyone. He pointed to the bag. "Do you have something special in there?"

She bent close to his ear. "I do. But let's wait until all of the children have gathered, so I can tell all of you at once. Why don't you tell the group I've arrived?"

A flash of disappointment crossed his face before he mumbled his consent and called the other children to the room designated for them.

While they took their places around the table, Laura withdrew drawing supplies, string, and paperboard from her bag. "To-day we're going to make thaumatropes. Does anyone know what a thaumatrope is?"

The children shook their heads as they eyed the supplies Laura had placed on the table.

"I don't think this sounds like fun. You promised you'd bring something we'd like." Lucy Wilson folded her arms in a defiant gesture.

Once more, Laura reached into her bag. This time she withdrew a thaumatrope she'd made to demonstrate to the children. "Look at the picture on each side of the cardboard disc." Laura showed them the picture of a bird on one side and then turned it over to reveal a birdcage on the other. A piece of string had been drawn through the small holes on each side of the disc. The children looked on as Laura tightly wound the circle disc and then released the circle. Their eyes grew wide as they watched the disc spin.

"It looks like the bird is inside the cage." Lucy pointed at the flying disc. "I want to do that. Can I, Miss Woodfield? Can I?"

"You may each give it a try, but then you're going to make your own."

Jumping up and down, they looked at each other with wide-eyed excitement, clapped their hands, and shrieked their enthusiasm.

Laura touched her pursed lips with her index finger. "Shh. I'm pleased you're happy, but we don't want to disturb the other class." The children circled around her. "You can decide on your pictures and then draw them on the cardboard discs. When you've finished, we'll poke holes in the cardboard and insert the string."

Lucy curled her lip. "I don't know what to draw. The older kids can draw better than me."

Laura pulled her chair to an empty spot beside Lucy. "Then let's think of something that isn't so difficult. What about drawing a spider on one side and a web on the other? I think you could do that very well, don't you?"

Lucy shrugged her shoulders. "It won't be as good as your bird."

"It will be wonderful. When you spin the disc, it will look like your spider is in its web." Laura handed her a disc. "You'll see. You're going to do a wonderful job."

As the children worked on their projects, Laura circled the table, offering help and a dose of affection where needed. The boys were slow to reveal any desire for love, but they beamed when she offered words of praise or when she gave them an encouraging pat on the shoulder.

She leaned over Kenneth's shoulder to look at his drawings. On one side he'd drawn a horse's head. On the other side he'd drawn a stall. "I think the horse will look like he's in the stall when the disc flies around, don't you?" he asked.

"Yes, Kenneth. I believe your design will work very well. That's a fine horse you've drawn. Let's make holes on either side and insert the string so you can try it."

One by one the children completed their thaumatropes, most revealing a little about themselves in the pictures. Margaret Reed, a somewhat melancholy little girl, had drawn an empty grave on one side of her disc and a woman on the other. Laura's breath caught as the girl spun the thaumatrope and the woman dropped in and out of the grave.

"That's my mother. She died when I was a baby. I just drew what I imagined she looked like since I don't remember her. Is that okay, Miss Woodfield?" Margaret didn't appear distraught. She'd seemingly accepted her lot in life, yet Laura couldn't imagine what it must be like to grow up without loving parents. Margaret nudged Laura's hand. "Did you hear me, Miss Woodfield? Is my picture all right?"

"Yes, of course. You're an excellent artist, Margaret."

Johnny Rutherford, a twelve-year-old, drew closer. "Why didn't you draw your mother in heaven instead of in the ground,

Margaret? Mrs. Tremble says if we believe in Jesus, our spirit goes to heaven when we die. Didn't your mother go to heaven?"

Margaret's lip trembled. "He's right. I should have drawn a picture of the sky with sunshine and fluffy clouds. I think my mama's in heaven, don't you, Miss Woodfield?"

Laura couldn't say for sure if Margaret's mother had gone to heaven. She hadn't known the woman or her beliefs. But one thing was certain: Laura wouldn't cause the child more worry. "I think your mother would be pleased if you drew a picture of heaven rather than a grave, and there's time to make changes to your thaumatrope, if you'd like." Laura handed the girl her handkerchief. "There's no reason for tears. With a few swishes of paint, you can easily adjust what you've already made."

After helping Margaret recreate her picture, Laura escorted the group into the adjacent classroom, where they presented their creations to the younger children. The older youngsters beamed as the little ones oohed and aahed over the spinning discs.

Mrs. Tremble stepped to her side. "You have such a way with children, Laura. I do hope you're giving my suggestion a great deal of thought and prayer. You have a gift, and I'd like to see it put to good use here at the orphanage — at least until you marry and have some little ones of your own."

Laura fixed her gaze on the young students. "I can't deny I find true pleasure coming here to spend time with the children, but I don't know what the future holds, Mrs. Tremble. Mother is selling the brickworks, and right now I couldn't possibly accept the position. However, you can continue to count on me as one of your volunteers." She turned and smiled at the older woman. "I'm sorry to disappoint you."

"Once things are settled with the sale of your father's business, you may change your mind. If so, the position will be available to you."

Laura snapped open the watch pinned to her bodice and startled. "Dear me, I didn't realize it was so close to twelve o'clock. I promised Mother I'd be home in time for the noonday meal. I'd best gather my things and be on my way."

Kenneth rushed after her as she strode into the other room. "I'll help you clean up, Miss Woodfield."

"Why, thank you, Kenneth."

"Could you leave some extra pieces of cardboard? I told some of the little kids I'd make a thaumatrope for them if you'd leave some supplies."

"That's very kind of you, Kenneth. I'll leave all of these things, and once you've finished, you can put any remaining items into the bag for me. I'll pick it up the next time I come." She ruffled the boy's blond hair.

"What you gonna bring next time?"

She chuckled. "I'm not sure, but I'll try to think of something you'll enjoy."

As she headed toward home, Mrs. Tremble's words resounded like a clanging bell: *". . . at least until you marry and have children of your own."*

Catherine was clearing the dishes after the noonday meal when a knock sounded at the front door. "You expecting more company, Miss Laura?"

"No, but you continue with your work. I'll go to the door. Maybe there was some problem with the papers and Mr. Hawkins has returned. Or perhaps it's Mr. McKay." She quickened her step and pulled open the front door. "Mr. Crothers, Mr. McKay, ladies. Good afternoon."

"I know we shouldn't have appeared unannounced, but I wanted a tour of the house," one of the women told her. "Hugh said it might take a while for you to get your

73

things packed up and moved, but I couldn't wait any longer before seeing it."

Laura's mouth gaped open as she stared at the group. Whatever was this woman talking about? "I assume you are Mrs. Crothers?" She turned her gaze to Kathleen. "And you are Mrs. McKay?"

Kathleen shook her head. "Nay. I'm Mrs. Crothers's sister, Kathleen. I'm not married."

"And neither is Ewan," Mr. Crothers added. "Sorry we are to barge in on you, Miss Woodfield, but my wife insisted on touring the house. She wants to measure for carpets and drapes."

"I think there's some misunderstanding, but please come in so we can discuss the house." Laura's head buzzed like a nest of irritated hornets. She directed the foursome into the parlor. "Please be seated and I'll have Catherine bring tea. My mother is resting, but I'm sure she'll be down before you depart. She'll want to make your acquaintance."

Mrs. Crothers took a seat on the divan. "So you and your mother plan to remain in the area?"

Laura frowned. "Of course. This is our home. Mother would never leave."

"Will you be moving into town, then?"

Mrs. Crothers's gaze drifted toward the parlor windows. "Any chance you'll leave the draperies? I like them, and it would be easier if I didn't have to replace them first thing."

"There's been some misunderstanding, Mrs. Crothers." Laura glanced at Mr. McKay. "This house was not included in the sale."

Mrs. Crothers jumped to her feet. "What's that you're saying?" She turned to her husband. "Did you hear what she's telling us, Hugh? Pull out those papers and show her we're the rightful owners of this house."

Laura shook her head. "There's no need. I know the contents of the contract, Mrs. Crothers, and this house is not included as a part of the sale."

Mrs. Crothers snatched the papers from her husband's hand and began tracing her finger down the first page. She turned to the second page and tapped her finger on the second paragraph. "There. See here? All those legal words describe the acreage and say a house is located on the property and is included in the sale."

"You're correct, it is, but —"

"You're talking out both sides of your mouth, lass." Mr. Crothers took the contract from his wife. "One minute you say the house is not part of the sale, and then you agree with me wife."

"Please let me finish, Mr. Crothers. There is a house included in the sale, but it isn't *this* house. The legal description on the second page of the contract is for the house my father had constructed when we first moved here."

Mrs. Crothers's face twisted with anger. "They've cheated us, Hugh."

"We didn't cheat you, Mrs. Crothers." Laura's stomach clenched.

How she wished that Winston would appear at the front door. Had he been in such a rush to complete the sale that he hadn't gone over the fine details with Mr. Crothers? But then, why hadn't Mr. Crothers read the contract for himself?

"A large frame house and barn sit on that piece of land. They are both in good condition. The home isn't fancy but is very suitable until you can build exactly what you want. We lived in that house until my father built this one."

"She can tell you whatever she wants, Hugh, but you need to talk to that lawyer. They'll not get away with this. I wanted this house, and if she's telling the truth, we don't own it. You need to get your money back."

Ewan rose from his chair and stepped to

his uncle's side. "We need to remember what is most important, Uncle Hugh. Our search was for a brickyard, not a house. We own the brickyard, and there's a suitable house on the land. I doubt you're going to be able to break the contract. Mr. Hawkins gave you sufficient time to read the papers, and he asked you several times if you had any questions. He even asked if you wanted to return and further explore the property before you signed the papers."

Laura exhaled a relieved sigh, thankful that Winston had been honest and thorough in his dealings with Mr. Crothers.

"Whose side are you on, Ewan? You take up her cause at every turn." Mrs. Crothers's face contorted with rage. "First you convince your uncle Hugh to pay full price for this place, and now you say that their contract was honest." She pointed the tip of her parasol at Laura. "Did that one pay your passage to America? Is she going to be your partner at the brickworks? You'd best be remembering who butters your bread."

"I am only stating the truth, Aunt Maggie. You can go to the lawyer, but it won't change a thing. And neither will your anger. This isn't the fault of Miss Woodfield or her mother. And, yes, I did encourage Uncle Hugh to pay full price and to settle here, but you said you loved this valley and wanted to make it your home, as well."

"Aye, that's true enough, but that's when I thought I'd be living in this fine house." Maggie thumped her parasol on the Wilton carpet.

"Stop with your thumping and shouting, Margaret. Ewan's right. The lawyer asked if I wanted to ride around the property so I could see exactly where the boundaries were located. I should have taken the time. Then I would have known this land wasn't included. But I didn't, and that cannot be changed." He narrowed his eyes and turned toward Laura. "But I can tell ya that I would not have paid full price had I known I was not getting this house. There are not many times I've gambled and lost, but this is one of them. Your lawyer has taught me a lesson, miss."

Laura squared her shoulders and met Mr. Crothers's steely gaze. "The purchase of this brickyard and the surrounding property was not a gamble, Mr. Crothers. If you operate the brickyard with the same diligence as did my father, you'll earn an excellent profit."

"Laura, I didn't know we had guests! You should have sent Catherine to fetch me." Mrs. Woodfield continued down the stairs and entered the parlor. She looked at her daughter and arched her brows. "You haven't served tea? What's come over you? Our guests will think we have no manners." Her mother smiled at the two women seated on the divan. "I am Frances Woodfield. We're pleased that we will have neighbors living close by. When you build your new home, I hope you'll choose a location that is within walking distance."

Mrs. Crothers stood and gestured for her sister to do the same. "I doubt we'll be visiting much. I do not think we're cut from the same cloth."

Mrs. Woodfield frowned. "I don't judge others by their social standing, Mrs. Crothers. I think friendships should be based upon trust and respect."

Margaret's lips curled in a wry smile. "So do I, but I have found nothing to trust or respect under this roof." That said, Margaret marched out of the room, with Kathleen following close on her heels.

"I apologize. Me wife has a bit of a sharp tongue." Hugh grasped Ewan by the arm. "Come along. We've some tall talking to do if we're going to smooth Maggie's ruffled feathers." The older man glanced over his shoulder as they departed. "It may take a while, but once she gets used to the idea that she doesn't own this place, Maggie will come 'round. When she does, she'll pay you more visits than you want."

Laura sighed and dropped to the over-stuffed chair, uncertain she would ever want Maggie Crothers to "come 'round."

CHAPTER 5

Ewan followed his uncle and the women to the carriage, thankful he'd ridden his horse. Maggie was insisting upon a visit to Winston Hawkins, a meeting Ewan didn't care to attend. Such a discussion would be a waste of time, but he realized Aunt Margaret wouldn't be satisfied until she heard those words from the lawyer.

He grasped his uncle's elbow. "I think it might be good for me to remain behind. I can go and see the house. That way, if it needs some repairs, we can make plans to have them completed as soon as possible. It might help if I can tell the ladies the house is in good order."

His uncle patted the gray gelding. "Aye, but you come to me after you see the place. If it's in bad shape, I don't want Maggie hearing it. I can extend our stay at the hotel if it needs fixing. I'll tell Maggie and Kathleen that you're riding down to the brickyard to look things over before you return."

"I'll head there right now. I wouldn't want you telling a lie on my account."

Hugh chuckled. "Always worried about telling a lie. Never seen the like. Take a look at the brickyard and then come back here and see if one of the ladies will give you a key to the house." His uncle lowered his head. "While you're riding down to the brickyard, you might ask the Almighty if He could strike your aunt dumb for a while. I could use some peace and quiet."

"I'll say a prayer that she'll be quiet on the ride back to town, Uncle Hugh, but I'm not sure it will help."

Hugh hiked a shoulder. "Aye, right ya are, my boy. Even the Almighty would have a time of it trying to silence Margaret." He patted Ewan on the back. "Go on with ya. We'll talk later."

Ewan shoved his boot into the stirrup and mounted his horse. As he headed off toward the brickyard, he could hear his aunt scolding Uncle Hugh. Little wonder the man had requested prayer. Urging the horse forward, Ewan settled into the saddle, glad for this opportunity to spend a bit of time on his own at the brickyard. Though he and his uncle had carefully examined the machinery and clay deposits during their earlier visit, this time alone would give him an opportunity to follow the workings from the clay deposits to the kiln. Though most brickyards were set up in a similar fashion, the layout could vary depending on the terrain.

He nudged the horse's flanks with his heels and urged him up a slope toward the clay deposits. What a beautiful place this was. Tree branches heavy with leaves of red and gold emblazoned the hillside while birds filled the air with their songs.

Ewan inhaled the crisp, fresh air as he dismounted. "Thank you, Lord. I am grateful you led us to this place." Leaning down, he reached his hand into the soil. "It is good to know I will soon be back to work."

He stood and surveyed the area. Mr. Woodfield had chosen a perfect site. The clay pits were to the rear of the yard. He'd been careful to leave plenty of space for the huge mounds of clay that needed to weather each winter. Ewan would need to find diggers as soon as possible. Men who knew how to handle a shovel. He wanted to dig before the first freeze so the clay would have exposure to as many freeze-and-thaw cycles as possible. Bricks made of thoroughly weathered clay made stronger bricks and were less liable to warp in the kiln. Ewan wanted to produce sound bricks.

Come spring, he wanted the clay weathered and ready for the pug mills. He walked off in the distance to the two horse-driven mills. Here, the clay would be ground and mixed with liquid to form a malleable mixture before delivery to the VerValen machine, where it would be formed into bricks. Then they would be set to drying in the shed before they could be fired.

They would need more drying sheds as they increased production, but there was still enough time to consider those plans. Late afternoon shadows draped the yard, and Ewan turned toward the hillside. If he didn't get back to Woodfield Manor soon, the ladies would be preparing for supper.

Riding toward the house a short time later, he spied Miss Woodfield on the porch. He removed his hat and waved in her direction. She stood and drew near the railing.

"We meet again, Miss Woodfield. I hope you do not mind, but I told my uncle I would take a look at the house he purchased. Is there any chance I could bother you for the key and directions to the place?"

Laura's lips curved in a generous smile. "Certainly. I'll go with you, if you'd like."

"I cannot think of a thing that would please me more, Miss Woodfield. Will you be riding a horse?"

"It's not far. If you don't mind walking, I'll get the key and my bonnet."

"A walk sounds good." Ewan swung down from the horse and tied the gelding to the post. "You behave yourself while I'm gone."

"Do you often talk to your horse, Mr. McKay?" Laura asked, coming from the house.

Ewan laughed. "Indeed. He listens and does not give any unwanted opinions."

Laura tied the strings of her bonnet. "Then I must remember to listen and give my opinion only when requested."

"Your ideas would always be treasured by me, Miss Woodfield."

"Is that a bit of the Irish blarney I've heard about, Mr. McKay?"

"Not at all. I'm speaking the truth. I value your opinion." He smiled and then gestured toward the dirt pathway. "The first time I came along this path, I wondered why your father had not lined it with bricks. My poor horse nearly lost a shoe in the thick mud."

"That's a good question, Mr. McKay, but I don't have the answer. Perhaps he didn't think it important, since the main road isn't much better. I'm afraid the trail leading to the house where you'll be living needs a bit of work, as well."

They'd walked about a half a mile when Laura pointed to a narrow trail leading off to the right. "This leads to the house. Mother is having the groomsman bring her over so she can go through it with us." She glanced up at him. "Mother wasn't happy I'd consented to an unescorted walk, but since I'd already told you I would go, she didn't fuss overmuch."

Ewan stopped short. "She could have walked with us. Did you not invite her?"

"She can't walk long distances. Her legs give out. And she didn't want to keep us waiting while Zeke hitched the carriage for her. No doubt she'll rush Zeke and be here soon."

"Is that the house up there in the distance?" Ewan gestured toward a hillock.

"Yes. It's a lovely setting. You can see most of the valley. The trees hide the brickyard from view, but you can see the river from two of the upstairs bedrooms." Laura turned at the sound of an approaching horse. "It appears Mother is going to get to the house before we do. That will please her. She would be completely disappointed in me if we entered the house unchaperoned."

"Aye." Ewan grinned and nodded. "I would not want to be the one causing your mother grief — or you, either."

They stepped to the side as the buggy approached, and Mrs. Woodfield called to the driver to stop. Leaning forward, she extended her hand to Laura. "Give me the key and I'll open the house. I'm sure it needs to be aired."

Ewan didn't care if the house was aired; he merely wanted to see the size and condition of the dwelling. If he could offer his aunt a good report, she might stop criticizing Uncle Hugh. Ewan needed his uncle's attention to remain centered on the brickyard, not on building a new house.

Once they arrived outside the structure, Ewan stopped and surveyed the exterior of the house. " 'Tis a fine dwelling. I can only hope that Aunt Maggie will agree and be satisfied until a new house that meets her every wish can be constructed."

Laura strode toward the steps leading to a generous front porch. "I think I may have detected a hint of disdain in your comment, Mr. McKay."

Ewan bowed his head. "Aye, and I do apologize for harboring and speaking unkind comments about my aunt. 'Twas not proper."

"No apology needed. Your aunt made an unforgettable impression." Laura waved him forward. "My mother and I both hope to forge a friendship with her, since your family will be living nearby."

Ewan mounted the steps. "I'm sure she'll be eager to visit, to ask your advice about the best places to shop, and to inquire about the guests she should entertain. My aunt has a strong desire to be welcomed into fashionable society."

Laura stopped outside the front door. "We will be pleased to help her. And if your aunt and her sister enjoy volunteer work, there are always positions to be filled."

"I know you helped your father at the brickyard, but is volunteer work how most society ladies fill their days, Miss Woodfield?"

"We all try to do our part. I'm thankful for the life my parents were able to provide me, so I want to help others who have been less fortunate. I think most of the ladies want to do what they can to ease the suffering of others."

"So what is it you do to help the needy, Miss Woodfield?"

"Since I enjoy children, I volunteer my time at the orphanage."

Ewan's lips lifted in a broad smile. "We have more in common than bricks, Miss Woodfield. To be sure, I think children are a blessing from God. I cannot imagine a life without children of my own, can you?"

His question hung in the air as Laura silently motioned him inside.

The area was large enough to greet several guests, though not nearly as large as the grand hallway at Woodfield Manor. A wide staircase boasting a hand-carved black-walnut banister rose from the left wall and a wide entrance led to the formal parlor to the right. Mrs. Woodfield had already opened the pocket doors, and Zeke was struggling to open some of the windows.

"Let me help with those. With all the rain, the wood has probably swelled a bit." Ewan crossed the room and soon had two of the windows open at the front of the house. Once Zeke had managed to raise a window along the side, a cross breeze soon drifted through the room.

Mrs. Woodfield inhaled a shallow breath. "That's a little better, but it will be several hours before we're rid of the stale air." She waved toward Zeke. "Open the rest of these downstairs windows and then go up to the bedrooms." Her forehead creased in a frown. "Maybe Zeke should spend the night here. He could leave the windows open, and it would be as fresh as a daisy by morning."

"Now, Mrs. Woodfield, you know I don't like sleeping anywhere but in my own bed."

The older man shuddered. "Maybe you should send Joseph. That young fella is always open to a bit of adventure. But me? I like my regular routine."

"Then we'll have Joseph come over." Mrs. Woodfield turned to Ewan. "Would you like to begin upstairs or continue here on the main floor, Mr. McKay?"

"Down here is fine. I was wondering about the workhorses your husband used to operate the pug mills. Is there any chance you still have the animals?"

"Zeke, do we still have those horses Mr. Woodfield used down at the brickyard?"

Zeke jerked and hit his head on the window frame. "Sure do." He rubbed his head. "Them are some mighty fine horses, Mr. McKay. Percherons. That's the only kind Mr. Woodfield ever used in the yard. He said that breed was hard workers. And they is. Charlie's good-natured all the time. Jack can sometimes be stubborn, but once you convince him who's boss, he'll give you a better day's work than any other horse you harness up to turn a pug mill."

"I was wondering if the horses were included in the sale, Mrs. Woodfield. I did not read the contract."

"Truly?" She arched her brows. "In the future, you may find it isn't wise to settle upon a contract without full knowledge, Mr. McKay."

"Aye, that's wise counsel, Mrs. Woodfield, but since my uncle was the one signing the agreement and paying the money, he did not believe there was any need for me to read the contents."

"But I thought you and your uncle were partners. Did I misunderstand?"

"We will become partners once I've earned my share in the company. My uncle expects me to oversee operations at the brickyard."

"I see." Her lips curved in a gentle smile. "I think it would be better for you to be the one acquiring contracts for the company, Mr. McKay. Unfortunately, your uncle's demeanor doesn't create a sense of trust. My husband always said that trust and dependability were the greatest assets a company could offer its customers. Perhaps your uncle should oversee daily operations, and you should travel to Wheeling and Pittsburgh to meet with building contractors." She tucked a wisp of her graying hair beneath her shirred russet bonnet. "Think about what I've said."

Ewan nodded. "Aye, that I will, but I do not think my uncle will be so quick to listen."

"Does he understand the operation of a brickyard, Mr. McKay?" Mrs. Woodfield asked, arching her brows.

"He does, but he's not keen on the idea of hard work now that he's got a bit of money in his pockets."

"Then maybe a visit with me will help. I think I may be able to convince him that my suggestions will benefit him."

Ewan didn't want to argue with the woman, but she'd not soon convince Hugh Crothers of any such thing. Uncle Hugh might take a stroll through the yard from time to time, but his plans didn't include overseeing the digging of clay or the molding of bricks. That's the reason he'd brought Ewan along. But if they failed to win contracts because of his uncle's abrasive behavior, there would be no need to burn bricks.

Mrs. Woodfield continued the tour, leading him from the dining room into a small library and an informal parlor. "Tell your uncle he should pay me a call." She hesitated for a moment. "Add that I have some helpful information to share with him." She gestured toward the hallway. "Shall we go upstairs?"

"I am still wondering about those horses, Mrs. Woodfield."

She chuckled. "Yes, of course." She strode

toward the kitchen and stopped in the doorway. "Zeke, do we have a need for those two workhorses any longer?"

Zeke's work boots clomped on the floor as he crossed the room. Ewan bent forward, eager to hear the response.

"I don't reckon we do, Mrs. Woodfield. They's been doing nothing but grazing and getting lazy since the brickyard shut down. Might take a bit of urging to get 'em back in working form. I told you last winter you should sell the both of 'em."

"I'm sure you did, but since we still have them, they'll be of use to Mr. Crothers and Mr. McKay." She turned and met Ewan's gaze. "When you tell your uncle I have some information for him, tell him I also have two good Percherons that are trained for the pug mill."

Ewan nodded. Mrs. Woodfield's behavior surprised him. She seemed to possess more familiarity with business affairs than he'd first thought. Either that or she'd become quite shrewd since meeting Uncle Hugh. Ewan hoped it was the former, for Uncle Hugh could sniff out a bluff in no time. The man had, after all, made his money gambling. He doubted whether Mrs. Woodfield would prove a match for Uncle Hugh, but he would pass along her messages and see what happened. He truly wanted — no, needed — those Percherons. The cost to purchase good workhorses should be enough to at least get Uncle Hugh to Mrs. Woodfield's doorstep.

The older woman traced her fingers along the bedstead that remained in the largest of the four upstairs bedrooms. "Isaiah insisted upon new furniture when we moved to Woodfield Manor. I wanted to bring this bed and the wardrobe, but he wouldn't hear of it. He said I deserved new furniture in my new house."

"Sounds as though your husband took pleasure in spoiling you a bit, Mrs. Woodfield."

Ewan could understand a man wanting to treat his wife well, but he couldn't imagine leaving all of this fine furniture behind — or the house, for that matter. Though it was no match for Woodfield Manor, this was a fine home. Perhaps those feelings arose from the life of deprivation he'd led in Ireland.

If Mrs. Woodfield planned to leave these furnishings, they could move in immediately. There would be no need to purchase furniture. A fact that would surely please Uncle Hugh.

"This is a fine house with a lovely view,

Mrs. Woodfield. Once my aunt sees it, I'm sure she'll settle in until a new house can be built."

"That's good news, Mr. McKay. It has never been my intent to deceive anyone. That was not my husband's method of conducting business, and it is not mine. I didn't realize there was any confusion about the ownership of Woodfield Manor until your family appeared on our doorstep."

Laura stepped to her mother's side. "Mr. McKay understands, Mother. He doesn't place any blame on our shoulders."

From the arch of her brows, she seemed to expect him to agree. "Aye. What your daughter says is true. I do not place any blame on either of you."

Ewan was careful to exclude his aunt and uncle from his answer. By now, he wasn't sure what his relatives believed. No doubt Mr. Hawkins had heard more than an earful of Aunt Maggie's dissatisfaction and would be pleased to have this misunderstanding settled.

Mrs. Woodfield descended the front steps. "I believe we're done here, Zeke. Let's get back to the house. After supper, Joseph can come over and spend the night. By morning, the house will be well aired."

"Um-hum." Zeke stroked his chin. "With

all them windows wide open, Joseph may be frozen stiff as an icicle by morning." Zeke helped the older woman into the buggy.

"I'll send extra blankets. It's not that cold yet." She pulled the key out of her pocket and presented it to Ewan. "Here you go. Now, you two should begin heading back to the house soon. If you have time before you start back to Bartlett, come in for a cup of tea, Mr. McKay."

"Thank you, ma'am." Ewan tipped his hat. "We'll be on our way in no time." After Mrs. Woodfield left, he looked at the key and then at Laura. "I was going to lock the door, but with all the windows open, I don't suppose there's any need to worry about that."

She grinned. "You're right. Besides, it will be easier for Joseph to get in if he doesn't have to climb through a window."

Ewan slapped his palm to his head. "I already forgot about Joseph spending the night. I don't want to make him feel unwelcome." He offered Laura his arm. "Shall we start back? I don't want your mother thinking we've been out here without a chaperone for too long."

"I think she trusts you, Mr. McKay." Laura slipped her hand through the crook of his arm. "I hope you and your family will enjoy as much happiness in this house as we did."

Right now, Ewan wasn't worried about the family being happy so much as he feared Aunt Maggie might have found some loophole in their contract. If she did, there would be no stopping her. They'd be on the next train out of Bartlett.

They'd walked only a short distance when the sound of hoofbeats thrummed on the road, and they turned to see Winston approaching on horseback. He reined the horse to a stop beside them and then fixed his gaze on Laura's hand resting in the crook of Ewan's arm.

Ewan tipped his hat. "Good afternoon, Mr. Hawkins. I hope your meeting with my aunt and uncle went well."

"Your aunt is not easily swayed. I'm still not certain she believes the contract is valid. When I finally excused myself, your uncle was talking to her." Concern creased his features as his focus returned to Laura's hand. "You're out here without a chaperone, Laura?"

"Mother was here until moments ago. Zeke took her home in the buggy." Laura dropped her hold on Ewan's arm.

Winston frowned and his eyeglasses slid from the bridge of his nose. Using his index finger, he shoved them back in place. "Even so, I'm not certain being unchaperoned out here in the woods with this . . . this Irishman would be considered acceptable by anybody." His eyes narrowed as he turned his gaze toward Ewan.

Anger cinched every muscle in Ewan's body. He fought off the urge to yank the lawyer off his horse and lash him. How dare he accuse Miss Woodfield of inappropriate behavior. He gritted his teeth as the memory of his promise to never again fight came to mind. Not since he'd made that promise to the Lord had he ever wished he could take it back — until now.

Ewan inhaled a deep breath. "I do not care what you say about me or my Irish kin, Mr. Hawkins, but you owe the lady an apology. She's as decent a lass as one could ever meet on this earth, and I do not think a true gentleman would ever accuse her of being any less." Laura held up her hand to protest, but Ewan shook his head and grabbed the horse's reins. "Nay, Miss Woodfield. None of us will be going any further until Mr. Hawkins offers an apology."

In spite of the cool air, perspiration trickled from beneath Winston's hat. "I apologize, Laura. I'll see you at the house." His jaw twitched as he yanked the reins from Ewan and rode off.

"Not much of an apology, but glad I am to see his back."

The two of them stared down the road for a moment before Ewan offered Laura his arm.

But this time she didn't accept.

CHAPTER 6

Moving at a slight angle, Laura managed to create a visible space between her and Ewan. From the wounded look in his eyes, there was no doubt she'd hurt his feelings.

"I hope I haven't offended you by keeping a distance between us, Mr. McKay. It's just that Winston was correct. It was improper of me to come out here without a chaperone." She inhaled a deep breath. "I tend to be careless when it comes to proper etiquette."

Ewan kicked a pebble along the path. "Is that what *you* think, or what Mr. Hawkins tells you?"

"Please don't think harshly of Mr. Hawkins. Winston fears my impulsive behavior might one day cause me some sort of social disfavor. He means well. That fact aside, he is only emphasizing what I already know."

"Since you're so quick to follow Mr. Hawkins's orders, I am guessing you're betrothed to the man."

Laura gasped. "You have guessed incorrectly, Mr. McKay. I am not betrothed to anyone, and I am not following orders."

"I did not intend to make you angry, Miss Woodfield."

"I am not angry." She enunciated each word.

Ewan grinned and hiked a shoulder. "You sound angry."

"Well, I'm not, so let's talk about something else." Her mind whirled as she attempted to change the course of their conversation. "What about the brickyard?"

"What about it?" Ewan's brows dipped low on his forehead, but then he laughed. "Now I understand. You want to talk about the brickyard rather than have me ask questions about your Mr. Hawkins. Is that it?"

Laura sighed. "He is not *my* Mr. Hawkins, but you are right. I would prefer talking about the brickyard. I'm sure you have some questions I might be able to answer."

"Aye, I'm sure there is much you could tell me. You said you sometimes acted as timekeeper for your father. Did you walk about the yard to spot the workers?"

She straightened her shoulders, pleased by his question. Though most women would never want to admit they'd performed a man's job, Laura took pride in the fact that she'd been the timekeeper at Woodfield Brickworks. The men had respected her and marveled at her uncanny ability to recognize each worker by his gait, clothes, habits, or pace. Each year there would be a group of transient laborers as well as the regulars, but it didn't take long for her to find some unique characteristic in each one.

"No. I could stand up on the hill as each stint ended and make the notations in my notebook. Of course, it helps to be good at fractions when you work as timekeeper, especially when some of the men work longer than a full day's stint." She grinned. "They don't take kindly to being under-paid."

"Aye, I'm sure they don't. I was hoping you could furnish me with a list of your workers — those who came back from the war and might be looking for work."

"I think I could." They were only a short distance from Woodfield Manor when Laura turned to see an approaching horse and carriage. "I believe that's your family, Mr. Mc-Kay."

Ewan nodded. "Aye, that it is." Ewan waved and walked toward the carriage. "Have you and Aunt Maggie come to see the frame house?" He glanced over his shoulder toward Laura. "Miss Woodfield and I just came from there."

"We've left the windows open to air the house because it's been closed since last spring. If you're going to stay the night, we won't send our handyman over." Laura gestured toward Woodfield Manor. "I can go home without you, Ewan. You should take your aunt and uncle to the house."

Mrs. Crothers's haughty look suggested she still bore a degree of animosity, and Laura realized her presence would only make matters worse for Ewan. Woodfield Manor was within sight, and she'd ventured much farther than this on her own. Though Winston would likely upbraid Ewan if he discovered she'd walked the short distance unescorted, she didn't plan to tell Winston or her mother.

Ewan shook his head. "I think I should go with you. My horse is still at Woodfield Manor. I can escort you the rest of the way and ride my horse back. It won't take long." He glanced at his aunt, but she merely pursed her lips in a tight knot and remained silent.

"I'll have Zeke bring your horse over. He won't mind. That way you can return to Bartlett with your aunt and uncle."

The knot in Mrs. Crothers's lips relaxed

and then disappeared. "I think that's the best idea, Ewan. Come along and let me have a look at the hovel your uncle has provided for me." Sarcasm coated her words.

Before turning to leave, Laura said, "Should you have any questions after you've toured your new home, please stop at Woodfield Manor. I'm sure my mother would enjoy visiting with you, Mrs. Crothers."

"Indeed we will. In fact, you may count on it. I believe your lawyer is going to be speaking with your mother about several matters that need attention."

Laura forced a smile and strode away without another word. She didn't want to make an unkind remark, but when she couldn't think of a pleasant response, she decided it best to head toward home. No need to fuel the woman's fire of hostility.

When she entered the house, muffled voices drifted from the parlor and she followed the sound.

Her mother looked up and smiled. "Ah, Laura. I'm pleased to see you're back. I was beginning to get a little worried. Winston said he'd stopped and spoken with you. We both thought you would have returned before now."

Why had Winston needlessly worried her

mother? "There was no need for concern. Besides, I'm sure Winston would have sought me had he been concerned about my safety." She turned her narrowed eyes on him. "Wouldn't you, Winston?"

"Yes, of course. And where is Mr. McKay? Has he ridden off without as much as a thank-you or good-bye for your mother?"

Laura crossed the room and sat down beside her mother. "No. His horse is still tied out front. His aunt and uncle met us on the path, and he went back to the house with them. I told him I would have Zeke take the horse over to the other house."

"I do hope she'll like it." Laura's mother set aside her needlework. "Winston tells me he had quite a time with Mrs. Crothers after they returned to Bartlett. She's insisting that I lower the price they had already agreed to pay. What do you think?"

"I'm your lawyer, Mrs. Woodfield, and it's my advice that you lower the price and we complete this matter as expeditiously as possible. There is no pleasing that woman unless she gets her way."

"I disagree." Laura folded her hands in her lap and met Winston's gaze. "They had every opportunity to go over all terms of the contract. The fact that they didn't inquire about the house is no fault of ours.

Surely she realizes we would have been asking a far greater price had this house been included."

"Do you think I haven't already told her that, Laura? I am, after all, accustomed to negotiating contracts."

Laura frowned. Winston's condescending tone startled her. "I'm aware you have a greater knowledge of contract law, Winston, but I don't think Mrs. Crothers comprehends the fact that our sale price is fair."

"Laura wasn't questioning your ability as a lawyer, Winston. She's merely stating what we all know: Mr. and Mrs. Crothers hope to gain the very most for their money." Mrs. Woodfield patted Laura's hand. "Of course, Laura and I want a fair price for our property, and I believe that is what we received under the terms of our contract."

Winston frowned and shook his head. "But Mr. Crothers signed the contract believing this house was included, so I think you should renegotiate, Mrs. Woodfield."

The older woman leaned forward. "Perhaps you should return to Bartlett, Winston. If Mr. and Mrs. Crothers return, I don't think there's any need for a lawyer. I believe we'll be able to come to an agreement that will satisfy all of us."

Winston argued against such a plan, but

when Laura's mother didn't relent, he stalked from the room. "When this entire sale falls apart, don't say that I didn't warn you."

Mrs. Woodfield followed him to the door. "To tell you the truth, I don't understand why you think the sale could go amiss, Winston. We have a signed and witnessed contract that you prepared. With your expertise, I'm sure any court would find in my favor." Mrs. Woodfield handed him his hat. "I think that after I've spoken with Mr. Crothers, he'll see things my way."

Winston shook his head. "You may convince him, but you'll never convince his wife."

Laura didn't want to agree with Winston but feared he could be right. Maybe they should lower their price a little. Then again, she'd wait and see what transpired when Mr. and Mrs. Crothers arrived on their doorstep.

When a knock finally sounded at the front door, Catherine was preparing supper. Laura jumped to her feet. "I'll go to the door, Catherine."

Mrs. Woodfield patted her hair. "I was beginning to think they weren't going to come. Shall I invite them for supper?"

Laura shook her head. "Not immediately. Let's first see what they have to say." She hurried down the hallway to the front door and stopped short when she saw Ewan and Mrs. Crothers departing in the carriage. "Mr. Crothers, your wife is not joining us?"

He doffed his cap. "Nay. Ewan said you wanted to speak with me, and I thought it might be better if my wife went back to town. She has a way about her that sometimes makes conversation difficult, especially when it comes to business."

Mrs. Woodfield waved him inside. "Do come in. I'm glad Ewan passed along my message." She gestured toward Laura. "I believe you saw my daughter not long ago."

"Aye, that I did." He nodded to Laura and then sat down. "The other house is to my liking, though it doesn't much please my wife. She wants something grand like this house. But the frame house will suit us until we build." He cleared his throat. "I think you'd have to agree that a man who thinks he's buying this fine mansion and then ends up with a small frame house might feel like he'd been cheated a bit, wouldn't you?"

Laura stiffened, but her mother only smiled. "I am not sure how I would feel, Mr. Crothers. I do know you had every opportunity to examine the contract, and you could have easily had another lawyer look at the papers and explain them, if you'd so desired."

"I don't hold much stock in lawyers. Most of the ones I've met are just like that Hawkins fella. They say what they think you want to hear, but later deny what they told ya. I've been around my share of double-dealers, and Hawkins fits in with the rest of those charlatans."

As Laura listened to Mr. Crothers disparage Winston, a surge of irritation swelled inside her like a river overflowing its banks. "Mr. Hawkins is a fine lawyer, and he's highly respected by members of the surrounding area. In fact, he has been nominated to run for a seat in our state senate."

Mr. Crothers tipped his head to the side. "Looks like I stepped on your toes, Miss Woodfield. You sound like a woman in love. I wouldn't have spoken so plain if I'd known you and Mr. Hawkins were . . ." He let the sentence hang there like a preacher waiting to hear *I do.*

"I defended Mr. Hawkins because your generalizations do not apply to him. He prepared a contract that was fair. You read and signed it. Rather than making him a charlatan, I believe you've shown yourself to be a poor businessman."

"Laura!" Mrs. Woodfield frowned and shook her head. "Mr. Crothers is our guest, and you will treat him with respect. If you cannot do so, please go out to the kitchen and help Catherine, or go up to your room."

Laura leaned back in her chair. "I plan to stay here. I won't say anything more, but I do want to listen so that Mr. Crothers can't later accuse you of double-dealing."

Hugh laughed. "You're a feisty young woman, Miss Woodfield, but you're no match for the likes of me. I don't plan on anyone double-dealing this evening, but I do plan on getting matters settled so that everyone is happy. Right now, my wife is unhappy, and so am I."

"Perhaps I can help with that, Mr. Crothers. Though I don't feel you've been cheated, I do believe I can help ease your unhappiness."

"You going to give me some of my money back?" He rubbed his thick hands together.

"No, not one cent. However, I do have two fine Percherons that are trained to work the pug mill. You are welcome to look them over. They're worth their weight in gold in that brickyard — unless you've already purchased horses." Her mother's lips curved in a gentle smile.

"No matter how fine the horses, I don't

know that they make up for the difference between the two houses. No offense, but I was hoping to hear something better than what you've offered."

Laura clenched her fists, then forced them to relax. Open and closed, open and closed. Over and over, she repeated the movement until she regained a sense of calm. Her father had taught her the maneuver years ago. Though Laura had never imagined her father a man with a quick temper, he'd told her otherwise. When he'd seen her become angry with a worker at the brickyard, he'd gently chastised her and then explained his past. The facts had alarmed her. Never had she pictured her father attempting to resolve disagreements with his fists, but she'd learned that during his early years he'd given and received many a blow. Only after he'd studied the Bible and made a choice to follow the teachings of Jesus had he changed.

Her father had gone on to demonstrate the method he'd learned to use when anger began to take hold of him. The same movement she was now using to control her temper and her tongue. Though she liked to justify her temper by telling herself she'd inherited it from her father, she knew that wasn't true. Resorting to anger was a choice that generally ended with poor results, another fact her father had explained to her years ago.

Laura's temper didn't flare when she was being wronged. But when she believed others were being treated unjustly, she was quick to anger. When the residents of western Virginia voted to pull away and form the state of West Virginia in support of the Union, she'd celebrated with her parents at a huge gathering in Wheeling, thankful to be among those who opposed the unjust practice of slavery. Her anger had swelled and she'd pressed local and state officials to action when the widows and orphans and returning soldiers of the War Between the States needed aid and none was forthcoming.

Although Mr. Crothers's actions were insignificant by comparison, the man was attempting to take advantage of her mother. His tasteless scheming stuck in her craw.

How she'd love to tell Mr. Crothers that Charlie and Jack were more than any other person would offer once a contract had been signed. Instead, she tightened her lips into a thin line and continued the exercise with her hands.

Laura's mother cleared her throat. "I believe the only other thing my daughter and I can offer you is a great deal of advice on how to make your brickworks successful." Mr. Crothers's mouth dropped open at the suggestion, but Laura's mother quickly continued. "Before you hasten to tell me that what I'm offering is of little worth, let me explain something to you. While I'm sure both you and Mr. McKay are capable of operating a brickyard, there is more to becoming successful than knowing how to burn excellent bricks. Laura and I can provide you with the names of men who are well trained in brickwork. We can also introduce you to my husband's business contacts in Fairmont, Wheeling, Pittsburgh, and Allegheny City — men who decide from whom they will purchase bricks. And I'm sure Laura would be willing to provide your bookkeeper and time-keepers with any assistance needed until they've become accustomed to their positions." Laura's mother leaned back in her chair. "Does any of this sound appealing to you, Mr. Crothers?"

"Aye. There's no denying we could use a bit of help securing contracts. If we can spend the winter months meetin' with these men you mentioned, we could begin making money come spring. I do believe my wife would take to the idea of meeting some of the wives, as well."

Laura flinched. Mrs. Crothers and her haughty attitude wouldn't enhance Mr. Crothers's opportunity to make a good impression and secure contracts. Then again, Mr. Crothers didn't possess much refinement, either. Did her mother truly expect these meetings to go well?

"For these initial meetings, I believe Mr. McKay would be a better choice. I know you are the owner, but I sense that Mr. McKay possesses a greater degree of passion about the brickworks. His excitement is rather spontaneous, and I think he would make a fine impression upon these men."

"And y'er saying I would not?" Mr. Crothers tugged on his vest. "There's an insult if ever I heard one."

Mrs. Woodfield twirled a handkerchief between her fingers, a sure sign her nerves were taking hold. At times it seemed her mother had become stalwart and strong, able to make difficult decisions and meet criticism without faltering. At other times, with only a word or two, men like Mr. Crothers managed to obliterate all the gumption she'd acquired since her husband's death.

Though she'd agreed to remain quiet, Laura couldn't sit by and do nothing. "My mother would never intentionally insult anyone, Mr. Crothers. She's merely offering you her very best advice, and you must admit that you and Mr. McKay possess very different dispositions." She watched Mr. Crothers for any sign of offense, but seeing none, she continued. "Given Mr. McKay's thoughtful temperament, Mother believes he would best represent your brickworks. Of course, you are not bound to take her advice."

Her mother nodded in agreement. "Laura is right. You may do as you wish." She inhaled a deep breath. "But I know I am correct about this."

Mr. Crothers slapped his thigh and guffawed. "I think you may be as spirited as your daughter, Mrs. Woodfield."

"I don't believe that's true." The aroma of roasted beef drifted into the room, and Mr. Crothers lifted his nose in the air. Mrs. Woodfield glanced toward the dining room. "Would you care to join us for supper, Mr. Crothers? We haven't completed our discussion, and Catherine will be unhappy if the meal is ruined."

"I thank you for the invitation. 'Twould be my pleasure to join you. I'm sure the rest of my family will have finished supper and gone to bed by the time I return to

Bartlett."

Laura winced at his response. Did Mr. Crothers intend to remain and wear her mother down so she would relent and agree to return a portion of his money? If so, he didn't know the women of Woodfield Manor.

CHAPTER 7

Ewan hurried down the hotel steps and into the dining room, eager to visit with his uncle. After supper last night, he'd waited in the lobby, but when his uncle hadn't returned by nine o'clock, Ewan surmised the older man had chosen to spend the night at their new house. He caught sight of his uncle seated at one of the dining tables and was pleased to see he was alone. Whenever Margaret and Kathleen were present, discussions regarding the brickworks quickly changed to talk of houses or furniture.

His uncle waved him into the hotel restaurant and motioned to an empty chair next to him. "Sit down, my boy. We need to talk."

Before Ewan had settled in his chair, a waitress hurried to the table and filled his coffee cup while his uncle slathered a biscuit with butter. The man appeared in good spirits, a sign things had gone his way yesterday afternoon.

After swallowing a bite of the biscuit, he wiped his mouth. "One thing is for sure, Ewan: Business dealings with men are a lot easier than with women. I'm thinkin' those two women had no need of a lawyer. They know how to fend for themselves."

Ewan's earlier optimism was now replaced by dread. His stomach roiled and he swallowed hard to keep the acidic taste of his morning coffee at bay. He was sure to receive a rebuke for suggesting the meeting with Mrs. Woodfield. Yet to ignore the woman's request would have been offensive.

"I'm sorry to hear you had a difficult time. So what do you plan to do? Meet with them again today?"

Uncle Hugh shook his head. "No need. I stayed last night, and we finally came to a meetin' of the minds. There's no way I'll convince 'em they should be giving me some of my money back, but I managed to talk them out of two good horses for the pug mill." He finished off his eggs and downed a gulp of coffee. "Also got 'em to give me names of experienced workers still in the area. Miss Woodfield agreed to help with the books and timekeeping for a spell. It took a bit of persuading, but she finally agreed we could take a look at all their records and contracts, too."

Ewan didn't mention that most of that had been offered to him yesterday. His uncle wanted him to think he'd come out ahead in the negotiations, and Ewan would let him. "Sounds like you struck a good deal, Uncle Hugh. There's real value in having access to those contracts and business papers from the Woodfield Brickworks."

His uncle stroked his mustache. " 'Course there is. That's why I went ahead and settled." His uncle leaned forward and rested his forearms on the table. "One more thing. They're willing to give us introductions to some of the big businessmen up in Wheeling and Pittsburgh." He grinned. "How's that for twisting their arms? I don't think they were real happy, but I insisted they take you along with 'em on their next visit. That way you can start to negotiate contracts before next spring. You'll need to be back here once we begin firing the kilns, but there's no reason you can't spend some time away from Bartlett during the winter."

His uncle had certainly put his own slant on the negotiations. He wondered what Mrs. Woodfield had said to convince his uncle. "So you don't want to travel to Wheeling or Pittsburgh to meet with the contractors? You think it should be me?"

"Aye. That's what I said, isn't it?" He

withdrew a paper from his pocket. "This here's a list of clay cutters and other workers." His uncle pushed the sheet of paper across the table. "We need to go and see about hiring as many of them as we can get. Thought you could begin today. The names with a check beside 'em are the men who still live in these parts."

Ewan didn't miss the fact that his uncle had switched from *we* to *you* when he mentioned beginning the process today. Now that he'd disclosed yesterday afternoon's happenings, he seemed eager to depart. Likely because he didn't want to answer any questions.

"Don't leave just yet, Uncle Hugh. I want to ask about going to Wheeling with Mrs. Woodfield and her daughter. If you expect me to travel with them, I need to know when they're planning to go and when we'll meet with Miss Woodfield to go over their old contracts at the brickworks. It would be good to review those before I try to negotiate new contracts." Ewan sighed. They needed to accomplish a great deal before they would be ready to begin production next spring. "There's a lot to be done in a short time."

His uncle hiked a shoulder. "There's no denying there's plenty of work, but I promised your aunt we could return to the house so she could make a list of things she'd be needin'. Once that's done, I need not tell ya that she'll be wanting to go shopping. Margaret will keep me busy. She's unhappy enough that I didn't manage to get her that mansion, but once she's settled in the other house, I'll be able to do more." He chuckled and placed his napkin on the table. "Besides, that's why you're my partner. I can depend upon ya to take over when I'm busy with other matters."

Ewan inhaled a deep breath. "But I'm not really a partner yet. That's something else we need to discuss."

"Heavens above, you sure are one for complaining. You'll be a partner as soon as the brickyard is turning a decent profit." Hugh removed his pipe from his pocket and pointed the stem toward Ewan. "The quickest way for that to happen is to get yourself busy hiring some of these men, especially the clay cutters." His uncle filled the bowl of his pipe with tobacco. "As for meetings in Wheeling and Pittsburgh with the Woodfield ladies, I cannot tell you what I don't know. If we happen to see either of them while we're out at the house, I'll ask."

Ewan nodded. "And ask them when we'll go over the contracts, as well. That's important, Uncle Hugh."

"Aye." His uncle patted his palm against his chest. "I'll carry your many questions close to me heart and report back with the answers."

Long ago, Ewan had become accustomed to his uncle's bristly comments and learned he ought not compare the man to his own father. Still, Uncle Hugh's sarcasm could occasionally cut to the bone. "If you expect me to do the work, then you need to make certain I have what I need. Otherwise you'll not get the results you want."

Uncle Hugh furrowed his brows. "Feeling a bit full of yourself this morning, are you?"

"I'm only saying what needs to be said. We both should be working to get the brickyard up and running. There will be more than enough time for shopping later."

"Tell your aunt Maggie and see what she has to say about that. You can be sure I won't be giving her that message." His uncle pushed away from the table. "When you go to the livery, ask the older fellow for directions. Miss Woodfield said some of the men live a distance away." His uncle stood and glanced toward the stairway. "I need to go upstairs and fetch your aunt. Good luck. I'll be looking forward to hearing a good report come morning."

Ewan stared at the list, uncertain how his uncle expected him to return with a good report by morning. Unless these men lived within a few miles of the hotel, it would take at least a week to contact all of them. He pushed aside his anger and strode out of the hotel. Resentment would only blur his thoughts and slow him down, and he needed to keep moving. The thud of his heavy boots echoed on the wooden sidewalk as he rounded the corner of the hotel. He stopped short as he came face-to-face with Laura Woodfield.

She gasped and took a backward step. "Mr. McKay. I'm glad you were more alert than I, or we would have collided."

As he looked into her sparkling blue eyes, his heart pounded a new beat. He wanted to say that colliding with her would be the best thing that could happen to him, but she'd think him an impolite fool. What kind of man would say such a thing? Especially to a woman he'd just met? He reined in his whirring thoughts and yanked off his cap. "I hope I did not frighten you too much."

"No, I'm fine." She pressed her palm down the front of her skirt.

A hint of jasmine lightly perfumed the air, the same scent he'd noticed the last time he'd been around Miss Woodfield. "Glad I am for that. I'm thinkin' I need to slow down going around corners in the future." He should let her continue on her way, but he couldn't let her go — not yet. He tapped the pocket where he'd placed the list of possible employees. "I was on my way to the livery. Off to locate some of the workers on the list you gave my uncle. I'm hopeful the stableman can provide me with directions for at least some of them."

Her lips curved in a winsome smile. "I'd be happy to help. Perhaps we could sit down somewhere and I could write out directions for the men who live some distance from town."

He plunged his hands into his pockets and tried to tamp down the thought that she might be attracted to him. She was a lady of social stature, and he was nothing more than a Scots-Irish immigrant with no land or money to his name.

Still, he could use her help, and he'd enjoy the added time with her. "We could go back to the hotel and sit in the lobby. There's a writing desk you could use."

"That would work perfectly." She matched his stride as they walked the short distance and then entered the lobby. "I suggest you begin by contacting the clay cutters first. They're the men you'll need to hire immediately." She glanced up at him as she sat down at the writing desk. Ewan pulled a chair next to hers. She withdrew a piece of hotel stationery from the drawer and said, "I'm going to write the names of the clay cutters and their addresses. I'll do my best to list them in the most direct route so you don't waste a great deal of time."

She carefully penned the names and addresses, stopping occasionally to tell him of a worker who might live near one of the clay cutters.

"If there's a hacker or an edger who lives nearby one of the clay cutters, you might do well to stop and explain that you've purchased the brickworks and are going to hire experienced workers in the spring. You could also ask to post a message at the general store. Mr. Lathrop keeps a board for that purpose."

She glanced at him and her smile disarmed him. He needed to concentrate or he'd forget everything she said before he walked out of the hotel lobby. Ewan forced himself to keep his attention focused upon Laura's comments, but each time he looked at her lips, his thoughts took flight.

"Explaining the systems would be easier if we had the books in front of us."

"W-what?"

"I fear I'm boring you, Mr. McKay. I was telling you about the bookkeeping system."

"Aye, the books." He bobbed his head. "I suggested my uncle ask you for a time when we could meet to go over the books and review your father's contracts."

"Aye. That he did." Hugh's voice boomed in Ewan's ear. He jerked and turned to see his aunt, uncle, and Kathleen surrounding them. "I told Ewan I would speak with you, but I see he beat me to the punch." His uncle squeezed Ewan's shoulder until he flinched from the pain. "What have the two of you been talking about without me, my boy?"

"Only what we've already discussed, Mr. Crothers." Laura tapped the piece of stationery. "I'm giving Ewan directions to the homes of the clay cutters so he can contact them today." Laura flashed a bright smile at the older man. "When did you wish to meet and go over the contracts and books? I'm sure that's foremost in your mind right now."

Aunt Margaret spoke up before Uncle Hugh had an opportunity. "We're eager to move out of the hotel, Miss Woodfield, and I've asked my husband to assist me for the remainder of the week. I fear there's much more to complete than I had anticipated."

His aunt's air of authority didn't surprise Ewan, yet she'd likely need to adjust her behavior if she expected to cultivate acquaintances among the upper crust of society. Otherwise, Mrs. Woodfield and Laura might think her too overbearing.

Laura dipped her pen into the ink. "That's not a problem, Mrs. Crothers." She twisted to look up at Ewan's uncle. "We'll set a time to meet without you, Mr. Crothers. I don't want to interfere with your already burgeoning schedule. I feel certain Mr. McKay will make time to go over the contracts and books." Her lips tilted in a rather insincere smile. "Besides, there's no need for you to be in the middle of things, since Mr. McKay will be in charge of contracting as well as hiring and seeing to the operations at the brickyard. Having to arrange for your presence will only slow progress, don't you think?"

Uncle Hugh narrowed his eyes and stroked his mustache — a sure sign he didn't know how to respond. " 'Tis true I want progress, but I do not want to be left out in the cold."

Laura's smile broadened. "We will be sure to include you if winter arrives early. We wouldn't want you to freeze."

"What's that supposed to mean?" Kathleen appeared completely confused.

"Don't worry yourself, Kathleen. I understand what Miss Woodfield is sayin'." Hugh returned her smile, then slapped Ewan on the shoulder. "And my nephew knows what I'm sayin', as well, don't you, boy?"

His uncle didn't wait for a response. Instead, he shepherded his wife and sister-in-law out of the hotel.

"Your uncle is an interesting man. I don't believe I've ever met anyone quite like him," Laura said. "I hope you don't think I was too forward with him, but I thought if someone else pointed out his misplaced priorities, he might see the error of his ways. He acts as though he's no more than a silent partner."

Ewan chuckled. "I don't think you could ever call Uncle Hugh silent. Believe me, he'll have his say about everything I do."

"And when the brickyard is a huge success, I'm sure he'll step front and center to take full credit. There are more than a handful of businessmen who act in the same manner. I'm thankful to say my father was not one of them. There wasn't a job in the yard he couldn't perform if needed. I saw him do everything from cutting clay from the hillside to sitting up at night to keep watch over the fires in the kilns." Laura handed Ewan the list of names she'd prepared.

"Thank you for this." He nodded toward the piece of paper. "I agree that it's a wise man who knows every measure of his business, but my uncle brought me along so he doesn't have to worry about those details."

Laura raised her eyebrows and pushed away from the desk. "I hope you don't let him take undue advantage, Mr. McKay."

"Laura! What are you doing here?" Winston Hawkins strode toward them. "I'm surprised to see you alone in the hotel lobby with Mr. McKay."

Laura's cheeks flamed a bright shade of pink as other guests in the lobby turned toward them. "You need not worry over my whereabouts, Winston. I believe my mother still claims that duty."

Winston's features went slack, obviously surprised by Miss Woodfield's terse reply, while Ewan fought off the urge to laugh aloud. He doubted Mr. Hawkins would be pleased by any form of levity.

Hoping to lighten the mood, Ewan hastened to explain that he and Laura had met by chance outside the general store.

He planned to tell Winston how they'd arrived at the hotel, but Laura interrupted him. "No need for all this explanation, Mr.

McKay. We are conducting business in a public place in the presence of many people. We've not breached any rules of etiquette." She looked up at Mr. Hawkins. "And should someone think my behavior improper, it does not concern me." Turning around, she picked up her pen. "Now, where were we?"

Ewan hoped her remarks would be enough to send Mr. Hawkins on his way, but the lawyer did not budge. Instead, he pulled a chair to Laura's right and sat down.

Lofty sycamores and poplars shaded the hillside where Ewan and Laura stood. Their position offered a clear view of the towering banks along the Tygart River, where the clay cutters he'd hired only days ago had begun their work. Ewan walked down the hill a short distance and shaded his eyes against the sun. No Irishman could slice into the face of a clay deposit with any greater skill. These brawny West Virginia clay cutters he'd hired were a sight to behold. They stomped on the rims of their razor-sharp hand shovels, and with the precision of acrobats, they balanced themselves just long enough for the shovel to cut through the layer of clay. The strokes were as fast and neat as those of an expert surgeon. Then, with a strong flip of the wrist, the heaping shovelful of clay would land in the dump cart. The driver held the reins taut, careful to keep the horses steady while the cart was being filled.

"They're good men. Treat them fair and you'll get a good day's work. When you begin production next spring, most of them will work an extra stint. They're always glad for the added wages." Laura stepped closer and pointed toward a muscular Negro man. "I'm pleased to see Jessie Sprolls down there. He's the best clay cutter in the state. I thought maybe he went to work over at the coal mine."

"He did. But when I told him I wanted to hire him, he said he'd rather work at the brickyard. Said working in a coal mine didn't suit him. He's the best cutter I've ever seen. Where's he from?"

Laura hiked a shoulder. "He just showed up one day looking for work. If you're wondering if he was ever a slave, I don't know, but I do know he fought in the war. He left Bartlett about the same time as my father. He has several children. They sometimes came and brought him lunch." When Ewan made no move, Laura touched his sleeve. "We should begin going over the books. I don't think Mother will want to stay here too long."

He gave a slight nod. "I'd much rather go down and shovel clay, but you're right. I need to begin learning."

Laura's mother had settled in a chair near one of the office windows overlooking the brickyard. She looked up from her knitting when Laura and Ewan entered the frame building. "Good morning, Mr. McKay. I know you're a trustworthy young man, but I thought I should come along to act as Laura's chaperone. I wouldn't want anyone to get the wrong impression."

Ewan grinned. Laura must have mentioned Winston's comment at the hotel several days ago. "I'm happy to have you join us, Mrs. Woodfield. I'll do my best to learn quickly."

"Laura didn't want to move all of the papers and books to the house, but if I grow weary, I fear you'll have to humor me. Unlike my daughter, I've never enjoyed being out here. I much prefer my home."

Several hours later, Ewan's shoulders ached from bending over the books. He stretched his arms and leaned back in his chair. "It's a good method you have, but I'm not as quick with figures as you."

She chuckled. "In time, it will become easier; it takes practice."

The click of Mrs. Woodfield's knitting

needles ceased. "If you're going to continue working, I suggest we go back to the house. It's nearly time for lunch. Catherine will be worried if we don't return soon."

Laura sighed. "You could return home, have lunch, and ask Catherine to pack a basket for us. I'd like to finish today, Mother. The only person who might come here would be someone looking for work. As I said earlier, I don't think you need to worry about maintaining social mores out here in the brickyard. There were many days when I worked alone in this office while Father was off negotiating contracts."

"Well . . ." Wrinkles creased the older woman's forehead. "I suppose you're right. Though I don't want to shirk my duty as a mother, I do want to go home for a while." She packed her yarn and knitting needles into a cloth bag. "If I decide I'm too tired to return, I'll have Zeke bring a basket lunch out, and he can stay here for the afternoon."

Laura stood, kissed her mother's cheek, and walked her to the door. "Whatever you think best, Mother."

Watching the love and friendship between the two women was a lovely thing, but as they bid each other good-bye, Ewan was struck with an undeniable longing for his three sisters. Leaving them in Ireland had been the most difficult decision of his life. Had his uncle not promised to bring the girls to America as soon as possible, he would have remained in Ireland. His sisters needed him. And he needed them.

"You appear to be pondering something significant. Is it my fractions, or has something else captured your thoughts? Something regarding your uncle, perhaps?"

Ewan forced himself back to the present. He didn't want to admit the fact that his thoughts had nothing to do with the business. She'd think him as indifferent as Uncle Hugh. "There is another matter you might help with. My uncle is still unhappy there is only one VerValen machine. He's determined to have at least two. I believe it's a matter of pride. He wants to have more and better machinery than other brickyards. I've convinced him to wait until we've secured orders, but he wants to move forward so the money is available once there's a need. He doesn't want a delay down the road. Earlier, Mr. Hawkins mentioned he would help with a loan, but when my uncle mentioned it to him, he said we should wait. Is there someone else who might help?"

"I feel sure Winston will reconsider and change his mind. He's on the board of the

Bartlett National Bank. Since he's familiar with the sale of the brickworks and your uncle's financial status, there should be no problem. I'd be happy to speak to him. I'm sure he'll change his mind."

Ewan didn't like the idea of asking for Winston's help, but he'd ask for her recommendation. He could hardly ask for another without giving a good reason. He could say he didn't like Winston because he feared the man was vying for her attentions. But such a comment might guarantee he'd never again see Laura Woodfield.

And he didn't want that to happen.

CHAPTER 8

Laura stood in front of the hallway mirror. After smoothing the black satin bow beneath her chin, she pinned her navy wool felt hat in place and stepped back from the mirror. The hat proved an unexpected match for her traveling suit with black braid trim. The red stripes in her white shirtwaist added a slight hint of cheerfulness to her otherwise plain suit. Perhaps she should have chosen something a bit more colorful. No. The suit would have to do. They'd be late to catch their train if she took time to change.

A pang of guilt shot through her as she completed her preparations. Since she couldn't be at the orphanage this week, she'd promised to stop by and deliver the kaleidoscope she'd received from her father years ago. Mrs. Tremble had agreed to oversee the children as they took turns viewing the various designs created by the instrument. A quick glance at the hall clock was enough to reveal there wouldn't be adequate time. Perhaps Zeke could stop at the orphanage and make the delivery after driving them to the station. Otherwise Kenneth and the other children would be sorely disappointed, and she didn't want that to happen. They'd all had enough disappointment in their young lives.

Stepping onto the front porch, she gestured to Zeke, who had the horse and carriage waiting for them. "You ready to leave, Miss Laura?"

"Mother will be down momentarily, but since we're running a bit late, would you stop at the orphanage and deliver this to Mrs. Tremble?" She held out the gaily decorated kaleidoscope.

Zeke stared at the object and nodded. " 'Course I will. But what is it, Miss Laura?"

"It's called a kaleidoscope. Hold it toward the light and look through this end." She pointed to the small hole at one end of the tube. "Then turn the other end near the glass and the designs will change."

While Zeke peered through the object, Laura hurried back inside to fetch her mother. She'd been looking forward to this trip for several weeks. Ewan had gone over all the contracts, and together they'd made a list and contacted architects and contractors in the Wheeling and Pittsburgh area to schedule meetings.

Eager to begin negotiations, Ewan had already met with a contractor in Fairmont. The man had agreed to consider purchasing from their brickyard, but not until he had an opportunity to examine some of their bricks. He'd promised to hold the bid open until after C&M Brickyard — the name they'd settled on for their business — began production in the spring. The news that the contractor would need bricks for the construction of a new hotel and office building had excited Ewan, but his uncle was unhappy that the man hadn't signed an agreement, and he blamed the lack of success on Ewan's failure to present the letter of introduction Mrs. Woodfield had offered.

Laura had seen the hurt in his eyes when Ewan reported his uncle's accusation. In an attempt to cheer him, Laura had expressed doubt that her mother's letter would have made a difference. She didn't tell him that knowing the right people could make or break a business, but so could a superior product. She'd assured Ewan that if the bricks produced by C&M Brickyard maintained the same quality as those made by Woodfield Brickworks, Ewan would eventually secure the contract in Fairmont. But

Laura and Ewan both knew it would take more than anything she said to impress Hugh Crothers. He wanted a signed contract.

"Has Zeke loaded our baggage into the carriage?" Laura's mother appeared at the top of the stairs in a violet wool suit adorned with narrow silk trim. "There isn't time to dally."

"Our trunk and bags are in the carriage, and Zeke is waiting on the front porch. I believe the only thing missing is you." Laura waved her mother forward. "Did you remember your headache powders?"

Her mother tapped her reticule. "They're in here. I want to keep them close at hand." She descended the stairs and came to a halt. "What are we waiting for? Let's be on our way."

Laura arched her brows. She'd been downstairs for the past fifteen minutes. "Mr. McKay is going to meet us at the train station."

"And Winston?" Her mother glanced over her shoulder as she exited the front door. "Will he be meeting us there or is he joining us later?"

"He plans to take the late afternoon train. There was a meeting he needed to attend this morning." Laura accepted Zeke's help into the carriage and sat down beside her mother.

The groomsman leaned close. "That's a mighty fine toy, Miss Laura. I'll be sure to get it to Mrs. Tremble, and I'll tell her to take good care of it for you."

"Thank you, Zeke." Laura smiled at him before turning back toward her mother. "Winston wanted us to wait and travel with him, but I thought you'd want sufficient time to rest, since we have two meetings tomorrow."

"I'm glad you didn't agree. You know how train rides affect me." The older woman patted her reticule. "I always need my headache powders and a rest once we arrive at our destination."

Laura patted her mother's hand. "You can rest as soon as we get to the hotel. It's good that we've divided the journey and will have several days in Wheeling before we go to Pittsburgh."

Her mother nodded. "I agree. I'm sure the meetings will bore me to tears, but I do want to help Mr. McKay. Since I told Mr. Crothers that his nephew was the better choice to negotiate contracts, I certainly don't want him to fail. If he doesn't meet with success, I doubt Mr. Crothers will ever let him forget." The leather carriage seat squeaked a protest when she twisted toward her daughter. "You did tell him to pack evening wear for the social events we'll attend, didn't you? I wouldn't want him refused entrance for being improperly attired."

"I told him when we first began planning the trip so that he would have time to make any necessary purchases. When I mentioned the need, he thanked me for advising him."

"Dear me, I do hope he doesn't appear in some sort of outlandish attire that he brought with him from Ireland."

"You talk as if people in other countries don't attend social gatherings or wear formal clothing, Mother. Don't tell me you've let Winston influence your opinion regarding immigrants."

"Of course not. I didn't mean to sound prejudiced against the young man. I simply don't want him to be embarrassed."

Laura gave her mother a sideways glance. "You don't want him to be embarrassed, or you don't want him to embarrass you, Mother? Your comment sounded like the latter."

"Do stop, Laura. You're exaggerating a trifling comment. I like Ewan McKay and don't think less of him because he's Irish. We have several acquaintances of Irish

descent. Now, does that settle the matter?"
Mrs. Woodfield pulled a handkerchief from
her reticule and blotted her face. She looked
at her daughter. "Aren't you warm?"

The October day was far from warm, and
her mother's question about the weather,
along with the heightened color in the older
woman's cheeks, alarmed Laura. Immediately regretting she'd taken her mother to
task, Laura placed her palm on her mother's
forehead. "You don't feel as though you
have a temperature. Did my comments
upset you, or are you fretting about the
meetings?"

Her mother shook her head. "No. You're
always permitted to speak your mind. You
know that. As for the meetings, I do find
them boring, but as long as they don't go
on too long, I'll be fine. Of course I'd much
rather have tea with my friends or go shopping for a new gown. Seeing the ladies at a
ball or social gathering doesn't permit time
for a genuine visit."

"I'll see if we can't make time for you to
have tea with a few of your friends while
we're here. I know you'll want to see Laurane, if possible. Did you write and let her
know we'd be visiting?"

Her mother and Laurane had been friends
since their school days in Wheeling, and

both had lost their husbands during the war. Laurane's first husband, John Bullock, had been a Union soldier and had died during the early months of the war, but the loss of Laura's father hadn't been until much later. The deaths had created an even stronger bond between the two childhood friends. Her mother had rejoiced when Laurane met and fell in love with Governor Boreman. Laura had accompanied her mother to Wheeling and attended the elegant yet simple wedding. With the country still suffering from the scourge of war, Laurane had insisted upon a quiet, very private affair. Though some of her friends had encouraged a gala wedding to cheer the public, Laurane's restraint had gained respect from her husband's constituents.

She'd offered comfort when Laura's father died, and even though her duties hosting formal gatherings and traveling with the governor kept her busy, the friendship between the two childhood friends remained strong.

Laura's mother tapped her reticule. "I received a return letter from her last week. She and the governor will be attending the ball tomorrow evening. She said once I had a better idea of my schedule, she'd be sure to make time for us to have a long visit."

Her mother frowned. "We'll see if that's possible. Laurane has more important social obligations than a visit with me."

When they arrived at the train depot a short time later, Zeke unloaded their baggage while Laura escorted her mother inside. "You can sit down over near the window. I'll see to our tickets."

Her mother made a slight turn, her gaze traveling every inch of the small depot. "Where is Mr. McKay?" The concern in her voice matched the worried look in her eyes.

"There's no need to fret, Mother. He'll be here. These meetings are important to him." With her mother settled on one of the wooden benches, Laura crossed the room to the ticket window. Before she had time to complete her purchase, the depot doors opened and Ewan entered, carrying a traveling bag in each hand. His gaze riveted on her, and her breath froze.

Over the past weeks, she'd done her best to deny the happiness that swept over her whenever Ewan entered a room, but her efforts had met with little success. Instead of remaining aloof, her stomach fluttered with anticipation at the sight of him. The reaction made her feel like a silly schoolgirl, yet she could no more control her feelings than she could stop the sun from rising in the east.

His lips tilted in a smile. Did he realize the slight curve of his lips enchanted her?

He rested his hand on the counter near her own. "I hope you weren't concerned. I had planned to be here earlier, but there was a bit of a misunderstanding with my aunt and her sister."

The railroad agent pushed Laura's tickets across the counter, and she tucked them into her reticule. "I do hope you had sufficient time to set things aright before departing. Leaving on a trip is always difficult if things are unsettled at home."

Laura remained at Ewan's side while he purchased his ticket and then accompanied him across the depot waiting room, where they settled beside her mother on the wooden bench. "Ewan had a bit of trouble at home, so he didn't arrive as early as expected." Since her mother had expressed worry over his late arrival, Laura thought it sensible to explain.

Ewan leaned forward. "I wouldn't say it was trouble — more a wee bit of confusion." His smile faded. "Aunt Maggie is known to take matters into her own hands from time to time, which is what happened this morning. Without discussing the situation with my uncle or me, she'd told Kathleen she could come along. My aunt decided that since the two of you were making the trip, it would be fine for Kathleen to join us."

Mrs. Woodfield placed her palm across her bodice. "Dear me. I'm pleased you managed to straighten out that bit of trouble — not that Kathleen is trouble. I didn't mean to imply that. But her name wouldn't be on the guest list for the social events, and it would have proved most embarrassing for all of us."

"That's what I explained to Aunt Maggie. While she didn't agree, Kathleen offered to remain home."

At the shrill sound of a train whistle, the three of them glanced toward the platform. Mrs. Woodfield stood. "I'll be glad when we're finally in Wheeling. I'm thankful for the speed of a train, but traveling is most taxing when you get to be my age."

"I'll say a prayer that our journey will not be too tiring, Mrs. Woodfield. And I hope you know how grateful I am for your help. I know it will give the brickworks a much greater chance of success, which is a matter that's also in my prayers."

"And in mine, Mr. McKay. I know your uncle still believes he didn't receive a fair bargain, but once you begin production, I think he will agree that the contract was more than fair."

"If there's anything that will change my uncle's mind, it's seeing a profitable return on his money, and I plan to do everything in my power to make that happen."

The train belched and wheezed to a stop outside the station, and a short time later Ewan assisted the ladies onboard. Once seated, Laura turned to Ewan. "While I understand you want to see the brickworks become profitable, I didn't realize you shared your uncle's intense interest in making money, Mr. McKay."

Ewan frowned. " 'Tis not making money that spurs me on, but a desire to provide a good life for my three sisters. The faster the brickworks turns a profit, the sooner my uncle will make me a true partner and I'll be able to claim a share of the proceeds. Providing for the three girls is a bit of a challenge, and I'd like to see that they have everything they need. For too long, Rose has had to worry over every farthing that passed through her fingers. I want the girls to enjoy what's left of their childhood." A melancholy expression came over his face. "But I fear that Rose already thinks she's fully grown."

"It's clear your sisters are very important to you. They are fortunate to have an older brother who cares so much."

"They might disagree with you. When I was at home, they were quick to remind me I was not their da." He chuckled. "O'course their comments did not stop me from having my say."

Laura fussed with the tassels of her reticule. "I have a dear friend who had to care for her younger siblings. She said it so tired her of children that she never wanted any of her own."

Ewan's eyes widened. "Truly? I cannot imagine such a thing. Having my sisters to care for has only increased my desire to have children of my own one day. After God, I believe having a family is the most important thing in life. Don't you?"

Laura pressed her palm down the front of her wool skirt. "Yes," she whispered.

"You don't sound completely convinced. I'm guessing that's because you didn't have any brothers or sisters when you were growing up, but once you have one child of your own, you'll want more."

"I don't believe this talk of children is a proper conversation, Mr. McKay," her mother cut in. "Please remember that my daughter is a single woman." She leaned forward an inch or two. "And you are a single man."

"I'm sorry, Mrs. Woodfield." Ewan leaned

a bit closer to Laura and whispered, "Why are we not supposed to speak about children?"

His breath tickled Laura's neck and sent a shiver racing down her arms. "You can talk about children, but not . . ." She hesitated a moment. "It is considered indelicate to speak about a woman bearing children."

Laura didn't miss his look of confusion, but her mother would only frown upon any further explanation.

"I'll need to be careful when I attend social gatherings. I don't want to be saying anything that would embarrass you ladies. Then again, if I'm not sure what is proper, how can I be careful?" His brows furrowed. "I may need to keep my talk to a minimum unless I'm discussing bricks."

"If you stay close to Winston, you should be fine. He'll give you a nudge if you begin to venture onto an inappropriate topic."

Ewan turned toward Laura. "Winston Hawkins is attending the meetings also? You didn't tell me he was coming."

She shook her head. "He won't be going to any of the meetings, only the social gatherings. I believe I mentioned he is going to be in the race for state senator. He's eager to meet with the governor and several others to help formulate his plans."

Ewan's features tightened. "Nay. You did not tell me of his plans to run for a political office or to be in Wheeling. When will he arrive?"

"Late tonight. He'll attend the ball tomorrow evening. You likely won't see him except at the social events, but Mother is right: If you have any concerns, you can feel free to ask Winston's advice. He'll be pleased to assist you."

Ewan didn't reply, and the conversation came to an abrupt halt for the remainder of the train ride. When the conductor passed through the train several hours later and announced Wheeling would be the next stop, Mrs. Woodfield perked to attention and smoothed the folds of her dress. "I'm so thankful we're nearly there. I'm weary of these close quarters."

Ewan accompanied the ladies into the train station. When Mrs. Woodfield spied a friend in the depot and they were alone for a moment, he turned to Laura.

"Why didn't you tell me Winston was going to be here?"

"I didn't think it was of consequence. We'll be conducting our meetings during the daytime while he's meeting with senators and testing the political waters. It worked to our advantage that we could all be here at the same time."

"Had I known you would have an escort, I wouldn't have rejected Kathleen's request to come along. If you were planning to make me feel like a fifth wheel on the wagon, you've accomplished your goal."

Laura recoiled as though she'd been slapped. She would never intentionally hurt another person. Her mother was the one who had encouraged Winston to join them. It wasn't until after he'd made his arrangements that Laura learned about the plans. She'd had no say in the decision.

For some time now, her mother had done everything possible to encourage Winston. Truth be told, her mother had been more delighted than Laura when he formally asked to court her. And the fact that all the single women in Laura's social circle thought her fortunate to be the one whom Winston had chosen only made matters worse. When several of her friends lamented the fact that Winston had overlooked them, Laura tried to discover why they were drawn to him. Perhaps a spark of love would be kindled if she could ascertain what she might have overlooked. He was an excellent lawyer and would likely become an excellent politician. Yet, try as she may, Laura continued to think of Winston as a friend, nothing more. She'd even spoken with her mother, but to no avail.

Instead of calling off the courtship, her mother had whisked away Laura's protests with a comment that love is sometimes slow to bloom. While she understood her mother's reasoning for the match, Laura would rather remain a spinster than marry a man she didn't love. Yet, for longer than she could remember, her mother had expressed regret that Laura had been without siblings to share her early years. As the years passed, her mother had made it clear that before she died, she intended to make certain Laura had a husband. And since her father's death, her mother's determination had increased tenfold.

Laura extended her hand toward Ewan. "Wait. I can explain if you'll give me a moment."

"You owe me no explanation. We're here to conduct business during the daytime, and Winston is here to be your escort and entertain you in the evenings. It's all very clear." He motioned toward the baggage being unloaded down the platform. "I'll go and make arrangements to have the baggage delivered to the hotel. No need for you and your mother to wait on me. I can come to the hotel once I've finished." He glanced across the depot. "I believe your mother said she wanted to rest as soon as we arrived."

Laura didn't want to leave him, but from the set of his jaw, she knew he would insist. He didn't want to hear her explanations, and he didn't want to ride to the hotel with them. He wanted to be alone and ruminate upon what he'd been told. It was clear he thought she'd deceived him. But if he wouldn't give her an opportunity to explain, how would he learn the truth?

She stared after him as he strode away. How she wished she'd told him before they'd departed. This journey could prove to be a disaster.

CHAPTER 9

Shortly after Laura and her mother departed the station, Ewan ascertained the hotel was only a half mile away. After arranging for delivery of the baggage, he set out on foot, stopping for his evening meal at a small restaurant along the way. A chance meeting with Laura and her mother in the hotel dining room was the last thing he wanted right now.

He couldn't deny the feelings of betrayal that had engulfed him when he'd learned Winston would be arriving in Wheeling. When Laura had arranged the trip to Wheeling, he'd assumed he would act as her escort. She'd never actually said as much. Then again, she'd never said he wouldn't. Why had she been so secretive? Was she one of those girls who enjoyed toying with men? He'd seen his share of those lasses in Ireland. One day they'd make you think you were the only man alive, and the next you'd see them on the arm of another lad. And he'd obviously read far too much into those invitations.

He'd wanted to believe that Laura might have an interest in him that went beyond helping to get the brickyard established, but her kindness had been nothing more than a bit of blarney. It was merely her attempt at making an immigrant believe he could be equal to someone like her father or Winston Hawkins. What a fool he'd been to think that someone as beautiful and refined as Laura Woodfield would ever cast a look in his direction.

He went to bed and reminded himself that the only females he should think about were his three sisters still living in Ireland. He must remember that he was responsible for them. Laura Woodfield had no need of a poor Scots-Irishman. She needed a gentleman of wealth and position. She needed Winston Hawkins.

The following morning, Ewan entered the dining room and requested a table by the window — a table with only two chairs. The waiter hadn't yet served him his coffee when Mrs. Woodfield tapped him on the shoulder with a delicate lace fan. "What are you doing sitting over here by yourself? Didn't you see us seated across the room?" She didn't wait for an answer, but immediately flagged the waiter. "I left word with the maître d' to seat Mr. McKay at our table." She glanced toward the pedestal at the dining room entrance and frowned.

"He wasn't there when I arrived, and I asked this waiter to seat me. 'Twas not the fault of the waiter, Mrs. Woodfield. If you're wanting to place blame, it belongs to me, not this poor fellow." The waiter scrambled behind them, fear shining in his eyes. No doubt the poor man worried he'd be without a job by day's end. Ewan glanced over his shoulder. "You need not worry. We'll be giving nothing but praise to anyone who asks about your service." The waiter held Mrs. Woodfield's chair for her. "Isn't that right, Mrs. Woodfield?" Ewan scrutinized the woman's face for some sign of agreement.

She offered a barely distinguishable smile. "Yes, of course. This isn't a matter of concern. You've been most helpful."

Though the waiter's spine remained as straight as a broomstick, his jaw relaxed a modicum. "Thank you, madam." He gave a slight bow and glanced at Ewan. "And my thanks to you, as well, sir."

"No need for thanks," Ewan said, giving the waiter a friendly pat on the shoulder.

The man hurried away from their table, most likely feeling quite pleased that his tables were in another section. After nodding to Laura, Ewan took a seat between the two ladies.

Mrs. Woodfield draped a linen napkin across her lap and leaned toward Ewan. "It is not proper etiquette to be overly friendly with the hotel staff. Touching them in any manner isn't acceptable." Ewan picked up the cut-glass pitcher and poured water into his goblet. When he attempted to add water to Mrs. Woodfield's glass, she quickly covered it with her hand. "You do not pour your own water, either. That is why they have waiters, Mr. McKay."

Ewan nodded toward the waiter. "If he's busy helping people at another table and I'm thirsty, why should I wait for him to pour the water? That makes no sense."

Mrs. Woodfield looked at Laura. Obviously she hoped her daughter would be able to explain. "Mother is trying to help you understand proper rules of etiquette so that you won't be embarrassed in the future. Many of the rules may seem foolish, but you'll soon grow accustomed to them." Attired in a lovely dress that accentuated her dark brown curls, she appeared to fit perfectly in these lavish surroundings, while he felt as uncomfortable as a fish on dry ground.

"Here you are! I'm glad for the opportunity to see you before you depart for your meetings this morning." Winston appeared at Laura's side with a smile as wide as the front door. He gave Ewan a faint nod and turned the remaining empty chair toward Laura.

Water goblet and silverware in hand, their waiter appeared out of nowhere and hurried to Winston's side. "I'm sorry, sir, I didn't realize another guest would be joining this group." He poured some water into Winston's glass. "Coffee?"

"I've already had my breakfast." Winston dismissed the waiter with a flick of his wrist.

After a slight nod, the waiter backed away from the table and returned to his position behind one of the nearby pillars, a spot where he could inconspicuously observe his assigned tables. With his back to Ewan, Winston continued to engage the ladies in conversation, inquiring about the suitability of their accommodations and assuring them he would do anything necessary to ensure their comfort. If it had been Winston's intent to shut him out of their small circle, he'd succeeded. Ewan felt as invisible as the restaurant staff. When the waiter arrived with their breakfast, Winston stood and offered Laura and her mother effusive goodbyes. The nod Winston directed at Ewan was so swift and negligible that he had no time to return the gesture. The message was clear: Winston wasn't happy to have another man present. The one commonality he and Ewan shared — beyond their interest in Laura, of course.

"May I offer thanks for our meal?" Ewan asked, looking toward Mrs. Woodfield for approval.

"Of course." She'd hesitated as if somewhat surprised by his request.

Uncertain if he'd overstepped propriety, he kept the prayer short. Perhaps giving thanks for one's food in a fancy dining room wasn't acceptable. When they were alone later, he would ask Laura if the practice was frowned upon. There seemed to be endless rules among these wealthy, fancy folks. He'd soon need a notebook to write them all down, so he could review them each time he came to Wheeling or Pittsburgh.

As their meetings progressed throughout the day, Ewan faced the fact that securing contracts wasn't going to prove as simple as he'd thought. Having Mrs. Woodfield and Laura along had gotten his foot in the door, but securing a deal fell upon his unseasoned shoulders. His meeting at a building site in Fairmont didn't compare to these conferences in wood-paneled offices with oversized mahogany desks and cigar-smoking men in expensive suits who immediately sniffed out Ewan's inexperience. Granted, he knew more about bricks than any of these businessmen, but his experience in Ireland had been supervising the brickmaking process, not negotiating contracts.

Spotting Winston waiting at the front door of the hotel when they returned only served to dishearten him further. No doubt Winston would take pleasure in hearing that Ewan had met with little success.

Winston looked to be in a good mood. "I hope your day was as successful as my own." He offered Laura his arm, but it was Mrs. Woodfield who sidestepped and grasped hold. He looked surprised, but he quickly recovered and patted Mrs. Woodfield's hand before turning toward Ewan. "Any luck with your meetings?"

"Nothing definite. The men appeared interested, but they're not willing to move forward until they have an opportunity to examine the product."

"I don't know why you don't just tell them a brick is a brick. We all know that one brick is about the same as any other. My guess is you lack the ability to convince them. They're accustomed to dealing with men who know how to drive a hard bargain, and it appears you waved a white flag." He shook his head. "Hard to gain respect after you've done that."

"I will have you know that a brick is not a brick, Winston, and Ewan did not wave a white flag." Laura's eyes flashed with anger. "Do you also believe that all shoes are alike?"

"There's nothing similar about shoes and bricks, Laura." There was a hint of disdain in Winston's voice.

Laura stopped short. "There *is* a similarity between shoes and bricks. A good shoe depends upon how the leather is tanned and on the talent of the cobbler. A good brick depends upon the quality of the clay and the talent of the brickmaker. If a brick isn't dried long enough before entering the kiln or if the burner doesn't know how to maintain a proper fire, the brick may look good on the outside, but crack under pressure." She tipped her head to one side and lifted an eyebrow. "I believe politicians sometimes crack under pressure, as well. Don't you agree?"

"I don't think there's time for a discussion regarding bricks or politicians right now. I'm eager to go upstairs and rest for a while before attending tonight's festivities." Mrs. Woodfield gestured to her daughter. "Judging from your peevish remarks to Winston, I think a bit of rest would serve you well, too, Laura."

"I don't think my remarks were peevish, Mother. I thought Winston's assessment completely inaccurate, and I merely set forth my position. I'm sure he's accustomed to being challenged. After all, he's required to debate his cases in the courtroom."

"True, but you're not his adversary, Laura." Her mother arched her brows at Laura as their waiter scurried to help with her chair.

As they prepared to depart the dining room, Ewan leaned close to Laura so the others wouldn't hear. "Thank you for defending me, but I'm sure your mother is correct. Your remarks appear to have troubled him."

Laura's shoulders lifted and dropped in a slight shrug. "Making Winston happy isn't why I've come here. I don't ever want my father's brickyard to fail."

Ewan remained beside her as they ascended the hotel stairs. "But it isn't your father's brickyard any longer."

"Perhaps not, but if it doesn't succeed, I will feel as though I have failed him. He would want you to experience great success, and so do I."

"Did I hear you wish me success, my dear?" Winston glanced over his shoulder as they arrived at the hallway leading to their rooms.

Ewan tensed. Was Laura Winston's "dear," or was Winston merely intent upon staking his claim when he deemed an adversary might be vying for her attention? "No, you didn't, but I know Mother is hopeful your political career will prove a great success."

When they'd come to a stop in front of the suite occupied by the two ladies, Winston turned to Laura. "I trust you desire the same success for me."

"I would wish failure only upon those who attempt to reach their goals by deception and fraud or at the expense of others. Since I doubt you fall into any of those categories, I wish you success." Her lips tilted in a fleeting smile before she stepped toward the door. As she turned to look over her shoulder, the abrupt movement caused the feathers on her hat to sway.

Her comment was a reminder that Ewan's uncle had accumulated the funds to purchase the brickyard by cheating at cards. If

Laura knew, what would she do? Would she ask her mother to renege on the contract?

Ewan's stomach clenched so tight he was overcome by a bout of queasiness. "If you'll excuse me, I'm going to my room." Without waiting for an answer, he hurried down the hallway.

"Don't forget to meet us downstairs at seven o'clock, Mr. McKay."

Ewan continued moving but waved to acknowledge Mrs. Woodfield's reminder. Right now he didn't want to think about a dinner party.

While they rode in the carriage to the governor's home, Laura quietly explained to Ewan what he could expect throughout the evening. She even encouraged him to watch her, should he feel uncertain about proper etiquette. She told him that if the governor wanted to give thanks for the meal, he'd do it himself, and Ewan should not offer. Knowing there would be many people present, he hadn't planned to ask, but he thanked her for advising him.

As they continued onward, Laura pointed out the state capitol. Ewan was disappointed. The building was nothing more than a rectangular brick structure, not the impressive building Ewan had anticipated.

When he stated that he considered the building rather uninspiring, Laura was quick to defend the choice. "You must remember that West Virginia wasn't admitted to the Union until 1863. During the war, the construction of an impressive capitol building wasn't important to the people of our state. We were focused upon winning the war. When the building that housed the Linsly School was offered, it seemed a perfect answer." Her lips curved in a generous smile. "Our legislators have been able to accomplish their work, and I'm not aware of any complaints — or any offers of money to build a new state capitol."

"I did not mean my remarks as an insult, but both Scotland and Ireland are countries where the gentry and our rulers possess huge castles. I expected something more massive and grand."

"No need for apologies. Perhaps one day we will have a beautiful capitol building, but this has served us well thus far. I think you've forgotten that America is a much younger country than either Scotland or Ireland. While you may see a number of forts in our country, I doubt you'll find any castles that compare with the ones in your homeland." Laura glanced out the carriage window. "Here we are. This is the governor's home. I do hope you'll enjoy the evening."

At dinner, Ewan was seated across from Laura and Winston, with an elderly lady to his right and a younger woman to his left. He did his best to make conversation, but the elderly lady couldn't hear, and the younger one was interested in the young man seated to her other side. For the majority of the dinner, he silently watched Laura's every movement and was pleased to receive an occasional nod of approval and smile.

After dinner, he followed the other guests up a winding stairway to a ballroom on the third floor of the home and leaned against a wall located near the doors to the balcony — a place where he could escape and gain a bit of fresh air if needed. When the music began, the governor escorted his wife onto the dance floor to lead the customary first dance. As soon as the governor signaled for their guests to join in, Winston and Laura were among the first couples to step forward. They swirled around the dance floor, her pale green gown shimmering in the candlelight. Her beauty captured the interest of every man and woman in the room. From his spot near the balcony, Ewan maintained a close watch and didn't miss the fact that Winston monopolized her time. Although she'd offered her dance card to

Ewan before they'd come upstairs, he had declined. He might know how to dance a Britannia two-step or a Circassian circle, but his knowledge of American dances wasn't any greater than his knowledge of their state buildings and rules of etiquette. Besides, making a fool of himself in front of all these people held no appeal.

After watching for a short time, he retreated to the balcony. He'd been there only a few minutes when Laura drew near. "I hope you're not planning to jump."

Ewan chuckled and shook his head. "Nay, but I heard two of the ladies mention the party would continue until the wee hours of the morning. If I'm required to remain until then, I might reconsider. Will we be here much longer?"

"I'm afraid so, but if you'd rather return to the hotel, you can thank Governor and Mrs. Boreman for their invitation and add your regrets that you must depart early. They will understand. You're not the only one who will leave before the party ends."

"What about the carriage?"

"You can have the driver take you back to the hotel and ask him to return and wait for us. An additional trip means more money. He'll be glad to take you."

"I'll be remembering your instructions

should I leave early." Ewan glanced over his shoulder. "Where's Winston?"

She nodded toward the dance floor. "His obligatory dance with the governor's wife."

He hadn't realized there were obligatory dances. A knot formed in the pit of his stomach. Why hadn't Laura told him? He glanced toward the ground below. "If I'm required to dance with the governor's wife, I may change my mind and leap off this balcony. These American dances are un-known to me."

"You're not required to dance with her. Winston hopes to impress both the governor and his wife, because he wants to gain the governor's support in the state senate elec-tion."

Ewan sighed. "That's music to my ears and further confirmation that I do not ever want to run for a political office." Ewan folded his arms across his chest and rested his hip against the railing. "You said politics don't particularly interest you, so I'm curi-ous why you would choose Mr. Hawkins as a steady escort. The two of you don't seem to be well suited."

"Really? I didn't know you were an au-thority on matchmaking, Mr. McKay." For a moment he thought he'd angered her, but he caught a glimpse of her smile in the moonlight.

" 'Tis true I'm not an authority on love, but I do know two people who share common interests and conduct, and I don't see similar aims between you and Mr. Hawkins." He pushed away from the railing. "So tell me — what it is that draws you to him?"

In the moonlight, he could see her knuckles turn white as she tightened her hold on the railing. "There are things that you don't know, Mr. McKay. If you did, you wouldn't ask that question. Suffice it to say that the thing that draws us together would be the very thing that would end a courtship for most couples." With a slight bow, she released her hold on the balcony rail, grasped the fullness of her gown, and turned toward the doorway. "Good evening, Mr. McKay."

Ewan remained on the balcony and stared at the starlit sky while strains of violin music wafted through the open door. He leaned his forearms on the railing and contemplated Laura's words. They made no sense. What would draw her to Winston but away from any other men? Could it have something to do with her mother, or perhaps with their finances? He doubted they could be in dire financial straits. After all, they'd recently received payment for the brickyard from his uncle. Perhaps there had been some promise between Laura's father and Winston — something untoward that most men would consider unacceptable. He pondered the idea through the remainder of the next dance set and then decided to leave.

Laura had been correct. Governor and Mrs. Boreman weren't offended by his departure, and the cab driver was pleased to end the evening with some extra silver in his pocket.

Arriving at the hotel, Ewan went directly to his room and to bed, but sleep eluded him. His thoughts remained on Laura and Winston, and on his inability to secure contracts.

Tomorrow afternoon they would board a steamboat bound for Pittsburgh and more meetings. Meetings he hoped would yield a contract.

CHAPTER 10

Ewan rested his forearms on the railing of the steamboat as it chugged up the Ohio River toward Pittsburgh. Moments later, the wind shifted and he turned to avoid the unpleasant river odors and dank early evening air. He'd remained on the deck since they'd finished supper, watching as they passed forested banks and small towns with houses hugging the mountainsides. The high-pitched whistle of an occasional passing boat overshadowed the constant chugging of the boat.

Thoughts of Rose and the twins overcame him as the moon ascended in the evening sky and cast a shimmering reflection on the murky river water. Were his sisters watching the moon right now? He hoped not. By his calculations, they should have been in their beds hours ago. While he was still aboard the ship coming to America, one of the sailors had spoken of the time difference and explained that time was earlier in America. At first Ewan thought the sailor was playing a joke on him, but he soon learned it was true. After that, whenever he thought of his sisters, he immediately estimated the time in Ireland. It helped him determine what they might be doing.

"Did you decide you preferred your own company rather than visiting with other passengers in the dining saloon?" Winston stepped to Ewan's side and leaned his back against the rail.

"I was seated at a table with five strangers, all of them old enough to be my parents and most of them hard of hearing. Between my accent and their hearing problems, I had to repeat everything I said two or three times. It's more relaxing to stand out here by myself."

"I thought perhaps you were brooding. Laura mentioned you were a bit discouraged by your inability to get any definite commitments at your meetings in Wheeling."

Ewan nodded. "That's true enough. I'm thinking my uncle will be more than a little discouraged by the news and will consider the trip a failure on my part."

"You may meet with greater success in Pittsburgh. I know Laura has scheduled some meetings there with a number of her father's former business colleagues." He removed a cigar from his jacket pocket and twirled it between his fingers. "Laura also mentioned the fact that your uncle could use help with a loan to buy another Ver-Valen machine. He spoke to me about the prospect of a loan, but I advised him I thought it prudent to wait. However, Laura asked that I reassess my position, and since I can't be much help with your meetings in Pittsburgh, I've agreed to do what I can to help with the loan. You can tell your uncle to pay me a visit at my office after we return to Bartlett. I'll take him over to the bank and make certain he gets whatever he needs to purchase additional machinery."

"That's good of you, but once he hears the results of my trip, he may not be as eager to acquire any loans." Ewan wanted to question Winston's motives, but that would likely muddy the waters. Obviously he wanted to please Laura. The thought troubled him, but if he said anything that caused Winston to withdraw his offer, Uncle Hugh would be less than understanding.

Winston shoved the cigar back in his pocket. Ewan gestured toward the lawyer's jacket. "You ever smoke that thing or just carry it around?"

"Laura doesn't like the smell, so I try to refrain. But I still keep one on me most of the time." He chuckled. "Old habits die hard. I'd better get back inside or Laura will think I've gone to bed and left her to fend for herself. Sure you don't want to come in with me? I think there are some young single ladies who would be pleased to keep you company."

Ewan shook his head. He probably should accept the offer, as it was the first hospitable exchange he'd had with Winston since he'd joined them in Wheeling. "Thank you for the offer, but I believe I'll turn in."

"I'm beginning to think you're a man who enjoys a good night's sleep more than a good party. Am I correct?"

"Aye, that would be right. I'm better at burning bricks than making idle chatter with strangers."

"There's much to be said for socializing, Ewan. You never know who you might meet. Could be someone sitting in that dining saloon who's eager to find a good brick supply. I've struck many a bargain at a fancy dinner party." He nudged Ewan. "And sometimes over a gaming table, as well."

"If you meet someone interested in bricks, you tell him to meet me for breakfast and we'll talk business."

After bidding Winston good-night, Ewan pushed away from the railing. He didn't want to return to the saloon and watch Winston fawn over Laura, and he didn't want to try to strike a deal with gambling or drinking men. His uncle might be as crooked as a barrel of fish hooks, but Ewan had no desire to share his reputation.

As they continued upriver the next day, the seating arrangements at meals remained the same, and Ewan saw little of Laura and her mother during the remainder of his time aboard the *Liberty Belle.* They were nearing Pittsburgh when Laura met him in the dining saloon. "I'm pleased I've finally located you." She sat down opposite him. "I was visiting with some other passengers last evening, and they suggested you become acquainted with James Laughlin. He's one of the owners of Jones and Laughlin, a company involved in the iron industry and coal mining."

"Is he in need of bricks?"

Laura grinned. "I don't know if he needs any bricks, but I do know he's Scots-Irish. Like you, he's from Ulster Province, and he could possibly help direct you to some people in the construction business." She touched his arm. "And you'll never guess what else Winston and I discovered."

"I'm sure I won't." The mention of Winston's name diminished the pleasure he'd experienced when she'd touched his arm moments ago.

"Then I'll tell you." Her voice trembled with excitement. "Thomas Mellon is Scots-Irish, as well. Isn't that exciting?"

Ewan wasn't sure who Thomas Mellon was or why that fact should be so exciting. Before leaving Ireland, they knew there were many Scots-Irish who had settled in this region. "And why should that be exciting?"

"He's an assistant judge in the Allegheny County Court of Common Pleas and is highly respected. Winston is going to have one of his friends try to arrange a meeting for you with Mr. Mellon."

Her voice bubbled with excitement, but Ewan remained confused. Why did she and Winston think meeting a judge or a man who owned an iron business would be of any great help? He needed to meet men who owned construction businesses or architects — men who needed bricks to perform their work.

"I appreciate what you're trying to do, but —"

"I can see you don't think this will be helpful, but trust me, it will. If these men recommend you, business will come your way without the need of much effort on your part." Her face radiated far more confidence than Ewan could muster.

He didn't want to hurt her feelings. After all, she was trying to help. "If you're able to arrange the meetings, I'll be pleased to discuss Ireland and my ancestry with your acquaintances." Secretly, he'd already decided the meetings would be a waste of valuable time.

"That's important, of course, but you need to discuss the business with them, too. These men understand investments and growth. They can offer sound advice as well as recommendations to their friends who are in the construction business."

Ewan did his best to appear enthusiastic when Winston stepped into the room and patted Ewan on the shoulder. "I told you that time in the dining saloon could be valuable. You should have listened to me."

"Aye, you were right." He wouldn't say anything more, but he feared this trip to Pittsburgh was going to be as fruitless as his time in Wheeling. "Shall we go out and take in the fresh air?"

Winston guffawed and pointed toward one of the windows. "I don't think you'll see much. Take a look out there. The closer to

Pittsburgh, the hazier the view. Right now, you can barely see the shoreline, and it will only get worse. Believe me, you won't need to step onto Duquesne Way to understand why folks refer to Pittsburgh as hell with the lid taken off. Some say living in Pittsburgh is good practice for those who are on their way to that fiery furnace the Bible promises."

When they disembarked a short time later, Ewan understood Winston's earlier description of the city. The pervasive effects of industry blanketed the city in a miasma that blocked out the sun and cast a murky pall in every direction. In Ireland, the gloomy days were caused by foul weather that eventually gave way to the sun. But here it was impossible for the sun to ever penetrate the dark covering that hovered over the city.

"I was right, wasn't I?" Winston asked. He didn't wait for an answer before hastening off to arrange for delivery of their baggage.

Ewan took note of the people who swarmed the riverfront. He appeared to be the only person amazed that the sun, clouds, and sky were blotted from view. Remarkably, neither the crews unloading freight from steamers nor the crowds scurrying along the waterfront seemed to notice the haze. He gave fleeting thanks that he would soon leave this city. He needed fresh air and a bit of sunshine; Pittsburgh was short on both.

Winston soon returned with news that the baggage would be delivered to the hotel. With a quick wave of his leather-gloved hand, he hailed a carriage. The man's ability to handle every detail left Ewan feeling as useless as a stove without fuel.

After assisting the ladies into the carriage, Winston leaned toward the driver. "Take us to the Monongahela House at the corner of Smithfield and Water Streets."

Ewan settled onto the leather seat beside Winston, with the two ladies sitting opposite.

"The Monongahela House is one of Laura's favorite hotels — isn't it, Laura?" Winston grinned at her as if to imply they shared some special secret. When neither Laura nor Ewan responded, Winston leaned toward Laura and urged her to explain why she favored the hotel.

"The Monongahela House hosted President Lincoln en route to his inauguration. He wasn't president when he stayed at the hotel, but he was a guest and gave some brief remarks the evening he arrived and a formal speech the following morning."

" 'Twill be an honor to have lodging at an

inn where your President Lincoln was once a guest. I can understand why you are fond of the place."

Winston snorted. "This isn't Ireland or the countryside, Ewan. The Monongahela House is a fine hotel, not an inn."

Laura frowned. "And if you were traveling in Ireland, would you know the proper name for every building, Winston? Your remark was offensive."

"And not particularly polite." Mrs. Woodfield pursed her lips in disapproval.

"You need not scold him on my account, ladies. I'm going to be staying in a fine hotel, and glad I am for that." Ewan brushed a piece of lint from his trousers. "I'm sure Winston didn't mean to be critical. That fact aside, I've developed a thick skin since coming to this country."

When the carriage came to a halt in front of the hotel a short time later, Winston straightened his shoulders and gestured toward the massive edifice. "I'm sure you understand why the president chose to stay here."

Ewan surveyed the five-story building constructed of blond brick and gave a nod. " 'Tis quite a sight. Many bricks were needed to construct this fine hotel. If things go well, perhaps I'll be making bricks that will be used to build some additional hotels in Pittsburgh," he said as he followed the others into the massive foyer.

The interior of the hotel featured white marble floors, black walnut stairways, and a ballroom lined with deep purple velvet curtains and topped with gilded ceilings. Though Ewan hadn't seen the ballroom, Winston was quick to mention the many features. "There will be a gala hosted in the ballroom tomorrow evening."

Laura stepped closer. "Mr. Laughlin and Judge Mellon will be present. We'll try to arrange for private meetings with both of them during the gala."

Ewan tried to match her excitement, but the most he could muster was a quiet thank-you. Dread hung over him as he ascended the stairs to his room on the second floor of the hotel. These final days of the journey were going to be no better than the first. He could feel it in his bones.

He'd been correct. There had been meetings with Mr. Laughlin and Judge Mellon, and Ewan had enjoyed talking about the homeland with both of the men. They'd been welcoming and kind, even eager to hear about the brickyard and Ewan's plans to make C&M Brickyard the finest in the country. They'd even alluded to future projects that would require large orders of bricks. Both men pledged their assistance in spreading the word to their colleagues and promised to maintain contact with Ewan. But, in the end, the meetings concluded without an offer to subsidize the brickyard with funds for additional equipment or a contract for bricks.

During the return from Pittsburgh to Wheeling, Ewan kept to his stateroom as much as possible. He appeared for meals, but otherwise avoided contact with other passengers. Now that they'd settled at the hotel in Wheeling for the night, he knew he couldn't avoid dinner with the others. Mrs. Woodfield had been clear when they arrived at the hotel that reservations had been made for all four of them in the main dining room.

Shortly before six o'clock, Ewan descended the staircase. He'd crossed the hotel foyer and turned to the right when Winston appeared and grasped his arm. "Since we didn't see much of you onboard the steamer, I'm surmising you weren't feeling well. I wanted to visit alone with you before now, but since I couldn't locate you, I decided to wait here in hopes we'd have a few minutes before joining the ladies."

"Something urgent to discuss?" Ewan

carefully avoided the comment about his health. He didn't want to admit that it had been his sour mood and not his physical health that had kept him in his stateroom during their time on the steamer.

"I haven't yet told Laura or Mrs. Woodfield, but I won't be returning until later in the week. There are a few other politicians I want to spend time with here. I know Laura will be disappointed, but she shares my political aspirations and will understand. I didn't tell them earlier because I didn't want to ruin the remainder of the trip for Laura."

Ewan attempted to digest Winston's remarks. Were Winston's political aspirations what had attracted Laura to Winston? She'd mentioned the fact that he'd only recently asked to court her. Had she waited until he told her of his interest in becoming a candidate before agreeing to be courted by him? Or had it been Mrs. Woodfield who'd been swayed by Winston's ambitions? In truth, Mrs. Woodfield appeared more interested in politics than Laura, but Ewan couldn't be positive. He'd learned that women had a way of hiding their true feelings from time to time.

Winston nudged his arm. "Are you listening? It doesn't appear you've heard a word I said."

Ewan startled back to the present. "I'm afraid I don't understand the reason why Laura will be disappointed that you're not immediately returning to Bartlett."

Winston pinned him with a scalding glare. "She will be disappointed because she enjoys my company and expects me to escort her home. When I arranged to meet the three of you in Wheeling, I told her we would be together for the remainder of the journey. Now I must break my promise."

"I see." Even though he pretended to understand, Ewan couldn't fathom why Winston thought Laura would be devastated by such an insignificant bit of news unless she cared for him more than she'd divulged.

She'd traveled to Wheeling without Winston at her side and had appeared perfectly content. Ewan had tried to understand the bond between Winston and Laura, but he'd not met with any success. Truth be told, he'd begun to wonder if he would ever understand any of these society folks.

"And why did you want to discuss this with me?"

Winston expelled a deep sigh. "I want you to assure Laura and her mother that you'll be there to look after their needs, if any should arise."

Confused by Winston's response, Ewan frowned. "Why would they need such an assurance? I'll be traveling with them."

"You were traveling with us on the steamer, but you were nowhere in sight. If they had needed assistance, they could hardly have come to your stateroom." Winston's retort bore more than a hint of annoyance.

Ewan could hardly mention it was Winston's presence that had caused him to retreat to his stateroom. "You have my word that I will make myself available to both of the ladies on our return from Wheeling to Bartlett." He wanted to add that they would be traveling in the same railcar, so the request was pointless, but Winston was already troubled. No need to agitate him any further.

As he'd both hoped and expected, Laura showed no despair when Winston announced he'd be remaining in Wheeling for additional political meetings. Mrs. Woodfield was delighted to hear there was additional interest in Winston's campaign, which didn't surprise Ewan. However, he was somewhat taken aback when Laura appeared pleased by the news. No matter how hard he tried, it seemed he couldn't unearth

Laura's true feelings about anything other than her father's brickyard.

As the meal came to an end, the older woman took Winston's arm. "We're going to be pleased to have a state senator in the family one day."

Winston chuckled and patted her hand. "Who can say? Perhaps one day you'll have a United States senator or a president in the family. I'm sure that would please you even more."

The older woman looked up at him and beamed. "Indeed it would, and I know you're inspired to serve our state as well as the nation."

Laura walked alongside Ewan. "You've undoubtedly noticed Mother enjoys associating with those involved in politics. When her dear friend married the governor several years ago, she became more interested in politics than previously."

"Aye. She does appear to be interested in Winston being elected to office." He grinned. "Perhaps she would like me a little better if I learned more about the American political system."

Laura shook her head. "Only if you were running for office."

"And what if I lost? Would she then lose interest in me?"

"In all likelihood." Laura kept her voice low as they neared the staircase.

"Maybe I should be praying that Winston loses his race for state senator. That might convince your mother he isn't worthy of you."

She tipped her head to meet his gaze. "I appreciate the thought behind your words, but my mother means well. She understands Winston, as well as what must be accomplished to advance his future." Laura hesitated a moment. "And my own."

Once again she'd made a subtle reference to something that required further explanation.

CHAPTER 11

Ewan was surprised when he stepped off the train at Bartlett and discovered Uncle Hugh, Aunt Maggie, and Kathleen all waiting at the station. His mouth went dry at the sight of them. No doubt Uncle Hugh had arrived to hear the outcome of his meetings in Wheeling and Pittsburgh. Ewan had hoped for an opportunity to speak privately with his uncle, rather than having his aunt involved in the conversation.

Before reporting that he'd been unable to gain even one contract, he had hoped to soften the blow by elaborating on his meetings with Mr. Mellon and Mr. Laughlin. He'd hoped that talk of Ulster and the wealthy Scots-Irish gentlemen would provide his uncle with a glimmer of hope and minimize his anger. Here in the train depot, Ewan would be hard-pressed to give any more than a quick account — one that would not please his uncle.

Fortunately for Ewan, Mrs. Woodfield took charge. Once greetings had been exchanged, she peered through the crowd and then tapped the tip of her parasol on the tile floor. Everyone turned in her direction. "Where is Zeke? Why hasn't he arrived? He was informed of our schedule and knew we would be arriving on this train." A frown creased her forehead. "He has never failed to . . ." Her frown faded and her eyes soon shone with concern. "Has something happened to Zeke? Is he ill?"

Uncle Hugh shook his head. "You need not worry on Zeke's account. He's fit as a fiddle."

"Has something else detained him? Zeke is far too reliable to have forgotten when we were scheduled to return."

"Pleased we are to meet the train and deliver you home, Mrs. Woodfield. Zeke was not easy to convince, but I told him there was no need for him to bring your carriage when we'd already made plans to meet Ewan." Uncle Hugh tugged on the hem of his vest, obviously pleased with himself.

Mrs. Woodfield gave a slight nod. "That's most kind of you, Mr. Crothers."

While Ewan's uncle and Laura's mother exchanged words, Laura maintained her grasp on Ewan's arm. The warmth of her hand seeped through his jacket and offered a bit of reassurance. If he was going to withstand his uncle's onslaught, Ewan needed all the comfort he could amass before the battle commenced.

"You appear worried." Laura gently squeezed his arm.

"Facing Uncle Hugh and his questions is enough to spawn fear in any man."

"Then perhaps it's good Mother and I will be riding in the carriage with you. Should he question you on the way home, I'll do my best to help calm him. If Mother and I add our support, he'll surely understand that the contracts will come once you begin production."

Ewan forced a smile, then bent close to Laura's ear. "Thankful I am for any help you can give, but I doubt your words or mine will soothe his temper."

When Ewan lifted his head, he noticed his aunt's eyes were fixed upon Laura's hand resting in the crook of his arm. His aunt stepped toward them, her gaze still focused upon Laura's hand. "We're all eager for a report of good news, Ewan."

While Ewan understood his aunt's anxiety over the business, he was surprised she'd been the first to mention a report. Perhaps Uncle Hugh had refused her some desired purchase or reneged on his promise of the new house while Ewan was away. Or maybe it was Aunt Margaret's old fears of poverty returning to roost. Ewan glanced at his uncle. Maybe he'd been gambling while Ewan was gone. Or perhaps he had mentioned the diminishing bank balances and caused his wife to dwell upon the days of her youth when starvation had knocked at the family door and stolen the lives of her two younger brothers. The woman could be a spendthrift one minute and miserly the next.

Her behavior had seemingly been shaped by the hunger and paucity of her early years. And while Ewan didn't completely understand her irrational actions, he did understand the cause. Unfortunately, Uncle Hugh's gambling had only served to intensify the woman's fears and illogical thinking.

Laura glanced at Ewan, then released his arm. "Perhaps you could check with the porter to make certain all of our baggage has arrived."

He was so thankful for an opportunity to flee, Ewan would have kissed Laura on the cheek had it not been completely improper. Rather than give his aunt a chance to prevent his escape, Ewan rushed off as though he'd been jabbed with a hot poker.

Though he felt like a coward, Ewan remained outside with the baggage porter until all of their belongings had been gathered and then assisted the man inside the station with the wheeled baggage carts. He would have pushed the cart himself, but the porter refused.

His uncle was assisting Mrs. Woodfield into the carriage when he stepped outside the station. "Sure I am that my nephew is going to have good news to tell me very soon, Mrs. Woodfield, for I'm remembering 'twas you who advised me that Ewan was better suited to running the business than me." He glanced at Ewan. "And for sure you said he was the better choice to go and speak to the businessmen up north. I'm going to be all ears when he tells us about the many contracts he negotiated and signed while he traveled with you."

Moments later, Aunt Margaret motioned Laura forward. "I'm sure you want to sit beside your mother, Miss Woodfield." She nodded toward her sister. "Kathleen will take the seat beside Ewan."

On the journey home, Ewan offered a silent prayer of thanks that there was no further mention of contracts. Laura's constant line of chatter made it impossible for his uncle or aunt to gain a foothold during the carriage ride. Shortly before they arrived at Woodfield Manor, Laura was adamant the family stay for the evening meal. "It's the very least we can do. Besides, it will give us an opportunity to discuss the business meetings. I've been so busy detailing the social gatherings, there's been no time to tell you about the fine impression Ewan has made upon all of the men he spoke with on the journey."

Uncle Hugh did his best to decline the offer, but Laura refused to take no for an answer. "Catherine always prepares enough for guests. Isn't that true, Mother?"

"Yes, of course. We insist upon having you as our dinner guests. Zeke can go and fetch all of the baggage. He'll be back before we've finished supper. It's a perfect plan." Mrs. Woodfield stepped down from the carriage and waved away the possibility of an objection.

A few days after their return, Laura spent the morning at the orphanage. Head bowed low, Kenneth shuffled to her side. "I'm sorry, Miss Laura. I didn't mean to break it."

"Break what, Kenneth?"

"Your kaleidoscope. Didn't Mr. Zeke tell

you?" When Laura shook her head, the boy sighed. "I was trying to see how it worked and took it apart, but I couldn't get it back together. All the pretty pieces of glass came out. I saved everything and gave it to Mr. Zeke. Mrs. Tremble told us we weren't to touch it without permission, but when she went to help some of the others with their arithmetic, I took it off her desk."

Reaching forward, Laura lifted the boy's chin with her index finger. The fear that shone in his clear blue eyes melted her heart. No doubt he'd been worrying for days now. "I'm proud of you for admitting you were responsible, and for being brave enough to tell me. I know it's very hard to be honest when we do something we shouldn't, but I also understand you didn't break the kaleidoscope on purpose. Perhaps it can be repaired."

"Mr. Zeke said he'd try to fix it, but he wasn't sure he could make it look the same as before." He inhaled a shaky breath. "Mrs. Tremble said it was a special gift from your father, and she was sure you'd be unhappy with me."

Laura stooped down in front of the boy. "Even if the kaleidoscope can't be repaired, I won't be angry. I liked it very much because my father gave it to me, but the

Bible tells us that it isn't our possessions here on earth that matter. I'm sure Mrs. Tremble has taught you that we shouldn't concern ourselves over worldly things."

Kenneth nodded. "She has, but I think that's because we're orphans and she doesn't want us to be jealous of other kids."

Laura met his intense gaze. "That may be part of it, but I also think she wants you to understand that the Lord has unimaginable rewards waiting for us in heaven. So while we're here on earth, things like kaleido-scopes shouldn't become so important to us that we don't forgive others."

Kenneth reached out and grasped her neck in a hug. "Thank you, Miss Woodfield. I'm sure glad you believe in Jesus, or you might have been really, really mad at me."

Laura laughed as she returned his hug and then stood. "Come along now. Let's go and tell Mrs. Tremble all is forgiven and see if the other children are ready to play the board game I brought today." She tapped the package beneath her arm. "I found this in a store in Pittsburgh and decided it would be an excellent help with geography."

She reached for Kenneth's hand, and together they headed toward the adjacent classroom. She'd couldn't help but wonder if the children had missed her as much as she'd missed being with them while she was gone.

The only saving grace since Ewan's return home had been his time at the brickyard, but now that winter had set in, all clay digging had come to a halt. The diggers had surpassed his expectations, and the pit was filled with rich clay that would weather over the winter months. The freeze-thaw cycle, a necessary process before pugging could begin, would make the clay soft and remove unwanted oxides that could discolor or weaken the bricks. While some of the diggers had secured work cutting ice or performing temporary jobs at one of the coal mines, others would remain jobless until the brickyard reopened in the spring. Men who had previously worked at the yard understood they should save money to meet their needs until the first thaw, but Laura had explained there were some who were always ill prepared for the long winter months.

For this winter, at least, Ewan wouldn't have to worry about his workers dealing with that particular problem. Only the diggers had actually been hired by the company, and before he employed them, Ewan made certain they were men who were experienced in more than handling a shovel. Come spring, they'd be the first men he'd bring back to work.

Ewan shoved another piece of wood into the stove that warmed the frame building Laura referred to as the office. In truth, it wasn't much more than a shack, but it did have a stove and windows that provided a good view of the pit. The weather would soon keep Ewan at home, and he dreaded that prospect.

Ever since he'd returned from his journey to Pittsburgh, he'd been forced to listen to his uncle's scathing remarks about his inability to gain even one contract so far. And Uncle Hugh hadn't been particularly pleasant with Mrs. Woodfield, either. Once he learned Ewan hadn't been successful during his trip, his uncle had told Mrs. Woodfield it would be the last time he took the advice of a woman. Both Laura and her mother had stated that the business contacts with the powerful men Ewan had met would soon help the brickyard, but Uncle Hugh was adamant: He considered the trip a failure.

Uncle Hugh had slightly tempered his words until they had departed Woodfield Manor, but during the carriage ride home he had exploded in a full tirade. Ewan attempted to convince his uncle that once they began production and the business-men could actually see the quality of their bricks, contracts would come. But his words had been to no avail. And nothing Ewan had said since that time had changed Uncle Hugh's perspective. Aunt Maggie's attitude hadn't helped, either.

She'd convinced Uncle Hugh that there was a romance afoot between Ewan and Laura. Ewan had denied the claim, remind-ing them that Winston Hawkins had been formally given permission to court Laura. But even that reminder had failed to stifle his aunt's accusations. Though he would have been pleased to say Laura Woodfield desired his attention, she'd never stated or even implied any interest beyond friendship and a willingness to assist him with the paper work for the brickyard. Her conduct had always been above reproach.

In an effort to deflect his aunt's accusa-tions, he'd invited his uncle to join them at the office, but the man had no interest in learning the book work or the timekeeping procedures. Today, Laura had told Ewan that his uncle Hugh's trips into town had nothing to do with the brickyard. Instead, he'd been busy attempting to locate men who would join him at the gaming tables throughout the winter months. Unbeknownst to Uncle Hugh, one of the men he'd approached was a good friend of the Woodfield family, who had, in turn, mentioned the matter to Laura.

She'd been apologetic for carrying the news to Ewan but feared his uncle might soon approach a banker or an investor, who would look askance at such behavior. Her words sent a clear warning to Ewan, one that he needed to convey to Uncle Hugh. At day's end, Ewan made certain the fire was out before locking the door to the shanty and heading back home. Rather than deal with these problems, he would have preferred sleeping on a cot in the shack. At least the shack would afford him a bit of peace and quiet — something that would be in short supply once he spoke with his uncle.

He took a deep breath as he opened the front door of Uncle Hugh's house. His aunt still complained about the home, impatient for the day they would move to a finer place, even though she'd never before lived in such a fine dwelling. Each time he thought there would be an opportunity to discuss the purchase of ship passage for his sisters, his aunt or uncle found some reason to take him to task. If he mentioned money for passage in the midst of an argument, his sisters would never board a ship.

They had finished their meal and were eating dessert — his uncle's favorite, bread pudding with rum sauce — when Ewan suggested the two of them have a talk in the library after dinner. Aunt Maggie continued to refer to the room as a library, though it contained very few books. When they sailed from Ireland, they'd filled their trunks with tools and clothing, not books. Still, the shelves that lined every wall in the room gave testament to the fact that the room had once been a well-stocked library.

"What do you have to say that can't be said here at the table?" His aunt's eyebrows arched like two question marks.

Ewan hadn't expected any objection, especially from his aunt. His jaw tightened as he met her gaze. "I'm remembering it must be at least one hundred times you've told us we are not to bring talk of the brickyard to your table. I was trying to abide by your rules."

Her features relaxed a modicum, but she continued to watch him. "You'd better not be trying to gain permission to call on Miss Woodfield. Your uncle and I agree that we do not want her marrying into this family. I know how those wealthy folks work. They think they'll keep our money and then marry right back into the business. Well, I'll not have it."

Ewan was uncertain how his aunt could speak with authority about wealthy people and how they thought or acted, as she'd been around very few in her lifetime. More likely she was ascribing her own behaviors and beliefs to the Woodfield women, behaviors he'd never observed by either of them.

"I've told you Mr. Hawkins is courting Miss Woodfield. This has to do with the machinery at the brickyard."

His aunt eyed him with suspicion. "You'd better not be telling your uncle there are problems with any of that equipment. If so, we'll have to go over and have a talk with Mrs. Woodfield and her lawyer. I'll see that contract set aside if they've tried to swindle us with faulty machinery or kilns."

How one woman could heap such condemnation upon others without any provocation was beyond Ewan. "No need to worry, Aunt Maggie. So far as I can tell, the equipment is working fine. We'll know for sure when we begin molding bricks and firing the kilns next spring. I'm sure if anything is faulty, Mrs. Woodfield will reimburse Uncle Hugh or have the equipment repaired. There was such a clause in the contract, wasn't there, Uncle Hugh?"

"Aye, but your aunt can always find something to argue about. With that sharp tongue of hers, a person would think she'd grown up working in a fish market."

"Or living with a husband who was willing to gamble away all his money." His aunt lifted a spoonful of bread pudding and held it in the air. "Here's to you, husband, the man who caused me to sharpen my tongue." She smirked, shoved the spoon into her mouth, and then licked it clean.

"No matter what you say, I know you hold nothing but love for me, dearie." Uncle Hugh matched her spoon salute with one of his own.

"Before you go off for your private talk, there's something I want to settle with both of you. We've all been invited to a social gathering — a harvest celebration. A silly name since this hilly country can't produce what I'd call a harvest. More like gathering a few vegetables from the garden. And if there'd been any harvest, it would have ended long before now."

His uncle ignored her critical remark, more interested in details of the gathering. "Who's hosting the party? And who's invited?"

"The Woodfields are hosting, of course, but I have no idea who else is attending. I didn't receive a copy of the invitation list, husband." Her words dripped with sarcasm, but his uncle didn't appear to notice or care.

"Let's hope there are some distinguished men present." Uncle Hugh leaned back in his chair and downed the remains of his coffee. "I'd like to meet a few men like those Ewan met in Pittsburgh. I think we'd have some common interests."

Ewan didn't respond. He doubted whether Mr. Laughlin or Judge Mellon would be interested in joining his uncle at the gambling halls, and that appeared to be his uncle's only interest right now.

Aunt Maggie straightened and gave a firm nod. "We can invite them to a party. Although I'd rather wait until our new house has been built, maybe we need to host a party before then. That way you can meet those men, Hugh." She tapped her fingertips on the table. "I think we should host a Hogmanay celebration to welcome in the New Year. We can invite folks and they can learn a bit about the Scottish tradition. What do you think, Hugh? We could serve steak pie. 'Twould not be a proper New Year's celebration without it."

Though their families had lived in Ireland for many years, the tradition of Hogmanay had continued to be celebrated among those who had long ago migrated from Scotland to Ireland.

" 'Tis true I want to meet those men, but I think it's early to be deciding on a Hogmanay party. 'Course, I know you'll do as you please, Maggie." He pulled his pipe from his inner pocket. "We both know you're not looking for my permission. Just remember that I'll not be playing bagpipes as part of your celebration."

Her lips curved in a slight smile. "Well, I've seen no pipes in this house, so I do not think you need to worry that I'll be asking you to play." She hesitated for a moment and then wagged her finger between Ewan and Kathleen. "Now, back to my earlier mention of the party at the Woodfields' — I'll be expecting the two of you to attend together as a couple. At the very least, dance and appear happy. Others need to regard you as a couple so invitations will come to both of you."

Ewan glanced at Kathleen. Deep crimson colored her pale cheeks. Ewan was annoyed with his aunt, but he didn't want to argue. It would only cause Kathleen further embarrassment. When Kathleen attempted to push away from the table, Maggie placed her hand atop her sister's and held her in place.

"I am sure both Kathleen and I will be invited to social gatherings without the need of acting as though we're a couple," Ewan said as pleasantly as possible. "No doubt Kathleen would prefer to find an eligible suitor of her choosing." He looked at Kathleen, hoping she'd affirm his remark, but she merely sat there. Silent as a stone. As though she'd lost her ability to speak. He leaned toward her. "Isn't that right, Kathleen?"

She shrugged and glanced toward her sister. "Whatever Margaret thinks is best." As the younger sister, Kathleen had always been overshadowed by her forceful older sister, but when she contracted consumption five years ago, she'd become completely dependent upon Hugh and Margaret. Since then, she seemed unable to break free of her older sister's domineering personality. Fear of being left alone in the homeland had eclipsed Kathleen's dread of sailing to and settling in a new country.

Ewan stared at the two women, uncertain what Margaret might be plotting. Never had he expressed interest in courting Margaret's sister, yet it appeared that was what his aunt was suggesting. The idea seemed almost ludicrous. The four of them had been living together as a family, and though he and

Kathleen were not related by blood, he thought of her as kin. He would act as Kathleen's escort — much as a brother or father might — but nothing more. If that was his aunt's intent, she would be sorely disappointed.

While Kathleen didn't possess her sister's abrupt personality, she and Ewan would never be a match. Kathleen had matured into a quiet young lady who seldom offered an opinion, likely because she'd learned her sister didn't appreciate opposing views. Even the two women's looks were as different as herring and trout. While Margaret was tall and thin as a rail, and twisted her dark hair in a knot atop her head, Kathleen was short and thickset, and swept her light brown hair into a severe mode that disappeared in a tight bun at the nape of her neck. Rather than hide the fullness of her face with a few thick strands of crimped hair, she wore a style that accentuated her plump cheeks and wide nose.

"You need to keep your thoughts of marriage channeled in the proper direction, Ewan, and I plan to help you." Margaret gestured to her sister. "Come along, Kathleen. Let's leave the men to their privacy so they may discuss the brickyard." She swept out of the room with an air of authority that left Ewan feeling as though he'd been hit by a tidal wave.

His uncle held a match to his pipe and puffed until the tobacco glowed red. Using the stem, he waved Ewan toward the library. "Best we get out of sight before your aunt has enlisted a preacher to marry you to her sister."

The words startled Ewan and he stopped short. "Marry her? What are you saying? I have no interest in Kathleen."

His uncle laughed. "If you do not want Maggie pushing you into a marriage with Kathleen, then you'd best keep your distance from the Woodfield lass. You know she's courting the lawyer, and so do I, but Maggie's made up her mind there's more than friendship between you and Miss Woodfield. And you know my Maggie when she gets something in her head."

Ewan didn't want to do or say anything that might hurt Kathleen, but he'd not permit his aunt to run his life. After following his uncle into the library, the two of them settled into a pair of worn leather chairs.

His uncle drew on his pipe. "So what is it that you need to discuss in private?"

Ewan rested his arms across his thighs and met his uncle's gaze. "I've learned you've been seeking company at the gaming tables."

His uncle merely shrugged. "No harm done. I'll be needing cards to keep me busy and a glass of whiskey to keep me warm during the cold of winter."

"You can't continue approaching strangers, Uncle Hugh. Even with Winston's support, no banker will loan money to a man he believes has a gambling problem, and there's already talk that you're more interested in gaming than operating a brickyard."

Hugh's teeth clenched so tight Ewan expected the stem of his pipe to crack. " 'Tis no one's business."

Ewan shook his head and sighed. "Either you cease your talk of gambling in town or you can kiss the hope of another VerValen good-bye. It's your choice."

His uncle dropped against the back of his chair. " 'Tis enough to scald the heart out of me. I'll do as you ask, but once we have that loan, I'll be doing as I please. Any more warnings for me?"

"Nay, but I'd like to discuss bringing my sisters over as soon as possible."

His uncle chuckled. "It's your aunt you'll need to convince. She's pulled the purse strings tighter than a hangman's noose. Why do you think I need to sit at the gaming tables?"

Expelling a breath, Ewan stood and strode toward the door. How could he possibly persuade his aunt? How could he soften a heart that had turned to stone?

For years Ewan had wondered over the relationship between his aunt and uncle, so opposite from that of his own parents. How had Uncle Hugh and Aunt Margaret ever decided to wed? Even more, how had they remained together all these years — and why? Several years ago, he'd gathered his courage and posed the question to his uncle. The answer hadn't been what he'd expected. His uncle had chuckled and said, "Because I love her, and she loves me. Nobody else would put up with either of us." Though the answer hadn't been particularly helpful, Ewan had decided there was a dependency that existed between the two of them. One that could neither be explained nor understood by others.

CHAPTER 12

Laura stood in front of the oval mirror and examined the fit of her gown. Brushing her fingers down the front of the plum-colored silk, she rearranged the folds and gave a satisfied smile. Her tear-shaped pendant earrings sparkled in the fading light filtering through her bedroom windows. She worried this evening might prove a disaster for Mrs. Crothers, but she wished her well with hosting her first party since moving to Bartlett.

When Laura and her mother had hosted their annual harvest celebration party, Mr. and Mrs. Crothers had seemingly enjoyed themselves, though they'd departed earlier than most of the guests. Ewan had never mentioned his uncle's behavior during the event, but she hadn't failed to notice Ewan had remained close to Hugh's side throughout the evening. On several occasions she'd considered asking if he'd warned his uncle to avoid inviting the other male guests to join him in future gambling forays, but there had been no opportunity.

Neither he nor Kathleen knew any of the dances, and their few attempts had been abysmal. She and Winston had offered to change partners and help them with their dance steps, but Mrs. Crothers had rushed to Kathleen's side and declined on behalf of the couple.

Since then, she'd seen little of Ewan, though she'd thought of him often. She attempted to refrain from such thoughts. To be thinking of another man was, after all, inappropriate. Yet she couldn't seem to cease comparing Winston and Ewan. They were so different. Winston, with his political ambitions and desire to mingle among men of power and money, had a distinct dislike of anything connected to manual labor and everyday life.

Ewan was quite the opposite. He held little interest in politics or acquainting himself with wealthy, influential men. Instead, with his feet slipping and sliding, she'd watched him run down the side of the hill to work alongside the men digging clay. Even at a distance, she'd seen his muscles flex and bulge beneath his tight chambray shirt. And though she should have averted her eyes, she didn't. The man fascinated her.

Over the months since they'd met, she'd tried to understand why she was drawn to him. He possessed an air of genuine kindness, exhibited an unapologetic faith in God, had proved honest in his dealings, and longed for success — not at the expense of others, but by his own hard work.

Using a delicate touch, she judiciously twisted a jeweled pin into her curls and gave herself one final look in the mirror. As she descended the stairs, Winston stood in the foyer gazing up at her with a frozen smile.

At that moment, the answer came to her: She was drawn to Ewan because he possessed the qualities she'd most admired in her father. Why had it taken her so long to realize the parallel between the two men? Of course there were some differences. Ewan was an immigrant and hadn't been reared in a well-to-do family, nor had he been educated in a fine school. Still, her father had known hardship, too. When he'd decided to go into the brick business, he'd met with strong disapproval from his father, but her father had persevered without the family's wealth to help him. And she was certain Ewan would, too. By connecting with friends from the early years, her father had gained a great number of customers.

The introductions that she and her mother were now offering Ewan would do the same for his business, unless his uncle managed to ruin everything with his gambling and crass behavior.

"You look lovely, my dear. Is that a new gown? I don't believe I've seen it before." He reached for her hand as she descended the final step.

"Yes, the seamstress delivered it early yesterday. I'm quite fond of the fabric and thought the color perfect for the holiday season."

Winston snorted. "Christmas is over, and I don't even claim to understand this Hogmanay celebration. The name alone is ridiculous. I know it has to do with the New Year, but the name is outlandish. Why didn't they simply call it a New Year's celebration?" He arched his brows as though he expected a response, but he didn't give her an opportunity to reply before he continued voicing his discontent. "I'm still not sure why you insisted we attend. I doubt any of our acquaintances will be present." He circled his index finger in the air, and she slowly turned. "Absolutely perfect. There isn't a woman in all the state who can compare with your beauty and charm."

His words should please her, but Winston's praise always sounded as though he was simply uttering proper and expected compliments. She didn't doubt that he thought her attractive and admired her social graces, but his comments didn't bear the emotion of a man in love. He'd likely perfected the art of hiding his true feelings while seeking candidacy for political office. Often enough, he'd told her that carefully chosen words could make or break a man during an election. There was no doubt he'd taken those words to heart in both his public and private life. To her, it seemed a sham. To him, it was telling people what they wanted to hear — anything for a vote. She thought the idea chilling and wondered if all politicians embraced that same belief.

Yet what right did she have to criticize Winston's behavior? Even though she'd first objected to his courtship, she'd eventually given in to her mother's wishes. Laura salved her conscience with the thought that she was saving her mother from the worry of leaving behind a spinster daughter. But wasn't that just as deceitful?

In truth, she and Winston were using each other — and they both knew it. Winston wanted a wife who would help him succeed politically. He cared about nothing else. As for herself, she wanted to ease her mother's fears, and her options were limited unless she married without telling her intended the truth. And she would never marry a man without detailing her past. But Winston knew her secret. He had actually been pleased when her mother presented him with the information. She should be thankful that he wanted to marry her, but there were times when she thought it might be better to remain a spinster than to live out her years in a loveless marriage.

Mrs. Woodfield appeared at the top of the stairs, wearing a dark blue gown trimmed with imported ivory lace. A jeweled brooch was centered on the neckline, and matching earrings gave the ensemble a striking final touch. "I'm sorry to keep you two waiting, but the older I get, the longer it takes to make myself presentable."

"You need not worry about your age, Mrs. Woodfield. You could pass for Laura's sister." He glanced at Laura and quickly stammered a retraction that only made matters more embarrassing.

Laura touched his sleeve. "No need to worry, Winston. I'm not offended in the least." She gave her mother a quick appraisal. "You look lovely, Mother. That color is becoming on you. It brings out the blue in your eyes, don't you think, Winston?"

"Absolutely." He helped Laura into her ermine-trimmed coat and then assisted her mother. "Have you thought about replacing Willis?"

Her mother made a quick turn to face Winston. "Why would I replace Willis? I have Zeke to take care of the stable and animals; Joseph takes care of any necessary repairs and whatever else Zeke needs done; Catherine and Sally take care of our household and personal needs. Willis took care of my husband's personal needs and occasionally performed a few duties as a butler. Had he returned from the war, I would have retained his services, but with both him and Isaiah in their graves, I see no need."

"I just thought it would be helpful to have someone assigned to answer the door, see to . . ." Winston grappled for the right answer, seemingly upset that he'd once again lodged his foot firmly in his mouth. Then he gestured to Mrs. Woodfield's coat. "To help with your coats and such."

"Why, that's exactly the reason we have an escort, Winston." Mother offered a charming expression as she brushed past him and continued out the front door.

During the short carriage ride to the party, Winston again voiced his displeasure that Laura and her mother had accepted the Hogmanay invitation. "I simply don't see why we couldn't have sent regrets."

Laura's mother looked at him as though he'd lost his senses. "Because it would be rude. These people are our neighbors. They purchased our business, and we want to support them in their first social event." She pulled her coat higher around her neck. "Once you see who is attending the party, you may be very happy we accepted the invitation."

Winston shot her a sideways glance. "I hope you didn't convince the governor he should attend. If so, I'm sure he'll be taken aback when he sees they've invited him to no more than a hovel."

Laura gasped. "A hovel? You've obviously forgotten we're going to the home where my family lived and entertained for a number of years."

Mrs. Woodfield chuckled. "You can't seem to keep your foot out of your mouth, Winston. I do hope your shoe leather is tasty."

Before Ewan could answer the knock, his uncle rushed forward and opened the front door. He leaned forward and, with a sweeping gesture, bid Laura and her mother entry. When Winston stepped across the threshold, his uncle grasped the younger man's shoulder. "Glad I am that you weren't the first man to arrive."

"Uncle Hugh!" Ewan nudged his uncle's arm.

Hugh lifted his shoulders in an exaggerated shrug. "No need to rile yourself. I was only referring to Mr. Hawkins's time of arrival. As you can see for yourself, it would not have been good if he'd appeared earlier and made first footing."

Winston immediately glanced in the hallway mirror and straightened his jacket. "Is there something unusual about my appearance this evening?" His eyes shone with a hint of concern as he turned and looked to the ladies.

"My uncle is only joking with you, Winston. In our homeland, there is a tradition on Hogmanay called 'first footing.' The first man to cross the threshold is supposed to have dark hair," Ewan said.

Hugh nudged Ewan with his elbow. "That's not the whole of it. First footing requires the first visitor of the New Year to be a tall, dark, and handsome stranger and come bearing a gift of coal to bring good luck for the coming year." His uncle broke into a hearty gale of laughter. "At least you're tall, but you do not have dark hair, and I'm not sure there are many lasses who would call you handsome." He glanced at Winston's hands. "And you did not bring me a lump of coal for good luck, so you see why I'm pleased you were not here to make first footing."

Winston's jaw twitched. "I was not aware of your ridiculous customs. In this country, coal is not considered a gift for good luck. Instead, it is placed in the Christmas stockings of children who misbehave. I'm sure someone must have placed coal in your Christmas stocking this year, Mr. Crothers, for your manners need much improvement."

Undeterred by Winston's brusque reply, Hugh clapped him on the shoulder and laughed. "You'll enjoy living your life a bit more if you do not take offense at every word that's said, my boy. I'm only having a bit of fun with you." Uncle Hugh gestured toward the other room. "Come on in, all of you, and have some refreshments. The music and dancing will begin in a wee bit."

Though Winston's jaw continued to twitch, he escorted the two ladies into the adjacent room. Ewan grasped his uncle by the elbow and nodded for him to move down the hallway, where they couldn't be heard.

"Are you trying to ruin your chances for a

loan at the bank?" Ewan clipped each word through clenched teeth. "Quit insulting Winston. You need his good will if you're going to get a loan from the bank in town."

Hugh shook off Ewan's hand. "I do not need you telling me how I can act in my own home. The only reason you're worrying about the loan is so there's money enough to get your sisters over here, not because you're worried about me being able to purchase more machinery." He punched his index finger against Ewan's chest. "And that's the truth of it, so don't be denying it to me."

Anger bubbled in Ewan's chest. His uncle could have gone to the bank before now, but he'd put off his visit after Ewan had mentioned passage for his sisters. "Not just my sisters, Uncle Hugh. We'll need more workers in the brickyard come spring, and the war has left this country with a shortage of men. Many who survived have already gone to the mines to make a living. They want work that will give them wages all year long, so unless you're willing to do tha—"

"Don't be preaching me a sermon about my business, boy. I know as much about the problems finding workers as you do, but I'll not be paying wages during the winter months. If they choose to kill themselves in those coal mines, so be it."

His uncle's quarrelsome attitude only fueled Ewan's anger. "If we don't have men to work in the yard, then you'll not make any money. I can't promise bricks if I don't have men to make them."

As music began to drift from the other room, his uncle's features softened. "Come on, now. It's time we joined our guests and enjoyed our party."

Ewan remained in place, blocking his uncle's path. "I don't want to begin the year without a promise that you'll bring my sisters and some of the other relatives over before spring, Uncle Hugh. And I want your word about when I will become a true partner."

His uncle stroked his jaw. " 'Tis not the time or place for this kind of conversation, Ewan, but we'll get it settled soon. I'll get your sisters and the other relatives over here like you're asking." Using his forearm, he pushed his way past Ewan. "Come, now, let's go into the other room and show these people how we celebrate the New Year."

The answer wasn't what Ewan had hoped for, but his uncle was right. This wasn't the time or place for the discussion. Still, it seemed there was never a time his uncle was willing to give Ewan answers. He followed his uncle into the parlor. He should have held his tongue. His outburst had accomplished next to nothing. Granted, his uncle had said he'd bring the girls to this country, but he'd said that before. Ewan wanted a definite date. Even more, he wanted to be there when his uncle sent the money for passage. But the money wouldn't be sent until they'd secured a loan. And a loan wouldn't be obtained if his uncle continued to insult Winston Hawkins.

Ewan strode into the room, determined to offer an apology to Winston, but his aunt and Kathleen waylaid him. His aunt grasped his arm in a viselike hold as Kathleen stepped to his other side. Margaret nodded toward the musicians. "You and Kathleen, along with your uncle and me, are going to show our guests how to dance the Circassian circle." She gestured to Uncle Hugh, who was speaking with the musicians.

Ewan glanced at their guests, who had all moved to the sides of the room to watch the performance. If he'd been in the brickyard teaching one of the men how to fire a kiln or mold a brick, he wouldn't have minded being the center of attention. But standing in front of everyone and performing a dance was another thing entirely. He inhaled slowly and hoped he wouldn't make a misstep. His uncle would enjoy making the fool of him in front of their guests.

Ewan grasped his uncle's arm. "We need more than four people to create a circle big enough to perform the dance. Why don't I see if there's another couple or two who will join us?"

Hugh addressed the guests. "My nephew thinks we'll be better able to teach the dance if we can have two more couples. Are there any volunteers?"

Two brave couples stepped forward. After giving them brief instructions, Hugh waved for the fiddlers to begin. The eight of them joined hands in a circle and, keeping time with the music, stepped forward until they met in the center and then stepped backward. While the men remained in the outer circle, the ladies stepped forward and as they stepped back, they crossed their arms and joined hands with their partners, circling in place several times. While continuing to hold their partners' hands, they reformed the large circle. After circling the room two times, they continued to repeat the steps.

Although the volunteers missed a few of the steps, they performed admirably, and when Uncle Hugh motioned for the musicians to cease playing, the crowd applauded.

Hugh smiled and waved to the crowd. "Come, now, and give it a go. I'll call out the movements during the first dance to make sure you remember what to do."

Kathleen glanced toward the far side of the room. "Do you mind if I dance with Terrance O'Grady? He asked me earlier, and I told him I would."

Ewan released Kathleen's hand. "Go ahead and enjoy your dance. I would not want to be the cause of a lady breaking her promise."

Kathleen hurried across the room toward the young man. Terrance's face creased in a smile as she approached, and Ewan watched the two take to the dance floor. He'd been surprised to see Terrance at the party. Ewan didn't know the man well, but he'd talked with him on a couple of occasions. They'd first met at the livery where Terrance worked, but had talked only a few times since then. The family didn't have the social standing or money that would have enticed his aunt to send them an invitation. Besides, he hadn't seen Mr. and Mrs. O'Grady this evening, only Terrance.

While the guests continued learning the dance, Ewan circled around the room to the punch bowl and helped himself to a cup of the cranberry drink. He'd barely lifted the cup to his lips when his aunt bounded to his side.

"What is Terrance O'Grady doing here, and why aren't you dancing with Kathleen?" Her eyes flashed like hot embers on a dark night. She nudged his arm hard enough that his punch splashed onto the linen tablecloth, but she seemed not to notice. She narrowed her eyes and continued to stare at him. "Well? Answer me."

"I have no idea why Terrance is here. I didn't extend any invitations for the party. If you didn't invite him, I suggest you ask Kathleen or Uncle Hugh." Ewan picked up a napkin and blotted the tablecloth.

"I told you to dance with her, so why is she out there making a fool of herself with Terrance?"

Ewan turned toward the dance floor. "I don't think she's making a fool of herself. Terrance is an expert at the Circassian circle."

His response further fueled her anger. "You know what I meant with my question. Why is she dancing with him instead of you?"

"Kathleen said he asked her to dance earlier in the evening, and she agreed. If you have further questions about Terrance, you need to speak to your sister, not me."

He gently touched her arm. "You might wait until after the dance is over. I know you're concerned about Kathleen making a fool of herself, so I wouldn't want you to interrupt the dance and embarrass yourself in front of the guests."

His suggestion was met with a hard look. If Ewan could have warned Kathleen, he would have, but there would be no opportunity. Margaret was standing at the edge of the dance floor, prepared to swoop to her sister's side the minute the music stopped.

"Are you enjoying yourself?"

Ewan spun on his heel to discover Laura standing behind him. "There are many things I enjoy much more than parties, especially one at which my uncle insults the guests and my aunt is angry with her sister and me."

Laura stepped closer and Ewan poured her a cup of punch. As he handed her the cup, he allowed his hand to linger on hers longer than necessary. She glanced across the room to the area where Winston stood talking to some of his political friends and then turned back to Ewan. "I know about your uncle's insults, but why is your aunt angry? I haven't seen you commit any social blunder."

He grinned. "My aunt wanted me to dance with Kathleen the entire evening, but Kathleen is more interested in dancing with Terrance O'Grady, a man who doesn't meet my aunt's expectations for her sister."

Laura leaned a bit closer. "Then perhaps she shouldn't have invited him."

"That's just it — she says she didn't. I have a feeling Kathleen invited him without my aunt's knowledge."

"Terrance seems to be a nice young man, and it appears Kathleen is enjoying his company. Perhaps your aunt should let time take its course. She may only push them closer together if she objects too much."

"I am sure that could happen, but my aunt does not take kindly to advice, especially from me." He took the empty cup from Laura's hand and placed it on the table. "May I have this dance, Miss Woodfield? While I was unfamiliar with the steps at your party, I do know how to dance a proper Circassian circle. I promise I won't step on your toes."

As they stepped onto the floor, she took hold of his hand. And his heart, as well.

CHAPTER 13

March 1869

Winter's frozen fingers continued to wrap a tight hold on the Tygart Valley River as March arrived. Laura had told Ewan of past years when the weather would surprise them, and almost overnight the frozen hillsides would thaw and birdsong would fill the air to announce the arrival of the new season. How he prayed that such would happen this year, too. The winter months had been long, and though he'd escaped to the brickyard office as often as possible, his only major accomplishment had been arranging a meeting at the bank.

Ewan wanted his sisters on board a ship to America as soon as possible, and Uncle Hugh insisted a loan was needed to pay for their passage. After hearing Uncle Hugh's remark, Ewan had determined to do everything in his power to ensure his uncle secured the necessary loan.

They'd met earlier that morning. Convincing Frank Swinnen, president of Bartlett National Bank, that Uncle Hugh would prove to be an excellent candidate for a loan had been no small feat, but Winston had been surprisingly helpful. He'd even suggested the bank loan a greater sum than Uncle Hugh had requested. Ewan had done his best to stand firm against that idea, but the lure of extra money had proved too great an enticement for his uncle. The sum Mr. Swinnen finally offered Uncle Hugh was much more than they needed for the VerValen machine and for the purchase of passage for their relatives.

The change in the banker's decision had seemed strange to Ewan. When they'd first arrived, Mr. Swinnen had been reluctant to make any loan at all. To subsequently agree on a much larger loan made no sense. There had to be something they weren't aware of in the paper work, but when Ewan objected to the additional funds and asked for time to read the contract, his uncle had ordered him out of the meeting.

Ewan had looked to Winston for assistance, but he'd simply shrugged. "Your uncle is the one who is taking out the loan. His signature is all that is needed." His lips curved in a thin smile. "No need to worry,

Ewan. Your uncle is the one responsible for repayment of the loan, not you."

During the buggy ride home, Ewan quizzed his uncle at length, but to no avail. Unwilling to accept the refusal, Ewan followed his uncle into the library. "I want to see the bank papers, Uncle Hugh. I have a right to see them. If I'm going to manage the business and one day become a partner, I need to know about the debts you're creating."

"You're not a partner yet, so you need to quit acting like you have a right to know everything I say and do." Hugh dropped into one of the leather chairs and glared at Ewan. "You made me look a fool in front of that banker."

"I don't know how I made you look like a fool. I only stated what he already knew. If we had needed more money, we would have asked for it at the start. Did you give any thought as to why he would offer extra? What he did makes no sense. I've never heard tell of such a thing."

"And you're an expert on banking practices, are ya?" His uncle pulled his pipe from his jacket and pointed it at Ewan. "That banker took a liking to me and was trying to give an extra bit of help."

"We had no need for that much, and you

should have told him so. I don't like the idea of starting out the business with so much debt."

"You'll just have to work a little harder. Besides, having the extra money allows us a little cushion in case those contracts don't come in as quick as you think. If that happens, you'll be thanking me for borrowing the extra money."

Ewan sighed and shook his head. "Can I read the bank note you signed, Uncle Hugh? I'm afraid there's something wrong with the way this was done."

His uncle yanked the papers from his jacket and tossed them at Ewan. "Have a look at them, but it will change nothing. My name has been signed and witnessed, so there's no going back."

His uncle filled his pipe with tobacco while Ewan began his examination of the paper work. Line by line, he read each word of the contract. When he came to the portion regarding security for the loan, he gasped. "Why did you agree to let them have the brickyard, all of the equipment, all of the acreage, and the house as collateral for the loan?" He traced his finger along the next line of the contract, and his unease was replaced by mounting anger. "You agreed that if we are so much as ten days late on one payment, they can seize everything. Everything!"

He stood and shoved the paper in front of his uncle. "Look at this." He rapped his fingers against the page. "Did you bother to read this clear through? You've done the same thing as before — you signed before you knew what you were agreeing to. Did you learn nothing the first time? Wasn't Aunt Margaret's ire enough to make you more careful?"

His uncle's eyes flashed with anger. "I read it, and I know exactly what it says. I objected at first, but Mr. Hawkins said there was nothing to worry about. The bank didn't want to own the brickyard. It's all a formality so they can make their books balance. Something about needing to have more collateral than the amount of money they loan so they have a correct audit or some such thing." He scratched his head and laughed. "I didn't know what all that meant, but it sounded right. Besides, I'm a gambling man, and I figured I'd place my bet on you making a go of things at the brickyard. You said you want a partnership, so now you'll be working for it."

"I was working for it before you put us so deep in debt." Heat climbed up the back of Ewan's neck. How dare his uncle place him in this position? The future of the entire family rested on his shoulders. "Tell me, Uncle, what would you do if I decided to walk away and leave you with this debt you've created? Could you negotiate contracts and manage the brickyard? Did you give any thought to the possibility I might leave you and go off on my own?"

His uncle leaned back and rested his elbow on the armrest of his chair. "I gave it about this much thought." He inched his thumb and forefinger apart by only a hairsbreadth. "I know your sisters are too important for you to try to strike out on your own. I'm the only way you'll get them over here. If they had to wait for you to earn enough money working at some brickyard, they'd all be spinsters before you could pay for their passage. And you forget that I've had enough years in a brickyard that I could run one if I had to."

His words stung Ewan's ears like pelting sleet on a winter day. Years of gambling had taught his uncle to use the vulnerabilities of others in order to win, and he'd learned to do that well. His uncle held Ewan in his grip. Like it or not, he wouldn't leave. His sisters were more important than his uncle's foolish business practices. Though Uncle Hugh had brushed off any concern regarding the late-payment clause, the provision caused Ewan immense anxiety. Being able to secure contracts and acquire enough income to make the payments on time would be left to him alone.

If he could keep his uncle's hands out of the till, the brickyard would succeed. Making bricks would be easy. Controlling his uncle could prove impossible. Only time would tell. Right now, he needed to reach an agreement with his uncle and get his sisters on a ship from Ireland.

"I want the money to secure passage for my sisters and the other relatives who want to come and work in the brickyard. Before you spend the money on anything else, I want their passage to America." Ewan grasped the armrests of his chair. If his uncle didn't agree, Ewan was prepared to argue. He would not leave this room until the matter was settled.

His uncle snorted. "I do not know what's gotten into you, boy. You act like we've taken up positions in opposite corners of the boxing ring."

"Sometimes that's how I feel. You promised to bring my sisters over here, but they're still in Ireland. You promised to make me a partner, but now you say we need to be operating at a profit before that can happen. You sign a contract that could cause us to lose the brickyard and all your acreage and home if we're late with one payment. None of these things make me feel that we're angling for the same prize."

His uncle took a deep draw on his pipe and stared at Ewan from beneath hooded eyes. "There's a wee bit of truth in what you're saying, but once I have your word that you're not going to run amuck on me, we'll get the family over here, just like I promised." His uncle blew a smoke ring that circled over his head like a lopsided halo. "Do I have your word that you're going to stay and manage the brickyard and make us some money?"

"You have my word that I'll do my best to make the brickyard a success, but I want your word that you'll make me a partner."

"You have my word. When the business is making a good profit, I'll make you a partner."

Ewan didn't question what a "good profit" might be. For now, he was more interested in his sisters and their future. "I want you to make the arrangements for my sisters by the end of the week. I want at least two of our male relatives to escort them, and I want them booked on a steamship, not a sailing ship. And do not book them in steerage. They should have a cabin, so they have some privacy and are not accosted by the sailors or other passengers."

"Would you like their meals served on silver serving platters?" His uncle shot him a wry grin.

Ewan grinned in return. "I would not object. I'm sure my sisters would be pleased to receive such fine treatment."

His uncle guffawed. "I am willing to put them in a small cabin, but that's as much luxury as I afforded my wife and her sister. I would not be hearing the end of it if your sisters' accommodations were better than what I purchased for my wife." He pushed up from his chair. "I'll ask Mr. Hawkins to make the travel arrangements for the family. I'm sure he can easily handle all of the details."

Ewan was sure he could make the arrangements as well as Winston, but he didn't argue. If his uncle wanted to pay the lawyer for handling the matter, so be it. "I want them here within six weeks."

"If train and ship schedules permit, Ewan, but let's not ask the impossible. I will tell Mr. Hawkins to do his best to get them here as soon as possible."

Unwilling to take a chance that his uncle would use any delay tactics, Ewan gestured toward the desk. "I'll write a letter to the girls today and tell them to prepare for their journey. And I'll be certain to check with Mr. Hawkins about the arrangements, as well. Are you sending for all twelve of your cousins and their families?"

His uncle shook his head. "Only ten. Byron and Robert don't have any experience working in the brickyard. I can bring them over later."

"They can earn their keep trucking off the pit and wheeling brick while they're being trained for the more difficult tasks. We always need men to do the heavy work, and both Byron and Robbie are strong fellows."

His uncle held a match to the bowl of his pipe. "Aye, and both of them have lots of hungry mouths to feed. At last count they each had six. By now, I'm guessing they each have another wee one or at least another one on the way. The passage for them, their wives, and their families is more than they'll ever be able to repay me."

Ewan frowned. "They're family, Uncle Hugh. Is it fair you leave them behind and bring only the others?"

"Nothing in this life is fair, and the sooner you learn it, the better off you'll be. If the brickyard makes lots of money and we pay off our debt, then I'll reconsider. We have to be careful with the money — isn't that what you said?"

Strange how his uncle had ordered Ewan out of the room and signed for the loan on his own, but now referenced the obligation as "our debt." His uncle had a way of twisting most anything to his own advantage.

"We do need to be careful with the money. After you pay Mr. Hawkins for travel expenses for the family, the balance should be placed in the business account. We can purchase the additional machinery and hold the remainder of the funds for a time as a safeguard until we begin receiving payments on our contracts."

"Aye, but first you must get the contracts." His uncle wagged his finger at Ewan. "We'll see if those friends of Mrs. Woodfield keep their word once you show them some of the bricks made in our brickyard."

Dread settled across Ewan's shoulders like a heavy yoke. His uncle would be present, but the burden to succeed would rest upon Ewan.

As the weeks passed and late April arrived, winter loosened its stronghold and spring made a glorious entrance into the West Virginia hills and valleys. The weather signaled a time of new beginnings and provided a promising foundation that would shape their future at the brickworks. So long as they weren't hindered by heavy spring rains and flooding, Ewan was confident he could develop the brickworks into a company with an even stronger reputation than it had carried under the Woodfield name.

They'd reopened the yard at a slower pace than normal so Ewan could learn the abilities of the men as well as any differences in how they performed their work. While seeking to purchase a brickyard, he'd visited enough yards to know that practices in this country didn't vary much from those in his homeland

Soon they moved into full production, with many of the men walking long distances along moonlit paths or through dew-drenched fields to arrive before the final morning whistle sounded in the cool spring air. The horses would already be harnessed to the pug mill, walking in an unending circle, their movement forcing sharp blades to cut through the mixture of clay and water in the giant tub until it reached the perfect pliable texture needed for the molds the Ver-Valen machine stood ready to fill.

Laura had been present a portion of each day since they'd begun operation. Mrs. Woodfield wasn't pleased by her daughter's early morning departures for the brickyard, but Laura soon convinced her that this time of transition was important for all of them. After that, there'd been no further objections.

Ewan was grateful to both of the women. He'd come to rely upon Laura's knowledge. Even more, he enjoyed having her at his side. He dared not admit that to Mrs. Woodfield. In truth, he barely admitted it to himself, for he feared he might say or do something that would jeopardize the arrangement.

Zeke appeared out of the early morning shadows and tipped his hat to Ewan as he neared the entrance to Woodfield Manor. "Good morning, Zeke. How are you today?" Each day, Ewan watched the front door, tamping down the fear that Laura might decide he no longer needed her help.

"I'm mighty fine, Mr. McKay." Zeke glanced over his shoulder at the front door as Laura appeared. He hurried to her side, escorted her down the steps, and helped her into the buggy.

Ewan had suggested that Zeke sleep in rather than rise so early to escort Laura to the buggy, but Zeke refused. The groomsman hadn't minced words and put Ewan on notice that escorting the ladies of Woodfield Manor in and out of their carriages was a part of his job, and he intended to do it himself. From then on, Ewan had remained in the buggy and waited while Zeke performed his duties. Far be it from Ewan to interfere with a man's job.

Laura settled beside him, her dark wool cape wrapped tight around her shoulders to stave off the morning chill. She shivered as the horses trotted away from the house, and Ewan nodded toward a lamb's wool blanket folded on the seat. "You're welcome to the blanket if you're cold. There's a bit of a chill in the air, but once the sun comes up, I have a feeling we'll be plenty warm."

Laura spread the blanket across her lap. "I'm sure you're right, but this blanket feels good right now." She tucked her hands beneath the coverlet. "Was your uncle pleased to hear about the contract for the hotel in Fairmont?"

Ewan hesitated. "He wasn't as excited as I had expected. Or had hoped." Last evening Ewan had shared the news that the contractor in Fairmont had inspected bricks from their first few burns and was pleased with their product.

The builder was returning today to sign a contract that Laura had prepared yesterday afternoon. She'd been careful to include all of the terms and conditions that her father always included in his contracts. Both Ewan and Laura were thrilled, but his uncle had shrugged off the accomplishment.

Instead of offering a bit of thanks and encouragement, Uncle Hugh had done the opposite. "Bricks for one small hotel are like a few drips of water in a river. We need a river, Ewan, not a few drips of water. I want those big contracts from Pittsburgh and Wheeling. The ones you said we would get once we started production." The words still rang in Ewan's ears.

When Ewan glanced in Laura's direction, the full moon revealed a hint of sadness in her eyes.

She met his gaze and slowly shook her head. "I'm sorry, Ewan. I truly don't understand your uncle, or how he could act in such a callous manner. Still, I have a bit of news that might make both you and your uncle happy."

"What's that?" He doubted anything less than a contract that would reap huge profits would please Uncle Hugh.

"Judge Mellon wrote Mother that a friend of his, a building contractor from Allegheny City, is arriving next week to visit the brickyard and to discuss some new projects with you. Isn't that wonderful?"

A rush of gratitude swelled in his chest. "Are you sure? What's his name? What time will he arrive? Did Judge Mellon say anything about the size of the projects?" He hadn't meant to flood her with questions, but they'd rushed out before he could stop himself.

She chuckled and clasped her palm against her chest. "Dear me, I don't know if I can answer all your questions, but I can tell you his name is Archibald Bruce. Judge Mellon said in his letter that Mr. Bruce performs almost all of the construction work for Campbell and Galloway, the largest architecture firm in the Pittsburgh area." Her lips curved into a tender smile. "Mr. Mellon added a postscript to his letter. He said he was certain you'd be pleased to know that Mr. Bruce, as well as the owners of Campbell and Galloway, is Scots-Irish and quite proud of his ancestry."

"Aye, that pleases me very much. At least we will have something in common, and by then I'm hoping we'll have the new frog designed for our bricks. I won't be able to have any burned by then, but I think Mr. Bruce will like it."

When Ewan was in Pittsburgh, Mr. Mellon had mentioned that most of the brickyards had begun using frogs that would identify the brickyard, usually using the name or initials of the yard. A frog would give builders a method to classify the durability of each brickmaker's product. During the winter months, Ewan had worked on a design they could use to mark their bricks. He wanted the initials C and M, but he wanted something more — something special — so he'd designed a simple burning bush beneath the letters. His uncle said it looked like three flames rather than a burning bush, but Ewan overlooked the criticism. His uncle had approved the design, which was all that mattered. Truth be told, it was the fact that they would use a little less clay in their bricks when they placed a frog in the bottom of the molds that pleased Uncle Hugh the most. If there was a way to decrease costs and increase income, Uncle Hugh maintained a tolerable attitude, but the only thing that truly made him happy was locating a gaming table where he was welcome. Fortunately, Aunt Margaret was keeping him in tow so far.

Over the past month she'd insisted he accompany her as they decided upon the location for their new house. Now that the location had been selected, she insisted that work begin immediately. No amount of explanation curbed her ongoing demands.

Both Ewan and his uncle pointed out they'd done their best to locate laborers. Except for a few itinerants, they'd been unsuccessful. There simply weren't any strong men who wanted to spend their days digging a foundation for the mansion. Most of the able-bodied men in the area who didn't want to cultivate their own hilly farms had gone to work for the coal mines, or Ewan had already employed them at the brickyard.

Uncle Hugh had promised Margaret that several of the newly arriving relatives could dig the foundation. A promise that annoyed Ewan and would likely cause problems for all of them.

CHAPTER 14

Ewan glanced down at Laura, pleased she'd agreed to come with him to the train depot. Shortly after he'd made the travel arrangements, Winston had delivered a list of times and dates when each of the relatives would arrive. He'd done his best to meet Ewan's request and arrange immediate travel for the girls, but to secure a cabin, they would have to leave earlier than the other relatives and travel by themselves. Two of Ewan's relatives would be following within a couple days of the three girls' departure, and the others would come two weeks later but without cabin accommodations. Ewan had considered all of the options, prayed fervently for God's direction, and decided his sisters should come alone on the ship so they'd have a cabin to themselves.

Laura had later explained the impropriety and the possible danger of the girls traveling by themselves, but Ewan had remained steadfast in his decision. His uncle could be as changeable as a spring storm, and Ewan hadn't been willing to take any chances by delaying their departure.

Laura lifted onto her toes and peered out the station window. "I do hope they're on the train. I don't want you to be disappointed."

"I've been praying for their safe travel and protection since before they stepped on-board the ship. I'm sure the Lord has brought them safely to me."

"I admire your unwavering faith, Ewan." She gave him a sideways glance. "I'm not sure how you maintain such certainty. Does God never disappoint you?"

Her question startled him. "That's a question no one has ever asked me, but I would have to say that there have been times when I have been disappointed in God's answer to my prayers. I prayed for my parents to live, but they did not. I prayed Uncle Hugh would let the girls come with us when we first traveled from Ireland, but he did not. There were other times, too, when God did not answer my prayers in the way I would have liked, but through my disappointment, I know He is divine and can see far beyond my limited ability. He knows what is best for each of us even when we can't imagine how death or suffering could be a good answer." Ewan touched his index finger to his temple. "I try to remember that we all must die and everyone must face certain tribulations in life. We live in a world filled with sin. 'Tis hard for us to understand the ways of a righteous God."

She looked at him with a faraway gaze. "I can't believe that everything that happens is good."

"I did not say it was good, but the Bible tells us that all things work together for good to them who love God, to them who are the called according to His purpose." He tipped his head to get a look into her eyes, hoping to see a glimmer of acknowledgment that she believed what he'd said. She looked down and avoided his gaze, but he decided to continue. "Good can come from evil. The apostle Paul suffered, but his suffering drew him closer to the Lord. Jesus was crucified, but His death offers us the gift of everlasting life. The Bible is filled with godly people who prayed they would not suffer or die, but they did. The stories of those martyrs strengthen our faith, don't you think?"

Finally she looked at him. "Perhaps. But prayers that are not answered as we hope can cause some to fall away from their faith."

Ewan turned to face her. "Has that happened to you, Laura? Have you lost your faith?" She looked so sad he wished he could pull her into his arms and assure her that God loved her and wanted only the best for her.

She forced a smile. "You see me in church every week, don't you?"

"Aye, but sitting in a church pew does not mean everything is right between you and God. A bird with a damaged wing can still fly, but until it is fully healed, it cannot soar." The crowd swarmed as the train drew closer to the station, but Ewan didn't move. He looked deep into her eyes. "I think you need to heal from something, too. You do not need to tell me what it is, but I will be praying that God will touch your heart and bring you back to Him."

As tears began to pool in her eyes, she turned away. "I hope He will answer your prayer." She gestured toward the platform. "Come. Let's wait outside and see if God has protected your sisters."

The minute the girls stepped off the train, Laura recognized them. Ewan had described them well. They were beautiful young girls, all with the same clear blue eyes as their brother. Although their hair was a shade lighter than Ewan's, the family resemblance was strong. The twins, Ainslee and Adaira, flanked their older sister, Rose, who was doing her best to keep them in tow. The minute the twins spotted Ewan, they charged down the platform and lunged at him. Had there not been a support post behind him, all three of them would surely have toppled in a heap.

Ewan embraced them in a giant hug and then turned his attention to Rose. "I am so glad you are safe, and we are together again. I've been lonely without the three of you."

Rose stepped forward and embraced her brother. "I have missed you, as well. Trying to keep these two in my sight and out of trouble during the journey was enough to make me wish we had traveled with the rest of the family."

Ewan gave the twins a mock frown. "Did I not tell you in my letter that you were to mind your sister and not give her any trouble?"

The girls' long braids bounced up and down as they bobbed their heads. "Aye, and we did our best," one of the twins replied. She turned her gaze on Laura. "Are you

Miss Woodfield? The lady Ewan has written about?"

Laura tipped her head to one side. "Yes, I'm Laura Woodfield. And you are either Ainslee or Adaira, correct?"

The girl smiled. "I'm Ainslee." She gestured to her sister's head. "Adaira is a tiny bit taller. That's how you can tell us apart."

Adaira giggled. "Unless Ainslee grows a wee bit. Then you'll have more trouble."

The girls were every bit as enchanting as Ewan had described. "Perhaps I should find some other ways to tell you apart in case that should happen."

Adaira drew close to Laura. "You're as pretty as Ewan said, and I like your dress."

"Adaira!" Ewan's face was a bright shade of red. "Not everything is meant to be repeated."

Her eyebrows dipped low. "I didn't tell anything bad." She looked up at Laura. "You didn't mind me saying that Ewan thinks you're pretty, did you?"

Laura bit back a grin. "I always enjoy hearing a lovely compliment, Adaira. However, I believe you've embarrassed your brother, so perhaps you shouldn't repeat anything else unless you first gain his permission."

She gave a quick nod. "Can we come and

visit at your house? Ewan says it's quite beautiful."

A look of defeat shone in Ewan's eyes as he stepped forward and gently tapped his sister's shoulder. "I'm wondering if you're having a problem with your ears, Adaira. Did you hear what I said only a minute ago? You're behaving like you've never been taught any manners."

"No need to chastise her on my account, Ewan. I'd be delighted to have the girls come visit as often as they'd like. If I'm at the orphanage or helping at the brickyard, I know Mother will enjoy their company."

"You work at the brickyard? What do you do? I know you're not strong enough to truck off." Adaira narrowed her eyes. "One time Ewan let me try to push a barrow of molded bricks from the machine to the dumpers, but it was too heavy and he had to help." She twisted the end of her braid and appeared to be deep in thought. "You don't edge or hack the bricks, do you?"

Laura was impressed by the girl's knowledge. She'd either spent her share of time at a brickyard or listened when her brother discussed his work. Perhaps women helped in the brickyards in Ireland. Laura had never asked Ewan, though she couldn't imagine a woman working alongside the men. "No. I help your brother with some of the office work, keeping the books and time-keeping — that sort of thing. My father never permitted children or women to work in the yard when we owned it, but a few of the children did bring lunch to their brothers and fathers who worked for us."

"After I begged and begged, Ewan took me to see the brickyard that he supervised back home. That's how I learned so much."

"That and asking lots of questions," Ewan added.

The girl's inquisitive nature reminded Laura of her own childhood behavior. During her youth, she'd been curious about everything, too. Her father had once accused Laura of having a secret machine that helped her dream up the many questions she posed each day. Young Adaira's questions might prove to be an even greater challenge, especially for Ewan.

"I want to know about the orphanage. What do you do there?" Ainslee stepped alongside Laura.

The girl's eyes shown with interest as Laura explained her volunteer work. "Perhaps you could come with me sometime and help with the little children. They love to play outdoors, but it takes many eyes to watch over them."

"Oh, I want to come, too," Adaira said, her lower lip protruding in a slight pout.

Ewan tapped Adaira on the shoulder. "We don't need to begin pouting about who is going to be doing what. For right now, you both need to get settled. If Miss Woodfield has time to take you to the orphanage sometime in the future, there will be time enough to discuss who goes with her."

"I thought Aunt Margaret and Kathleen might come to meet us." Rose turned away from the baggage car long enough to glance at her brother.

"I told them it was not necessary. Besides, it would have taken me longer to fetch them since I came here from the brickyard."

"If you were at the brickyard, how come you're not dirty?" This time it was Ainslee who posed the question.

Ewan chuckled. "Because I was working in the office."

"With Miss Woodfield?" Adaira's lips curved in a teasing grin.

Rose gestured to one of the wooden baggage carts. "I see our trunks. I worried they might not make it onto the train. We had very little time when we changed trains in Wheeling." She sighed. "I'm surely happy we've come to the end of our journey.

"The other relatives are eager to leave

Ireland. Uncle Darach said their ship would sail two weeks after ours, so it won't be too long before they arrive. The whole lot of them are worried about where they'll be living. Aunt Margaret wrote Aunt Elspeth and said Uncle Hugh would try to locate enough housing for all of them but they might have to share living quarters for a time. Is that right? Will we be living with Aunt Elspeth and Uncle Darach once they arrive?"

Ewan grasped Rose by the hand. "Nay, of course not. You'll be staying with me at Uncle Hugh's house."

Ainslee wrinkled her nose. "I'd rather stay with Aunt Elspeth. She's much nicer. You know Aunt Margaret doesn't like having us around. She thinks we're a bother." The girl ignored her brother's warning look. "Kathleen wrote and said Aunt Margaret wants her to marry you."

"What?" Ewan ducked his head when several people turned around. "I'm sorry. I didn't mean to shout, but it seems Adaira isn't the only one who has forgotten her manners."

Ainslee frowned and folded her arms across her chest. "You should be angry with Kathleen instead of me. I'm only repeating what she wrote in her letter. I told Rose I didn't believe a word of it. Didn't I, Rose?"

Ainslee nudged her older sister.

"Aye, she did. Truth is, none of us thought you'd consider taking Kathleen as a wife." Rose winked at her brother. "We know the two of you would be a terrible match, but I don't think Kathleen would ever defy her sister. I think she's afraid of Aunt Margaret's temper."

Ewan raked his fingers through his thick brown hair and gave a shrug. "If these three continue jabbering, you're going to hear all of the family secrets before we ever get out of the train station."

On the ride home, the girls peppered Ewan and Laura with a multitude of questions. Laura didn't mind their inquiries, but Ewan grew increasingly tense.

Laura touched the sleeve of Ewan's jacket as they neared the turnoff to the house. "Perhaps you should take me home first. I'm sure your family would like some time to get reacquainted in private. Besides, I promised Mother I'd write out invitations for a tea she is hosting in a few weeks."

The twins objected to Laura's departure, but she held fast to her decision. Hearing Margaret Crothers was devising plans for Ewan to wed Kathleen had sealed her decision. Laura had been around Margaret enough to know that an unwanted guest on her doorstep could bring out the worst in the woman, and Laura didn't intend to be that unwanted visitor.

The girls begged to come inside when they arrived at Woodfield Manor, but Ewan refused. "We have to get home. I don't want Aunt Margaret to send Uncle Hugh looking for us."

"You're all three welcome to come over tomorrow afternoon, but only if you have your brother's permission. There's a short-cut through the woods he can show you." She smiled at the girls. "I'm delighted to meet each of you and pleased you're going to make your home in West Virginia. I hope we'll become good friends."

As the girls' chattering voices followed Laura up the front steps of the house, a repressed longing for family washed over her like a giant wave that threatened to drown her. Her heart ached for what she could never have.

Once inside, she leaned against the cool wood of the front door and forced herself to inhale slow, steady breaths. This feeling would pass — it always did. It had to.

CHAPTER 15

A few days later, his uncle, aunt, and Kathleen were already seated at the breakfast table when Ewan entered the dining room. The moment he crossed the threshold and sat down, Aunt Margaret rang a small bronze dinner bell she positioned beside her water goblet during each meal. Adaira rushed from the kitchen and hurried to the buffet for the silver teapot his aunt now used at every meal.

Ewan gestured to his sister and pushed away from the table. "The last I looked, my arms and legs were still working just fine, Adaira. I can serve myself. You don't need to wait on me."

Aunt Margaret glowered at him. "She has assigned duties, Ewan. As do Rose and Ainslee. You can't walk in here and change my orders. I run the household, and I want our meals served to us so the family becomes accustomed to formal dining."

"The family? My sisters are as much your family as I am. I do not object to having them help with the household chores, but I'll not have them treated different from anyone else in this house. Uncle Hugh has already said he plans to withhold money from my wages to pay for their room and board, so they should be doing less work than Kathleen, who is not paying anything to live here." He looked at Kathleen. "I'm sorry to bring you into this bit of disagreement, Kathleen, but I do not like what's happening here."

"Do I tell you how to run the brickyard?" His aunt's scowl deepened. "Of course not. And you'll not be telling me how to run my house." She leaned forward and turned her frown on her husband. "Tell him, Hugh."

"Oh, stop with your highfalutin ways, Maggie. We can all pour our own tea and fill our plates with rashers, eggs, and boxty. We do not need the girls rushing about carrying platters and serving us with that fine silver you bought. You've gone and started a bit of nonsense." He leaned back and met his wife's harsh stare. "You can quit giving me the evil eye, too. By now you should know it has no effect on me."

Ainslee stepped into the dining room with a plate of boxty and curtsied as she offered the platter to her brother. " 'Boxty on the griddle, boxty on the pan; if you can't make boxty, you'll never get a man.' " She grinned at him. "You'll have to taste my boxty and tell me if you think it's good enough to get me a husband one day."

He smiled and helped himself to several of the potato pancakes. "You're too young to worry about getting a man, but I already know you make the best boxty in all of West Virginia."

"Tell your sisters to come in here and join us for breakfast, Ainslee." Uncle Hugh waved his fork toward the kitchen.

The girl glanced at her aunt, then looked at Ewan. She stepped from foot to foot, her misgivings evident. "Do as your uncle said. Go and tell your sisters to join us for breakfast."

"Shall we leave Fia in the kitchen alone, then?"

Fia and Melva had been chosen for the two spaces in steerage on a ship sailing a few days after Ewan's sisters had departed. The two had been selected because Margaret desired a cook and a housemaid as soon as possible. No matter that the women had to sail without their families. If they desired a new life in America, they must do Margaret's bidding.

"Aye. Fia's being paid to do the cooking, so let her cook. There's only four of us at the table. It does not take one person to cook for each of us, now does it?" Uncle Hugh forked a bite of eggs into his mouth while Ainslee scuttled into the kitchen and fetched her sisters.

Rose and Adaira came into the dining room. The kitchen's heat had heightened the color in their cheeks, and Rose wiped some perspiration from her forehead with the corner of her apron. Uncle Hugh pointed his knife at the empty chairs. "Sit down, girls, and eat your fill. You do not need to work in the kitchen. I pay Fia to cook and Melva to clean, and with your aunt overseeing the two of them, that should be plenty of help." When Margaret tried to object, he waved away her protests. "Ewan is right. He pays for their room and board. They aren't here to serve you, Margaret."

"Very well, but I don't want to hear complaints if you're unhappy with your meals or the house isn't tidy. My time is better spent at the building site, making sure the men do their work. When I'm not there, they dawdle about and nothing gets done."

Uncle Hugh sighed. "Those men are good workers, Margaret. If St. Peter himself stepped down from heaven to oversee the

261

project, you'd still find fault."

"There's no need for your irreverent remarks, Hugh. Maybe if you'd check on them once in a while, you'd see what I'm talking about. From what I'm able to find out, you're not spending your time at the brickyard, and you're not overseeing the new house, so where are you all day?"

Ewan looked at his uncle from beneath hooded eyes. Ewan had questioned his uncle regarding his whereabouts on several occasions, but each time Uncle Hugh had told him to tend to his own business. The man had made it explicitly clear: He didn't want or need a guardian. Ewan wasn't so sure that was true, and his uncle's lack of involvement at the brickyard hadn't helped to ease Ewan's concerns.

"Taking care of the finances so we don't sink any further into debt, which is proving to be no easy task, what with all the things you've been ordering for the new house. You don't need to order all of those expensive frills before the foundation is even completed, Maggie."

Rather than let Aunt Maggie buttonhole him, Uncle Hugh had manipulated the conversation to put his wife on the defensive.

"Mrs. Woodfield said that sometimes it

takes a very long time to receive orders from the city, especially when the items have to be custom-made. I was only following her advice. We don't want to end up with a brand-new house but no furniture or draperies."

"You can hang bedsheets over the windows as far as I'm concerned. We got by all our lives without special-ordered furniture." He pushed away from the table and gestured to Ewan. "Time we got down to the brickyard, don't you think?"

Ewan nodded. The older man had deftly avoided his wife's question and escaped out the door. His uncle winked as they descended the front steps. "And that, my boy, is how it's done." As if by some unexplained foreknowledge, Joe appeared with his uncle's saddled horse and held the reins while Uncle Hugh mounted. He gathered the reins into his hand and tipped his hat. "Have a good day, Ewan. I'll see you at supper."

Joe, the groomsman his uncle had hired, stood beside Ewan and the two of them watched Hugh ride off. "You have any idea where he's off to, Joe?"

The groomsman shook his head. "Naw, he don't tell me nothing 'cept what time I'm supposed to have his horse ready for him each morning." Joe nodded toward the barn. "I got the buggy ready for you. Didn't think you'd be leaving quite this early or I would have brought it from the barn when I brought Mr. Hugh's horse."

"I'm in no big hurry, Joe. I'll walk down to the barn with you."

The two men walked in silence, Joe likely thinking about all the chores he needed to accomplish by day's end, while Ewan thought about Mr. Bruce. On his original visit, the contractor had been pleased with their operation, but he wanted bricks that were a more uniform shade of red and said he'd return when Ewan could show him something more to his liking. Ewan hoped that would happen today. If the brickyard was going to support all of the men and their families, he needed to secure additional contracts. Though he had expected his uncle to be present when Mr. Bruce arrived, it didn't appear that would happen. Once again, full responsibility would fall upon Ewan's shoulders.

During the many weeks that followed, the entire family had undergone a number of changes. The other relatives had arrived from Ireland, and the men had already begun work. The three single men had taken up residence in local boardinghouses, while the married men and their families had settled in some of the vacant houses near Bartlett. Ewan's uncle had arranged rental agreements for four houses, but he'd purchased three as well. He'd been clear with all of them: They would be paid wages for their work, but would pay rent and all of their living expenses. Each man also signed an agreement to reimburse Uncle Hugh for their passage, plus interest. For the single men, repayment would be easy, but it would be a burden for each married man with a wife and children.

Ewan had argued against requiring any of the men to pay interest on the money, but to no avail. His uncle was quick to point out that the bank required interest on loans and his relatives needed to know they could not take advantage of him. Ewan had laughed at the comment. No family member had ever succeeded in taking advantage of Uncle Hugh. There'd been a few who'd tried, but Uncle Hugh had always beaten them to the punch.

Before the girls had an opportunity to knock on the front door, Laura heard their laughter and hurried to the hallway. Since their arrival, the three girls had become almost daily visitors to Woodfield Manor. On one of their first visits, the twins had admired some of Mrs. Woodfield's tatting, and she'd offered to give them lessons. Their attempts were heartfelt, but the girls hadn't yet conquered the art.

"Good morning!" After opening the door, Laura ushered the threesome inside. "You're a little earlier than usual."

"We finished our breakfast early and Aunt Margaret said we could leave," Adaira said as she removed her shuttle and thread from a small cloth bag and handed it to Mrs. Woodfield. "I've been practicing. I think my tatting is much better than Ainslee's, but she doesn't practice much."

While Laura's mother examined the tatting projects, Laura motioned Rose toward the porch. "It's such a beautiful August morning. Why don't we sit outside and visit while Mother helps the girls with their tatting."

As long as the twins were busy with their handwork, they didn't mind if Laura and Rose disappeared for a private chat. During their visits, Laura tried to provide a bit of respite for the older girl. Rose had become a mother figure to her young sisters, and though she never exhibited an aversion to that role, she seemed to relish a bit of time away from the twins.

Instead of choosing the cushioned wicker furniture, the two of them settled beside each other on the porch swing, which had become their favorite visiting spot.

Using the toe of her shoe, Rose gave a slight push and set the swing in motion. "I thought you might be at the brickyard this morning. Ewan seems a wee bit anxious because a contractor is coming from Pittsburgh today."

"Yes, Archibald Bruce is supposed to arrive early this afternoon. I told Ewan I'd come to the office after lunch." Laura smiled at the girl. "There's no reason for your brother to be concerned. I think Mr. Bruce is going to be very pleased with the bricks, and I'm sure he'll sign a contract large enough to relieve Ewan's worries over the brickyard." Laura scooted back on the swing. "Once there are a few happy customers in Pittsburgh and Wheeling, word will quickly spread, and the men will be working overtime to keep up with the orders." She patted Rose's hand. "Just you wait and see."

"I know Ewan is determined to make it a success, but sometimes it's difficult when he doesn't have the final say in things. I see how he worries when Aunt Margaret insists upon having some of the relatives working on her house instead of down at the yard."

"How are your relatives adjusting to all of the changes here in America? Do they like it in West Virginia?"

"Uncle Darach says some of them are unhappy and have already gone to work at the coal mines. They can make more money there than Uncle Hugh will pay them."

"Dear me, that isn't good news." Laura attempted to withhold her surprise, for Ewan hadn't said a word to her. Perhaps he held out hope he could convince them to return, or that he could convince Hugh to raise their pay. "I thought they all signed agreements with Hugh that they'd repay him."

"They did, but they said they didn't agree upon where they would work. They told Ewan they didn't feel Uncle Hugh was being fair with them, and I think Ewan agrees. But he's hoping the rest of them won't quit any time soon. I know he's thankful Aunt Margaret finally agreed they would use the first bricks they burned for her house. After she saw the deep red ones the man from Pittsburgh requested, she tried to convince Ewan to make all new deep red ones for her, but he refused."

Laura smiled. "I hope she didn't upbraid

him when he turned down her request."

"Nay, but she did go to Uncle Hugh and ask him to overrule Ewan's decision." Rose chuckled and shook her head. "Uncle Hugh said she should be glad Ewan had offered up any of the bricks. So that was the end of it." Rose touched her fingers to her lips. "I'm just like my sister — telling tales that shouldn't be repeated." She gave the swing another push with her toe. "Ewan says when Aunt Margaret and Uncle Hugh move to their new house, we'll get to remain in the old one. I'm glad we'll have a place of our own. I'll be happy to do the cooking and cleaning."

Laura put her foot on the floor of the porch and brought the swing to an abrupt halt. "I almost forgot. I was going through my wardrobe and discovered some dresses I think will fit you, if you'd like to try them."

Rose's eyes sparkled as she jumped up from the swing and strode toward the door. "Oh, I'd love to. Do you think Aunt Margaret will object?"

"Why should she? You're the only one the dresses will fit. If she's displeased I gave them to you, she can speak with me. I'll be happy to set her mind at ease." Laura grasped the hand-carved walnut railing as she led Rose up the stairs and down the hallway to her room.

After entering the sitting room that adjoined Laura's bedroom, Rose pivoted in a full circle. "This is so beautiful." She rushed across the room and looked out the window. Turning to look at Laura, she said, "If this were my room, I would look out every morning just to see the mountains."

The girl's enthusiasm was contagious. "I'm very fortunate to have beautiful views from all of the windows. That's one of the reasons my father chose this spot to build Woodfield Manor." Laura opened the wardrobe along the west wall of the sitting room. "I keep my out-of-season dresses and those I no longer wear in these two wardrobes."

Rose peeked around the corner into the bedroom. "You have three wardrobes in your bedroom." Astonishment shone in her eyes. "I didn't know anyone owned enough clothes to fill so many wardrobes. God has blessed you for sure, Laura."

Laura's stomach cinched in a knot. "Not so much as you might believe, Rose. Just because I have wardrobes filled with dresses doesn't mean God has favored me."

The girl tipped her head to one side. "You live in a beautiful house and want for nothing, and you think God's love isn't shining down on you? If you'd been in Ireland with the twins and me, you'd feel different."

"When important things are missing in your life, material possessions don't seem significant."

" 'Tis true heartache can be hard to bear, but when your stomach meets your backbone from lack of food or your fingers are so cold they turn black, you forget the ache of grief and long for a bit of food and a stove to warm yourself." Her eyes shone with a faraway look. "For sure, you think God has deserted you when you'd fight your own sister for a crust of bread." A tear trickled down her cheek. She swiped it away and inhaled a deep breath. "I'm sorry to turn melancholy on you. Let's look at the dresses."

Laura lifted several day dresses from the wardrobe and placed them across the settee. "I think all of these will fit you."

Rose stepped across the room and traced her fingers down a raspberry and tan print dress with shell buttons centered down the front of the wide skirt. "This is beautiful. I've never owned anything so lovely. I do like this print very much."

"The raspberry color suits you, and I think this aqua shade will be pretty on you, as well." Laura held a sleeve of the aqua dress near Rose's face. "Yes. It's a lovely color for you."

Rose stood in front of a large oval mirror and held the dress close to her body. "It might be a little long, but Kathleen is good with a needle. I'm sure she'd help me hem it."

"How is Kathleen? Except at church, I've seen little of her."

Rose shrugged. "She's unhappy most of the time. She argues with Aunt Margaret about a fellow she likes very much. Kathleen says he's quite wonderful, but Aunt Margaret won't let him call on her. I would never tell on Kathleen, but I've seen her sneak out at night. I think she goes to meet him. If Aunt Margaret ever finds out, the sound of doomsday will be ringing in Kathleen's ears." Still clasping the dress in front of her, Rose made a small pirouette and beamed as the skirt of the dress swished and then settled and pooled at her feet. "I think what the twins said at the train station remains true: Aunt Margaret would be pleased if Kathleen and Ewan would marry."

Laura's breath caught. She had hoped Margaret had set aside such a notion. She couldn't imagine Kathleen and Ewan as a couple. Even more, she didn't want to. In truth, she didn't want to think of him with any woman. Yet what did she expect? Ewan was a handsome man who would one day be part owner of a profitable business. If he invested his money wisely, he'd likely become one of the most successful men in the county before he was thirty years of age. There were some young ladies who would refuse to be courted by an Irishman, but wealth and good looks had a way of winning affections. Before long, Ewan McKay would have women vying for his attention. Why was Margaret determined he marry her sister? Wouldn't an alliance with a young lady from a wealthy family be more advantageous? Margaret hadn't hidden the fact that she hoped to move into the proper social circles. She appeared to be overlooking the easiest route.

"What does your brother think about your Aunt Margaret's ideas regarding marriage to Kathleen?" Laura held her breath as she waited for Rose's answer.

"He says he hasn't decided who he will marry, but Aunt Margaret will not be making such a decision for him." Rose pressed her palm down the sleeve of a blue velvet basque, decorated with jet beads. "One thing is sure. The lady Ewan marries must love children, for he's always said he wants a houseful."

Rose's words wrapped around Laura like a tight cord and strangled her longing for the future — a future she'd been picturing with Ewan McKay.

CHAPTER 16

Long after the girls departed, Rose's comment plagued Laura. The words raced through her mind like a dog chasing a rabbit. Yet why did hearing Rose tell her that Ewan wanted a houseful of children cut so deep? From time to time, he'd said as much himself. Hadn't he told her that other than God, family was the most important thing in his life? During the passing months as she worked alongside him at the brickyard, she'd done her best to forget Ewan was a man intent upon having a large family. In truth, he was everything she desired in a husband, and he possessed the kindness and loving spirit to be a wonderful father. He'd certainly exhibited fatherly skills with his three sisters.

Yet the very thing he desired the most, she could never give him. Or any other man, for that matter. The sadness of that knowledge dismayed her much more today than it had when she'd first heard the doctor's proclamation at thirteen years of age. Back then, she'd been more devastated to hear she couldn't return to boarding school for the remainder of the year. The life-altering injuries she'd incurred when thrown from her horse were more significant now than she'd ever imagined during her childhood.

She'd been teetering on the fringes of consciousness when she'd overheard the doctor report the extent of her injuries to her parents. At first, she fought to maintain consciousness for increasing periods of time. Then, learning to walk again became her goal. After that, returning to full health and getting back to boarding school took precedence. Not until discussions of marriage and children became topics of discussion between Laura and her school friends did she begin to realize what impact the doctor's prognosis would mean for her future.

Her friends had looked at her with such pity and expressions of sorrow that finally the significance of her situation became clear. If she was honest with her suitors, they would judge her a poor marriage prospect. Lucy Martin had burst into tears when Laura explained her condition, and Laura had never forgotten Lucy's mournful decree: "You'll never marry, Laura. Every man of wealth and social position expects his wife to bear a son to carry on the family name." Lucy had wiped her tears and looked deep into Laura's eyes. "Don't ever tell any man who courts you. It's the only way, Laura."

For a time, Laura considered Lucy's advice and had spoken to her father about remaining silent on the subject of children when a young man requested permission to call on her. But her father had counseled against the idea. "Better that I have a discussion with any young man who asks to court you, Laura. Be it friendship or courtship, deception is not the way to enter into a relationship." He'd patted her hand and advised that if God intended her to marry, He would send the right man. And though she knew her father was correct, all of the young men who'd asked to court Laura had withdrawn their requests after a talk with her father.

Until Winston came along. He'd actually been pleased by the news. Laura had been stunned when her mother relayed the details. At first, Laura doubted Winston understood her condition, but on their first outing, he'd been frank with her. He disliked children, had no desire for any, and thought a child would be nothing more than a deterrent to his political aspirations.

She had doubted his truthfulness, but her mother believed him, and eventually so did Laura. He was friendly to children when it could advance him in the eyes of political benefactors or influential businessmen. Otherwise, he either ignored or avoided them all together. But then, he did the same with adults. Those who could further his political ambitions received his full attention; others were snubbed.

She disliked his attitude and behavior, and given her way, she would discontinue their relationship. But her mother wanted a match for Laura — and not just any match. She wanted Laura to marry a man of wealth and influence. Little matter that her own husband had not been such a man when they'd wed; she wanted better for Laura. And marriage to a man who could immediately provide a life of ease could help alleviate her childless state. At least that's what her mother believed. But Laura knew better. Marriage to a man she didn't love would only feed the ache in her heart.

After changing into a walking suit, she descended the front stairs and stopped at the parlor door. "I'm going to the brickyard. Ewan asked that I be there for the meeting with Mr. Bruce."

Her mother glanced over her shoulder and frowned. "I didn't realize he was coming to Bartlett today. Why didn't you mention it?"

Laura slipped on her gloves. "He's coming for a meeting with Ewan, not a social visit. I didn't think it would be of any great importance."

"Perhaps not to me, but you know Winston would like the opportunity to visit with Archibald. His influence with folks in Pittsburgh is vast. Invite him to join us for supper this evening, and I'll have Zeke ride into Bartlett and extend an invitation to Winston. We'll have a small dinner party. Won't that be fun?"

"Do you want me to invite Ewan, as well?"

Her mother hesitated. "If you think he'd enjoy dining with us, he's more than welcome, but I don't want anything to detract from Winston's visit with Archibald."

"I don't know if Ewan will accept, but I'll let him know it's an impromptu dinner party. Shall I send Catherine in so the two of you can plan a menu?"

"Oh yes. Thank you. And tell Zeke to ride into town and speak with Winston after he's delivered you to the brickyard. Is Archibald staying at the hotel in Bartlett? How is he getting from the train station to the brick-yard?"

"I have no idea, Mother. Mr. Bruce likely made the arrangements for his travel and hotel, but I can ask Ewan if Mr. Bruce sent word of his plans."

"Do let Archibald know that he's more than welcome to stay with us." Her frown returned. "Oh, I do wish you had let me know he was arriving so I could have invited him to stay with us. This all makes me feel very uncivil."

Laura sighed. "As I said, Mother, he's arriving for a business meeting with Ewan. This was never intended to be a social call. However, I will pass along your messages."

The cook wasn't pleased to receive news of the evening dinner party, and when Laura told Zeke he had to go into Bartlett, he didn't hesitate to tell her he had other work that needed doing this morning. Laura wanted to tell them both that she wasn't happy with the turn of events, either, but confiding in the help was inappropriate. A rule she'd been taught long ago.

Ewan turned and stood when she entered the office. "I was beginning to worry you'd forgotten." He glanced at the clock. "Mr. Bruce is due to arrive in about a half hour."

"That answers my first question."

His features creased in a puzzled look. "And what are your other questions?"

"Mother asked if you'd made arrangements for Mr. Bruce to travel from Bartlett to the brickyard or if I should have Zeke wait for him at the train station. She also wanted to know if he'd arranged for a room in town. She'd like him to come for dinner this evening and stay at Woodfield Manor if he hasn't already reserved a room at the Bartlett Hotel."

Ewan turned both hands palm side up and shrugged. "He sent a telegram saying he would meet with me at the brickyard office at two o'clock. I do not know any more than that. Was I supposed to offer him a ride from the station and a room for the night?" His question was tinged with a note of alarm that matched the fearful look in his eyes.

She regretted having caused him further anxiety. "No, you weren't expected to do any of those things. I merely wanted to know if Mr. Bruce had notified you of his plans. There's no need for concern. I'll go out and give Zeke instructions and then return." She hoped her smile offered a bit of reassurance.

When she strode back inside, Ewan was

pacing the length of the office. Back and forth. Back and forth. Finally Laura could no longer watch him. She pointed to a chair. "Please sit down. There's no reason to be anxious. Mr. Bruce wouldn't be taking the time to return if he didn't think you were going to produce a top-notch product."

"I don't know how you can be so sure. We have no idea what the other brick companies have presented to him, or at what prices. If he can strike a better bargain with some other company, he has no reason to offer a contract to our brickyard."

"He's returning because he liked what you showed him the first time he was here. My guess is that he'd already seen what others had to offer and he was most impressed with the C&M Brickyard."

Ewan came to a halt near her chair. "Do you really think so, or are you just saying that so I'll relax?"

Laura laughed and shook her head. "I'm not given to telling lies, Ewan. If I didn't believe he had great interest in contracting with C&M, I'd tell you." Her words seemed to calm him enough that he quit pacing. "I almost forgot. Mother asked me to extend a dinner invitation to you, as well. I do hope you'll accept."

He hesitated a moment and then gave a

nod. "But what if Mr. Bruce has other plans for dinner? Then what will your mother do?"

She chuckled. "Then you'll get to eat several servings." For a moment she considered telling him Winston would be there but changed her mind. She'd wait to tell him.

A short time later, Mr. Bruce arrived. He'd accepted Zeke's offer of a ride as well as her mother's dinner invitation. However, he'd already registered at the hotel, so he declined the invitation to stay at Woodfield Manor. "I do appreciate your mother's hospitality. I enjoy her company very much."

"Then you must visit more often. We don't see enough of our friends and always enjoy company."

Mr. Bruce clapped Ewan on the shoulder. "Well, if this young man and I are able to sign a contract, I'm sure you'll see a bit more of me. I always like to visit the companies where I do business. Much more personal than letters or telegrams, don't you think, Mr. McKay?" He turned his focus on Ewan.

"Aye, much better. I want to please our customers, and I want to hear for myself what they have to say. If they are unhappy, better they tell me than spread the word to my competitors, right?"

"Exactly! I knew I liked you, Ewan. We

think much the same way." Mr. Bruce stepped to the window and looked down at the yard. "I see you're working at full production. I'm eager to see the color you've developed and the completed frog." He rubbed his hands together like a child anticipating a Christmas surprise. "Let's go down to the yard."

Ewan didn't mind the request, but he'd wanted Laura present during any talks with Mr. Bruce, and the yard was no place for a lady, especially one dressed as fine as she. He worried she'd leave and go home to help her mother with arrangements for dinner, so he stopped in the doorway. "You'll be here when we return?"

"Of course. Now go on and show him what fine bricks you're making down there."

Her smile warmed his heart. He strode forward and led Mr. Bruce down to the yard with renewed confidence in his step. "I think you're going to like the color. We worked to get the right combination of clay and hematite to produce several different shades of red. If you decide to use our company, I've carefully recorded the amount of hematite to clay so that we can immediately begin production. Of course, burning can make a huge difference in the color, too, so I've been working long hours training the men I hired to work as burners."

Laura's father had been thoughtful in his layout of the yard. While allowing space for expansion, he'd also made certain the supply of clay would be close enough to the pug mill to make the use of one-horse carts economical.

Once the path into the yard widened, Mr. Bruce came alongside Ewan. "So you're mixing the hematite into the clay while it is being tempered in the pug mill rather than mixing it with the molding sand."

There was no doubt that Mr. Bruce knew a great deal about the brick-making process. Ewan didn't know if he was being singled out and put to a test or if Mr. Bruce asked detailed questions at every business he visited. Ewan hoped it was the latter and Mr. Bruce wasn't feeling doubtful about Ewan's ability to meet deadlines with an excellent product.

Ewan nodded. "Aye. Too much of the molding sand is rubbed off while the brick is being handled, which can result in loss of hematite and the red coloring you desire. I would never use that method unless a customer insisted."

Mr. Bruce appeared pleased by the answer but immediately followed with another question. "How long does it take to temper the clay in your pug mill, and how many bricks do you yield from each mix?"

Ewan pointed to the semicylindrical trough with long knives set spirally around the circumference. Mr. Bruce watched as clay was loaded at one end of the trough and mixed by the knives until it reached the other end and was discharged from the machine. "We use a closed pug mill because there is more uniform pressure on the clay while it is being tempered, which gives us better mixing results. With this machine, it takes about ten hours to temper enough clay for sixty thousand bricks." He pointed to the nearby idle pug mill his uncle had recently purchased. "That one will produce about the same amount."

Mr. Bruce arched his brows. "But you're not using it?"

"I don't need it right now, but I hope one day to have both pug mills operating every day from early spring until early winter. Everything depends upon how many orders we receive."

"I'm surprised you'd purchase machinery before it's needed, Ewan. That doesn't seem particularly prudent."

Ewan nodded. "I do not make the decisions regarding how the money is spent, Mr.

Bruce. I manage the brickyard, but my uncle is the owner, and he decides what will be purchased and what will not. I'm expected to bring in enough contracts to cover the expenses and make a tidy profit, as well."

"I'd say you have the difficult end of that bargain. I hope your uncle is paying you handsomely."

Ewan refrained from answering that remark. Instead, he directed Mr. Bruce to the VerValen machine, where the bricks were being molded. "I'm sure you're familiar with this piece of equipment."

"Indeed. The VerValen has changed the course of brickmaking." Mr. Bruce picked up one of the six-brick molds bearing the new frogs Ewan had designed. "I like this very much. I understand the C&M initials, but why the burning bush? A reference to burning the bricks?"

"There are two reasons. You've touched upon one of them. The other is because the burning bush reveals a living God. I wanted to use something in the design that symbolized my faith."

"And the faith of your uncle, as well?" Mr. Bruce traced his thick fingers across the design.

"I cannot speak for the faith of any other man, Mr. Bruce. Sometimes we can be fooled by outward appearances. Deceiving humans is not difficult, but deceiving God is impossible. Only He knows the true heart."

Mr. Bruce clapped Ewan on the shoulder. "You're a perceptive young man, Ewan. When anyone asks about the design, it will provide an opportunity for you to share your faith, a topic most of us are reluctant to discuss with others."

Ewan hadn't considered that possibility, but it pleased him to think his bricks might be a way of sharing God's faithfulness with other people. The idea continued to take root as he and Mr. Bruce watched a teenage boy sanding the molds before placing them in the machine.

Ewan moved closer to the workman adding sand to the molds and pointed to a spot in the wooden form. "Be sure you sand them well so the bricks don't stick. See here in the corners? You need to make sure those are sanded as well as the middle of the molds." Ewan added a little more sand and tilted the mold until every spot had been coated with sand.

The boy's hand trembled as Ewan returned the mold. "I try to be careful and do a good job, Mr. McKay. My pa's gonna be angry if he finds out I'm making mistakes."

"No need to worry. We all make mistakes from time to time." Ewan was surprised the young man hadn't been corrected by the molder, who scraped off the top of the molds as they came out of the machine, or by the off-bearer, who took the mold from the delivery table and placed it on a two-wheeled barrow. Ewan had asked the experienced men to help the younger or untrained workers, but it seemed he'd need to have another talk with them.

They stepped aside as two truck men scurried back and forth from the VerValen, pushing the wooden carts filled with molded bricks to the yard, where they dumped the bricks onto the drying floor for the mold setters to arrange in a herringbone pattern to begin the drying process.

"Looks like you have quite a number of hardworking men," Mr. Bruce said as they continued toward the drying floor.

"Aye. We were fortunate to hire almost all of the men who returned from the war and had worked for Mr. Woodfield. And all of our relatives my uncle brought over from Ireland had worked in brickyards, either in Scotland or Ireland, so they are well trained in the craft. Unfortunately, only one was an experienced burner, other than myself, so that has been the biggest challenge."

"How many arches in your kilns?"

Ewan followed Mr. Bruce's gaze. "Fifteen arches made up of thirty-five to forty thousand bricks. I prefer the arches to be about forty courses high. Since we're burning with coal, we start the fires on the windward side so the smoke will blow through the arches."

The two of them continued onward until they neared the far end of the drying yard. Ewan directed Mr. Bruce to a small covered section. "So you've covered only a small area?"

Ewan nodded. "Eventually, I want to have both an open and a covered yard, but right now we have only a small section covered. The bricks we created for your inspection are in this section."

Mr. Bruce leaned down and picked up one of the deep red bricks. "Did you test the water absorption on these bricks?"

"Except for the salmon bricks, all of these are at less than 10 percent absorption. On that particular brick, it is 5 percent. The bricks were weighed before they were placed in water for twenty-four hours and weighed as soon as they were removed."

"Salmon and green bricks always absorb more, but I'm glad to hear these deep red ones are below 10 percent. I think they will be my choice for the row houses in both Allegheny City and Pittsburgh." He placed the brick back on the pallet and picked up another, one shade lighter. "This one for the churches, libraries, and office buildings in Pittsburgh. The one over there for all industrial buildings, and this one for business buildings, churches, and libraries in Allegheny City." He glanced at Ewan. "You should write this down so you'll remember what bricks to produce when I send word we're going to be constructing a new bank in Allegheny City or row houses in Pittsburgh."

Ewan's pulse quickened. "You're going to sign a contract with us?"

"I am." Mr. Bruce gave a firm nod. "You know how to make a fine brick, Ewan. As long as you meet our deadlines and continue producing bricks of this quality, you won't need to worry about keeping your men busy." He gestured toward the hillside. "Let's get back up there and sign the contracts and then go and enjoy dinner at Woodfield Manor."

Ewan's heart pounded a new beat. He wanted to race up the hill and yank the contracts from his desk, but he forced himself to slow his steps and keep pace with Mr. Bruce. He offered a silent prayer of thanks. Signed contracts and sharing a cel-

291

ebratory dinner with Laura would make for a perfect ending to this day.

CHAPTER 17

"What do you mean we weren't invited?" Ewan's aunt stood in front of him, hands perched on her hips. With her beady eyes flashing and her elbows angled like wings, she reminded him of an angry hen ready to peck anyone who approached.

Margaret remained in her henlike stance at the foot of the stairs. If Ewan was going to get upstairs and dress for dinner, he'd either have to convince her to move or vault overtop of her. The thought caused him to grin, which only worsened the situation.

She extended her hand and pointed her index finger beneath his nose. "This is no laughing matter, Ewan McKay. Not only has your uncle been snubbed, but Mrs. Woodfield has slighted our entire family with her lack of an invitation."

"I don't think there was any slight intended, Aunt Margaret. Mrs. Woodfield didn't know Mr. Bruce was coming to town until today, and the invitation to dinner was arranged at the last minute. I'm sure I was included only because of my meeting with him today." Ewan didn't add that he assumed Laura had been the one who'd included him in the arrangements. That admission would only compound his aunt's anger.

"Your uncle is the one who owns the brickyard. If anyone attends the dinner, it should be him. And me, of course." She lifted her nose and sniffed.

"I believe this is a social dinner rather than a business gathering, Aunt Margaret. Mr. Bruce has known the Woodfields for many years, and they share a number of the same acquaintances. Since we've already signed the contracts, there's not going to be a need to discuss business." Ewan took a step to the right, hoping he could edge around her.

"I'll tell you what I believe." His aunt placed her palm against his chest and stayed him. "I believe those Woodfield women have cooked up a plan so they can remain involved in the brickyard — especially Laura. She's been keeping her nose in things ever since they sold the place to us. You think I don't know how often she's over at that office with you?"

The longer his aunt talked, the more

Ewan's excitement faded. His aunt's caustic remarks were enough to wilt the bloom off a rose. Maybe if he didn't respond, she'd cease her angry diatribe and move aside. As if to announce how little time he had, the hallway clock chimed the hour.

"Laura Woodfield thinks if she marries you, she'll still be able to keep her fingers in the business." His aunt's brows dipped low as her face creased into an angry frown. "You can tell her for me that she'll never have any part of our brickyard again. And if you want to stay in your uncle's good graces, you'll heed my words and stay away from her."

Ewan sighed. Laura had offered tremendous help to them — help they would have had to pay for if they'd purchased a brickyard from anyone else. And he'd already explained to every member of the family that Laura was being courted by Winston Hawkins. If Winston would drop out of the running, Ewan would request permission to court Laura, but he'd never divulge that information to Aunt Margaret.

"You can cease your continual worries about Laura Woodfield. Why do you find it so difficult to believe that she's helping only because she wants us to be successful?"

His aunt's cackle echoed down the hallway. "I know women better than you ever will, young man, and you can mark my words — she has an ulterior motive. No one volunteers all that help without expecting something in return."

Nothing Ewan said would convince his aunt otherwise, and he was wasting valuable time arguing with her. "Please step aside, Aunt Margaret. I need to change clothes and leave. It would be rude to arrive late."

"What's rude is that we weren't invited. Invitation or not, if your uncle were here, I'd demand we attend that dinner. But since he's not, I'm going to insist you take Kathleen." His aunt gestured toward the parlor.

Ewan turned toward the room. Apparently, Kathleen had been quietly sitting and listening to their entire conversation. He didn't know what offended him more — the fact that she'd been eavesdropping or the fact that his aunt expected him to take her sister to the dinner.

"She is not invited, and I'm sure Kathleen doesn't want to embarrass herself by appearing at a dinner party when she's not received an invitation." He tightened his jaw and looked at her. "Do you, Kathleen?"

Kathleen glanced back and forth between her sister and Ewan and soon decided to take her sister's side in the matter. "I can change my dress and be ready in short order, Ewan. I'm sure Mrs. Woodfield won't mind an additional guest."

Ewan's stomach clenched. He wanted to object, but it would serve no purpose. His aunt would continue with her silly argument until she won. Throughout the years, she'd used this same ploy with his uncle, and her smug look only increased Ewan's irritation.

Ewan sighed. "Even if she is offended by our rude behavior, Mrs. Woodfield is far too proper to ever let on."

His aunt grasped his arm. "Are you saying that I'm not a lady?"

"Nay. You're putting the words in my mouth, Aunt."

He shook loose of her hold and bounded up the steps before she could detain him any longer. Escorting Kathleen to the dinner would prove an embarrassment to both of them and an inconvenience to Mrs. Woodfield. His thoughts raced as he tried to formulate an appropriate remark he could make when he arrived at Woodfield Manor with Kathleen at his side. By the time he met Kathleen downstairs, he'd still thought of nothing. Perhaps she'd have a helpful suggestion.

The carriage was waiting for them when they stepped onto the front porch. Aunt

Margaret had thought of everything. She'd made certain Ewan couldn't use the lack of a carriage as an excuse and ride off to Woodfield Manor on his horse.

They'd gone only a short distance when Kathleen grasped Ewan's arm. "I know you're angry that I didn't object when Margaret insisted I attend the dinner party, but there was a reason."

Ewan glanced in her direction. "Do you care to share your reason with me, or am I to guess?"

Her lips trembled in a slight smile. "I want you to take me to Terrance O'Grady's house and return for me after the dinner party. Please, Ewan? We care for each other, but my sister won't give him permission to call on me. She has her mind set against him, but it doesn't change how we feel about each other. Once he's making enough money to support a wife, we'll get married, but until then I need to continue living with Margaret and Hugh, which means I must do as my sister says."

Ewan wasn't surprised to hear Aunt Margaret wouldn't grant Terrance O'Grady permission to court Kathleen. Though his aunt had never said it aloud to him, Ewan had come to the realization that she wanted him to marry Kathleen. In fact, he was sure his aunt would do everything in her power to see her sister wed to her nephew. But that would never happen. Not that Kathleen wasn't a nice young woman; she was. But he'd never be attracted to her as anything other than a friend — not now, not ever.

"So you and Terrance have been seeing each other without Aunt Margaret's approval?" He didn't wait for an answer. "How long has this been going on?"

"Quite some time now. It's easy enough to slip out after everyone is asleep. Now that it's warm, we meet near the hillside leading down to the brickyard, but please don't tell Margaret."

He was surprised to hear Kathleen would secretly meet Terrance O'Grady, or any man, for that matter. Even more troubling was the fact that she wanted him to be a part of her plan to meet Terrance this evening. "I understand your plight, but I cannot play a part in your deception, Kathleen. If something should happen to you, your sister would never forgive me. And that means Uncle Hugh would never forgive me, either."

"I thought you would be willing to help." Her angry tone faded as she began to plead with him. "Even if something should happen while I'm with Terrance, Uncle Hugh's anger would soon vanish. You know he can't operate the brickyard without you. His only real interest is money, so he's not going to do anything that would cause the brickyard to falter." She tightened her hold on his arm. "No one needs to know. Please change your mind, Ewan. I would do the same for you if you ever asked. It's not like this is the first time I've gone to meet Terrance, but I'd enjoy spending more than an hour during the middle of the night."

He shook his head. "I would not ask you to lie for me, Kathleen."

Her features tightened into a frown. "Then don't help me, but I'm not going to any dull dinner party with you. When we arrive at Woodfield Manor, I'm going to leave and walk to Terrance's house, and you can't stop me. If you try, I'll make a scene that the Woodfields and their guest will never forget. I'm sure you don't want that." She shifted on the carriage seat. "There's far more chance I'll come to harm while walking to the O'Gradys' than if you took me there in the carriage and then called for me after dinner. If Aunt Margaret ever finds out, I'll tell her I was going to create a scene if you didn't do my bidding."

He was torn by his lack of options. While he didn't want to take her to the O'Gradys', neither did he want trouble when they arrived at Woodfield Manor. From the set of Kathleen's jaw, he was certain she'd hold true to her promise. If he tried to force her inside, she'd create a scene. If he didn't, she'd walk to Terrance's home. Neither was a good option.

The young woman's plight tugged at Ewan. Little Kathleen did or said ever met with her older sister's approval. Margaret consistently berated Kathleen's artistic talents, her choice of clothing, her supposed lack of social graces, and her inability to gain Ewan's attention as a suitor.

With a tug on the reins, he turned the horses toward the O'Gradys' house. "I'm doing as you've asked, Kathleen, but not because I want to or because I think it's what you should do. I fear this is a terrible mistake, but you're a grown woman, old enough to make your own decisions."

"There's no need to worry. Everything will be fine; I promise you won't regret helping me."

By the time he arrived at Woodfield Manor, Ewan had forgotten the exhilaration he'd experienced earlier in the day. From the moment he'd arrived at home, there had been nothing but cross words, veiled threats, and outlandish accusations.

Ewan stepped down from the carriage and handed the reins to Zeke. Being an amiable dinner guest was going to require an abrupt change of attitude. Ewan inhaled a deep breath and tried to recapture some of his former excitement.

Laura met him at the front door, wearing an evening dress of pale plum silk with velvet trim, her beauty undeniable. Her blue eyes sparkled as she greeted him. "I was beginning to think you weren't going to join us."

"I'm sorry for the delay. There were a few matters at home that required my attention. I hope I didn't keep your mother and Mr. Bruce waiting."

"No. We're all visiting in the library. Dinner won't be served for another half hour." She gestured for him to follow.

Being with Laura was enough to raise his spirits. Perhaps he shouldn't have been so harsh with Kathleen. She wanted to spend time with the man she loved. Couldn't he understand her position?

For different reasons, they shared the same problem. Although he tried to tamp down his increasing feelings for Laura, he still longed to be with her. If Winston weren't her beau, he would ask for permission to call on her, for try as he might, there was no denying what he felt for her each time he was in her presence. He followed her down the hallway, his mood improving with each step.

"Ah, you've finally arrived." Winston stood with his elbow resting on the black walnut mantel.

The moment he heard Winston's voice, Ewan's spirits plummeted. Laura hadn't mentioned he would be present this evening. This was the second time she had surprised him this way. His thoughts raced back to her unexpected announcement on the train to Wheeling that Winston would be present to attend social gatherings while they were there seeking contracts. Ewan had been unhappy she hadn't forewarned him, and he was every bit as displeased to be caught once again unawares.

Winston's sullen tone was enough to alert Ewan that his own presence displeased Laura's suitor. Winston moved from the mantel and sat down beside Laura, making it clear he would occupy her time this evening. Knowing in advance that Winston had been invited wouldn't have changed Ewan's acceptance, but being informed would have given him time to steel himself against the pain of seeing them together.

Forcing aside his dejected attitude, Ewan greeted Mrs. Woodfield and Mr. Bruce

"I'm a bit outnumbered with two Scots-Irish in the room." Winston looked at Ewan and leaned a bit closer to Laura.

"Aye, that you are. And the only way you'd find better company in all of West Virginia would be for Ewan and me to add a few more of our clansmen to the dinner party." Mr. Bruce's exaggerated accent caused Ewan to smile.

"I've read there's a great deal of fighting between the north and the south in Ireland," Winston said.

Mr. Bruce cast a soulful look in Winston's direction. "Seems much the same as what happened in this country, does it not? North fighting against south. Of course the warring is based upon different reasons. We're not fighting due to slavery in Ireland."

"Then again, our war has ended while yours has gone on for years and years, has it not?" Winston seemed determined to gain ground in an argument that served no purpose. If he angered Mr. Bruce, he might lose political support from the man and from his wealthy Scots-Irish friends in Pittsburgh and Allegheny City, as well.

Mr. Bruce nodded. "Quite true, Winston. Our war has gone on far too long, but I fear

Judge Mellon may be correct. He once said that the only way to settle the Irish question would be to sink the island. I hope it will never come to that." His lighthearted response broke the tension in the room.

Ewan sighed with relief and hoped there would be no further discussion of the north and south — in this country or in Ireland.

Throughout the rest of the evening, Winston remained by Laura's side like a dog protecting a bone. Much to Ewan's surprise, Winston didn't accompany the two of them to the front door as Ewan prepared to depart. Probably because Mrs. Woodfield followed them down the hallway. Had Winston known the older woman would take the opportunity to go upstairs and refresh herself, he likely wouldn't have been so careless.

Ewan stepped close to Laura's side as she opened the front door. He turned to her and gave a slight shake of his head. "I am truly baffled that a woman who professes your Christian beliefs would ever consider Winston Hawkins as a suitor. Surely you can see that the man is no more than a dogmatic hypocrite with regard for no one other than himself. If you stand at his side, people will think the same of you, Laura. If you've never considered that notion, perhaps it's time you gave it some thought."

He didn't look back as he strode down the front steps.

CHAPTER 18

Fortunately, Kathleen and Terrance were waiting when Ewan arrived. The dinner party had been painful. Watching Winston boast about his suitability to become a leading member of Congress one day had been as irritating as squealing pigs hungry for slop, and he'd said as much to Laura before he departed. He'd been disappointed when she simply nodded and offered a weak defense for Winston's ingratiating behavior.

Ewan didn't know which had bothered him more: Winston's conduct or Laura's willingness to defend and accept such a man. She deserved much better, yet she seemed unable to comprehend her own sense of worth. The realization saddened him.

When Terrance approached the carriage, Ewan stared down at him. "Don't expect that I'll be bringing Kathleen to meet you again. I don't approve of this sneaking around. If you cannot gain my aunt and uncle's approval, you need to find some other woman to court."

Terrance ducked his head as though dodging bullets. "I do not think they will ever agree, but I'll do me best to speak with Mr. Crothers when I get a chance."

The man's weak response surprised Ewan. He'd expected Terrance to fight for the right to court Kathleen. If she'd been telling the truth, they'd met more than a few times. By now, Terrance should have at least attempted to speak with Hugh.

Still, Ewan understood Uncle Hugh could be formidable. No doubt the thought of coming face-to-face with Uncle Hugh was enough to put the likes of Terrance O'Grady in mortal fear, but if he cared for Kathleen, he needed to make an attempt. If he and Kathleen eloped, there'd be no end to Aunt Margaret's wrath. In spite of her sister's controlling behavior, Kathleen loved her sister, and being estranged would come to no good end for either of them. Yet, he knew Aunt Margaret. Her stubborn nature would take hold, and she'd never forgive. It had happened before with other relatives, and it could happen again with Kathleen.

"I don't want the two of you to do anything foolish. You do not want to suffer the anger of Margaret Crothers, and neither does Kathleen. If you start down that path, there's no turning back, and it can only lead to pain. If you fear talking to Hugh, let me see if I can ease things a bit. Perhaps then he can get his wife to come 'round and let you call on Kathleen. Maybe together we can handle this. Will you give me a bit of time to see if I can help?"

Terrance raised his eyebrows a notch. "I do not think you should become involved, Mr. McKay. I'm thinking it'd be better if I spoke to Mr. Crothers without you stepping between us." He turned his gaze on Kathleen. "Don't you agree, Kathleen?"

She dutifully nodded. "Whatever you think is best, Terrance."

"I thank you, Mr. McKay. But in good time, I'll speak to your uncle and see if he will give me permission."

"Whatever you think best, but the offer remains open. You come see me if you change your mind."

"Aye, that I will." Terrance pulled his soft cap from his back pocket and settled it atop his head.

Kathleen waved to Terrance as Ewan flicked the reins. He liked Terrance, but he'd been surprised by the young man's refusal of help. Perhaps Ewan had misjudged him.

Maybe Terrance possessed an inner strength that wasn't immediately noticeable. Still, it likely would make things easier for the young man if Ewan spoke with Uncle Hugh beforehand. At least his uncle could help calm Aunt Margaret. Even then, he doubted it would change the woman's mind. She didn't want her sister to marry a man who worked in a livery. Aunt Margaret wanted her sister to marry him, an event that would never occur, for Ewan could be as headstrong as his aunt. He didn't love Kathleen, and he would never enter into a loveless marriage.

They'd gone on a short distance when Kathleen grasped his arm. "Thank you, Ewan. I appreciate your offer to try to help us." She sighed. "If only Margaret would meet Terrance, I think she would like him. He's kind and funny and a hard worker. He possesses far more good attributes than Hugh. She'd see that if she'd give him a chance."

"Aye, but we both know that changing your sister's decision will be as likely as moving one of these mountains."

"I know. The Bible says if we have faith as small as a grain of mustard seed, we can move a mountain, so my faith must be very weak. I've prayed and tried to have faith that she'll change her mind, but each time I mention Terrance's name, Margaret becomes angry. I've told him how she feels, and that's why he's so hesitant to speak with Uncle Hugh."

"I doubt his conversation with Uncle Hugh will go well, so I think you need to be prepared to end your relationship. I know you don't think it's possible to forget him. But eventually Aunt Margaret will match you with a young man who will be pleasing to both of you."

Kathleen protested, but Ewan shook his head. "We don't have time to argue about this. I need to tell you about the happenings at Woodfield Manor this evening."

"I don't care about that silly dinner." Moonlight draped across the carriage and painted a silhouette of Kathleen with her lower lip protruding like a pouting child.

"You need to care. If your sister questions you about what was served for dinner or what Mr. Bruce discussed, what are you going to tell her?"

"I hadn't thought of that. I suppose you'd better tell me. Our details will need to match."

"Aye." Ewan was glad she finally understood the seriousness of what had happened this evening. If Margaret became suspicious, they'd both be in very hot water.

For the remainder of their ride home, Ewan described everything from the spring vegetable soup to the seasoned chicken with rice and stewed mushrooms to the sweet strawberry cake. After he'd described the menu, he detailed the conversation that had taken place throughout each course. "I hope your memory is good."

"It's passable. I think I can remember what you've told me, but I'm interested in hearing more about Winston Hawkins's appearance at the dinner. I thought you and Mr. Bruce were the only invited guests."

"So did I, but there he was, big as life, leaning on the fireplace mantel like he owned Woodfield Manor. The man is so full of himself, you'd think he'd explode."

Kathleen nodded. "Aye, but the sun shines on the likes of him, while the rain falls on our heads. Why is that, Ewan?"

"I do not know, Kathleen, but I cannot offer up any loud complaints. I have a better life now than ever before. My sisters are with me, and they'll have a better future here than if we'd stayed in Ireland. And one day I'll be a partner in the brick business. Even though I do not understand why Laura finds Winston Hawkins a man worthy of her time and her future, I cannot say the

Lord has not been good to me." He tipped his head in her direction. "And you cannot say that, either, Kathleen. Coming here with your sister has given you a much better life than you had before. Aye?"

"Aye, but it still does not make it easy to live with Margaret. Nothing I say or do meets with her approval. She's as rigid as an iron stake, and she's never willing to change her mind. I do not wish to marry a rich man. I wish to marry Terrance. He's the man I love."

"For now, you'd best keep that to yourself."

The next morning, Ewan's words still rang in Laura's ears. How she'd longed to tell him that she understood his assessment of Winston. Yet that would only complicate the situation. Ewan rightfully questioned her capacity to love a man of Winston's character, but she'd maintained her silence. He wouldn't understand her willingness to continue in a relationship with a man she'd not yet learned to love.

Before she met Ewan, she'd nearly accepted the idea of marrying a man she didn't love. Even now, she didn't consider such a concept impossible. She loved her mother, and if nothing else, her marriage to

Winston would ease her mother's anxiety over her daughter's future. Winston would provide for Laura and love her, even if she couldn't love him in return.

For a brief time, she'd considered severing her relationship with Winston, but listening to his sisters over these past months, she'd come to realize that family was very important to him. The girls had told story after story about their lives in Ireland, and many of those stories included Ewan and his goodness to them. Their reflections also included his deep desire to have children of his own one day. The girls didn't realize that each comment added another wound to her already scarred heart.

She'd done her best to think of Ewan as no more than a friend, but with each encounter it proved more and more difficult, this evening being the most heartrending. His departing words had felt accusatory, as though he questioned her judgment and integrity. And why shouldn't he? Winston made no effort to hide his willingness to do whatever was necessary to achieve political success. Even Mr. Bruce had appeared taken aback by several of Winston's self-serving comments.

In all likelihood, she should distance herself from Rose and the twins, yet the very thought caused her physical pain. The girls brought her such pleasure, she couldn't imagine calling a halt to their visits. However, she did wish she hadn't made plans to spend time with them today. Would Ewan have said anything about Winston's unexpected appearance last night? Would he have criticized her in front of the girls?

Ewan wouldn't intentionally belittle her to his sisters, but he might have said something about Winston's unexpected presence to his aunt or uncle — something derogatory that the girls might have overheard. She shook off the idea and stopped by the parlor door.

"I'm going to meet the girls. They want me to see the progress that's been made on Crothers Mansion. And we may go over to the orphanage afterward."

Her mother looked up from her knitting. "Crothers Mansion? Is that what they've christened their new home?" She chuckled. "Margaret is determined to make her mark, isn't she?"

"She is, indeed. From what the girls tell me, it won't be much longer before they move into the portion that's been completed. I do wonder where she'll direct all her energy once the house is finally completed."

"I'm sure she'll devote herself to entertaining and volunteering to help the needy. She's been clear she wants to be accepted by the community, and there's no better way than to help others." Laura's mother continued her knitting.

"Let's hope so. There are certainly more than enough needs to be met in Bartlett and the surrounding area." Laura stepped to the mirror and pinned a brooch to her neckline. "I should be back by late afternoon. I told the girls they could return here for tea. I hope you don't mind."

"Of course not. I enjoy their company. The girls are unpretentious, sweet young ladies."

"They truly are. And the children at the orphanage enjoy their visits. The twins are always eager to lead them in outdoor games."

"I'm glad they enjoy going with you," her mother said. "I think I heard Zeke bring the carriage around. You'd better go, or he'll be unhappy for the rest of the day. You know he dislikes waiting."

Laura greeted Zeke as she stepped onto the porch. He appeared relieved when she said she'd drive herself. "I'm picking up the McKay girls, and we won't have enough room for you to join us, Zeke." She grinned.

"I know you're disappointed."

"Yes, ma'am. Nothing I like better than sitting around waiting for young women to get done visiting, but jest this once, I'll try to overlook being left behind." He offered a wry smile as he assisted her into the carriage.

"In that case I'll make sure it doesn't happen again." Laura laughed as she flicked the reins and waved good-bye.

The three girls were sitting on the porch swing when Laura arrived at the old house that had been her home as a young girl. She'd loved spending summer afternoons on that swing and was glad to see someone had taken time to give it a coat of paint and hang it for the girls to enjoy. The girls jumped up when she came to a stop, and the swing bounced for several seconds as they raced toward her carriage.

She leaned forward and glanced at the door. "Do you need to tell someone you're leaving? I don't want your aunt or Kathleen to worry over your whereabouts."

Ainslee was the first to settle inside the carriage. "Aunt Margaret knows we're going with you. Rose told her first thing this morning."

Adaira followed close on her sister's heels and bounded onto the leather seat beside her. "She has a headache, so she went to rest after lunch."

"I think she's glad we're leaving. She said she'd be glad for the peace and quiet." Ainslee giggled. "She says our chattering tires her out."

Rose followed her sisters and stepped up into the carriage. "What sort of stories are they telling you?" She glanced over her shoulder at the twins and smiled.

"We just told Miss Laura that Aunt Margaret has a headache and is glad we're leaving." Ainslee scooted forward and leaned her head between Laura and Rose. "Uncle Hugh says the workmen will be snapping their suspenders for joy when they hear Aunt Margaret won't be checking on them this afternoon."

Laura couldn't contain a burst of laughter. The twins were such a delight. They didn't realize there were some things that shouldn't be repeated outside of the family circle. On the other hand, if their uncle didn't want his remarks repeated, he shouldn't make them in front of his nieces.

Rose frowned. "Ainslee! No need to tell everything you hear."

"Everything I said was true. You told me as long as what I said was the truth and didn't hurt anyone, I didn't need to worry about getting in trouble."

"You're not in trouble." Rose sighed and looked at Laura. "Sometimes I feel more like a mother than a sister."

Laura gave a slight nod. "I know it's difficult, but you're very good with the twins. They're fortunate to have you."

The few words of praise appeared to allay Rose's concerns over her dual role with the girls. "Thank you, Laura. You always know exactly what to say."

"I wish that were true. There are many times when I find myself at a loss for words." The response had barely escaped her lips when she caught sight of Ewan standing near the construction site. "I didn't know your brother was going to be here today."

Laura's ears filled with the roaring sound of her beating heart. Though she tried, she couldn't control the surge of emotion that engulfed her when she was drawn into Ewan's presence. After his parting words of disapproval last evening, she wondered how he would react to her this afternoon.

He turned as the carriage approached and stepped forward to help her down. "I see the girls have convinced you to entertain them again today." He glanced at the twosome sitting in the back seat of the carriage.

"It's my pleasure. They wanted to see the progress on the house, and since I've never been here, I was pleased to bring them. Besides, they're going to help me at the orphanage afterward." She lifted her gaze to the structure. "What wonderful advancement the workmen have made. It appears your aunt and uncle will be able to move into this wing very soon." She shaded her eyes against the sun. "Or is there still a great deal of work to be completed inside?"

Ewan shook his head. "Nay, not in this section, but my aunt is determined the house is to be much larger, so several wings will be added before she's satisfied." Laura's breath caught as he stepped closer and brushed her arm. "Aunt Margaret wants to be certain her house is the largest home in this portion of the state." The twins and Rose had already proceeded toward the house when Ewan lightly grasped her elbow and directed her forward. "Come along. I'll give you a tour."

The area buzzed with activity, with all of the men scurrying to and fro like ants building a colony. "I see your uncle has hired additional help."

"Aye. When he continued taking men from the brickyard and bringing them over here to work, we had a long talk. He said if

I could find additional workers for him, he'd send any of the trained brickmakers back to the yard. I had good luck locating some freed slaves, who were pleased for the work. They're good workers, and many have experience with construction. I even hired two fine carpenters who have carved some beautiful woodwork for the house."

"That's excellent, but I thought your uncle was overseeing construction of the house and you were charged with operating the brickyard. Has that changed?"

"Nay, but I think you know Uncle Hugh is sometimes brash with others. One of the carpenters and four other good workers threatened to quit, so Aunt Margaret decided I should step in and assist. I'm helping out here some of the time, and he's at the brickyard more than he'd been in the past. I'm not so sure the men at the brickyard are happy, but I cannot divide myself in two. 'Tis bad enough that some of the relatives have left to work in the mines. I can only hope others don't follow them."

Laura could well understand the workers' dissatisfaction with Mr. Crothers. His abrasive manner was enough to send the most dependable workers running for the hills. "With the brick orders you'll need to fill for Mr. Bruce, as well as the orders for the proposed hotel in Fairmont, is it a wise use of your time to be here rather than the brickyard?"

"Nay. 'Tis a very bad idea." He hiked a shoulder. "If I had the final say in things, I would be at the brickyard every waking hour, but my uncle is the owner, and he makes the final decisions."

"I'm sure you'll do an excellent job with both the house and brickyard. Your relatives know you're a competent leader."

Ewan gave her a sidelong glance. "The girls need me to support them, so I can't walk away from all of this no matter how unfair."

They continued toward the front of the house, where the girls were waiting. The black walnut double porches were almost an exact replica of the ones at Woodfield Manor. "I would not want the girls to suffer for any of the decisions I've made in the past or the ones I make in the future. I've prayed a great deal about the future, but so far I haven't gotten any clear answers." He smiled as Ainslee waved for them to hurry. "Enough of this talk. Let me show you the house. We can start in the basement."

Laura surveyed the basement of the house, where quarried stone had been cut and mortared to form the foundation. The stones outlined the exterior of the house as well as the division of rooms in the lower area. A dividing wall and hallway were built to separate the areas into rooms, likely for food storage and work rooms for carpenters. There were three outside entrances to the basement. Perhaps Mrs. Crothers planned on using the rooms as living quarters rather than work rooms. There were also two sets of stairs leading to the interior of the upper level of the house.

Laura gestured toward the basement rooms. "Are these spaces where some of the hired help will live, or are they for storage?"

Ewan shrugged. "I'm not sure what Aunt Margaret has decided about these rooms. This portion of the house was completed under Uncle Hugh's supervision, although the bricks were made at the yard. The walls are four bricks thick from the basement to the attic. Some of our softer bricks were used on the insides of the walls, with hard bricks on the outside. The house should stay cool in the summer and warm in the winter." Ewan motioned to the twins. "Let's go upstairs."

Ainslee wrinkled her nose. "I think it's cozy down here. Can't we stay here and play for a while?"

"I suppose, but don't open the windows."

Ewan furrowed his brow. "I mean it, Ainslee."

As they were walking upstairs, Ewan explained that not long ago Ainslee had stacked some bricks that had been left in the basement and opened one of the windows. "The windows are hinged to open inward, so I didn't notice when we left. A skunk got inside the house."

Laura clamped a hand to her lips. "Oh no! I'm sure that didn't sit well with your aunt."

Ewan chuckled. "Nay. Worse yet, she blamed a worker, and if I had not discovered Ainslee was to blame, she would have fired the poor man." At the top of the stairs, Ewan directed Laura to turn to the right.

"I notice a number of similarities to Woodfield Manor. I'm flattered your aunt wanted to replicate so many of the details of our home."

Ewan chuckled. "My aunt is competitive. She wants this house to be similar, but much larger. That's why she's adding the extra wings. Fortunately for the girls and me, Uncle Hugh, Aunt Margaret, and Kathleen will move into this portion of the house as soon as work is completed."

"From what I've seen so far, it appears that will happen soon." The main stairway leading to the second floor had also been constructed of black walnut with a curving banister and intricately carved newel post.

"If all goes according to plan, we should be done soon. However, Aunt Margaret is unwilling to move in until the brown plaster is covered with plaster of paris and painted or papered."

Laura concurred that the brown plaster made by mixing sand with pigs' hair was unattractive, but it wouldn't be enough to stop most people from moving into a house. The walls could be completed after a move. Ewan had spoken of living conditions back in Ireland, so Laura was surprised at Mrs. Crothers's decision.

They walked through the door leading to the upstairs porch. "There's a traveler's room over there." Ewan gestured to the west end of the porch. "The outer stairway at the west end allows access to the porch, but the room doesn't have access to the interior of the house." Ewan had thought the room unnecessary, but while staying at the hotel, his aunt had overheard two ladies discussing such a space being added to a house in Wheeling. The room was used to offer hospitality to travelers while also retaining privacy in the main house. Naturally, his aunt had insisted upon mimicking the idea.

"I've never before seen such a room, but I suppose if someone arrived that wasn't well known to the family, it could prove useful."

Ewan shrugged. "I doubt it will get much use unless one of the servants should request it. Given the location of the house, I doubt there will be many itinerants knocking on the door."

Laura walked to the porch rail and looked out over the valley below. "This is a lovely spot for a home. The view is spectacular."

"For sure, it is."

Laura turned and met Ewan's gaze. Her heart fluttered as he looked deep into her eyes, leaned toward her, and wrapped one arm around her waist. Without a word, he pulled her close, lowered his head, and captured her lips in a kiss that quickened desire in her until it melted her resolve to resist him. His kiss was intoxicating, and when he at last lifted his head, she leaned against his chest.

"This won't work, Ewan."

He leaned back and looked down at her. "We will find a way. I promise."

CHAPTER 19

Ewan shoved his foot into his horse's stirrup, then swung up and into the saddle. After turning the horse toward the brickyard, he once again asked himself the same question. Why had he been so bold? Over the past three weeks, Ewan had asked himself that question a thousand times. Though Laura had seemed to enjoy his kiss and had leaned against his chest and murmured his name, moments later she'd hurried away. No doubt she hadn't believed him when he said they'd find a way to make things work, for only moments later she and his sisters were hurrying off in the carriage. He'd seen or heard nothing from her since. Now that Ewan had an understanding of the daily record-keeping process, as well as the financial and contract issues, Laura no longer came to the office.

He missed her visits, but Uncle Hugh had begun spending more time at the brickyard, so it was probably better she wasn't offering to help. Ewan couldn't be certain why Uncle Hugh's recent suspicion of Laura had developed, but he assumed Aunt Margaret was involved.

He'd hoped to hear his aunt admit that she'd been wrong about Laura, but her feelings seemed to have intensified. However, she was planning an elaborate party to celebrate the completion of the first wing of Crothers Mansion, and she needed the help of the Woodfield women. The Crothers name wasn't well enough known to receive an automatic acceptance from the cream of society, but a properly placed word from either Laura or her mother would ensure the acceptance of influential members of the upper class — people Aunt Margaret wanted to count as friends.

He tied his horse and strode toward the brickyard office before the first whistle sounded. Perhaps he'd have a chance to set the office aright before his uncle arrived. Over the past days, Hugh had been going over the books and leaving the office in a state of disarray. But when Ewan had attempted to help or offered to answer any questions, his uncle brushed him aside. He'd dug through the files like a woodchuck digging a burrow, though Ewan could never find a reason for the sudden interest.

He expelled a sigh when he caught sight of his uncle dismounting only a few minutes later. The man was seldom out of bed so early. Ewan picked up the record book containing the employee time records and strode toward the door as his uncle approached. He extended the book toward his uncle. "The first group of men will be arriving soon. Care to act as timekeeper today?"

His uncle tugged on his mustache and frowned. "Keeping time is not to my liking. You know I cannot cipher those fractions."

Ewan remained in the doorway. "You don't need to do anything except make a notation of when they arrive and when they complete their stint. Who was keeping time on the days when I was overseeing construction at your house?"

"I told each of the foremen to keep a log and give it to me at the end of each stint. They complained, of course, but they did it. A person standing watch up here at the top of the hill seems a bit silly to me." His uncle brushed past Ewan and entered the frame building that served as the office.

" 'Tis not a job for the foremen." Ewan turned and followed him. "It won't seem silly when the foremen lose track because they're busy performing their duties and the workers complain because they've been shorted on their hours. We need every worker we've got down there, and I don't want any problems because of timekeeping."

His uncle dropped into one of the wooden chairs. "You worry too much, Ewan. Your cousins, Ian and Darach, are both good foremen who can do what's asked of 'em, and so can the other foremen. Why pay them if they canna do what's assigned? Besides, things are moving along just fine. The bricks are being shipped out on time and we're not receiving any complaints about the quality. And we have two new Ver-Valens and two more kilns. According to my figures, we've got about a hundred arches in those kilns, more than most brickyards. There are still a few yards in the Hudson River Valley that have more arches than we do, but we'll catch up real soon."

"I know Ian and Darach are both good foremen, but they can't be expected to be foremen and timekeepers at the same time. And you need to remember those yards in the Hudson Valley have been in business much longer." Ewan glanced over his shoulder. "We can wait to expand until we've been here a little longer. I want to be sure every load of bricks that bears our insignia meets with satisfaction. Word of mouth can make or break our business. We need to be careful. If we grow too fast, we may become sloppy."

"There you go with your needless worrying again. Sit down and relax. The men can take care of things in the yard." His uncle leaned back in his chair and pulled out his pipe.

Ewan didn't sit down, but he moved closer and looked down at his uncle. "If you're so pleased with the way things are going, why don't we discuss my partnership? You said that once we were established and making a profit, you'd see to having the papers drawn up and we'd become full partners. I agreed to less pay and have worked long hours here at the yard to get this operation going, and you should not be forgetting I was the one who secured contracts that will keep us busy for at least the next two seasons. Our company is named C&M Brickyard, but the *M* does not mean anything until I am a partner. If you're pleased with things, then I think we should speak about the partnership papers."

"We're doing well enough that the men do not need you watching over them like a mother watching over her wee laddies, but I said we'd be looking at a partnership when the company was making a profit. This company still has a great deal of debt, so no one in his right mind would think we're making a profit."

The muscles in Ewan's neck tightened. He didn't want to lose his temper, but his uncle's reply came as a blow. When Uncle Hugh had signed for the bank loan, he'd used Ewan's sisters as pawns. Because of Ewan's deep desire to get the girls to America, he'd been willing to set aside his arguments over the bank loan, but he hadn't expected his uncle to go this far.

Unless the company made great strides, it would be years before Ewan could consider a part of this company his own. His uncle's wily ways hadn't changed at all. The man had felt no compunction when he'd purchased the brickyard with money he'd won cheating Lyall Montclair, and he didn't feel any right now. If it meant a greater share in his pocket, Uncle Hugh was willing to cheat Ewan out of his partnership until the debt was paid — and, who could say, maybe forever.

"You're the only one who would look at our books and say we're not making a profit, and that's because it means more money in your pocket." Never before had Ewan spoken to him in such a manner, but he was not going to let his uncle think such behavior was acceptable.

Anger continued to knot in Ewan's chest. He clenched the record book in his hand, stepped outside, took his position at the top of the hill, and systematically checked off the names of the men appearing in the yard. These were the men who always arrived early and tried to complete their work before any of the other groups. They prided themselves on being first to complete their jobs and leave the brickyard.

Most days they'd make some heckling remark to the others as they swaggered out of the yard to go into town and enjoy themselves at the local tavern. In some ways, they reminded him of Uncle Hugh. Always wanting to be first to depart, they gave little care as to how they reached their goal. However, their shoddy work was beginning to affect the number of good bricks that could be shipped to Pittsburgh.

On several occasions, Ewan had spoken with the men and asked them to slow down, but he'd met with little success. In their rush, they occasionally tipped over a barrow of bricks, ruining them, or the edgers in their group didn't straighten and turn the bricks to make certain the surface was smoothed during those important first two days of drying.

However, it was the men assigned to hack the bricks who were least careful. Once the bricks had dried for two days, the hackers stacked the bricks in herringbone fashion to dry further. They were instructed to leave a finger's width between the bricks but often failed to do so. Such habits resulted in improperly dried bricks that didn't burn sufficiently when fired in the kiln and were dubbed "pale bricks," while bricks that burned too hot were dubbed "lammies." The pale bricks and lammies couldn't be used to fulfill their contracts and had to be sold for a much lower price. Though Ewan realized they would always have some unacceptable bricks, he wanted to see that number decrease significantly in the near future.

Still holding the record book, he strode into the yard. He tipped his cap to one of the men. "Have you been taking care when you hack the bricks, Tom?" When the man hesitated, Ewan stopped short. "Be careful with your answer. I plan to go over there and take a look for myself before the setters and wheelers begin to set the arches."

Tom's eyebrows pulled together, and his features creased in a frown. "I been working bricks all me life, Ewan. You do not need to be checking on me work."

Ewan stiffened at the retort that sounded much like what his uncle had said only a short time ago. He wheeled around to face the worker. "Last firing, we had more than an arch of pale bricks. That's about thirty-five thousand bricks I had to sell for half the price we receive for good bricks. How would you feel if I cut your wages in half, Tom?"

Several of the men who were listening shouted their disapproval. "Aye, well, that's how I feel when we burn fifteen arches and a full arch isn't worth the cost it took to make it. I expect better from you men. You say you've got years of experience. Prove it by doing better. There will be no pay raises so long as there's no improvement in your work. Getting done before the other men isn't what's important. If you want an honest day's wages, then give me an honest day's work."

He gestured to Tom. "Come with me and let's have a look. If the hacking is done well, you'll have my apology."

"And a pay raise?"

The conversation with Uncle Hugh had put Ewan in foul humor. Tom was asking for a pay raise for performing mediocre work, while Uncle Hugh had decreased

Ewan's wages. Truth be told, Ewan was now paid less than the burners working for him. Granted, he lived in a fine house he didn't have to pay for and ate food he didn't purchase, but he worked longer hours than any man he'd hired — and he was the boss — at least when Uncle Hugh wasn't around.

"I'll need to see improved work more than one time for a pay raise."

The two of them had gone only a short distance when a din rang out that split the morning air. Ewan sucked in a breath and turned on his heel. The number one VerValen machine being used by the early morning crew had squealed to a grinding halt. Cupping his hands to his mouth and running toward the men, he shouted, "What happened?"

"The VerValen!" one of the workers called out. "The mold pusher misjudged the empty molds and dumped his sander."

Ewan grimaced as he examined the machine. "I'm no mechanic, but from what I can see, we'll need new parts before this machine can be repaired." He looked at the man. "You work at this machine every day. How did this happen?"

The man hiked a shoulder. "I was talking to Henry and didn't check before I dumped the sander. We all make mistakes. It was an accident."

Ewan wasn't an expert, but he understood the workings of the huge machine as well as did most of the men in the yard. Dumping a filled sander into the machine would cause enough damage to put the VerValen out of use until it could be completely cleaned and tested.

Ewan shook his head. "For sure it was an accident, but one that could have been avoided if you'd been tending to your work instead of talking to Henry. You men think I am being hard on you, but there is a reason why you need to do good work. If we default on our contract, I cannot pay the bank. If I cannot pay the bank, the brickyard will close down, and there will be no jobs for any of you. So it matters if we have an arch of pale bricks in every kiln, and it matters if a machine is out of operation for a week or two. It is important to me, but it is just as important to all of you."

None of the men met his gaze, staring at the ground instead. He gestured to the mold setter. "Move to machine number two, and from now on, tend to your work. You can visit while you eat lunch."

He didn't like being hard on the men, but their careless ways had to cease or this brickyard would fail. How he wished his uncle hadn't purchased the extra equipment and pushed for so many contracts. How he wished they could have made a slow and steady gain in the business. But wishing wouldn't change anything, so he and the men had to accept that they all needed to give their best effort, just as he'd had to accept that he wasn't going to become a partner any time soon.

Ewan trudged up the hill and found his uncle in the same spot where he'd left him. "Did you not hear the ruckus down in the yard, Uncle Hugh?"

"Aye, but I figured you were down there and would take care of any problem that needed attention." He took a long draw on his pipe. "What happened?"

Ewan gave his uncle a quick explanation before stepping to the desk and withdrawing a file. "I don't know how long it will take to get it cleaned and operating again, but for sure it will slow production."

"Guess that's a bit of confirmation there'll be no need to ask about a partnership for a while longer." His uncle grinned and pushed up from his chair. "I trained a new burner while you were supervising over at the house. He's a good man and learned fast — I got him scheduled for tonight."

Ewan massaged his forehead as his uncle

departed. He hoped they'd complete setting the final arch in one of the kilns today and set the fires later today. It took an entire day for four truck men to wheel the bricks from the drying yard to the kiln while the two setters set an arch of thirty-five thousand bricks. Maybe he could assign a couple more men as wheelers. Ewan preferred to have enough men to set all fifteen arches in three days, but unless he had enough trusted setters on the job, burning had to wait. Firing without a full load was a poor use of resources that Ewan tried to avoid, but he'd rather burn a half-full kiln than one that wasn't properly set.

Ewan could only imagine how much training his uncle had given the new man he'd hired. If they completed setting the final arch this afternoon, Ewan would stay at the yard to watch and make certain the new hire understood how to start proper fires in the arches.

For the remainder of the day, Ewan's mind was in a whir. He spent more time than usual in the yard, mostly overseeing the mechanic who was charged with taking apart the VerValen to see if it could be cleaned and put back together without a need for any new parts. From the man's dour face, Ewan held out little hope the machine would be back in operation any-time soon. The one bright spot of the day occurred late in the afternoon when one of the setters ran across the yard and, with hair matted to his head and perspiration beaded on his forehead, panted news that the arches were ready to fire.

"Signal me when the new burner gets here, and I'll come over to watch him set the fires."

The man swiped the perspiration from his face and gestured toward the kiln. "He got here 'bout five minutes ago, but I told him not to do nothing till I let you know we was ready."

After instructing the mechanic to keep working, Ewan strode alongside the setter and into the kiln. He looked at the setter. "Did you make sure there's no mistakes in the setup? We can't afford any more prob-lems."

"It's good, Mr. McKay. We should get a good burn with all fifteen arches." He nod-ded to the other side of the kiln. "That's Rudy Banks over there, the new burner."

After thanking the setter, Ewan strode across the width of the kiln and introduced himself to the new employee. "I'm Ewan McKay. My uncle informed me this morn-ing that he'd hired and trained you as a burner. Have you had any experience before coming to work for us?" Ewan hoped so, for his uncle's experience as a burner was limited, and Ewan doubted his uncle had given the new man much training.

"Rudy Banks." The man extended his hand. "The foreman said the arches are ready, so I thought I'd go ahead and set the fires, unless you wanted to check 'em again."

Ewan shook his head. "Nay. I don't plan to check them any further. Why don't you show me how you plan to start your burn."

Ewan didn't miss the fact that Rudy hadn't answered his question about previous experience, and that bothered him a great deal.

Rudy gestured toward one of the arches. "I'll start with this arch first. Your uncle said to set a fire in the mouth of each arch." He grinned as though that bit of knowledge alone should be enough to convince Ewan that he knew what he was doing.

"Aye." Ewan nodded. "You go ahead and I'll watch."

The fellow had more confidence than experience, and Ewan had to stop him several times when he started to set the fire downwind rather than on the windward side of the kiln. "You need to always start the fire on the windward side so the smoke will blow through the arches." Ewan pointed to the other side of the arch. "You need to start another fire there so the two fires build slowly and meet in the middle. Did my uncle tell you that?"

"He did say I needed to set one on each side."

The man didn't add that he remembered he was supposed to set another fire, and Ewan had his doubts the man remembered much of whatever Uncle Hugh had told him. Or maybe Uncle Hugh had gone through the steps so quickly the man couldn't remember. But having an inexperienced burner begin without overseeing him for the first few times was asking for trouble.

"It will take between forty and sixty hours for the fires to cross the arches and meet. The steam needs to escape evenly around the top." Ewan continued alongside the man as he set each fire.

"Ewan!" Martin O'Donnell, an experienced burner, ran toward the kiln. "Sorry I'm late, Ewan. My wife's sick and with all the wee ones at home 'twas hard to get away."

"I'm glad you made it. This is Rudy Banks. My uncle hired him, but he doesn't have much experience as a burner, so you'll need to help him. He needs to learn how to watch the burn and how to increase or ease up the steam." Ewan turned his attention back to Rudy. "Once the fires are increased enough that the steam becomes a bluish-black color, the kiln will be hot, but it takes a lot of hours before that will happen."

Martin rolled up his shirtsleeves. "We want to get the kiln hot, but it's important to increase the heat gradually, so that means you need to watch the fires and the steam to make sure the kiln isn't heating too fast. Elsewise, the bricks will stick together, run, or get twisted out of shape and cracked, and we'll end up with lots of bricks that can't be shipped to fill our contracts."

Ewan gave a firm nod. "And it also means you will have an unhappy boss."

Martin turned back toward Rudy. "Once the kiln is hot, the burning will take about six days, and then all the doors must remain sealed to prevent any air from getting in. The kiln has to cool for several days. After that, the bricks are approved and loaded onto the barges."

Ewan stayed with the men while Martin continued to explain the process to Rudy. If Uncle Hugh had trained Rudy, he'd done a poor job, for Rudy didn't seem to know what would be expected of him.

"I'm not so sure I like the amount of work

that goes along with this job. Don't you have something that doesn't need so much attention?"

"You can speak to my uncle. Since he hired you, he's the one you need to talk with about a change. He should be back in the morning. In the meantime, you need to continue helping Martin set the fires."

Ewan strode away from the kiln and back to the office. He wouldn't wait for Rudy to speak with his uncle. Once he got back home tonight, he'd tell Uncle Hugh the man wasn't suited to be a burner. They could use additional setters, but Ewan doubted Rudy was a man who would be careful even with that task. Perhaps he could be a wheeler, but he'd best be ready for a cut in pay. A man pushing a barrow of bricks couldn't expect the same wages as a burner, and Rudy should realize as much after witnessing the process.

CHAPTER 20

Since the Crotherses' move to the area, Ewan's aunt had met with little success of being accepted by the wealthy families of Bartlett. For more than a month, she'd been struggling to orchestrate a housewarming at Crothers Mansion. As the date for the party arrived, she'd made it clear they were all to be on their best behavior, for she expected the event would not only hail her as an excellent hostess, but gain her a foothold among the genteel members of society. Other than from the Woodfields, invitations to social events in the area hadn't been forthcoming. A fact that increasingly distressed her.

Although his aunt and uncle were still in the throes of moving to their new house, Uncle Hugh had been unable to convince his wife to wait another two weeks before hosting the party. Aunt Margaret had rebuffed his advice, but when she finally accepted the fact that she couldn't accomplish both the party and moving, she'd called a halt to the move and proceeded with plans for the party at the new house.

Ewan would be pleased when his aunt and uncle were finally into their new home. He'd tired of the grumbling that steadily increased with each passing day. He looked up from his breakfast as Uncle Hugh entered the dining room with a scowl on his face. "Half my clothes are in one house and half in the other. One day I may walk into this dining room wearing a shirt and no trousers."

"Hugh Crothers, that's no way to talk. There are young ladies at the table." Aunt Margaret's brows knit into a frown that matched her husband's scowl.

"I see there are young ladies at the table, but that doesn't change the fact that my clothes are spread between two houses and I can never find what I need. When are we finally going to be moved?"

The couple continued their bickering throughout breakfast while Ewan, his sisters, and Kathleen remained silent, their focus upon their eggs, rashers, and boxty. Uncle Hugh and Aunt Margaret loved nothing more than to convince another family member to take their side during an argument. But Ewan, his sisters, and Kathleen had learned to avoid being drawn into the fracas.

The couple was stopped short when someone pounded on the front door and Melva ran down the hallway to answer.

"Who could be calling at this hour of the morning?" Aunt Margaret's lips pursed into a knot of irritation. "With the party tonight, I have too much to accomplish today for any unexpected interruptions."

Melva scurried into the dining room. "One of the workers from the brickyard is on the porch, Mr. Ewan. He says you're to come quick. There's trouble at the yard."

Ewan jumped to his feet and his uncle followed close on his heels. Martin was wringing his cap between his hands and looked up as soon as Ewan arrived at the door.

"We got two full kilns of ruined bricks." Martin's face was ashen. No doubt he'd not wanted to be the one to deliver the bad news.

His uncle pushed in front of Ewan and grasped Martin by the front of his shirt. "How's that possible? Are you the burner responsible?"

Martin's eyes shone with fear as he shook his head. "No, sir. It wasn't me."

"Let loose of him, Uncle Hugh. He won't

be able to tell us anything if you scare him out of his wits." Ewan nodded to Martin. "Tell me what happened."

"It was that Rudy fellow you hired, Mr. Hugh. I've been working to get him trained proper. He said he understood he had to keep a watch on the fires, and I stayed with him when we did three burns in other kilns, but he was alone last night after we set the fires. Guess he decided he could drink whiskey and still keep a watch on the fires. I don't know how much he had to drink, but he was still sleeping it off when I got to work this morning, and the fires were burning way too hot."

Ewan dropped into one of the chairs on the front porch. "We won't meet our quota for the row houses in Allegheny City, which means we won't get our money on time to meet the bank payment."

"No need to be takin' on the fear of doomsday. We'll get down there and take a look about. It can't be as bad as all that."

Anger swelled in Ewan's chest as he jumped up and stood looking down into his uncle's eyes. "What did I tell you the day you hired Rudy?" Ewan clenched his jaw until it ached.

"I know you did not think he was worth his salt, but I thought he was smart enough.

348

If you thought he was so bad, you coulda fired him yourself."

Ewan's chest felt as though it would explode. "I'm not going to stay here and argue, but you may recall that when I said I was going to fire him, you told me I had no right because you were the owner and you hired him."

Hugh tugged on his mustache. "Seems I do remember saying something like that, but I didn't figure you'd listen."

Ewan gestured to Martin. "Come on. Let's get back down there and take a look."

Before they'd stepped off the porch, Margaret came to the door. "Don't you leave and go to that brickyard, Hugh. I need your help getting ready for the party."

Ewan gave a dismissive wave. "Right you are, Aunt Margaret. Your party's more important than two kilns of ruined bricks."

"I don't know what's gotten into Ewan. He used to be courteous and well mannered back in Ireland. Now that he's running the brickyard, he's as brash as an Irish fishmonger."

His aunt's words carried on the breeze, but Ewan didn't turn to respond. Keeping Uncle Hugh away from the brickyard was probably best. He'd only spend his time attempting to justify the fact that he'd hired

Rudy. For the life of him, Ewan didn't understand why he'd not fired the man. Though he'd expected Rudy to be gone when they arrived, he was sitting near one of the kilns, his knees drawn close to his chest.

He looked up at Ewan with bloodshot eyes. "I'm real sorry, Mr. McKay. I get the shakes if I don't have me some whiskey every day. I needed a drink real bad. Guess I had a few too many, 'cause I fell asleep. Next thing I knew, Martin was yelling at me and it was morning."

"Do you have any idea what you've cost me because you got drunk and passed out? If you knew you couldn't make it through the night without drinking, why didn't you tell someone? Anything would have been better than allowing two kilns of ruined bricks. Do you understand what you've cost us?"

Rudy remained silent, staring at the ground. There was nothing more Ewan could say, nothing that would change the horrid circumstances. An invisible band cinched around his chest and threatened to cut off his breath as he appraised the situation.

"I told Mr. Crothers I wouldn't be good for this work, but he said burners made more money than any of the others in the yard, and I could pay him back faster."

The man's words startled Ewan and he stopped short. "You owe my uncle money?"

Rudy nodded. "We got into some gambling, and I owed him more than I could pay. He said I could come to work and pay him out of the wages I earned here."

Hiring Rudy to pay off a gambling debt might have made some sort of sense to his uncle, but his uncle's ridiculous decision might cause them to default on their note at the bank. There simply was no end to Uncle Hugh's poor judgment.

After telling Rudy he'd have to find some other way to pay his debt to Hugh, Ewan gave the men instructions to let the kilns cool until the ruined bricks could be removed and new arches set. As soon as he'd given the men their orders, he raced back up the hill, mounted his horse, and rode for home.

He was surprised when he caught sight of his aunt's carriage and Uncle Hugh's saddled horse outside the house. He'd expected his uncle to immediately depart for the mansion in order to avoid a confrontation before this evening's festivities. Perhaps he thought Ewan would remain at the brickyard much longer.

With a slight kick of his heels, Ewan urged his horse onward. Only moments later, he spotted Rose and the twins sitting on the front porch. Ainslee waved and called to him as he dismounted.

"You girls enjoying your morning?" He attempted a smile but failed.

Ainslee shook her head. "Not so much. We're waiting for Aunt Margaret. She said she needs our help getting ready for the party at the other house. I wish we could stay here and read instead. I don't know how to fix things for a party."

The words had barely escaped his sister's lips when their aunt stepped onto the porch and locked gazes with Ewan. "I need your uncle's help. Don't detain him with talk of the brickyard." Her sweeping gesture brought all three girls to their feet. "Get into the carriage, girls. We have much to do before this evening's party." She sent a warning look in Ewan's direction. "Don't forget what I've said: I need Hugh's help. And if you're not doing anything, you can come and help, as well."

A rush of anger swelled in Ewan's chest. How could she possibly even think he had time to assist with party preparations when they'd just lost two kilns of bricks? Adaira peeked around the side of the carriage, a

352

reminder he needed to keep his temper in check. "I believe the problem at the brickyard will require my time and attention, Aunt Margaret, and I believe Uncle Hugh will feel the same once he hears my report."

She tightened her lips into a thin line. "Do not detain him, Ewan. This party means a great deal to me."

He longed to tell her the brickyard should mean much more than the party, since that was where she'd gained the funds to pay for her gala. And if they didn't set things aright with the bank, there would be no more parties, and she'd possibly lose her mansion. However, to say such things at the moment would only cause anger and mayhem. Besides, Aunt Margaret wouldn't believe him. She thought they had more money than she could ever spend.

"I'll talk as quickly as my tongue will permit, Aunt Margaret."

When she pursed her lips and gave a tiny shake of her head, he knew she'd heard the sarcasm in his voice. Thankfully, she didn't offer a retort. He silently chastised himself for the childish behavior, for it would serve no good purpose. He marched up the front steps and crossed the threshold as his uncle was descending the staircase.

His uncle stopped midway down the steps.

"I didn't expect you back so soon. I hope Martin didn't know what he was talking about. I cannot believe we lost two full kilns."

"I'm afraid you'll need to believe every word of what Martin said. Both kilns burned far too hot all through the night, thanks to your friend Rudy Banks."

His uncle's face turned ashen. "Now, don't be makin' this my fault. There may be some truth to the fact that I didn't train him well, but you had Martin working with him. If anyone beyond Rudy's to blame, it's Martin."

"How can you foist the blame on someone else? I told you the man needed to be fired, and when you wouldn't do it, I begged you to assign him to some other job." Ewan pointed his finger at his uncle. "You refused to do that, as well, and today I discovered why. Rudy told me about the gambling debt he owes you and how you figured he'd pay you back by working as a burner."

Hugh's knuckles turned white as he tightened his hold on the banister. "I was trying to help the man. He has a family to feed, and I thought —"

"You thought you'd get your money out of him one way or the other. Your plan made no sense at all." Ewan tapped his finger to the side of his head. "Did you ever stop to think he was paying you back with your own money?"

"I'm not a fool, Ewan. I know the pay Rudy received was my money, but he had to work for it. He had no job, and there was no other way to show him that a man has to pay his debts." Hugh finally descended the remainder of the steps.

"That's very true, a man does have to pay his debts. Right now, I'm wonderin' how we're going to pay our debt at the bank. Maybe you need to be thinking on that for a while, for we won't be receiving our money from the contractor in Allegheny City until he has the bricks he's been promised, and we can't get two more kilns shipped before the money's due."

His uncle stepped around him. "You worry too much, Ewan. You forget there's a party this evening. The president of the bank will be attending, and I'll talk with him. Once Frank knows the money will be coming his way in a month or so, he'll be fine." His uncle gestured toward the door. "Now, I need to get over to the mansion, or Margaret will have my hide."

Ewan didn't believe a few words to the bank president would solve their problem. Frank Swinnen had to answer to a board of directors, who would likely jump at the opportunity to seize the brickyard. "And are you remembering that the contract you signed permits a seizure if we're ten days late with our payment?"

His uncle patted his shoulder. "I'm thinking you were born under a worrying star, Ewan. Seems you're not happy unless you've got something to fret about."

The condescending comment further irritated Ewan. How could his uncle remain so unconcerned? "You're not even going to come down to the yard and take a look for yourself?"

"Going down there will not change anything. Besides, 'tis your Aunt Margaret who's in need of my help. You take care of the brickyard, and I'll take care of straightening things out with the bank."

His uncle walked out the front door with a wave and a jaunt to his step that left Ewan speechless.

Could this be retribution for his uncle's offense with Lyall Montclair back in Ireland?

Though he'd worked hard throughout the day and every muscle in his body ached, Ewan knew he would not be excused from this evening's party. No amount of cajoling would gain a pardon from his aunt. She expected to show off her new home in fine style, and there would be questions if Ewan wasn't present, inquiries that would doubtless lead to talk about the brickyard rather than her garishly decorated mansion. And that would never do.

When he descended the stairs, he was pleased to see his sisters sitting in the parlor, each of them dressed in finery he'd never before seen. He stopped in the parlor doorway. "The three of you look lovely. I am guessing Aunt Margaret took you shopping."

Ainslee stood and twirled in front of him. "She insisted on dressing Adaira and me in the same dresses, even though we asked for different ones. She said people think it's darling to see twins dressed alike."

Adaira curled her lip. "Maybe when the twins are babies, but not when they're our age. I feel silly."

Ewan grinned. "You're not so terribly old, and you look very nice. Maybe if you stand on opposite sides of the room, no one will notice there are two of you in the same dress. As I recall, you used to enjoy using your matching appearance to play tricks on everyone."

Rose stood and motioned to her sisters.

"Come along. Let's be on our way. Aunt Margaret will be angry if we're late. She said we should all be at the mansion before the first guests arrive."

Ewan glanced around. "So they've already dressed and gone?"

"Yes, they left about a half hour ago," Rose said. "Kathleen asked to wait and go with us, but Aunt Margaret wouldn't let her."

The carriage ride to the mansion took only twenty minutes. Ewan pulled out his pocket watch when they arrived and checked the time. "We're here fifteen minutes early, so we shouldn't be in any trouble." He followed the girls inside, where his aunt was shouting commands to anyone who drew near. "Maybe it would be wise to hide somewhere until time for the party."

The twins giggled and Adaira grasped his hand. "I know. We can go to the upstairs sitting room and watch out the window to see when the first carriage arrives."

Ewan was more than happy to agree to the plan. After today's events, he needed a bit of peace and quiet before joining the evening's festivities.

CHAPTER 21

Laura walked down the stairs, surprised Winston had arrived so early. She hadn't expected him for another half hour. Wearing his black tailcoat, heavily starched white shirt, low-cut black vest, and tidy white bow tie, he looked the perfect gentleman.

"You're fortunate I'm not one of those women who is always late, or you'd likely become very bored waiting on me."

"You look lovely, as usual." His comment didn't sound sincere, but she'd become accustomed to the disingenuous remarks he made to everyone — including her. "I thought we'd have time to visit for a short time before going to the party." He grimaced. "I do dread spending an evening with those people."

Laura slipped her hands into a pair of lace gloves. "Exactly who are you referring to when you say 'those people'?"

Winston waved a dismissive hand. "All of

them. I find their company boring, and I can't imagine that Crothers woman has the slightest ability when it comes to hosting a dinner party and ball. Then again, perhaps it will provide an opportunity for a bit of laughter and a chance to hear how Ewan McKay plans to solve the dilemma of paying his banknote."

Laura stepped into the parlor and sat down. "What are you talking about? Why would there be a problem with the bank? Ewan secured ample contracts for the brickyard to sustain itself in fine fashion."

"I'm surprised you haven't heard. As often as those McKay girls visit, I thought you'd have already heard the news." Winston sat down on the divan. "You're correct about the orders, but his uncle isn't a very clever businessman, and that will likely prove to be McKay's downfall." Winston went on to explain what had happened at the brickyard and the contract clause that permitted seizure of the business with only a ten-day default.

"Surely the bank won't attempt to seize the business if they're only ten days late. I can't believe Mr. Swinnen would do such a thing." She straightened her shoulders. "You're on the board of directors. You can speak with the others and convince them their money will be forthcoming." She exhaled a small sigh. "I feel better already, knowing you'll be able to help."

"I'm not so sure I can do that, Laura."

Winston reached for her hand, but she jerked back at his response. "Why couldn't you? There's no logical reason for the bank to move so quickly. It's unfair."

"Not according to the contract Hugh Crothers signed. He agreed to the terms, and the bank has every right — in fact, every obligation — to seize the brickyard if they can't make their payment on time. The members of the board are required to protect the bank's stockholders."

"I think a word of assurance from you would help a great deal, Winston. If Ewan McKay was your friend, you'd do everything in your power to help. I know you would."

"Ah, but it's you that he's befriended, Laura — not me." His eyes flashed with spite before he looked down and tugged on the corner of his black vest.

On several occasions after the purchase of the brickyard, she and Winston had argued about the time she devoted to helping Ewan and Winston's desire that she refrain from going to the yard. When Laura didn't acquiesce to his request, he'd gone to her mother and planted the idea that her time at the brickyard could cause people to talk and possibly place a blot on Laura's good name. When her mother didn't immediately agree, he'd gone a step further and said he couldn't marry a woman whose reputation might cast embarrassment upon him and jeopardize his political career.

Mother had done her best to convince Laura that any hint of scandal would end her future with Winston, but Laura hadn't been swayed. She'd promised to help Ewan and refused to go back on her word. Now Winston was going to use his position at the bank to punish both Ewan and her.

"We've discussed this before, Winston. The time I spent with Ewan was to help acquaint him with the paper work and to show him how Father had run the brickyard. You've made our acquaintance into something it isn't."

"Acquaintance? I think it's more than an acquaintance. I see the way he looks at you, and his sisters are over here all the time. Whether you care to admit it or not, there's more going on than meets the eye. I'm no fool."

"Is that what you think? That I've been making a fool of you? If that's the case, why have you continued to court me?" Her simmering anger had reached the boiling point.

"You're even more controlling than I suspected if you believe I should refrain from visits with the McKay girls just because they're Ewan's sisters."

Winston pushed his glasses tight against the bridge of his nose. "I didn't say you were making a fool of me, and I certainly do not consider myself to be controlling, but I didn't approve of you keeping company with Ewan at the brickyard, and I think it unwise for you to form a bond with his sisters."

"How can you be so callous?" Laura shook her head and frowned. "Have you considered what it must be like for those three girls to be living in a new country with no mother or father, their brother working long hours, and Margaret Crothers treating them like excess baggage?"

"No. I've given no thought to that at all, and neither should you. Those girls aren't your problem, and they certainly aren't mine. Let them spend their time with some of those relatives Hugh brought over here to work at the brickyard."

"Some of those relatives you intend to put out of work! Have you taken into account how many people will be affected if the bank seizes the brickyard, Winston? There is much more wisdom in giving Ewan time so that he can fulfill the orders and pay the banknote than there is to seize the yard."

Winston leaned back and looked down his nose at her. "You simply don't understand the fine details of banking, Laura. There's so much more involved, and I don't want to tax you with the boring details. Suffice it to say, the die is cast. Unless Hugh Crothers or Ewan McKay can pay their banknote within ten days of the due date, the brick-yard will be seized."

He'd spoken to her as though she possessed little more intelligence than that of a gnat. "Then suffice it to say that I will do everything in my power to make certain the bank isn't successful."

He blanched, but before he could respond to the curt retort, her mother fluttered into the parlor. "Dear me, have I kept you waiting? I could have hurried along if I'd known." She glanced back and forth between Winston and Laura. "Has something happened? The two of you look positively piqued." Her eyebrows dipped low as she focused on Laura. "Is there something we should discuss in private before we depart?"

Winston jumped to his feet. "Not at all, Mrs. Woodfield. There's no need for concern. Laura and I have a small matter of disagreement, but I'm sure we'll be able to reach an amicable resolution before the evening's end."

Laura pinned him with a stern look. If he thought they were going to reach an amicable resolution, he'd be the one making all the concessions. There were few issues where she would go to such lengths, but saving the brickyard from ruin was one. She would not stand by and do nothing while the bank seized the brickyard.

Instead of taking Winston's arm, Laura assisted her mother to the carriage and leaned close once they were seated inside. "We need to talk."

Her mother gave a slight nod. "We'll find time at the party. I hope this isn't serious."

Laura hoped her mother would align with her rather than Winston. Surely she wouldn't support any action to seize the brickyard. Perhaps Mother could convince Mr. Swinnen to act in a reasonable and Christian manner. If not, all of Ewan's dreams could be destroyed.

The dinner astounded Laura. Mrs. Crothers had seen to every detail, and the food had been sumptuous. From the chicken consommé that began the meal to the fruit trifle at the end, each course had been prepared and served with meticulous care. When they'd finished their dessert and coffee, Laura silently chided herself for thinking Margaret lacked the skill to carry off a dinner party for guests with such exacting tastes and expectations, for other than requesting addresses for the invitations, Margaret hadn't asked for any help from Laura or her mother.

Yet when they'd first met, Margaret had been clear that she'd never hosted large formal gatherings. The woman possessed hidden talents if she'd accomplished this feat without advice and with such expert ease, especially since her permanent staff consisted of distant relatives from Ireland, who'd likely never been charged with serving a formal dinner. Perhaps Margaret had befriended one of the other guests and requested assistance with the details.

As the men retreated to the library after dinner, Laura and the other women were escorted to a formal parlor, where a talented pianist treated them to music that ranged from Hermann Goetz's Concerto no. 2 for Piano in B-flat Major to "The Blue Danube" and "The Man on the Flying Trapeze." Laura learned from Mr. Swinnen's wife that the pianist had traveled from Wheeling with some of the other guests attending the party.

Mrs. Crothers leaned close as the pianist completed her final selection. "Isn't she wonderful? Mrs. Blount suggested her name to me."

Laura arched her brows. "Really? I didn't know you and Naomi Blount were acquainted."

"I discovered it only takes a name dropped here or there among the socially elite before your own name becomes quite well known among those in the group." The older woman's lips curved in a cunning smile. "Please excuse me. I need to speak to Naomi and thank her for her wonderful suggestion."

Laura stared after the woman. If determination could win her a place among the socially elite, Mrs. Crothers would soon be on the social register in the states of both West Virginia and Pennsylvania.

Feeling no compunction, Laura waved Rose to the empty chair beside her. No doubt Winston would be unhappy if he saw Rose visiting with Laura, but she cared not a whit what he might say. Rose's dress of soft blue silk looked lovely against her pale skin and dark hair. "You look lovely this evening. The blue of your dress makes your eyes even more beautiful. Once the dancing begins, I'm sure you'll have lots of fellows

367

filling your dance card."

The color in Rose's cheeks heightened. "I don't know how to dance very well, so I may refuse unless it's a waltz. Kathleen taught me how to waltz, but our dances in Ireland are not the same as those here in America."

"Who taught Kathleen how to waltz?"

Rose glanced around and then leaned a little closer. "I'm not supposed to tell, but it was Terrance O'Grady. He's been in the country longer, and he's learned quite a few of the dance steps."

"I see. Well, it was kind of her to teach you. I'll be sure to keep your secret. Next time you're at the house, I'd be happy to teach you some new steps." Laura squeezed the girl's hand. "The dinner was quite lovely, don't you think?"

Rose nodded. "I wish Aunt Margaret would have given Ainslee and Adaira permission to eat with us. They worked very hard completing every task Aunt Margaret assigned them and were sorely disappointed when she said they'd have to eat in the kitchen because children weren't permitted at the party.

"Ainslee argued that it was Aunt Margaret's party and she could let children be seated with the adults if she wanted, but Aunt Margaret would not change her mind.

I'm happy we'll soon have a house to ourselves. I think Ewan is pleased, too."

Rose had spoken his name only moments before Ewan approached. "I see you've been keeping Laura company. I thought the women were to have some sort of entertainment while the men were in the library."

Rose smiled up at her brother. "We did. There was a piano recital."

Laura kept her gaze trained on Ewan while Rose detailed the happenings of the past hour. His usual good nature wasn't shining through, and she wondered if the conversation in the library had revolved around problems at the brickyard.

Once Rose finished telling her brother how some of the women had joined in to sing the lyrics to "The Man on the Flying Trapeze," Laura turned in her chair. "I understand there was a terrible mishap at the brickyard last night."

"I'm afraid so." Ewan ran his hand through his hair. "We lost two full kilns, which is a terrible blow. I don't see how we're going to make the bank payment within the allotted grace period. Uncle Hugh says I'm too quick to toll the death knell, but after talking to Mr. Swinnen in the library, I'm afraid that unless the good Lord grants us a miracle, we'll lose the brickyard." Ewan stepped around the row of chairs and sat down on the other side of Laura. "I tried to reason with Mr. Swinnen, but he wasn't willing to hear a thing I was saying."

Weariness gathered in shadowy pockets beneath his eyes, and she longed to say something to comfort him. "Maybe someone needs to point out that having the brickyard sit idle is going to have a terrible impact on lots of folks in Bartlett. There are men who gave up their jobs in the coal mines and others who've moved here for work. Now they'll be without any means to support their families. The stores in town will suffer, as well."

Ewan nodded. "You're right. And we'll be able to make the payment within six or eight weeks at the most, but Mr. Swinnen didn't seem to care. He says the bank has to look out for the stockholders."

Laura bristled. The bank president was giving Ewan the same response she'd gotten from Winston only a few hours ago. "If you'll excuse me, Ewan, I need to go and speak with my mother."

He pushed to his feet as she stood. "I'm sorry. This is a party, and here I am talking about my problems at the bank. Forgive me."

"You weren't boring me, and you don't need to apologize. I'm the one who brought up the brickyard." She glanced across the room and signaled her mother. "However, before we left Woodfield Manor, I told Mother I needed to speak with her."

She pointed to the dance card on her wrist. "A lady isn't supposed to mention empty lines on her dance card, but I'd be pleased if you'd fill in a few of mine."

He grinned and gave a nod. "I'd be delighted, so long as you don't mind having your toes stepped on several times."

"I'll be pleased to take my chances." She held out her dance card, and his fingers rested on her hand for a little longer than necessary. Her pulse quickened as she looked into Ewan's eyes and remembered his kiss. That moment had confirmed what she'd tried to deny since she'd first met him. Her feelings for him went much deeper than friendship. This was one time Winston would not be pleased he'd been correct.

Laura escorted her mother to the upstairs parlor that had been set aside for the women to refresh themselves throughout the evening. Several ladies sat in front of mirrors, carefully repinning their coiffures or checking lip rouge while they exchanged the latest gossip. Laura grasped her mother's arm and pointed toward a brocade settee in the far corner. "Let's sit over there, where we won't be overheard."

Her mother feigned a look of alarm as she clasped a hand to her bodice. "Oh, this does sound like it's going to be a clandestine conversation. How exciting!"

"Don't make fun, Mother. What I'm going to ask of you truly must be carried out in the strictest of confidence. Otherwise, the consequences will be life altering for many of those in attendance here."

Her mother leaned back into the cushioned settee. "You've certainly managed to gain my attention. Don't keep me waiting any longer, or my heart may fail me."

CHAPTER 22

Four days after the party, Laura was surprised when Kathleen Roark arrived at the front door of Woodfield Manor not long after breakfast. Laura was so amazed that she peered around Kathleen, certain Margaret Crothers must be following on her sister's heels. Though Kathleen seemed a sweet young woman, Laura hadn't had much opportunity to visit with her. Kathleen's previous visits to Woodfield Manor had always been in the company of Margaret, who overshadowed her younger sister and afforded Kathleen little opportunity to interact.

"Will your sister be joining us?"

Kathleen shook her head. "Nay. I'm alone."

Laura stepped to the side. "Do come in. I'm pleased to see you."

Kathleen obviously did not realize that proper etiquette required an invitation before paying a call so early in the day. Otherwise, a written note requesting a visit and allowing ample time for acceptance or refusal should have been delivered.

Catherine hurried from the kitchen, wiping her hands on the corner of her white apron. "I'm sorry, Miss Laura. I was kneading dough, and you got to the door before me."

"No need for an apology, Catherine. When you have a moment, could you bring us something cool to drink?" The maid scurried back to the kitchen, and Laura waved Kathleen toward the parlor. "Please sit down. You look overheated."

The midmorning sun had ascended over the towering trees in the yard and promised another surprisingly uncomfortable day for late September. The heat had colored Kathleen's cheeks crimson, and perspiration dotted her forehead. Her black leather shoes and the hem of her plaid skirt were coated with a fine layer of dust.

She dropped into one of the overstuffed chairs, snapped open her fan, and flapped it with a vengeance. "I didn't realize it was so warm, or I would have chosen to arrive earlier."

Laura bit back a grin. If Kathleen had arrived any earlier, she would have been on their doorstep in time for breakfast.

Kathleen leaned forward and lowered her voice to a conspiratorial tone. "I didn't want Margaret to know I was going to pay you a visit, so I had her carriage driver deliver me to Ewan's house and then sent Margaret's carriage back home. I had planned to have Ewan's driver bring me here but discovered he and the girls had taken the carriage into town." She sighed and sank deeper into the chair. "I had no choice but to walk here in this terrible heat."

Laura didn't mention the fact that Kathleen could have waited until after the sun had begun to lower in the western sky. Then again, she was likely expected home before then. Catherine returned with glasses and a pitcher of lemonade.

The maid glanced at Kathleen before turning to Laura. "I made up this pitcher special for your mother, but she's resting. Says she has a headache."

"It's fortunate for us that you made the lemonade, but I'm sorry to hear Mrs. Woodfield isn't well." Kathleen didn't wait for Catherine or Laura to complete their hostess duties. Instead, she grasped the pitcher handle and proceeded to fill the two empty glasses to the brim. After downing a large gulp, she placed the glass back on the tray.

"That's delicious. I apologize for my lack of etiquette, but I was parched."

She fidgeted with the pleats in her skirt. "Margaret says she can't take her eyes off me when we're out among her friends. She says I'm truly an embarrassment, but I can't remember all those rules. Truth is, I don't know how Margaret learned 'em all so fast, but she's got her a mind like a steel trap." Kathleen tapped the side of her head. "Once something gets in there, it stays forever."

"Your sister is very fortunate to have an excellent memory, but I don't think you've ever exhibited bad manners in front of me, Kathleen. You poured a glass of lemonade for me, so I don't think your manners could be considered lacking by anyone." Laura reached forward and patted the girl's hand. "Besides, I'm certain you were very thirsty."

Kathleen continued to fidget. Several times she wiped her handkerchief around her glass to remove the condensation, straightened the pleats in her skirt, and glanced about the room as if she needed to catch sight of something that would calm her.

When Laura could stand the tension no longer, she set her glass on the tray and looked at Kathleen. "I'm delighted to have you visit, but I have a feeling there's something in particular that's brought you to Woodfield Manor. Am I correct?"

"Yes, that's right." Kathleen didn't look up from wiping her glass.

Laura could only surmise this was going to be a game of cat and mouse, but she didn't know if she was the cat or the mouse. "Did you wish to speak with my mother?"

Kathleen shrank back. "Oh no. I could never talk to Mrs. Woodfield about my problem."

At least Laura had been able to discover there was a problem and Kathleen needed to discuss it with her. Now, if she could just pry the girl out of her shell and get her to reveal the problem . . . "Have things been chaotic at home since the mishap at the brickyard?"

"Aye. My sister has been on a blithering rampage. What with all the money she's spent building the new house and buying all the furnishings, she's worked herself into quite a frenzy. Of course, her greatest fear is that she'll lose all the worldly belongings she finds so important. But she's also fretting about what people will say if the brickyard is seized by the bank. She says we'll all have to leave the state if that happens."

Laura shook her head. "I think your sister

may be overreacting a bit. There are other people who have suffered business losses, and they've managed to continue living in West Virginia. Besides, I'm hopeful financial matters can be rearranged so that there's no seizure at the brickyard." Laura took a sip of her lemonade. "Is that what brought you for a visit today? Concern over your sister?"

"Aye, but not regarding the matters I mentioned. There's another bit of a problem. One that I've not yet mentioned to my sister." Kathleen's fingers trembled at the mention of her sister. "I fear if I tell Margaret, she'll burst forth in a hurricane of rage that won't soon be forgotten. I remember how she ranted at Hugh back in Ireland when —" The sad-eyed girl stopped short and gave a slight shake of her head. "I should not be tellin' family secrets. It's not proper, and that's not the reason I came here."

Laura wished Kathleen would speak up, but she didn't want to push her. The young woman appeared ready to swoon each time her sister's name was mentioned. "Whatever the reason, I'm glad you decided to pay me a visit. Rose and the twins come over quite often."

"Aye, they've told me about their visits. Margaret doesn't want the girls to come,

378

but Ewan told her that he'd make the decisions regarding his sisters." She straightened her drooping shoulders. "And I say good for Ewan! He's the only one who's ever had the courage to stand up to Margaret." She covered her mouth with her fingers. "I shouldn't have said that."

"You need not worry, Kathleen. The girls have already told me that Margaret isn't fond of having them visit Woodfield Manor, though I don't understand why."

"You do not know?" When Laura shook her head, the girl's eyes grew as large as silver dollars. "My sister fears you want to continue to have a say in the brickyard. Hugh has told her the idea is foolish, but she says if you'd had a husband, you would never have sold the business. She thinks you hope to marry Ewan so you can gain control of the business, and she's decided you're trying to win the girls over in order to win Ewan's affection." She ducked her head. "Margaret even tried to make a match between me and Ewan, but he was quick to tell her she'd not be choosing his wife. I was thankful for his courage. I couldn't have been as firm with Margaret, but Ewan is not the man I want to marry."

A rich shade of pink returned to Kathleen's cheeks at the mention of marriage.

Was that why she'd come to visit? Did she fear telling Margaret she was going marry? Did she need help planning her wedding? Laura's mind swirled with that possibility.

"Do you have a beau you're planning to marry? Do you want me to help you with your wedding plans?" When the girl didn't immediately respond, Laura let out a slight gasp. "It's Terrance O'Grady, the young man who danced with you at the Hogmanay party." Laura grinned. "Am I right?"

"You're partly right and partly wrong." Her shoulders drooped back into their earlier slumped position. "I do love Terrance, but I've not come to ask you about planning a wedding." She inhaled a long breath. "The truth of the matter is . . . I'm going to have a baby."

Laura grasped her lemonade glass in a tight hold. She needed to remain composed and supportive. The last thing Kathleen needed was a barrage of criticism from her. Margaret would be sure to voice her condemnation in a loud and lengthy discourse. "If you are to have a child, then it seems a wedding is what's needed. Don't you agree?"

"Aye, 'tis true, but I've not told anyone but you. Terrance does not know, and I'm not so sure he's going to look fondly on the news." Her voice warbled and she swallowed hard. "We began to secretly meet each other a few weeks before the Hogmanay party, and he promised to speak to Hugh about courting me, but after all these months, he still hasn't gained the courage. He hasn't come to meet me for several weeks now." She folded her hands in her lap. "By my reckoning, the babe will be born in March."

"I see." Laura searched for something more to say, but the girl's announcement caught her off guard.

Shame clouded Kathleen eyes. "Margaret is going to be as mad as a wet hen. There will be no mollifying her once she finds out."

"Just because you haven't seen Terrance doesn't mean he won't do the right thing. After all, your sister has made it clear he's not welcome to call on you." Laura couched her words with as much hope as she could muster, but she knew Margaret would prove a formidable opponent to the idea of a marriage to Terrance. Still, with a baby on the way, what other choice was available to the girl? Margaret might not like the idea, but she would have to accept the marriage.

Kathleen's lips curved in a slight smile. "Maybe you're right about Terrance. He used to sneak over to see me after the others were in bed, but I've waited for him most every night lately, and he hasn't come back. Maybe Margaret discovered we were meeting and had Hugh go and tell him to stay away."

Laura didn't miss the glimmer of hope in Kathleen's eyes. "I believe the first thing you must do is talk to Terrance. Tell him about the baby and make him understand that no matter what Margaret or Hugh says, you want to become his wife."

Minutes crawled by before Kathleen slowly nodded. "I know you're right. And I know I must talk to him right away, but . . ." She wrung her hands together. "Would you go with me? Could you have your driver take us to the livery in town?" Apprehension clung to her words like thick molasses.

Laura's mind reeled. She hadn't expected to be drawn further into Kathleen's plight, yet how could she refuse the girl? "I'll have Zeke bring the buggy around to the front. In the meantime, let me go upstairs and tell my mother that I'm going to be leaving the house for a while."

When she returned downstairs, Kathleen was pacing the front hallway, her footfalls muffled by the Axminster carpeting. "You didn't tell your mother about me, did you?" Worry lines creased her forehead.

Laura pulled on her gloves as they walked

outside, where Zeke stood beside the horse and carriage. "I merely said that I was driving you into Bartlett and wasn't sure when I would return. Since she's suffering one of her headaches, she'll likely be in bed most of the day. She waved me off without any questions, though she may have a few when I return."

They hadn't gone far when Kathleen suggested they stop at the mercantile. "Then you can tell your mother we went shopping." She fidgeted with her reticule. "I have enough money to purchase some thread. I wouldn't want you to tell a lie on my account."

"Don't worry about what I tell Mother. I can worry about that. Instead, why don't you decide what you're going to say to Terrance when we get into Bartlett."

"Aye. 'Tis true I need to give that some thought."

Late summer and early fall had been unusually warm and dry. Dust plumes rolled from beneath the buggy as they continued along the sunbaked dirt road. Silence stretched between them like a yawning chasm. Kathleen's hands never stilled during the ride, a sure sign she continued to fret about her meeting with Terrance.

When they approached the outskirts of

town, Kathleen turned pale. "What if he isn't there? What if he won't talk to me?"

"I'm sure he's going to be thrilled to see you." She hoped her words offered a bit of reassurance.

Truth be told, Laura couldn't even imagine the fear that Kathleen likely felt at this moment. She pulled back on the reins and slowed the horse as they entered town and rode past the mercantile, the bank, the milliner's shop, and a host of other businesses that lined Bartlett's main street. Laura glanced at Kathleen. The girl sat with her shoulders tensed and her stare fastened upon the unpainted frame building that housed the livery. Kathleen didn't move a muscle once the buggy came to a halt.

Laura patted the girl's hand and offered an encouraging smile. "I'll wait here until you make certain Terrance is inside. If he's there, step to the door and wave me on. I'll go to the mercantile, and you can walk over when you've finished talking to him."

"Aye." She didn't appear capable of uttering anything more.

Laura watched as Kathleen disappeared inside the livery and then reappeared and waved. Laura had offered a silent prayer that Terrance was at the livery and their talk would go well. Perhaps she and Kathleen would be purchasing fabric for a wedding dress before they left town. The thought pleased her. Though not the best of circumstances to begin a marriage, Laura hoped the two of them would find happiness in spite of any obstacles Margaret might place in their way.

In the mercantile, she made her way down several aisles before stopping to admire some lace that would add a lovely touch to a dress for Kathleen.

"I thought that was your buggy I saw outside."

Laura startled and discovered Winston was standing only a few steps away.

"Looking for something special?" His gaze fell on the lace. "That appears to be lace edging for a wedding gown." His lips curved in a knowing smile. "Have you begun making your wedding gown without including me in your plans?"

His remark was so startling that she was momentarily rendered speechless. She'd been clear about her intentions the other night. Although Winston had attempted to divert their conversation away from problems at the brickyard, she'd been clear that she wanted the bank to give Ewan additional time to meet the financial obligation. When they parted, she'd been even more explicit, so now to hear him speak of marriage and act as though she were shopping for wedding gown fabric only served to annoy her further. Surely he realized his inapt remarks wouldn't sit well with her.

Laura rested her hand on a bolt of fabric. "You must have misunderstood our conversation before we parted the other night, though I believe I was very explicit. Our beliefs are far too disparate for me to ever consider a future with you. I could never marry you."

His lips curled in a sneer. "And do you believe you'll find a husband willing to accept you with your little *problem*? I doubt Ewan McKay will want to marry a woman who can't bear him an heir."

Laura gasped at his cruel words. "I'm shocked you would speak to any woman in such a vile manner." She took a backward step and inhaled a deep breath as she attempted to digest the pain Winston had so willingly inflicted. "Ewan McKay has nothing to do with my opinion about you and your behavior, but if it eases your mind, please know that I would never marry a man without being honest."

The anger in his eyes seared her. "You're determined to make a fool of me, but in the end, we shall see who is truly the fool."

Winston's words sizzled with bitterness as he turned on his heel and stormed down the aisle of dry goods and out the front door. His heated response pulsed in her ears, and she leaned against the display counter to gain her bearings. She could only imagine how he would have acted if he'd known she'd enlisted her mother to help Ewan secure financial aid to make the bank payment.

Convincing her mother to help had required a great deal of finesse. While her mother didn't want to see the brickyard fail, she wasn't thrilled to lend help to Hugh or Margaret Crothers, both of whom had proved to be untrustworthy. However, Laura's gentle persuasion and a mention of Christian duty had convinced her mother that the many employees, as well as Ewan and his three sisters, would suffer dearly if the brickyard failed. Laura's mother had finally agreed that her distaste for Hugh and Margaret Crothers and their unseemly behavior should not color her decision.

Once she agreed to lend her help, Mrs. Woodfield had done everything in her power to maintain secrecy in the negotiations. Still, Laura and her mother both understood how businessmen tended to talk about business ventures — even when they'd agreed to keep matters private — and Laura feared word might leak out at any time. Her mother remained certain their plan would remain a secret, but her mother's confidence hadn't eased Laura's concerns. However, the fact that Winston hadn't seemed to know gave her hope that her mother was correct.

A short time later, Laura turned and caught sight of Kathleen as she entered the store. After taking a slow breath, Laura forced a broad smile. She didn't want Kathleen to know this trip into town had resulted in a confrontation with Winston.

As Kathleen drew closer, Laura noted the girl's splotchy complexion. She'd obviously been crying. Laura reached forward and grasped her hand. "Do you need to sit down?" The girl appeared as though she might faint at any moment. Laura glanced about, hoping to locate a chair.

"Nay. Please, I want to leave." When Laura didn't immediately move toward the door, Kathleen tugged on her hand. "I don't want to stay here."

Laura placed her arm around Kathleen's waist and escorted her to the buggy. Once she was ensconced inside and they'd traveled beyond the outskirts of town, Kathleen began to cry, and soon her soft weeping intensified until her entire body was heaving with uncontrollable sobs.

Unable to console the girl while driving the buggy, Laura pulled to the side of the road, then drew Kathleen into an embrace. "Tell me what happened. I can't help you unless I know what you and Terrance decided. You did speak to him, didn't you?"

She sniffled and gave a slight nod. "He doesn't want to marry me." Her voice hitched and her tears once again flowed.

Laura was sure Kathleen had misunderstood. Surely Terrance hadn't understood the depth of Kathleen's dilemma — of their dilemma. "Did you tell him about the baby?"

She nodded. "He said he's going to marry Jenny O'Malley. They were seeing each other before he ever met me. He says it's her that he loves, not me." Her voice was laced with tears as she continued the tale. "When I told him about the baby, he said he doubted it was his, and that a girl that was as easily bedded as me had surely been sleeping with every man she ever met." Her wails cut through the scorching heat.

Laura snapped open her fan and waved it back and forth in front of Kathleen's face. "What a despicable thing for him to say! What kind of man is he that he'd treat you in such a manner?" Laura placed an arm around Kathleen's shoulder.

"Promise you won't tell anyone until I have a chance to talk to Margaret and Hugh. I don't want them to find out from someone else."

Laura patted her hand. "You have my word, but you must try to calm yourself. Please know that I'll do whatever I can to help you."

CHAPTER 23

The afternoon sun beat down across the brickyard and blended with the thick humidity to produce torturous weather that continued to take its toll on the men. Though the workers attested to the fact that the weather was odd for September, they'd affirmed they'd experienced hot Septembers in the past. They'd also mentioned those hot Septembers had been followed by early winters, a fact Ewan wasn't pleased to hear. He wanted as much time as possible to produce the necessary bricks to fulfill all pending contracts.

Ewan strode down the hillside to check on the progress of the afternoon shift, a task he'd taken on since they'd begun the nearly nonstop operation at the yard. The men who worked the early shift arrived while darkness shrouded the hillsides, and the men who worked the late shift arrived when the sun was beginning its descent. They were the fortunate ones. The men working during the heat of the day suffered the most. Ewan disliked requiring them to work in these conditions, but if they didn't make up for the two kilns of ruined bricks, the company wouldn't survive. There was no time for resting in the shade during the heat of the day.

He continued to work at a frenzied pace, all the time realizing his efforts would be in vain if they couldn't meet the deadline for the bank note. On the other hand, his uncle had adopted a somewhat complacent attitude that Ewan failed to understand. The money invested in the brickyard — the money that would be lost if they didn't meet their financial obligation — had belonged to his uncle.

Ewan had gone only a short distance when the pounding of horse hooves caused him to turn. From atop his horse, his uncle gestured. "Get on up here, Ewan. I need to have a word with you."

With a sigh, Ewan trudged back up the hillside to the office, where his uncle stood tying his horse. His uncle had remained away from the brickyard for days, but the moment he appeared, he expected everyone to do his bidding — Ewan included.

Ewan was still a short distance from his

uncle when he gestured toward the yard. "I need to go down and check on progress. Have you managed to secure the money we need to make the bank payment?"

"That's why I've come to talk to you, so get yourself up here, where I don't have to strain me voice."

Though he knew his uncle had overextended his assets with the construction of a new home and the purchase of expensive furnishings, Ewan wasn't certain he had depleted all of his funds. The man tended to hide his true state of financial affairs, so Ewan held out hope his uncle possessed at least enough money to stave off the bank's promise of seizure.

His uncle pushed his hat back a few inches, withdrew his handkerchief from his pocket, and wiped the perspiration from his forehead. "Not enough to meet the full payment, but I'm still working on it."

While Ewan and the men at the brickyard continued to labor, Ewan relied upon prayer to keep himself from dwelling on the possible loss of their business. His uncle usually came up with money, albeit not always in a legal manner. Even though the man had indicated he didn't have money to make the full bank payment, Ewan wasn't sure he'd been told the truth. He hoped his uncle continued to exaggerate his lack of funds in order to curtail Aunt Margaret's spending.

"Exactly how are you working on it, Uncle Hugh? Are you meeting with some businessmen who might offer a short-term loan? If so, you can tell them we're working overtime to meet our orders and they can expect repayment as soon a —"

"Hold your britches, boy. Since when am I needing your advice on how to conduct business?" Hugh tugged on the end of his mustache and pinned Ewan with a look of disdain.

Ewan's weariness and his uncle's sharp words joined together, and Ewan said forcefully, "You needed my advice a long time ago, but you were too proud to take it. If you would have listened to me before you signed that contract giving us so little time to make our payments, we wouldn't be in this position. And you shouldn't have hired Rudy Banks, either. It's your doing that's landed us in this kettle of fish, so you shouldn't be acting so high and mighty when I ask about the bank loan." He waved toward the brickyard. "The men are working in the heat of the day to try to make a go of this, so I hope you've been doing as much to help with the problem."

He'd seen little of his uncle since the

calamity at the brickyard, but they lived in separate houses now, so there was no telling whether Uncle Hugh had been lazing about or if he'd actually been attempting to secure the necessary funds. But Ewan wanted to know. Mrs. Woodfield had sent word she wanted to meet this afternoon — likely to know what was happening with the brick-yard. No doubt she worried her late hus-band's business would once again lay idle. And though the closure might cause her a certain degree of distress, it would cost Ewan a great deal more.

"I've used all my resources and managed to come up with only a little less than half of what we need. Folks around here don't part with their money as easily as those liv-ing around the large cities. I'm having a hard time locating anyone willing to join me at the gaming tables."

Ewan sighed. He had hoped his uncle would seek help from legitimate business-men, but it seemed Uncle Hugh wasn't go-ing to give up his old habits easily. "I had hoped you'd seek help through another bank or speak to some of the businessmen you've met since we've arrived."

"Aye, and if you think I would have had a bit of luck with those ideas, you're daft in the head. There's no one in this town who's going to loan me money, and you can be sure all those businessmen you're talking about are friends of Winston Hawkins and his banker friends." His uncle's eyes glazed with anger. "There's about as much chance of that happening as there is of the Lord answering all them prayers of yours."

"The Lord answers all of our prayers, Uncle Hugh — maybe not the way we'd like, but He always answers. Trouble is, you want to take credit for the good things that happen in your life and blame others, God included, for the bad that happens. I don't know when you strayed so far from the beliefs you learned years ago, but you need to turn back and put God first in your life."

"I don't want to be listening to your preachin' any more than I want to hear Margaret nagging me for money." His uncle shifted around and pointed toward the yard. "You got enough bricks down there that if I found a buyer, we could go ahead and sell them outright?"

Ewan stared at his uncle in disbelief. "Those bricks, along with the ones we're continuing to make, are promised under the contract made with Mr. Bruce. We can't sell them to someone else."

Hugh hiked a shoulder. "If we don't sell what bricks we've got ready, we won't have enough money to pay the bank. You can tell Mr. Bruce we'll get his shipment upriver as soon as we can, but he shouldn't expect it for at least a month."

"They're waiting on those bricks to complete their apartment buildings, Uncle Hugh. We can't sell the bricks to someone else."

"Mr. Bruce won't pay until he has the full amount called for in the contract, am I right?"

"You're right, but that doesn't mean we can sell bricks we've made for them to another buyer just because we don't have their full shipment ready. We'll put their project so far behind they won't be able to complete their buildings before winter sets in."

"Maybe I should talk to Mr. Bruce and tell him his options." Uncle Hugh pulled his pipe from his jacket pocket. "Maybe then he'd pay us enough to meet the bank loan."

Ewan shook his head. "Even if he agreed, we'd never get another contract from him. Who wants to do business with a company that would do what you've suggested? Besides, word would quickly spread among all the other builders in Pittsburgh and Allegheny City, and we'd never again be offered large contracts. Without those large contracts —"

"That's enough! I do not want to hear any more of your blathering." His uncle swatted the air. "I know what you think, but you've not come up with any way to solve the problem, so don't be condemning me for trying to find a way to fix it."

"What you're suggesting is not a solution. It's only going to make the problem worse. Don't do anything until we talk tonight." When his uncle turned to study the bricks stacked in the yard, Ewan grasped his arm. "Please! Don't offer those bricks for sale to anyone else until after we talk this evening."

His uncle's lips dipped in a frown. "I'll wait until tonight, but unless you can think of something better, I'll be trying to sell what bricks we've got on hand whether you like it or not. 'Tis better than having the bank seize the entire yard."

By the time his uncle had ridden off, Ewan was certain there would be no good solution to their dilemma. Not unless Mrs. Woodfield came to their aid. She'd requested he pay a visit this afternoon, but there had been no indication of assistance in her message. Merely a brief note saying it was important she speak with him.

He'd been praying their meeting would

somehow offer a solution to the dilemma, yet why should Mrs. Woodfield help them? Uncle Hugh and Aunt Margaret had done nothing to endear themselves to the woman, and the success or failure of the brickyard would not affect her.

Still, as he rode to Woodfield Manor a short time later, he continued to hope and pray that Mrs. Woodfield would offer some form of assistance or advice. Zeke hurried to take the reins of his horse when he dismounted. Preoccupied by thoughts of his uncle's earlier visit to the yard, Ewan didn't notice Laura sitting on the front porch until he neared the door.

"Good afternoon, Ewan." She smiled, and desire swelled in him and melted his resolve to resist her.

He had no right to feel this way about a woman being courted by another man, but her beauty and compassion were intoxicating. She possessed all of the attributes any man would desire in a woman — in a wife.

"Good afternoon." The words stuck in his mouth like thick molasses. "I'm supposed to meet with your mother."

She closed her fan and attached it to a silver chatelaine clipped at her waist. "I know. I'm going to join you for the meeting." Her smile broadened. "I hope you won't mind."

He shook his head in answer but hoped the motion would clear his mind, as well. "No, not at all." He followed her inside and down the hallway to the library, where her mother sat visiting with a man whom Ewan had never met.

Mrs. Woodfield greeted him with a pleasant smile. "Good afternoon, Ewan. I'd like to introduce you to an old friend of mine, Herman Lofton." She waved toward Ewan. "This is Ewan McKay, the young man I've been telling you about, Herman."

Mr. Lofton stood and extended his hand. "I'm pleased to make your acquaintance, Mr. McKay."

Ewan reached forward to shake Mr. Lofton's hand. "Please call me Ewan."

"Good enough. And you may call me Herman, if you'd like."

The older man returned to his chair, and Laura stepped across the room and took a seat beside her mother. "Do sit down, Ewan. I believe Mother was going to have Catherine serve some lemonade. Would you like a glass?"

While Ewan appreciated the pleasantries and knew it would be rude to decline refreshments, he would have preferred to know why he'd been summoned to this meeting. Even more, he was curious to learn about Herman Lofton and why he was there.

"A glass of lemonade would be most refreshing, thank you." Ewan sat on the edge of his chair, his arms resting across his thighs, his shoulders hunched forward.

"You look as though you're preparing to take flight, Ewan. Do relax. I don't have plans to do you harm." Mrs. Woodfield chuckled and glanced at Mr. Lofton before returning her attention to Ewan. "There's no reason to be on edge. We're hoping to arrive at a solution to help you save the brickyard from being seized by the bank."

Ewan wasn't certain what to think, but he wanted to believe this was an answer to his prayers. Using his index finger, he waved an imaginary line from Laura to her mother, and then to Mr. Lofton. "The three of you want to help me?"

They bobbed their heads in unison. "Is that so difficult to believe?" Mrs. Woodfield asked.

"After the way my aunt and uncle have behaved, I can only believe you are an answer to my fervent prayers. Otherwise you wouldn't attempt to help us."

"Helping wasn't my idea, Ewan. Laura convinced me that I had a Christian duty to lend a hand — and she was correct. While I'm not particularly fond of your aunt and uncle, I know you to be a commendable young man who should not bear the burden of an uncle who makes poor decisions. Besides, far too many people will be affected if the brickyard closes, so I don't think I can let that happen." She straightened her shoulders. "That's why I called upon my friend Herman. I needed the advice of someone who hadn't been associated with any of the previous dealings regarding the brickyard. I needed someone who could give me unbiased advice, so Herman is the person I called upon to help me — and you."

Ewan leaned forward. "I'm eager to hear what measures the two of you have planned."

Mr. Lofton chuckled. "I'd hardly say we've made any arrangements, Ewan. Much will depend upon you and, unfortunately, your uncle, since he is the owner of the brickyard. We wanted to discuss this first with you and, if you are in agreement, we suggest you have your uncle return with you for supper this evening."

Ewan listened as they laid out their idea. Though he would have agreed to most anything they suggested that would save the brickyard, he thought the plan fair and workable. For sure, it was better than anything he or his uncle could devise within the next few days. But whether Uncle Hugh would agree was entirely another matter.

CHAPTER 24

Being excluded from the dinner invitation hadn't pleased Aunt Margaret, and Uncle Hugh had expressed no desire to meet with Mrs. Woodfield. But after he revealed that his afternoon of gambling had resulted in more losses than gains, Ewan pointed out that they were without any other options. Given their state of affairs, his uncle finally relented.

As the two men rode side by side toward Woodfield Manor, Hugh's agitation steadily increased, and his frown deepened when Ewan wouldn't reveal the details of his earlier meeting with Mr. Lofton. "I want to know more about this man who's so willing to help us. There's got to be something he hopes to gain out of all this. He best not be thinking he's shrewd enough to pull the wool over my eyes with some complicated contract."

Ewan bit back a laugh. "Why would anyone ever think such a thing, Uncle Hugh?"

His uncle snorted. "Scorn me if you like, but I'll not fall prey to the same trickery again."

"Mr. Lofton wants to propose a way of saving the brickyard, but if you do not like what he has to say, then you can let the bank have it. Remember, there is likely little room for negotiation and even less time. We must do something right away."

His uncle scowled. "I know. I know."

Hugh's demeanor was less than contrite when they entered the house. As soon as introductions had been made, he did his best to take control. "My nephew tells me you have an offer to make regarding the financial problems at the brickyard." He glanced at Mrs. Woodfield. "While I do appreciate the offer to have dinner with you, I'd first like to hear the proposal. Otherwise, I do not think my stomach will settle enough to enjoy the meal."

Mr. Lofton turned to their hostess. "I must leave that decision to you, Frances. You're more aware of whether the preparations will be ruined if we have our meeting before dinner."

"I believe we can hold dinner until after the meeting." Mrs. Woodfield turned to Laura. "Would you let Catherine know we won't be dining for another half hour?" She arched her brows at Mr. Lofton. "I think that should be sufficient time to go over your idea, don't you?"

Mr. Lofton nodded. "If we need time for more details, we can continue our discussion after dinner, don't you agree, Mr. Crothers?"

"Aye. It's the meat of your proposal I'm wanting to hear before we have dinner, enough so I know if your idea will even bear my consideration."

Had it not been inappropriate, Ewan would have jabbed his uncle in the side. How dare he make such a pompous remark when there were no other options available?

Mr. Lofton remained surprisingly unruffled. "Indeed, I wouldn't want you to accept my offer unless you felt it was the best thing for you, your employees, your family, and your business, Mr. Crothers."

The faint scent of jasmine wafted through the air as Laura returned from the kitchen and sat down in a chair next to Ewan. Her gown of pale green satin heightened the color in her cheeks, and though he did his best to concentrate on Mr. Lofton, her nearness distracted him.

"Are you listening to this, Ewan?" His uncle poked his arm. "Mr. Lofton says he's willing to pay the bank note in full."

"Aye." Ewan nodded.

Mr. Lofton held up his hand. "That's the first part, Mr. Crothers. Listen closely while I explain the rest, for I don't want there to be any misunderstanding." He inhaled a deep breath. "I will use my funds to buy your obligation to the bank. You will then owe me the payments we shall agree upon, which shall not exceed those in your current contract. I will, of course, permit you a greater period of grace to make those payments. You will pay me the same interest you've agreed to pay the bank."

"This sounds like it will work, Mr. Lofton." Hugh slapped his knee and smiled, but moments later his smile faded and he shook his head. "This is too easy. There's got to be something more to it that you're not telling me. Why would you offer to save the company at the same rate of interest, give us a more generous grace period, and not ask for something beyond what we promised in the old contract? It makes no sense."

Mr. Lofton folded his hands across his protruding stomach and smiled. "Why is it when someone offers something good, we think there must be some hidden scheme? Is it because that's what we would do in the same circumstance?" Instead of looking at Uncle Hugh as he asked the question, he let his gaze travel among all of them.

Uncle Hugh was first to respond. "Exactly right. So that's why I'm asking why you'd make such an offer to strangers. You know Mrs. Woodfield, but she won't lose anything if the brickyard goes under. So I'm thinking there's something more to all of this."

"Since you've asked, Mr. Crothers, there is something more that I'll ask of you. But first let me tell you why I'm going to make that request." Mr. Lofton met Uncle Hugh's suspicious gaze. "A long time ago, a businessman helped me when I hit a streak of bad luck. Truth of it was, I didn't deserve his help or the help of anyone else."

Uncle Hugh appeared unmoved. "Why's that?"

"Because in the past, I'd been party to some rather shady dealings. I'd been willing to do whatever it took to get ahead without giving thought to those I cheated along the way. I truly warranted any trouble that came my way. But that businessman said he was still willing to help me as long as I paid him back as promised, and on the condition I'd lend a helping hand to others who might have a need in the future." He looked at Mrs. Woodfield. "That man was Isaiah

Woodfield. I paid him back, and I've tried to keep my promise to him to help others whenever I could. So when Frances asked me to consider this loan, I couldn't refuse."

Uncle Hugh's complexion paled, and he pinned Ewan with a hard stare. "Has my nephew been telling tales about me, Mr. Lofton?"

The balding man shook his head. "The only thing your nephew has lamented in regard to your conduct is the fact that you signed your original contract without proper diligence, and that you don't spend much of your time at the brickyard."

" 'Tis true I rely upon Ewan to run the brickyard while I've been building a house for my wife, but I'll have more time to give to the business in the future."

As if on cue, Catherine stepped to the doorway and announced dinner. While Hugh and Mr. Lofton continued to discuss a time when they could sign the contract, Laura leaned toward Ewan. "I hope this will set your mind at ease so you won't have to worry about the future for yourself and your sisters. Herman is an honorable man, and I know he'll be fair."

Laura's smile and the reference to his sisters warmed Ewan's heart. "I do not doubt that he's a good man. When I was alone with him earlier today, he spoke of his past misdeeds. He also told me your father had spoken to him about his belief in the Lord and that your father's words had convinced Mr. Lofton to change his life and become a Christian. I hope Mr. Lofton can have the same effect upon Uncle Hugh. I've tried to point him toward Christ's teachings, but he will not listen to me."

"Sometimes it's easier to listen to a stranger speak the truth than to a relative or close friend. Herman has a way with people, so he may influence your uncle."

Ewan forked a piece of roasted potato and nodded. "Let's pray that will happen."

After dinner, Mrs. Woodfield gestured toward the hallway. "Why don't we finish our discussion over coffee in the library?"

Laura hesitated a moment. "I don't believe Ewan and I need to be present. It's rather warm, so I thought we'd sit in the garden out back."

When Mrs. Woodfield didn't object, Laura grasped Ewan's arm. "I hope you don't think me bold, but I wanted a few minutes to speak with you alone."

Ewan's throat closed around his response. He would like nothing more than to spend time alone with Laura, yet he dare not say such a thing aloud. With his heart pounding in his ears, he sat down beside her on the wrought-iron bench and tried to gather his thoughts. He should thank her for helping arrange the meeting with Mr. Lofton. He was sure she'd played a part in the arrangement, but when he opened his mouth to speak, she turned toward him, and his thoughts once again muddled.

"There's something I want to tell you." She tucked a tendril of hair behind her ear and hesitated for a moment. "Recently I was in town and had occasion to see Winston while I was there. We had a rather heated discussion."

Ewan's heart plummeted. He didn't want to hear about Winston. He forced a smile. "And did you want to tell me about that conversation?"

Laura nodded. "Winston will no longer be courting me. We have far too many differences." A slight sigh escaped her lips. "Winston embraces many ideas and opinions that I could never accept. We would not make a good match." She folded her hands in her lap. "I should never have agreed to the courtship, but I wanted to please Mother."

"Your mother thought he would be a good husband for you?"

"She thought he would be the only man willing to accept me." When Ewan opened his mouth to interrupt, she held her fingers to his lips. "Let me finish, and then you'll understand."

His thoughts whirred as she told him that Winston's only aspiration was to become a politician and he believed children would be a hindrance to his political career. "Mother thought we would make a good match because . . ." Her voice faltered. "Because I cannot have children. I fell from a horse years ago, and the doctor informed my parents the injuries were such that I could not bear children. I know this isn't something I should speak about with you, but eventually Winston would have told you, and I feared you would feel I'd been hiding the truth from you."

Ewan let her words seep into his consciousness. "So your mother decided no other man would find you acceptable because you could not bear children?"

He appeared to find her explanation unthinkable. "Think about it, Ewan. I don't know any man who doesn't want to have a son — an heir to carry on the family name. After spending time with you and your sisters, I know family is very important to you. The same is true of most men. Even when they marry for love, they also hope for children. When that hope is snuffed out before marriage . . . well, you can see why my mother thought Winston and I would be a good match."

Laura's eyes reflected a haunting pain, and he wanted nothing more than to erase her fears.

He reached for her hand. "If you believe I would not marry a woman because she could not have children, then you do not know me very well."

"Ewan, you deserve to have a family."

"I have a family." He squeezed her hands. "And Laura, it is more important to me that true love exists between husband and wife than any expectation of children. Besides, who can say what God will do in such a situation?" He reached up and cupped her cheek in his hand. "I am pleased to know Winston is no longer competing to win your heart. That is one job I do not want to share with any other man."

He leaned forward and lightly brushed her lips with his. When she made no move to stop him, he embraced her and deepened his kiss, wishing the moment could go on forever.

CHAPTER 25

His uncle reined his horse close to Ewan's as they started toward their homes. "I suppose you're waiting for me to say I owe you some thanks for this evening's turn of events."

Ewan gave a slight shrug. "I think your thanks should go to Mrs. Woodfield, Mr. Lofton, and Laura. Without all three of them, saving the brickyard would have been impossible."

"For sure, I owe Mr. Lofton a debt of gratitude, and I understand Mrs. Woodfield is his friend and she asked him to help, but why am I to feel thankful toward Laura Woodfield?"

Ewan thought he might be joking until he noticed his uncle's baffled look. "Because Laura is the one who convinced her mother to seek help for us. If she hadn't gone to Mrs. Woodfield, you wouldn't have been able to sign a new contract this evening, and we wouldn't be meeting Mr. Lofton at the bank next Friday to pay off the debt."

"I'll admit this evening's events have given me a lot to think about. After hearing Mr. Lofton tell about his past and the changes he's made, I was feeling my own shame for having left Ireland with Lyall Montclair's money in my pocket. Maybe that's why things have gone awry with the brickyard." He arched his brows. "Do you think that might be true?"

The horses continued their slow gait along the dirt road. "There's no way of knowing, but I'm certain our situation was worsened by your gambling and the hiring of Rudy Banks." Ewan had given thought to the incident regarding Lyall Montclair, as well. Still, there was no way to be sure if his uncle's behavior had truly caused their problems at the brickyard. However, Ewan could at least use this moment to emphasize the ill effects of gambling. "There's nothing good that comes from gambling, Uncle Hugh. I'm hoping that what's happened has finally brought an end to your time at the gaming tables."

"I told Mr. Lofton I'd do my best to stay away from gambling in the future, but I can't say it will never happen again. I can't explain what it's like for me, except to say that there's a real sense of excitement when the wager could end in financial disaster. If you've never had the experience, you can't understand what it does in here." Hugh placed his fist against his chest. "Your heart beats so fast and hard you think your chest will explode, and then when you win . . ." He expelled a long breath. "There's no greater thrill."

Ewan had hoped the problems at the brickyard would be enough to break his uncle's gambling habit, but hearing him talk about his love of the gaming tables only served to deepen Ewan's concern. Gambling had a stranglehold on his uncle, and along with prayer, Ewan would need to keep a close watch over his uncle and the business.

"Come back to the house with me before you go home, and we can give Margaret and Kathleen the good news. It will be more enjoyable if you're there when I tell them."

Though he would have much preferred to part ways at the fork in the road and head for home so he could share the news with Rose and the twins, he didn't want to deny his uncle's request. If Ewan was to see changes in his uncle, he'd need to be accommodating, even when it wasn't convenient.

"I can't stay long. I promised Ainslee and Adaira I would be home before they went to bed."

"Aye. We'll give them the good news as soon as they greet us at the front door." They rode in silence for the remainder of the distance to Crothers Mansion. A short time later they dismounted and tied the horses near the front of the house. Hugh strode up the front steps and entered the front door, with Ewan following close on his heels.

"Margaret! Kathleen! Where is everyone?" Fia peeked around the corner of the kitchen, then hurried toward them, her eyes wide with fright. "The missus and Kathleen are upstairs. They've been having a terrible row. I don't know when I've ever seen the missus so angry." Fia cowered, as though she expected Margaret to appear at any moment.

Hugh expelled a long sigh. "I'm sure there are plenty of times I've seen her temper flaring far more than it is tonight, Fia." He waved toward the stairs. "Go up there and tell them Ewan and I are down here and we have good news to share with them." When she hesitated, he frowned and stomped his right foot. "Go!"

Fia scuttled up the steps like a frightened

rabbit with its ears laid back. The sound of high-pitched voices drifted down the steps, followed by clattering footfalls as Fia returned at breakneck speed. "The missus says they'll be down straightaway and you best be prepared for some bad news to go along with any good news you have for her."

"You should thank the good Lord you're still single, Ewan. If you ever take a wife, you'll soon discover nothing is ever the same. Truth is, there's no end to the commotion a woman brings to your life." Hugh raked his fingers through his dark hair. A door slammed upstairs, followed by the sound of heavy footsteps. Moments later, the two women came down the stairway. Margaret first and then Kathleen. Their faces were blotchy and their eyes swollen. There was no doubt they'd both been crying.

At the bottom of the stairs, Margaret gave her sister a slight push toward the parlor. "Go on in there and tell your brother-in-law what you've done to disgrace this family." When Kathleen didn't move, Margaret grasped her sister's arm and directed her toward the other room. "I said, go into the parlor!"

"It appears there's a bit of a problem, and I'm thinking I should go home so the three of you can talk in private." Ewan took a backward step toward the door.

"Stay right here, Ewan." Margaret's shrill voice echoed in the wide hallway. "You're a part of this, too."

Ewan didn't know what part he might have in the argument between Kathleen and Margaret, but making any further attempt to leave would only make matters worse. He looked at Hugh and shrugged as they followed the two women into the parlor.

Margaret pointed to the hallway. "Close the pocket doors, Hugh. I don't want Fia or any of the other servants hearing this."

"Do you think they've not already heard you screaming at me for the past hour, Margaret?" Kathleen reached for her handkerchief and blotted her eyes.

Margaret's shrill voice could be heard as clearly as a screeching red-tailed hawk, but Hugh did as he was instructed and closed the doors leading into the hallway.

After taking a position in front of the large windows covered with specially made brocade draperies that darkened the room even on the brightest summer day, Margaret folded her arms across her chest. She glared at Kathleen, her face now contorted with anger and disgust. "Tell them how you've shamed this family."

Kathleen pulled her shoulders together and hunched forward, appearing to wilt before their eyes. "I'm going to have a baby."

She'd spoken so softly, both Hugh and Ewan had to lean forward to hear her. Hugh remained silent, obviously uncertain what he should say, but Ewan moved to the divan and grasped Kathleen's hand. "You're sure?" She nodded. "Is Terrance the father?"

"Of course Terrance is the father." Margaret stomped forward and came to a halt in front of the divan. "And you took her over there to be with him, Ewan. What were you thinking?"

Kathleen turned toward Ewan. "It didn't happen the night you took me to meet Terrance, but she won't listen to me."

"Shouting and pointing blame will do none of us any good, Margaret." Ewan squeezed Kathleen's hand, hoping he could transmit a bit of strength to the trembling woman. "I'm sure Kathleen is feeling enough remorse without all of us adding to her heartache."

"I know this is not the best of circumstances, Kathleen," Hugh said, "but there's been many a wee one born to a couple before they've been married for nine months. Folks forget these things and the child is loved no matter when it arrives.

Have ye already talked to Terrance and made some arrangements for a preacher to perform a quiet weddin'?"

Hugh's kindness stunned Ewan, and his compassion created a new flood of tears from Kathleen, which surprised him even more. "There's no need for more tears, Kathleen. Uncle Hugh is merely suggesting a quick wedding would be best."

Tears streamed down Kathleen's face as she looked at her sister, who stood before them with her hands perched on her hips. "Go on. Tell them." Margaret glowered at Kathleen.

"Terrance won't marry me. He's already engaged to a girl who lives in town." Her voice quivered. "They were courtin' before I ever met him, but I didn't know about her until I went to town with Laura."

Ewan sparked to attention. "Laura? How did she become involved in this?" And why hadn't she mentioned it to him this evening when they'd been alone in the garden?

Kathleen explained how Laura had taken her to meet with Terrance and offered to help in any way she could. "I made her promise she wouldn't tell anyone." She glanced at her sister. "I didn't want Margaret and Hugh to hear this from anyone else."

Margaret snorted. "Not that it makes it any easier hearing it from your own lips. I can't believe my own sister would find herself in this horrid situation. Ever since we arrived, I have worked very hard to establish a good name so that we would be accepted in the proper social circles. Now, with your unseemly behavior, you've managed to wipe out everything I accomplished."

"I doubt everyone is so small-minded they'll consider Kathleen's impropriety a reason to banish you from their parties and sewing circles, Aunt Margaret." Ewan forced a smile.

"Easy enough for you to say, Ewan. You can distance yourself from all of this." She waved her hand toward Kathleen, then moved to a nearby chair. "She lives under our roof, so Hugh and I must bear the embarrassment of her unseemly conduct."

Each time Margaret spoke, Kathleen's weeping intensified until Ewan could no longer bear the situation. "I have a solution to your problem, Margaret."

"What's that? Are you going to marry her? That would be the gallant thing to do. I've thought the two of you should marry since before we sailed from Ireland."

Ewan shook his head. "Marrying Kathleen

might be the gallant thing to do, but I don't love her and she doesn't love me. The marriage would be unfair to both of us. However, I'm going to take Kathleen home with me. She can stay in her old room, and she'll have Rose and the twins to keep her company."

Margaret's face creased in a haughty sneer. "It isn't proper for her to be staying in the home of an unmarried man. That would only give rise to more rumors and gossip."

"Rose and the twins are there, so I don't think anyone would find it unusual for me to stay there." Kathleen's voice hitched and immediately sent her into a bout of uncontrollable hiccoughs.

Margaret snapped open her fan and waved it at a frantic tempo. "This is all too much for me. I feel as though I might faint." When no one responded, she glared at her husband. "Did you hear me, Hugh? I said I feel faint!"

Hugh tugged on the end of his mustache and pierced her with a stern look. "Anyone who has enough breath to shout isn't about to faint, Margaret. Now, gather yourself together and quit acting like you're the one in trouble. It's Kathleen who's faced with a problem, not you." He turned to look at

Kathleen. "I say if you want to go and stay with Ewan, that's fine, but the decision is yours."

"It is not her decision. I've already told her that I don't want her living under this roof bringing any more shame on me."

Ewan shrugged. "If you've already told her to move out, then you should not be offering objection to her living with my sisters and me. This is your sister and she's in need of help. If you don't want to give it, then I will." He released Kathleen's hand. "Go and fetch what you'll need for tonight, and you and Rose can return tomorrow to gather the rest of your belongings." The three of them sat in silence as Kathleen departed the room.

Moments later, Hugh shifted in his chair and frowned at Margaret. "Sure and you've taken the wind out of my sails. I come home thinking to tell you that an agreement has been reached to save the brickyard, and I'm greeted by nothing but angry words and a family divided."

"Did you expect me to keep all of this to myself?" Margaret returned her husband's frown.

"I know better than to think you'd keep bad news to yourself." He shook his head. "Remember what I told you, Ewan —

there's no end to the commotion a wife brings to your life."

Before Margaret could respond, Hugh stood and stalked out of the room.

CHAPTER 26

Over breakfast Sunday morning, Laura detailed Kathleen's plight to her mother. "When Margaret disowned Kathleen and ousted her from Crothers Mansion, Ewan immediately came to her aid. She's staying with him and the girls at the old house."

Mrs. Woodfield stirred a dollop of cream into her steaming coffee. "While I commend Ewan's kindness, I'm not certain living with him is the best decision for Kathleen." She took a small sip of her coffee and blotted her lips. "Ewan and Kathleen are not related by blood, and there could be talk that would lead to suspicions the child is his. You know how people enjoy weaving together a few strands of gossip and passing it on as fact."

Laura's eyes widened. She hadn't expected such an uncharacteristic reaction from her mother. "What would you have him do, Mother? Leave her out in the cold of winter to fend for herself?"

The older woman pursed her lips and tsked. "Of course not. You know I'm not prone to such uncharitable actions, my dear, but I think there is a better solution to this situation. To have her live with Ewan and the girls is, simply said, not proper."

Laura was eager to hear her mother's proposal. She hoped it wouldn't consist of a plan to move Kathleen to some distant foundling hospital until the child was born. The young woman had already suffered being rejected by Terrance and disowned by Margaret. If Kathleen now had to endure the thought of being sent away, Laura doubted the girl would survive. She simply didn't have the inner strength to be alone at some distant institution during her confinement.

Her mother spread orange marmalade on her toast and then lifted her gaze. "I believe the best thing is to have her come here and live with us. She can use the largest of the guest rooms at the far end of the upstairs hallway, where I believe she'll be quite comfortable. Any members of the family who want to visit her may do so, yet there won't be any question of impropriety." She sat back and beamed at her daughter. "Well, what do you think of my idea? It's a good one, is it not?"

The thought of moving Kathleen to Woodfield Manor hadn't crossed Laura's mind. Yet she couldn't deny the solution was perfect. "Yes, Mother, it's an excellent idea. I don't know why I didn't think of it myself."

Her mother chuckled. "I'm glad you didn't. Once in a while, it's good to let us older folks have an opportunity to solve problems. We can speak to Ewan and Kathleen after church this morning, and I'll notify Dr. Balch that we'll have need of his services. He can come to the house so Kathleen won't have to make trips into Bartlett." Her mother rubbed her hands together. "Oh, I do think this is going to be perfect. Kathleen will be well cared for, and she can then make plans for the future without interference from Margaret."

"But we must be careful, Mother. I don't want to force Kathleen to come here against her will. It must be what she wants. If she'll be more comfortable remaining with Ewan, then promise you won't attempt to persuade her otherwise. Kathleen has been pressured enough by her sister. I don't want her to think she'll receive more of the same from us."

Her mother pushed away from the table. "You're right. Though I don't think Rose should be burdened with looking after

Kathleen, it must be Kathleen's decision. I don't intend to force my idea upon her."

Laura followed her mother into the hallway and carefully arranged her hat.

Disappointment etched her mother's face when they entered the church. Ewan, Rose, and the twins were seated by themselves in their regular pew, but Kathleen was nowhere in sight. Laura assisted her mother into their pew and sat down beside her. "Do quit looking about, Mother. Kathleen isn't here."

Her mother pursed her lips. "I'm merely attempting to see who is sitting in the pews behind me."

Laura grinned. "The same people sit in the same pews every week, Mother. We both know you're looking to see if Kathleen is somewhere at the rear of the church. She'd be sitting with Ewan if she were here. I imagine she's afraid if she attended, Margaret might cause a scene."

After craning her neck to gain a better view, her mother nodded toward the pews along the west side of the church. "I see Margaret and Hugh aren't sitting in their regular pew. They've moved over to the other side of the church. I do hope it isn't because Margaret wanted to distance herself from Ewan and the girls."

The pastor entered and gestured for the

congregation to stand. Throughout the service, Laura stood and sat down on cue, but her thoughts weren't on the preacher's words. Instead, they hopscotched among Ewan, Kathleen, Hugh, Margaret, Winston, Ewan's sisters, and her mother. So much had happened in such a short time that it was difficult to digest. She hoped that the problem between Kathleen and Margaret wouldn't affect the brickyard in any way. It had taken a great deal of finesse on her part to suggest Herman Lofton as a possible solution to the financial problems at the brickyard, and she didn't want anything to ruin this opportunity to set things aright. Ewan didn't deserve for his hard work to end in failure.

Yet she didn't believe Margaret Crothers was farsighted enough to understand that the problems she created between Ewan and Hugh could lead to her own financial downfall as well as destroy the woman's hopes of becoming an accepted member of polite society. Whenever things didn't go her way, Margaret's desire for reprisal seemed to outweigh her vision for the future.

When the church service ended, the twins wiggled around Ewan and headed back toward Laura. Adaira was the first to arrive at her side. "Did you know Kathleen has come to live with us?"

"I did. Does it please you to have her?" Laura straightened the bow fastened to the neckline of the young girl's dress.

Adaira shrugged. "She cries all the time, so it isn't much fun. She didn't want to come to church this morning because she thought Aunt Margaret would be angry with her." The girl ducked her head. "I think Aunt Margaret will be fuming when she finds out Kathleen stayed home. We're not supposed to miss church unless we're sick, and I don't think Kathleen is sick."

Ainslee came alongside Laura and took up where Adaira had left off. "I don't think she's sick, either, but Ewan says she has some kind of problem. When I tried to talk to her, she started to cry, so Ewan said we shouldn't bother her with our questions."

Before Laura could respond, Ewan approached with his gaze fixed on his twin sisters. "Are you two busy telling tales?"

Adaira shook her head. "Nay, we were telling the truth. I told Laura about Kathleen crying all the time."

Laura's mother stepped into the aisle and grasped Ewan's arm. "I was hoping for an opportunity to speak with you and Kathleen. Laura and I have an idea that might prove helpful to all concerned. I was going to invite you to come for lunch, but since Kathleen isn't here, perhaps you could bring her for tea this afternoon. I trust she isn't ill?"

"Nay, not ill. Just a wee bit sad." Ewan gestured for Rose to take the twins to the rear of the church. "She feared she would break down and cry during church and make a spectacle of herself." He glanced at Laura. "I would be very pleased to come to Woodfield Manor for tea. I'm sure it would cheer Kathleen, as well."

"Tea at Woodfield Manor, is it?" Margaret Crothers had approached as silently as a fox stalking its prey. "Was this an invitation to the entire family I've just heard?"

Laura's mother didn't hesitate for even a moment. "I'm afraid today's invitation is only for a select few, Mrs. Crothers."

Margaret glared at Ewan. "I see my sister has decided to remain at home rather than show her face in church. She should know that she can't hide her sin much longer. Soon it will be evident for all to see."

"Aye, that's true enough, Aunt Margaret. But even if she could cover her mistake, I'm sure you'd not let her forget." Ewan's words cut through the air with an icy chill, and his aunt marched out of the church without a backward glance.

Hugh gave a slight nod to Laura and Mrs. Woodfield, then patted Ewan on the shoulder. "Don't provoke her too much, Ewan. If we don't openly disagree with your aunt, perhaps she'll have a change of heart and realize even she has made mistakes from time to time. Besides, I wouldn't want her urging me to evict you and the girls from your house."

Ewan grunted. "I hope you wouldn't consider anything so drastic, Uncle."

"I'm not sayin' I would, but it would be best to tread lightly around your aunt Margaret. There's been no calming her since she found out about Kathleen." He glanced toward the doors at the rear of the church, sighed, and marched off.

Ewan hadn't expected Kathleen's objections. For the past half hour, he'd done his best to assure her that Mrs. Woodfield wasn't going to say or do anything to embarrass her. "She said she and Laura had an idea that might be helpful to all of us. You trust Laura, don't you?"

Kathleen wiped her eyes and bobbed her head. "Yes, but I barely know her mother. I don't think I want to discuss my condition with her."

"I think you'll feel better if you get out of

the house for a while. I'm sure it will be a pleasant hour. It's not good for you to sit in your room and brood." He lightly grasped her elbow and directed her toward the hallway. "I'm going to insist you come with me, just this once."

She walked out the front door, still sniffling. "I can hardly refuse, since you've been good enough to let me come here and stay with you."

He disliked being forceful with Kathleen. Most of her life, she'd had someone pushing her one direction or another, which was probably why she'd been so easily swayed by Terrance O'Grady. Instead of gaining a voice now and objecting to tea at Woodfield Manor, he wished she would have gathered her strength to say no when Terrance had come sneaking around and taking advantage, but there was no need to dwell on that.

What had happened couldn't be undone, and Kathleen would have to make the best of the situation. Perhaps by the time the wee one arrived, Margaret would soften her ways. If not, Kathleen was going to have to make some difficult decisions regarding her future and that of her babe.

Since the weather had cooled, Ewan suggested they walk the short distance to Woodfield Manor. He hoped it would give

Kathleen time to compose herself before they arrived.

Kathleen came to a halt when they neared the front porch of the Woodfield home. "Is my face splotchy?"

Ewan looked down at her and smiled. "Nay. You look fine, Kathleen." He grasped her elbow as they mounted the steps. Her shoulders were as rigid as a board. "Try to relax. These are friends, not enemies. I think Laura and her mother want to help you."

They hadn't yet crossed the porch when Laura appeared and opened the front door. "Welcome! We're so glad you agreed to come for tea. Do come in."

The tension in Kathleen's shoulders eased when Laura reached for the girl's hand. "It's kind of you to invite us. I didn't want to intrude, but Ewan insisted. He said you and your mother want to talk to me." She leaned a little closer to Laura. "Does she know about the baby?"

Laura nodded. "She does, but it's fine. There's no reason to worry about Mother."

A short time later as they were drinking their tea, Mrs. Woodfield settled her gaze on Kathleen and gently proposed she move into Woodfield Manor for the remainder of her confinement. "As time progresses, you can decide about your future. Laura and I will be glad to help in any way we can, and my physician will see to your care. Besides, Rose has her hands full with the twins."

"You're right," Kathleen agreed. "It isn't fair to burden Rose, and even though Ewan says it doesn't matter, I know it's improper for me to live in the same house with him. I've already done enough to bring shame on the family. I don't want to do any more harm by injuring Ewan's reputation." Bright pink colored her cheeks.

Ewan leaned forward and rested his arms across his thighs. "You do not need to worry yourself about me, Kathleen. You make your decision based upon what you want to do. If you think you'll be more content at my house, then we'll not worry about what anyone has to say, but if you'd like to come here to Woodfield Manor, then I'll bring your few belongings from my house and gather the rest from your sister and deliver them. Whatever you decide is fine with me."

Kathleen looked back and forth between Mrs. Woodfield and Laura before she finally turned to Ewan. "I think it would be best for all of us if I stayed here with Laura and Mrs. Woodfield."

Ewan gave a slight nod. "If you're sure that's what you want."

Kathleen forced a feeble smile. "I think

it's best for all of us."

"Then I'll go home and get Rose. Together we can go to your sister's house, pack up your clothing and other belongings, and bring them back here before nightfall." He glanced at Mrs. Woodfield. "Is that arrangement fine with you?"

The older woman gave a firm nod, and once they'd finalized their plans, Laura escorted Ewan to the front porch. "I'm so glad Kathleen decided to stay with us. I know Mother will see that she has the best medical care. Mother sometimes seems a little brusque, but she'll make certain Kathleen is well settled and as happy as she can be, given the circumstances."

Ewan smiled down at Laura. "I do not doubt your mother's kindness or her good intentions. I'm thankful she offered to help Kathleen. Rose told me she was a wee bit worried about being alone with Kathleen when her time draws near. This will set Rose's mind at ease and allay some of the twins' many questions — at least for the near future."

"The girls are always welcome here. In fact, I'll be glad to have them come after school each day. I've been missing their daily visits now that school has begun."

Ewan reached forward and clasped her

hand in his. "I had a few moments alone with your mother recently and asked for permission to court you." His heart quickened as he awaited her response.

She squeezed his hand. "I can't think of anything I would like more."

Her eyes glistened in the afternoon sunlight, and the warm smile that curved her lips melted his heart. Did this woman have any idea of what a treasure she was? She'd stood by him, extended a welcoming hand to his sisters, and now was opening her home and heart to a woman she barely knew — a woman who was carrying an unwelcome child when Laura herself so desperately longed for such a gift.

Stepping closer, he placed his hands on her waist and drew her toward him. He lowered his head and met her soft full lips in a lingering kiss that swept over him like a raging summer storm.

He forced himself to take a backward step. "I'd better go or I may never leave your side." His voice cracked with emotion as he traced his finger along her cheek, then hurried down the front steps.

Chapter 27

Although they remained silent, there was a sense of anticipation and solidarity between Ewan and his uncle as they rode to Bartlett on Friday morning. Today they would meet Mr. Lofton and pay off the existing debt on the brickyard.

Ewan's optimism mounted as they neared the hotel. Once the money was paid to the bank, he'd finally be relieved of the ongoing anxiety that had plagued him for months. The Bible told him he should cast all of his cares upon the Lord — and he had tried. Night after night, he'd prayed to be released from this weight of concern, but his unease remained. In less than an hour, he'd be free of further financial worry.

As they neared the bank, Uncle Hugh pulled back on his horse's reins while Ewan urged his horse onward. Leaning forward in the saddle, his uncle hollered, "Where are ya goin', boy?"

Ewan glanced over his shoulder. "To the hotel. Mr. Lofton said he'd meet us in the hotel lobby, and we'd go to the bank together."

"Nay. Are ye sure? I thought he said to meet at the bank."

"I'm sure." Ewan slowed his horse until his uncle came alongside. Truth be told, Ewan didn't think he'd forgotten even one word of those meetings with Mr. Lofton. They'd been far too important to the survival of their business.

As the two men entered the hotel lobby, Ewan darted a glance around the room. When there was no sign of Mr. Lofton, he strode into the restaurant. Perhaps the older man was indulging in a final cup of coffee after breakfast.

His uncle stepped to his side. "He must be waiting for us at the bank."

Ewan shook his head. "He said to meet him at the hotel." Turning on his heel, he rushed to the front desk and gestured to the desk clerk. "We were to meet Mr. Lofton in the lobby this morning, but I don't see him. I need his room number so that I can check on him."

The clerk traced his finger down the hotel registry, then shook his head. "It appears Mr. Lofton had a reservation, but he never arrived."

Panic seized Ewan, and he grabbed the book. He had to see for himself. When it was clear Mr. Lofton hadn't registered, Ewan lifted his gaze and met the clerk's annoyed stare. "He has to be here. We have a meeting this morning. Is there a message for me?"

The clerk reached for the registry and returned it to its proper place on the desk. "Your name?"

"Ewan. Ewan McKay. Or maybe Hugh Crothers. If you could check under both of our names, I'd be grateful." He glanced at his uncle as he attempted to hide the grim feeling that had settled in his chest.

The clerk riffled through a stack of messages and shook his head. "Nothing here for either of you, sir."

His uncle patted his shoulder. "Do na get yourself too worked up, Ewan. I'm guessin' Mr. Lofton arrived on the early train and is already waiting for us at the bank. There's no need to wait around here any longer."

Ewan agreed there was no reason to wait at the hotel, but he didn't share his uncle's thought that they'd discover Mr. Lofton waiting for them at the bank. Strange how the two of them had changed perspective. His uncle was the one who usually adopted a negative attitude. Today, Ewan had assumed that position. As they walked toward the bank Ewan silently prayed God would give him peace and eliminate his increasing dread.

The moment they stepped into the bank, Ewan surveyed the area and shook his head. "Mr. Lofton's not here. What do you think has happened to him?"

"I do na know, but I'm hoping that he'll soon appear on fairy wings and set both our minds at ease."

Winston was already seated in Mr. Swinnen's office when Ewan and his uncle were directed into the bank president's office. Mr. Swinnen leaned his ample body forward and gestured toward the two empty chairs. "Have a seat, gentlemen. I'm glad to see you're punctual with your appointments, even if you're not going to be punctual with your payment."

Ewan lowered himself into a chair that afforded a view of the street where he'd be sure to see Mr. Lofton if he should arrive.

Hugh glanced at Ewan. "You go ahead and do the talkin', Ewan."

Ewan jerked around and gave his uncle a questioning look. What could he possibly say to the banker? His stomach roiled as Winston and Mr. Swinnen turned to face him. He cleared his throat and once again sent a silent prayer heavenward. "My uncle and I had made arrangements to pay off the debt this morning. However, there's been a bit of confusion and our meeting will need to be rescheduled for a later date."

Instead of Mr. Swinnen taking the lead, Winston moved to the edge of his chair. His eyebrows pulled together and deep creases settled across his forehead. "Do you honestly expect us to believe you've located a benefactor who is willing to pay off your debt?"

"Aye. I expect you to believe me, because it's the truth I'm telling you. I'm sure you both have your doubts, but if you'll give us a bit more time so we can discover what's happened, you can be sure the debt will be paid."

Winston rubbed his forehead. "We agreed before you arrived this morning that the bank is willing to give you two weeks to move from the property. We believe that amount of time is extremely generous. Though I doubt you have a benefactor or you'll have the money to pay off your debt, we won't extend that period of time. In truth, you should likely use the time to begin moving from the property."

Winston and Mr. Swinnen exchanged a

quick look before the banker took up the conversation. "I understand you want additional time, but in order to protect the stockholders, we must have the property on the market as soon as possible. I simply cannot agree to more than the two weeks. Either you pay off your debt by then, or you must vacate the premises."

Winston steepled his fingers and leaned forward. "Tell me, Ewan, who is this benefactor you've mentioned?" His lips curled in a wry smile. "I'm trying to think of anyone you may know who is financially capable of paying off your debt. For the life of me, I can't think of a soul." His brows dipped low, and he hesitated for a moment. "Please tell me Frances Woodfield hasn't decided to fund the brickyard she sold you less than a year ago."

Ewan pushed up from his chair. "Put yourself at ease, Winston. It isn't Mrs. Woodfield, but I'll say nothing more about our benefactor."

Winston guffawed. "Well, one thing is certain — he's as invisible as a snowstorm in July."

"Let's go, Uncle Hugh." Ewan nodded to Mr. Swinnen. "We'll be back with the money before the two weeks is up, so don't make any plans to sell the business."

The banker cleared his throat. "I feel I should tell you that we've located a prospective buyer, Mr. McKay. He's eager to take possession of the brickyard, so don't be late with your payment."

"And who is this buyer, Mr. Swinnen?" Hugh jumped to his feet. "Seems strange there's someone chompin' at the bit to buy the brickyard when Winston was having a terrible time trying to sell the place when we were looking for a suitable brickyard."

Winston didn't give Mr. Swinnen an opportunity to respond. "When the yard was sitting idle, it was a hard sell. But now that you have it up and operational, there's greater appeal." His words carried an undeniable air of pomposity.

"I didn't hear a name mentioned in your answer, Mr. Hawkins." Hugh turned toward the door. "Or is your buyer as invisible as a snowstorm in July?" Hugh snorted and waved to his nephew. "Come on, Ewan."

Winston stood and frowned. "Joke while you may, Hugh, but it's I who will have the last laugh."

They'd walked only a few steps out of the bank when Winston called Ewan's name. He turned and waited as Winston stalked toward them. He glanced at Hugh. "I'd like a word alone with Ewan."

445

The older man arched his brows in question. When Ewan gave a slight nod, his uncle returned the gesture. "I'll meet you back at the hotel."

"What is it you want, Winston?" Ewan's world was crumbling around him. He truly didn't want to talk to Winston. If the man hoped to ply the name of their benefactor from him, he was going to be very disappointed.

"It's Laura that's been trying to help you arrange for payment of the bank loan, isn't it?" His words were laced with venom. "I know she fancies you, and you may think you've won, but you haven't." His eyes shimmered with hatred. "I'd wager Laura hasn't told you she can't ever bear you a child. Believe me, she's not the prize you think she is." He sneered and gave Ewan a slight shove. "Go ahead and ask her. She'll know I've told you, and she'll have to admit the truth."

Ewan shook his head. "You're a pitiful shell of a man, Winston. Laura has already told me about the accident that happened years ago and what the doctor told her parents. None of that matters to me. I love Laura and hope to marry her. Whether she can have a child is not what influences my love or desire to spend my life with her.

With or without children, I believe our love will sustain us."

Winston snorted. "Love? We'll see how long that lasts. Have you taken time to consider that the two of you have nothing in common? She is a woman who has had many advantages, and her associations are with people of a different — shall we say higher — class than you and your family. Do you truly think she will remain happy in the surroundings you'll provide?" He shook his head and sneered. "Whether you're able to pay off your debt or not, I see the makings of a disaster."

"Disaster?" Anger welled in Ewan's chest, and he squeezed his hands into tight fists. He longed to wipe that sneer off Winston's face, yet such behavior would be breaking his promise to God. Violence in any form would only reinforce Winston's misguided beliefs. There was nothing Ewan could say or do that would change the man's skewed thinking. Ewan shrugged one shoulder. "Bring your prediction to me after we've been married for ten years. Then we'll see who is right."

Under other circumstances, Ewan might have spoken with more conviction. But after this morning's debacle, he wondered if Winston was right. Once Laura learned Mr. Lofton hadn't appeared and the brickyard was still in jeopardy, would she still consider a future with him? He wanted to believe it wouldn't matter, yet he knew she was committed to the success of the brickyard. And there was no denying she was accustomed to a life of ease among the wealthy. He couldn't expect her to marry him if they lost the brickyard.

Panic and sadness took hold as he continued toward the hotel. If Mr. Lofton didn't keep his word, how would they survive? He could seek work as a brick burner at one of the brickyards they'd surveyed during their journey to West Virginia, but he hadn't come to America to work as a brick burner for the rest of his life. He'd never earn enough money to own his own business or give his sisters the life he'd promised them.

"Pick your lip up off the ground, boy. We've got only two weeks, so we do na have time for sulking and cryin' over spilt milk." Hugh grasped Ewan by the arm. "Leave your horse. We need to make a stop before we head for home."

Side by side, the two of them walked the short distance to the telegraph office, where the operator prepared and sent a message to Mr. Lofton. Ewan's insides roiled as he dictated the message. What if Mr. Lofton

448

didn't respond? Surely he'd intended to meet them, or he wouldn't have made a reservation at the hotel. Ewan clung to that tiny thread of hope as they departed the office.

His uncle donned his hat and straightened his shoulders as though nothing had gone amiss. "We should hear something back within the next couple of days. With the two weeks the bank gave us, there's still plenty of time to get things settled before Winston comes knocking on our door with his legal papers."

His uncle's affable conduct was so out of character that Ewan came to a halt. "Do ya not realize how serious this is, Uncle? What if Mr. Lofton has decided he doesn't want to help us?"

"Now don't be talking such nonsense, Ewan. I don't recall the last time I was so impressed by a man. I'm thinking he had some sort of urgent situation and missed his train. Once we hear from him, we'll have the matter settled." His uncle chuckled. "If not, I may have to break my word and go back to the gaming tables." Ewan opened his mouth to protest, but his uncle held up his hand. "Don't get yourself all riled up. I was only joking with ya."

Ewan gave his uncle a sideways glance. "I

449

hope so, Uncle Hugh. The gaming tables will only cause more problems." After mounting their horses, Ewan came alongside his uncle. "I think I'll stop at the orphanage. Laura's helping there this morning. She may have some idea of why Mr. Lofton didn't appear."

Hugh nodded. "I might as well come along. I'd like to know what she has to say, as well."

"If she has any advice, I'll stop by your house on my way home." Ewan hoped to talk to Laura alone and discover whether this turn of events would affect their future. If Mr. Lofton didn't pay off their debt, Ewan feared losing more than the brickyard. But broaching the subject of their future with Laura would be impossible if Uncle Hugh was at his side.

"Na. 'Tis easier if I come along with ya. I've never been in the orphanage, so it will give me a chance to have a look at the place."

His uncle's desire to look at the orphanage was as strange as his demeanor had been when they'd sent the telegram. Ewan considered questioning the inexplicable changes he'd observed in his uncle's behavior but decided this wasn't the right moment; he simply didn't have the strength.

The bell over the front door of the orphanage brought Mrs. Tremble scurrying to the entrance. She smiled at Ewan. "So good to have you with us again, Mr. McKay." Though he'd only visited the orphanage with Laura on a couple of occasions, Mrs. Tremble greeted him as though he'd been a frequent visitor.

She glanced in Hugh's direction. "Good morning, sir. I don't believe we've met. I'm Sophia Tremble, the director of the orphanage."

"Hugh Crothers," Hugh said with a smile. "Pleased to meet you, Mrs. Tremble."

"I was hoping to have a word with Laura, Mrs. Tremble. Is she in the other room?" Ewan glanced over the director's shoulder.

"She is. It's story time, but I can get someone to take over for her. If you'll wait for a moment, I'll tell Laura you're here."

Ewan nodded, but Uncle Hugh stepped forward. "I'd be pleased to have a look around, Mrs. Tremble. If it wouldn't interfere too much."

Her lips curved in a warm smile. "We're always pleased to have visitors view our facility, Mr. Crothers. Follow me."

Ewan stared after his uncle's departing form. The man's behavior continued to baffle him. Nothing he'd said or done throughout the morning fit his uncle's usual character. It was as though Uncle Hugh had gone through some wonderful transformation. Had his uncle truly made a change, or was this merely an act of some sort?

"Ewan! I didn't expect to see you this morning." Laura grinned. "And I certainly didn't expect to see your uncle visiting with the children and touring the building. He seemed very interested. Perhaps Kathleen's condition has caused him to think about fatherless children."

Ewan shrugged and shook his head. "I'm not sure what's come over him. Even with all our bad news, he's been a different man this morning."

Laura glanced over her shoulder as she led him toward the simple wooden chairs that lined the stark room. "What bad news?" She frowned. "Did the bank attempt to add additional charges to your loan? If so . . ."

He shook his head and met her puzzled gaze. "Nay. I wish it had been as simple as that." For the next several minutes, Ewan detailed their meeting at the bank. As he spoke, he watched and weighed her every movement, hoping to distinguish what she was thinking, what all of this would mean for their future.

"Now that you've sent the telegram, I

452

don't think there's anything more that can be done except await Mr. Lofton's response." She reached forward and grasped Ewan's hand. "I'm certain there's some good reason why he didn't appear. Mr. Lofton isn't a man who goes back on his word."

"I'm not thinkin' he is, but the fact remains that we have only two weeks. Do you think I should take the train to Wheeling?"

"No. If need be, you can go to meet with him in Wheeling after you've received word back from him. Right now, I think it's best to wait."

Her troubled countenance worried him. "And what if this arrangement with Mr. Lofton doesn't take place? What happens to us if we lose the brickyard, Laura?"

She stood and glanced toward the doorway as Mrs. Tremble and Hugh strode toward them. "We're not going to even consider such an outcome, Ewan."

Moments later Uncle Hugh was at his side.

There would be no further questions about the future today.

CHAPTER 28

Throughout the night, Ewan had prayed — and worried. He'd hoped to receive a telegram today, but none had been forth-coming. And there would be no telegram on Sunday — the telegraph office was closed.

Sunday he sat in church, but in spite of the pastor's sermon, he was unable to cast his cares upon the Lord. He tried. His desire still remained strong. Yet he simply couldn't turn loose of the fears that besieged him at every turn. What if Mr. Lofton didn't respond? What if Laura returned to Win-ston? What if the girls were relegated to a life no better than they'd left in Ireland? What if all the men who worked at the brickyard ended up jobless and unable to support their families? What if, what if, what if. His head throbbed with a thousand ques-tions, but no answers.

He and Uncle Hugh agreed that if they

didn't receive a return telegram by Wednesday, Ewan would travel to Wheeling. Ewan would have preferred to leave on Tuesday, but his uncle hadn't agreed. "Give the man time to respond. I'm sure we'll have word by Wednesday."

And though there hadn't been word from Mr. Lofton himself, Uncle Hugh received a telegram on Wednesday morning before Ewan departed for the train station. "Not the best news," he said as he extended his hand and offered the telegram to Ewan.

Ewan's fingers trembled as he unfolded the piece of paper and read the contents. The blood rushed from his head, and he swayed for a moment before grasping the edge of the table. "What now? Am I still to go to Wheeling?"

His uncle hesitated for only a moment. "Aye. 'Tis best for you to be there. If nothing changes by the middle of next week, I'll seek Mrs. Woodfield's help."

"Nay. You should go and talk to her today. We don't know what the future holds. It will be better if we're prepared. She may have some other plan to help us hold off the foreclosure." The clock struck the hour and Ewan glanced toward the door. "I need to be on my way or I'll miss the train."

When he arrived at the station, he was

surprised to see Laura waiting for him.

"I was hoping you'd heard from Herman and you wouldn't appear," she said.

He forced a grim smile. "Uncle Hugh received a telegram early this morning from Mr. Lofton's butler. While on the way to the train station on Thursday, Mr. Lofton suffered a seizure of some sort. He's been unconscious since then."

Laura clasped a hand to her bodice. "How tragic. Mother will be devastated to hear this news." She touched his hand. "This truly creates a difficult situation for you and your uncle. I'm glad you're going to Wheeling. Be sure to send word of Mr. Lofton's condition once you arrive."

The train chugged into the station, the wheels screeching on the iron rails as the brakes grabbed hold and brought the train to a halt. Laura remained at his side while he purchased his ticket. Together they walked to the platform.

He longed to ask her what would happen between them if they didn't find some way to save the brickyard, but the words stuck in his throat. Right now, he was afraid to hear her answer.

Day after day, he visited Mr. Lofton's hospital room. Day after day, Mr. Lofton's

456

condition remained the same. Ewan prayed, but he felt as though his prayers were no more than hollow words. Utterings that went no further than the four walls of the hospital room. Each day he'd sent a telegram to his uncle. Each day it said the same thing: No change. Tomorrow he would return to Bartlett. His uncle had sent instructions for him to return if there was no change by Monday evening.

His hopes dashed, Ewan boarded the return train early Tuesday morning. He had hoped to carry some bit of encouraging news back home. Instead he would be the bearer of bad news. Uncle Hugh hadn't mentioned any alternate plan, but he hoped his uncle would greet him with a solution to the pending disaster they would face on Friday morning. There was little doubt they would lose everything.

Uncle Hugh was waiting when he stepped off the train. "Do ya have any good word for me, boy?"

"Nay. I wish that I did, but Mr. Lofton was the same when I left him as the day I arrived. The doctor said he could be this way for months, but there's always the chance he'll wake up from his deep sleep at any moment. No one but the good Lord himself knows for sure." Ewan sighed. "I hope you've come up with some other solution while I've been gone." His uncle's grim expression said it all. On Friday, they would lose everything. "Did you speak to Mrs. Woodfield? Did she have any ideas?"

"We had a good talk and between us tried to come up with another way we might save the yard. She's willing to go with us tomorrow and speak to Mr. Swinnen. She isn't sure it will help, but I think we should accept the offer." His uncle clapped him on the shoulder. "I haven't been to the gaming tables, but there's a game this evening. I think it's our only chance."

Ewan shook his head. "I'd rather lose everything than have you go back to your old ways, Uncle Hugh. I think it might be better if we spend our night in prayer rather than at a card table."

The nighttime hours moved as slow as molasses in winter. Ewan paced the length of his small room and longed to find answers to the questions his sisters had asked upon his return. Were they going to return to a life of poverty? Would they have to leave Bartlett and Miss Laura? If so, where would they live? Would Uncle Hugh and Aunt Maggie be angry with them forever? Would Uncle Hugh have to move from his big house? They'd peppered him with question upon question until he'd retreated to his room with a throbbing headache.

He'd finally dropped into bed, but the night had been fraught with nightmares that left him feeling as though he'd not slept at all. Dark circles rimmed his eyes when he entered the dining room the next morning.

"What's going to happen to us, Ewan?" Adaira met him in the doorway, her eyes shining with fear.

He leaned down and embraced her in a tight hug. "I don't know, Adaira, but you must remember that we are a family, and no matter what happens, we'll be together. As long as we have each other, we can face whatever happens."

Ainslee rushed to her sister's side. "What can we do to help, Ewan?"

Their obvious desire to help touched him. "The very best thing you can do is pray that all goes well at our meeting this morning."

He ached to give them greater assurance, but how could he? At the moment, he feared his nightmares would become reality. Mrs. Woodfield's offer to attend the meeting had given Uncle Hugh hope and encouragement, but Ewan didn't share those feelings. She'd hold no sway over a banker set upon helping his stockholders, and her attendance would likely set Winston on edge. At first, Uncle Hugh had disagreed with Ewan's assessment, but he finally relented. After all, there was little she could do. She'd secured help from Mr. Lofton. They should ask no more of her.

Ewan insisted upon a stop at the telegraph office before going to the bank. "It makes little difference if we're a few minutes late. It will change nothing, and I want to be certain no word was received from Mr. Lofton earlier this morning."

He'd done his best to keep his hopes tamped down, but when the telegraph operator smiled at him, he took it as a good sign. The man tipped his head. "Morning, Mr. McKay. I s'pose you and your uncle are still looking for a telegram from Wheeling."

"We are, and I hope that smile means you have a telegram for us."

The telegraph operator's lips dipped into a frown. "I always smile at customers when they come in the front door, but that doesn't mean I have a telegram for you. Truth is, I've not received any messages all morning."

Ewan's chest caved as he let out a long sigh and turned to his uncle. "Let's get this over with. No need to prolong the agony. It seems the Lord has said no to our prayers."

His uncle matched Ewan's gait as the two men strode to the bank. "Aye, it would seem that way." Hugh pulled out his pocket watch. "And to make matters worse, we're five minutes late. Winston will be in a foul mood for sure."

A clerk stood near the front door waiting to escort them into Mr. Swinnen's office. He tugged on his vest and shot a disapproving look at Ewan. "You're late. You've kept Mr. Swinnen and the others waiting."

Ewan hadn't taken note of the clerk's reference to the "others" until he entered the bank president's office. There was a stranger seated across the desk from Mr. Swinnen. Ewan had never before seen the man. Was this then the man interested in purchasing the brickyard?

Hugh stepped into the room behind Ewan and glanced around. "Who have we here? I don't believe I know this gentleman."

The small-framed man popped to his feet and extended his hand. "Edward Glasco, Mr. Crothers." He nodded at Ewan. "You must be Mr. McKay."

"Aye, that I am," Ewan said. "Have you been invited to this meeting for some special reason, Mr. Glasco?"

Winston glanced back and forth between

Ewan and Mr. Glasco. "We didn't invite him, and he won't tell us why he's here. We assumed you'd invited him."

"I'm Mr. Lofton's secretary. He instructed me to come here on his behalf."

Ewan drew close to Mr. Glasco. "How is Mr. Lofton's health? When I was in Wheeling —"

"Mr. Lofton is doing much better, but obviously his physician advised against traveling. He's been most concerned about your circumstances. He read the letter you left for him at the hospital and was thankful you'd received the additional time to pay your debt." Mr. Glasco reached into his breast pocket and withdrew an envelope. "He asked that I deliver this to you." He extended the envelope. "That concludes my business here, so if you gentlemen will excuse me, I'd like to catch the next train to Wheeling."

Mr. Swinnen and Winston both remained silent until Mr. Lofton's secretary exited the room, and then both turned toward Ewan. Winston pointed to the envelope. "What's this about? Did Laura and her mother convince Herman Lofton to come to your aid?"

Ewan reached into the envelope, withdrew the bank draft, and handed it to his uncle.

Hugh gave a firm nod, then handed the draft to Mr. Swinnen. "I believe that concludes our business, gentlemen. You can now set aside your concerns over the brickyard."

Hugh nudged Ewan as they departed the bank. "You were wrong about that answer, my boy — and so was I, but I have to say the good Lord sure did make us wait for His answer this time!"

CHAPTER 29

January 1870

Using the arm of the divan to help propel her forward, Kathleen struggled to stand. The girl's swollen feet would no longer fit into anything other than a pair of soft slippers Laura had knit for her. "The doctor says this swelling isn't a good sign, and I shouldn't use salt on my food, but even that hasn't helped."

Laura offered a slight smile. Kathleen's feet looked like overstuffed sausages ready to burst from their casings. "Perhaps you should prop up your feet. Did the doctor mention anything other than decreasing salt?"

Kathleen shuffled toward the parlor door. "Nay, but I'm weary of sitting. I do wish I could go for a long walk, but just these few steps cause pain."

Laura stood and hurried to Kathleen's side. "Then let me help you down the hallway. You can sit on your bed with your feet propped."

Once settled, Kathleen grasped Laura's hand. "I want to speak with you and your mother when you have a little time." She rested her hands on her protruding stomach. "About the future."

The baby was expected in March, and Kathleen had grown increasingly uncomfortable as time passed. Mrs. Woodfield had recently transformed the library into a bedroom so the young woman wouldn't have to climb the cumbersome stairway to the second floor. Also, the library provided a lovely view of the mountains.

Later, when Laura carried the message to her mother, the older woman frowned. "I hope this has nothing to do with the message she received from her sister yesterday." Mrs. Woodfield shook her head. "Though she tried to hide her tears from me, I'm afraid the note from Margaret caused Kathleen a great deal of pain." She steadied her gaze on Laura. "Did she reveal the contents to you?"

"Not a word. She merely said she wanted to talk to us about the future."

Mrs. Woodfield massaged her forehead. "I wonder if Margaret has seen the error of her ways and wants Kathleen to return to

Crothers Mansion before the baby is born. If Kathleen leaves, I hope Dr. Balch will agree to continue her care."

"No need to worry, Mother. We both know it doesn't help a whit."

"Easier said than done, my dear." Mrs. Woodfield stepped to the kitchen door and instructed Catherine to bring tea to the library and then waved Laura to follow her. "Let's see what Kathleen wants to discuss."

Kathleen was standing and gazing out the French doors leading to the garden when Laura and her mother entered the room. She turned toward the two women while supporting her back with one hand. "My lower back seems to ache no matter whether I'm sitting, standing, or lying in bed. I suppose all women go through this."

"Some more than others, I think," Mrs. Woodfield said. "Would you like to sit down? We can adjust a pillow behind you. I really think it's better if you keep your feet propped."

Kathleen agreed. While Laura placed a pillow and a thin folded blanket behind the young woman's back, Mrs. Woodfield sat down on the divan. "Laura tells me you want to talk about the future."

A fleeting look of hesitation shone in Kathleen's eyes, but she nodded her head.

She reached to the table beside her chair and picked up an envelope. "I'm sure you know my sister had a message delivered to me yesterday."

"Yes, though I have no idea of the contents." Mrs. Woodfield glanced at Laura.

"Nor do I, but Catherine did tell us you'd received a message from Crothers Mansion." Laura wanted Kathleen to understand that the household staff kept them apprised of anything delivered to the house, but no one had read or ever would read her private mail.

The girl forced a smile. "I think I should tell you the contents of the message." Her voice hitched. "Margaret wrote to tell me that Terrance O'Grady was married a few days ago." Her body quaked as she attempted to hold back her sobs. "Margaret said she wanted me to know so that I wouldn't hold out hope that Terrance might change his mind and marry me before the babe is born. She said it would be best for all concerned if I no longer lived in the area. Why did she feel the need to put a knife in my heart?"

Mrs. Woodfield sighed. "Perhaps we should give Margaret the benefit of the doubt. Rather than attempting to hurt you, she may have hoped to soften the blow by sending the information before anyone else carried the news to our doorstep. Right now, you must focus on your health and that of the unborn child. Becoming distressed won't serve you or the child well at this time."

"I know you're right, Mrs. Woodfield, but ever since I came here, I've been praying Margaret would change her mind and welcome me back home. When the letter arrived, I thought maybe . . ." Kathleen sniffed as unbidden tears flowed down her cheeks. "I should have known better. Now that I know she will never accept me or the baby back into her home, I've made some decisions." Kathleen reached for Laura's hand. "I will need help from both of you to carry out my plan, but please don't agree unless it is truly what you think is best for all of us.

"Shortly after I arrived, your mother mentioned a friend who owns a millinery in New York. She offered to write the woman and see if she'd be willing to train me so that I could learn a skill and support myself. I do think it would be easier for me to begin over if I moved away from here."

Laura wasn't surprised by her mother's generosity. Kathleen would need to support herself, and without proper training, it would be difficult. She could seek work as a housekeeper or maid in Fairmont or Wheeling, but many of those positions were already being filled by war widows.

Kathleen glanced toward the door as Catherine stepped into the library with a tea tray, then quietly exited. "If I remain here, I can't support myself or the child, and there would be nothing but heartache for both of us. I think it would be best if I left."

"And the baby?" Laura's gaze moved to Kathleen's swollen belly. "How will you care for the child and complete your training at the millinery shop?"

She squeezed Laura's hand. "That's the part I must discuss with you. I know you and Ewan plan to marry, and it is my hope that the two of you would raise my baby as your own."

Laura's breath caught. She and Ewan had spoken of marriage, and they both acted as if marriage was in their future. Still, Ewan hadn't formally proposed. "I would be honored to raise your baby, and it would give me great joy, Kathleen, but Ewan hasn't yet asked me to marry him, so I can't give you a definite answer to the question you've posed."

Her mother sighed. "Ewan hasn't yet

asked for your hand, but he spoke with me recently, and I gave my blessing to your marriage." Laura's mouth dropped open, but before she could speak, her mother hurried on. "I know I've ruined the proposal for him, but I don't think he would want Kathleen fretting about the future of the baby." Mrs. Woodfield looked at Laura. "And we both know he loves children and will be delighted to raise Kathleen's child."

Laura didn't know what surprised her more: Kathleen's request that she and Ewan raise the baby or the fact that Ewan had already asked and received her mother's permission for them to wed.

When Laura had finally gathered her thoughts, she turned toward Kathleen. "Even though my mother and Ewan have spoken, I would like an opportunity to talk with him and gauge his reaction. I'm sure that Mother is correct and he will be more than delighted to raise your child, but I do think we should talk before I accept on his behalf."

"I think that's best, as well." Kathleen glanced at Mrs. Woodfield. "If Ewan agrees, will you send word to your friend?"

"I must be truthful with you, Kathleen. I took the liberty of writing to her shortly after we first discussed the matter. I've recently received her answer. She said she'd be delighted to have you as her new assistant. Her letter states that there are living quarters above the shop that she no longer uses, and you may live there as long as you'd like." Mrs. Woodfield leaned back in her chair, a pleased expression on her face. "I know you will learn quickly and be an asset to the shop."

A slight blush colored Kathleen's cheeks. "Thank you, Mrs. Woodfield. I can never repay the kindness you and Laura have shown me."

"If we've helped you, then I suggest you do the same for someone else if the opportunity should ever present itself in the future." Mrs. Woodfield smiled at the girl. "That was my husband's philosophy. He helped any number of people during his lifetime, and those same people are now helping others. I hope you will do the same."

"And is that *your* philosophy as well, Mrs. Woodfield?" Kathleen searched the older woman's face.

"I agree with my husband's idea, Kathleen, but I prefer the verse in the book of Luke that says, 'And as ye would that men should do to you, do ye also to them likewise.' " Mrs. Woodfield lifted her cup and took a sip of tea. "It's not always possible to do something tangible, but we can always treat others with dignity and grace."

Laura nodded her agreement, but her thoughts weren't on the philosophy of either her mother or father. Rather, she'd slipped into a somewhat bewildered state over what might transpire during the upcoming months. She'd told Kathleen she would speak with Ewan, but how would one go about bringing up such a delicate topic without seeming like a besotted spinster hoping to land a husband by any means available? Ewan had certainly expressed his love for her, and he'd asked her mother for her hand in marriage. So why hadn't he spoken to her? He could have had a change of heart by now.

Laura's palms turned damp at the thought of mentioning marriage to Ewan and being rejected. She could think of no reason he might have changed his mind, but he'd had ample opportunities to ask for her hand. So why hadn't he?

"Ewan is coming for dinner this evening, so Laura can speak with him tonight, Kathleen."

Laura snapped to attention at her mother's comment. "Tonight?" Her voice cracked, and she swallowed hard. "Perhaps it would be better to wait a few days until we've all had time to . . . to . . ." She struggled to think of some reason that would make sense to the other two women. They both continued to stare at her. "To digest what we've decided," she finally said.

"Nonsense. There's nothing to digest, Laura. It's not as if we've eaten a large meal. What is there that needs any further thought? You need to speak with Ewan this evening so Kathleen can set her mind at ease."

Kathleen nodded her agreement while Laura downed the remains of her tea. "I believe I'll go upstairs and decide what I shall wear for dinner this evening."

Her mother beamed. "That's a wonderful idea. You should consider the violet gown with the deep rose ribbons. It's lovely with your complexion, and I don't think Ewan has seen it."

Laura made her way to the library door. She'd mentioned the matter of clothing only as an excuse to leave the room and formulate her thoughts. She doubted whether her choice of gown would be foremost in Ewan's mind once she broached the subject of marriage and the adoption of Kathleen's child. If only she had a little longer to contemplate the proper way to handle this matter. Then again, there was no proper way. Etiquette books simply did not give instructions on how a woman should propose to a man!

CHAPTER 30

Laura stood in stunned silence when the maid escorted Ewan and Hugh into the parlor. Ewan's sheepish look revealed his discomfort over the situation. Hugh hadn't been invited to dinner, and his appearance was completely unexpected.

Catherine hesitated for a moment and glanced toward the upper hallway. Mrs. Woodfield hadn't yet come downstairs, and the maid was obviously flummoxed over the appearance of an extra dinner guest. "Shall I set an extra place for dinner?" Her gaze traveled between Laura and Mr. Crothers.

Hugh didn't wait for Laura to respond. "Why thank you. I'd be pleased to join you for supper. I have some exciting news to share with the ladies, and enjoying a good meal will make it all the better."

Catherine glanced at Laura and shrugged. Laura knew the maid would do her best to stretch the meal. She'd learned to serve smaller portions to the ladies when an unexpected guest arrived. Still, Laura didn't understand why Ewan hadn't sent one of the girls over to the house to let them know in advance. Or why Hugh hadn't sent a note, for that matter.

For the past two hours, she'd been rehearsing what she would say to Ewan. But with Hugh present, it would likely be impossible. Now that she'd finally gathered her courage and prepared her speech, she found Hugh's appearance annoying.

Laura gestured for the men to be seated as she sat down in a chair facing the stairway. "I can't imagine what is of such importance that you believed it necessary to join us for dinner, Mr. Crothers."

Hugh guffawed. "Is that a polite way of saying you're unhappy I appeared uninvited, Miss Woodfield?"

Heat climbed up Laura's neck. "I wouldn't go so far as to say I'm unhappy. Rather, I would say I was taken aback. Since we live in such close proximity, I merely assumed someone would have sent word in advance."

Hugh bobbed his head. "Aye, that would usually be the way of things, but circumstances worked out in such a way that I have the pleasure of dining with you and your fine mother. When I arrived at Ewan's house, he was leaving to come here. And since I wanted to share my good news with your mother and you, I decided there was no time like the present." He leaned back and smiled like a cat that had discovered a bowl of cream.

"Well, I'm pleased to hear it's good news you have to share with us." At the sound of her mother's footfalls on the stairs, Laura glanced toward the hall. "I do believe Mother is going to join us."

The two men stood as Mrs. Woodfield entered the room. Though her mother quickly recovered, Laura hadn't missed the fleeting look of disbelief that shone in her eyes when she spotted Hugh. "Isn't this a surprise! I didn't realize you were joining us, Hugh."

" 'Tis a bit of a surprise for all of you. I caught Ewan as he was leaving home to come here and invited myself to come along. I'm not one to often stick me nose in where it isn't wanted, but I have some news that wouldn't wait — good news."

"I'm pleased to hear it's good news. Did you plan to share it with us now?" Mrs. Woodfield sat down and folded her hands in her lap.

"I'll share it whenever you'd like, but I was first going to ask about Kathleen. I know it doesn't appear anyone cares about the girl, but I'm truly sorry that Margaret has taken such a hard position with her sister. I've made enough mistakes that I think Margaret should welcome the girl back home, but she'll not hear of it. I was maybe hoping to see her for a minute or two so's to cheer her a wee bit."

Mrs. Woodfield's shoulders stiffened. "After we've finished dinner, I'll ask Kathleen if she'd like to visit with you. If she's willing, I certainly have no objection."

Catherine stepped into the parlor and whispered in Mrs. Woodfield's ear and then disappeared down the hallway. The older woman gestured to the three of them. "Catherine tells me dinner is ready. If you'll follow me?"

After they had finished the first course, Catherine began to clear their soup bowls. Laura turned her attention to Mr. Crothers. "When you arrived, you said you had some good news to share. I'm eager to hear what it is, Mr. Crothers."

The older man settled back in his chair. "Glad I am to share this with you before news spreads throughout all of Bartlett."

Mrs. Woodfield perked to attention. "You've piqued my interest, Hugh. Is there something afoot in Bartlett that has slipped

478

by me?"

"I'm sure it has, though you'll likely be asked to join in the effort very soon." Hugh tugged on his mustache, obviously enjoying his moment of importance. "You remember that Mr. Lofton told me about how your husband had helped him and that he'd helped others since that time?"

"Yes, of course I remember." Mrs. Woodfield leaned back as Catherine placed the serving bowls on the table. "He instructed you to do the same when you had an opportunity."

"Aye. And that's what I'm here to tell you. I'm doing me own bit of good to help others."

"And what might that be, Uncle Hugh?"

"You recall the day I went with ya to the orphans' home?" When Ewan nodded, Hugh grinned. "Mrs. Tremble walked me through the place, and the building is in a terrible state of disrepair. That frame building has seen better days, and the roof is in terrible shape, as well, so I've given me pledge to supply all the bricks to construct the Bartlett Widows and Orphans Home." He leaned back in his chair and smiled at each of them. "I think it's the least I can do, since Mr. Lofton was so good to help us with the brickyard." While Mrs. Woodfield quietly spoke to the maid, Hugh lowered his voice and leaned closer to Ewan. "And maybe it's me way of making amends to Lyall Montclair, as well."

"I'm guessing Montclair would rather have his money, but I'm pleased you're finally acknowledging the error of your ways, Uncle Hugh."

Mrs. Woodfield returned her focus to Hugh and Ewan. "I'm sorry for my lack of attention, but Catherine requested a bit of instruction." The maid immediately picked up the platter of roast chicken and passed it to Mr. Crothers, who forked a generous serving onto his plate.

"I must say that I am truly surprised by this news. I'd heard nothing of constructing a new facility that would house both widows and orphans, but I think it is an admirable project. I'm delighted to hear that you've offered to donate bricks for the building. Such a significant gift will surely permit construction to begin in the spring." She motioned to Catherine, who handed the bowl of potatoes to Hugh. "Have they selected a piece of land or are they hoping someone will step forward and donate the property?"

Hugh spooned a large helping of potatoes onto his plate. "Mrs. Tremble tells me there was a piece of land donated to the orphanage some years ago. It's located on the edge of town, in walking distance to stores and to the school. I did not see the land for myself."

"I'm pleased you shared this news with me. I believe our Ladies of the Union group will want to be of help on this endeavor as well. We've been looking for projects where we can be of assistance. Who should I contact to offer our help?"

Hugh hesitated a moment. "Josiah Pritchett."

Laura looked up and met Hugh's gaze. "Josiah Pritchett? The man who's running against Winston for the legislature?"

Hugh grinned. "Aye, the very same. I'm thinking it might give him a bit of an edge here in Bartlett, so we're planning on moving as quickly as possible." He nudged Ewan's arm. "Once spring arrives, you may have to keep the lads working overtime on this one,"

"We'll do what we can, Uncle Hugh, but I wish you would have talked with me first. We already have a lot of orders to fill, orders that will pay our outstanding debts."

"Let's don't be talking business in front of the ladies, Ewan. There's time for that tomorrow. Right now, I think we need to be pleased at the good that will come from building this home for them that's in need. I'm even thinking it might be a place where Kathleen might find a bit of work and be able to care for herself and the wee one."

Mrs. Woodfield poured a dollop of cream into her coffee and stirred. "I don't think you need to worry over Kathleen or the baby. We're happy to have them living with us. I believe she's already seeking out her own plan for the future. Not that I'm discounting what you're doing, Mr. Crothers, but I think Kathleen is going to want to do more with her life than clean and cook in a home for widows and orphans, don't you?"

Hugh grunted. " 'Tis honest work and nothing shameful about what I'm suggesting. The home will be a fine place, and it will give the wee one other children to play with. There are many living in much worse circumstances. She could make an honest living and not have to worry about safety for herself or the child."

Mrs. Woodfield took a sip of her coffee. "That's true, but Kathleen deserves the opportunity to discover her talents. Of course, the final decision rests with her, but it's nice to hear that you were thinking of her."

"I'm not as coldhearted as you might

think, Mrs. Woodfield. If it was up to me, Kathleen would still be living under our roof. But the girl is Margaret's sister, and I agreed to abide by Margaret's decision. I was thinkin' that if Kathleen should go to work at the widows and orphans home, maybe Margaret will one day see the error of her ways and bring Kathleen and the child back home."

"I don't mean to imply you are cold-hearted, Hugh, but from what Kathleen has told me, it doesn't appear your wife will ever accept her back into the family fold." Mrs. Woodfield trained her gaze upon Hugh. "To return Kathleen and the child to your home could prove painful for both Kathleen and the child, since your wife has been clear about her position. She believes Kathleen and the child are a blight upon the social status of your family."

Hugh twirled the end of his mustache. "I will not disagree that Margaret is determined to be accepted into society. I blame her deprived childhood for what you consider improper behavior, and I tend to make allowances where I sometimes shouldn't. But I must remember that she has had to make allowances for my bad choices, as well."

Mrs. Woodfield's shoulders sagged at his

rebuttal. "I do not mean to judge you or your wife, Mr. Crothers. That was not my intent. I only wish to see Kathleen and her child have a peaceful and happy life. I do not think that will happen in the Bartlett Widows and Orphans Home, nor do I think it will happen at Crothers Mansion."

Hugh shrugged. "The girl does not have many choices. I doubt you want her to remain under your roof until she dies of old age." He arched his brows. "Or do you?"

"I'm pleased to assist Kathleen with her future plans, but I don't think she will be living here that long." Mrs. Woodfield gestured toward the parlor. "I can't ask you to join me for brandy and cigars, gentlemen, but if you'd care to join Laura and me —"

Before Mrs. Woodfield could finish, Hugh pushed away from the table. "You said you'd ask Kathleen about visiting with me. I'd like to see her now if she's willing."

"Of course. Why don't you have a seat in the parlor? I'll go speak with her."

Laura escorted the men into the parlor, her discomfort increasing as the minutes slowly ticked by. She grappled to make conversation, but Hugh was more interested in pacing than talking. After Laura's final attempt to engage Hugh in a polite exchange, Ewan leaned close and whispered, "Please relax. There's no need to fret."

She wondered if he would encourage her to relax if he knew the speech she had planned for him this evening. Even more, she wondered if she would be saved from the embarrassing talk. Maybe Kathleen would want Ewan nearby while Hugh visited with her. Or maybe Kathleen wouldn't want to see either of them. If that happened, she imagined Hugh would insist the two of them depart. Being rejected by Kathleen would not sit easy with him.

Laura sighed with relief when her mother finally reappeared. Hugh ceased his pacing and crossed the room in several long strides before coming to a halt in front of Mrs. Woodfield. "Well? May I go and visit with Kathleen?"

"She is willing to see you." When Hugh took a step to the right, Mrs. Woodfield touched his arm. "However, she asked that I be present during your visit."

Hugh clenched his jaw. "Why is that? Does she think I'll harm her? She knows I would never do or say anything to intentionally hurt her."

"She thinks it would be improper to receive you in her condition without another woman present. Surely you understand her delicate condition."

Hugh grunted. "Delicate? Back in Ireland, the women work until the day their babe is born."

"But we're not in Ireland, Mr. Crothers. Do you want to see Kathleen or not?"

"Aye." Deep ridges creased his forehead. "Lead the way, Mrs. Woodfield."

Laura's mother stepped to the doorway, then glanced over her shoulder. "This would be a perfect time for you and Ewan to have your little chat, Laura."

Laura's stomach roiled. Why did her mother have to interfere? Broaching the subject would have been much easier without Ewan knowing she had something specific to discuss with him. Her thoughts scrambled as she attempted to recall her carefully prepared speech.

Ewan turned toward her, his lips curved in an alluring smile. "What is it you want to talk about?"

She swallowed hard, her mind reeling. "Will you marry me?"

CHAPTER 31

Unable to maintain his composure, Ewan's mouth dropped open. He'd been struck dumb by Laura's unexpected question and could do no more than stare at her. When she finally nudged him, he cleared his throat and rubbed his jaw. "I always thought that was a question a man asked a woman. Are things different here in West Virginia?"

A deep crimson colored Laura's cheeks, and she turned away from him. He reached out and gently cupped her cheek, turning her head back until she looked into his eyes.

"You're right. A marriage proposal is almost always made by the man, but I was afraid that if I made the speech I had prepared, I'd never ask. So I blurted out the most important question of that speech. I'm sure you think I've lost my mind."

"I would never think such a thing. I think you're quite brave, but I must admit that you caught me by surprise." He chuckled.

"Now that you've asked the most important question, why don't you give me the rest of that speech you prepared. I want to know what was important enough to inspire you with such bravery."

He leaned back, excited to hear what Laura would tell him. He couldn't imagine what would have elicited her proposal, but Mrs. Woodfield obviously had known of the plan, which surprised him. After all, he'd already told Laura's mother of his desire to marry her and had received the woman's blessing. Although he hadn't mentioned a specific date for the proposal, he assumed Mrs. Woodfield would let him choose the proper moment. Obviously, he'd been wrong.

"Recently Kathleen has been making plans for her future and has discussed those ideas with Mother and me."

Ewan nodded. "I'm glad she's giving thought to what she will do once the wee one is born, for there isn't much time before the blessed event will take place."

"Exactly." Laura twisted her handkerchief between her fingers. "There's no other way to say this than to be rather abrupt. Kathleen wants us to raise her child."

"She does?" Understanding slowly washed over him. "I see. You agreed, and now you have proposed."

Laura shook her head. "It's not exactly like that. I didn't agree. I knew I couldn't speak on your behalf, and I told her we weren't even engaged, but Mother said you'd already spoken to her and she'd given her blessing, so I told Kathleen I'd ask you about the baby, but then I proposed, and —" She'd not taken a breath yet and inhaled a gulp of air before continuing. "Then I realized I should have made my proper speech, but —"

He leaned toward her and gently lowered his lips to hers. "You don't need to say anything more, my love." Wrapping her in a warm embrace, he captured her lips in a passionate kiss. When he finally released her, he looked deep into her eyes. "I would marry you this very night, if it were possible."

At the sound of footfalls, they pulled from their embrace and looked toward the hallway. Mrs. Woodfield entered and glanced at the two of them. "I hope we aren't interrupting the two of you."

"We have some additional matters to discuss, but they can wait a bit longer." Ewan looked at his uncle. "Did you have a good visit with Kathleen?"

His uncle twisted the end of his mustache.

"She is content here at Woodfield Manor, and I can see she is cared for quite well. I thought she would be pleased to hear about the widows and orphans home, but it seems she's satisfied with the plans she's already made for her future. She did say that if her arrangement didn't go as hoped, she would give my suggestion consideration." His uncle shrugged his shoulders. "She wasn't willing to share her plans with me. Seems all of it isn't quite settled just yet, but she said when everything was in order, she'd give me the details."

Ewan gave Laura a sidelong glance. "Does Aunt Margaret know that you planned to see Kathleen this evening?" Although his uncle had told Aunt Margaret of his plan to donate bricks, Ewan doubted she knew he was coming to Woodfield Manor or that he would speak with Kathleen.

Hugh shook his head. "And don't you be tellin' her, either. The last thing I need from Margaret is another tongue-lashing." He waved for Ewan to follow him. "Come along, boy. Time we went home."

Ewan remained beside Laura. "You go ahead, Uncle Hugh. It's not far for me to walk. Laura and I haven't finished our talk, but I'll want to visit with you at the brick-yard in the morning."

His uncle hesitated. "About the bricks for the widows and orphans home?"

"That and another matter, as well, but it can wait until tomorrow. Better you get home to Aunt Margaret than to have her worrying about where you might be spending the evening."

"Right you are on that one, my boy." He donned his hat as Mrs. Woodfield escorted him to the front door.

When she'd returned to the parlor, she sat down opposite Ewan and Laura. "I trust you two have had your talk and can now set Kathleen's mind at ease regarding her child."

Ewan smiled at her. "We've gotten as far as me accepting Laura's marriage proposal, but you and Uncle Hugh returned before we'd actually agreed upon raising Kathleen's babe." He reached for Laura's hand. "But I think Laura knows me well enough to realize that I'd be more than happy to call the wee one our own." He inhaled a deep breath. "So since we are soon to become parents, I think the wedding should be taking place as soon as possible." He glanced at Mrs. Woodfield. "Don't you agree?"

"We don't have much time with the baby due to arrive in early March — at least that's what the doctor has predicted." Mrs. Woodfield sighed. "There won't be adequate time to prepare for the elaborate wedding I've always hoped to give Laura."

"I don't want a large wedding, Mother. Something small and intimate here at home would be my preference." She turned to Ewan. "What do you think?"

"I think whatever pleases you will please me. You just tell me the day, time, and place, and I'll be there. Unless you need my help, I'll let you ladies take charge of the wedding."

For the next hour the three of them discussed the wedding, but before Ewan departed, he and Laura went to Kathleen's room and shared their decision with her. The young woman beamed with pleasure when Ewan told her how much he would enjoy raising her child. "Be it boy or girl, Laura and I will raise the babe like our own, Kathleen. You've made a difficult and unselfish decision that will bring us great joy. We can't thank you enough."

Kathleen wiped away a tear. "Thank you both for being so kind and generous. I hope that one day I'll make all of you proud of me." She rested her hand on her stomach. "I know Margaret will never forgive me, but I've asked God to forgive me, and I've asked

Him to show me what was best for the baby and for me. I believe He wants only the best for this child, and I think the two of you are His answer to my prayers."

Ewan stepped forward and placed a kiss on Kathleen's cheek. "You're a brave young woman, Kathleen. I know this has not been easy for you. I've been praying that Aunt Margaret will soon see that she's made a terrible mistake and the two of you can reconcile."

"Whether we reconcile or not, I plan to carry through with the arrangements Mrs. Woodfield is making for me. And no matter what, I know the baby will have a good home with you and Laura."

Laura took Ewan's hand. "I think we should let Kathleen rest. It's been a long evening for her."

Ewan bid the young woman good-bye and walked beside Laura toward the front door. "I think I'd best get back home to the girls. I'm sure they're trying to convince Rose to let them stay up as long as possible." Ewan placed his hand on the ornate bronze doorknob. "Do you want to tell them the news or should I?"

"Why don't we wait and tell them to-gether?"

"You always have the best ideas." He

gathered her in his arms, leaned down, and tenderly kissed her lips.

"I think your idea was even better than mine."

He chuckled and pulled her close. "Then I'd better have one more kiss before I leave for home." Happiness swelled in him as she melted into his arms.

When Hugh didn't appear at the brickyard the following morning, Ewan waited until noon. After placing William McDougal in charge, Ewan advised the foreman that he'd be at Crothers Mansion for a short time. Moments later, Ewan mounted his horse and rode off. His thoughts churned as he urged the horse to a trot. Why did Uncle Hugh have to be so cantankerous? Ewan had been clear last night. He'd told his uncle that he needed to talk to him this morning, so why couldn't the man do as requested this once? Ewan thought they'd parted on good terms last evening, but perhaps his uncle had been angry when Ewan didn't leave with him. By the time he arrived at his uncle's house, Ewan thought he'd considered every possible scenario, and none of them was worthy of his uncle's failure to keep his word.

He lifted the brass knocker on the front

door and banged it several times. Melva was out of breath when she pulled open the heavy door. "Sorry to keep you waiting, Mr. Ewan, but I was cleaning the silver." Though Ewan had told Melva several times that she didn't need to call him Mr. Ewan, Margaret insisted on the practice. Having a distant relative address him in such a manner seemed foolish and demeaning to the woman. Melva stepped close and lowered her voice. "You picked a poor time to come visiting. Mr. Hugh and the missus are having quite a row." She glanced over her shoulder as the sound of escalating voices drifted down the hallway. "You want to come back later?"

Ewan shook his head. "Nay. I want to talk to Uncle Hugh. He was supposed to meet me at the brickyard this morning, but he never showed up."

"Of that, I'm sure. He's been arguing with the missus ever since she came downstairs this morning. I heard Kathleen's name mentioned, and the missus went into one of her tirades."

Ewan nodded. Margaret had been known for her mean-spirited behavior long before she left Ireland, and those who had suffered her wrath stayed clear of her whenever possible — all except her husband, of course.

"Do you want to tell Hugh I'm here, or shall I enter unannounced?"

Dread shone in Melva's eyes. She likely feared she'd become the target of Margaret's fury if she interrupted the couple. "If you do not mind, I'd rather not be the one to disturb them. If you're determined to see Mr. Hugh, you'll find him in the library."

"Thank you, Melva." Before he could change his mind, she scurried off toward the dining room to complete her silver polishing. Ewan shook his head at the idea of Margaret having a maid polish silver. How much her life had changed since moving to West Virginia.

He stood outside the library until there was a slight lull in the argument before he tapped, then immediately opened the door. "Good afternoon." Hoping to ease the tension in the room, he greeted them with a broad smile.

Margaret glared at him. "What are you doing here? Where's Melva? I told her we were not to be interrupted."

Ewan shrugged. "I told her I wouldn't leave. She did her best, so direct your anger at me, not Melva."

"Don't you think I won't. And maybe it's good that you've showed your face, because

I have more than a few words to say to you, too. I hear you were over having dinner with Hugh and the Woodfields last night." She turned an angry look on her husband. "Seems Hugh can't get enough of being charitable, what with building an orphanage and offering to give Kathleen a job and a place to live."

Ewan rested his hip against the large library table. "I don't know what difference it makes if he offered help. She refused, so nothing has changed."

Margaret wagged her index finger back and forth. "It is the principle, Ewan. If you can't see that, then you're not as smart as Hugh thinks. Were you in there talking to Kathleen, too?"

Ewan gave a nod. "I talked to her after Uncle Hugh left the house. She's doing quite well."

"I don't give a whit how she's doing."

Hugh cleared his throat. "Maybe it would be best if you let us finish in private. I'll come down to the brickyard later this afternoon."

"You said you'd be there this morning. This won't take long, and Margaret might just as well hear it, too. Laura Woodfield and I are going to marry within the next six weeks. I want you to move forward with our partnership prior to the marriage. I've been more than patient, and I think it's time for an agreement to be signed."

The blaze in the fireplace was no match for the fire in Margaret's angry eyes. "There! You see, Hugh? I told you that woman was going to weasel her way back into the business. She's convinced Ewan to marry her and has him pushing you for a partnership before the wedding." She dropped to the settee and blotted her upper lip with her handkerchief. "I do feel like I'm going to faint."

Hugh arched a brow and drew close to Ewan's side. "We need to speak privately, Ewan. I've got no quarrel with you marrying the Woodfield woman, but you know how Margaret feels. You should never have brought this up in front of her."

"Better she knows from my lips than to hear it around town, don't you think?"

"Aye, but you picked a bad time."

Ewan hiked a shoulder and lowered his voice. "Then maybe you should be the one to tell her that Laura and I are going to adopt Kathleen's child."

"Sure and you've done it now, Ewan." Hugh grasped his arm and led him toward the door. He glanced over his shoulder as they neared the doorway. "I'm going to show Ewan out, Margaret." He continued to hold onto Ewan's arm as they strode toward the front door. "She'll never forgive this, Ewan. You're making me life more difficult by the minute, and you're not helping yourself any, either. She'd get over your marrying Laura Woodfield because of the social connections, but adopting Kathleen's child — you're taking it too far, me boy."

"Are you thinking of the child or of yourself, Uncle Hugh? I know Aunt Margaret will be difficult to live with when she finds out, but I'm praying she'll soon see that her actions only make her look small in the eyes of others. Kathleen has asked forgiveness for what she's done, but Margaret won't even acknowledge that her behavior toward her sister is offensive and wrong." He tapped his uncle's chest with his forefinger. "And you know it is, Uncle Hugh."

"Aye, but I must live with the woman. I've tried to talk to her, but you can see how far I get. Don't say anything about the babe just yet. Let me tell her in due time."

"Don't wait too long or she'll hear it from others, and that would be even worse."

Hugh sighed. "Can you not keep news of the babe to yourselves for a wee bit longer?"

"I suppose we can. I haven't told the girls.

Laura and I agreed we'd speak to them together. I'll explain to Laura and ask her to refrain from telling any of her acquaintances. Of course, I don't know if Mrs. Woodfield will tell anyone of our plans, but I think she'll cooperate. Right now, she's more interested in the hurried wedding arrangements."

His uncle's shoulders relaxed. "And that's as it should be. The wedding is the most important thing right now."

"And the partnership agreement. You'll see to it before my wedding day?"

Hugh patted Ewan on the shoulder. "First I have to get Margaret settled to the fact that you're marrying Miss Woodfield. Then I'll see about the agreement. You'd better get back to the brickyard. Don't want any more accidents happening."

Hugh turned and stepped back inside. The click of the closing door resounded in Ewan's ears.

Chapter 32

Ainslee, Adaira, and Rose, wearing dresses of burgundy velvet, led the procession down the stairway of Woodfield Manor. Wearing her mother's reconstructed ivory satin gown, edged with fine Irish lace, Laura followed Rose down the steps. Laura's mother had moved mountains to make certain the gown was a perfect fit for Laura — and completed on time. Seamstresses in Bartlett had worked day and night to recreate Mrs. Woodfield's wedding dress into a slightly more modern gown. Wearing the rather ornate dress had been Laura's one concession to her mother. Mrs. Woodfield had prepared a long invitation list, but Laura had held fast to her decision for a small wedding at home. Her mother finally agreed to the arrangement but only after Laura agreed to wear the fancy wedding gown.

In truth, both women knew there hadn't been adequate time to organize a large wedding before the baby's birth. Laura now believed her mother had prepared the long invitation list only as a ruse to gain Laura's approval of the wedding gown. And it had worked.

An invitation had been sent to Hugh and Margaret, and though Margaret refused to attend, Hugh agreed he would be present. Hugh had apologized for Margaret's refusal, adding she still held fast to the idea that Laura was marrying Ewan to regain an interest in the brickyard. In addition, his wife believed that Ewan and Laura were attempting to cause her pain and embarrassment by adopting Kathleen's child.

Neither allegation was true, but Margaret remained unconvinced and unwilling to attend the marriage ceremony. Ewan still hadn't received his partnership agreement, but Hugh promised it would be waiting for him when he returned from their wedding trip to Pittsburgh. Laura wondered if Hugh's promise was sincere, but only time would tell. Unless Margaret convinced her husband to break his promise, Laura held out hope that Hugh would finally keep his word.

Ewan stood near the fireplace in the grand parlor, looking more handsome than ever in his black formal wear. Since his uncle had deemed it impossible to stand as Ewan's best man, his cousin, Ian, agreed to do the honors. Mrs. Woodfield had seen to proper attire for Ian, but the poor fellow still looked as out of place as a stem of thistle in a bouquet of roses. The preacher was positioned near Ewan's side, and tall gold urns filled with fresh evergreens flanked either side of the fireplace. The three girls took their places to the left of the minister as Laura stepped forward to stand beside Ewan.

He tipped his head close. "You look beautiful."

She smiled up at him, her heart swelling with joy and thankfulness that this fine man wanted to become her husband, that they would soon become parents of a newborn babe, and that Rose, Adaira, and Ainslee would become more than her friends. They would now be her sisters, and she and Ewan would have the family they both desired.

The preacher led them through their vows. After they had each promised to love and cherish the other for the remainder of their days, he pronounced them husband and wife. "Ewan, you may kiss your bride." The preacher smiled at the couple as he closed his Bible.

"This is the moment I've been waiting for

all day." Ewan grinned at Laura, then lowered his head and kissed her with such passion that the preacher cleared his throat. Ewan released his bride and turned to the preacher. "Is there something wrong?"

The preacher chuckled. "The rest of us would like to partake of the refreshments. I was afraid the food would grow stale if I didn't interrupt that kiss."

Ewan laughed and patted the preacher on the shoulder. "After conducting such a fine wedding, I would not want you to eat stale food." He waved to the others. "The preacher is going to lead you to the refreshments."

Mrs. Woodfield stepped to Laura's side. "You and Ewan are supposed to go first, my dear, not the preacher."

"We're not in any hurry, Mother. We've already broken with many wedding traditions, so why not this one, as well?"

Mrs. Woodfield grasped the preacher's arm. "Very well, then. Come along, everyone. There are refreshments to be enjoyed."

Darach and Elspeth remained close to Ian and his wife as they followed Mrs. Woodfield into the other room. In the end, neither Uncle Hugh nor any of the other Irish relatives had appeared. Ewan wasn't certain why, but he assumed Uncle Hugh feared

Aunt Margaret's wrath, and the others feared losing their jobs at the brickyard. Though he would have liked to have them there to celebrate and witness his marriage, he wouldn't let their absence ruin their day. Herman Lofton had appeared to witness the marriage, along with several members of Mrs. Woodfield's social circle.

Ewan grasped Laura's hand and kissed her palm. "Remember the day Rudy Banks failed to watch the fire in the kilns and the damage we suffered at the brickyard?"

His question puzzled her. "Why would you think of that terrible event on our wedding day?"

"There's a good lesson to be learned from all of the ruin we suffered that day." He ran his finger across her lips. "The adversity at the brickyard was a reminder to me that love and bricks both need a slow, steady burn in order to become strong and withstand the test of time. I promise to tend the fire of love between us and never let it go out."

He cupped her cheek in his palm, traced the curve of her cheek with his thumb, and once again claimed her lips, just as she had claimed his heart.

Laura held her hand to the light and

watched the sun glint off the gold band on her finger. *Mrs. McKay. Mrs. Ewan McKay.* She turned and smiled at her bridesmaids, who'd gathered in her bedchamber to help her prepare for her wedding trip. "You all will need to teach me how to be a sister. I haven't any practice."

Ainslee flopped on the bed. "We'll make sure you know all the basics."

"And what would those be?"

"How to share secrets. How to giggle half the night. How to have a good cry."

"Girls." Rose held up the claret traveling dress Laura had chosen as her going-away outfit. "There will be plenty of time to tell Laura all those things when she returns. Her new husband is waiting."

Adaira sank onto the bed beside her twin. "And how to put up with a bossy big sister." She stuck out her tongue in Rose's direction.

Laura chuckled and asked the girls to help her change. She didn't want to keep Ewan waiting on their wedding day. Once dressed, she pinned her matching hat in place and twirled in front of her new sisters. "How do I look?"

Ainslee crawled off the bed. "Too good for Ewan."

They shared a laugh. The first as sisters,

506

and it warmed Laura's heart.

A knock on the door startled them. "Are you all kidnapping my bride?" Ewan called.

Rose managed to stifle her laughter. "She'll be right out."

Laura held out her hands and wiggled her fingers, asking the girls to join her. The four of them formed an intimate circle. "I want to thank you all for loving and accepting me into your family. You each mean the world to me, and I promise I will do my best to make our home one that is filled to the brim with love and faith."

"And babies?"

The hope in Adaira's eyes sent a familiar jolt of pain through Laura. "There will only be the one baby, I'm afraid. I had an accident when I was about your age. The doctor said I would never be able to have children."

Beside her, Rose sucked in a breath, then squeezed Laura's hand while Adaira shrugged. "It's just as well. One screaming baby will be more than enough." Ainslee slipped her arm through Rose's. "And it just means Rose will have to get married a lot sooner."

The four of them made a second procession down the staircase to where Ewan waited impatiently for his bride. He met her at the foot of the stairs. "Our trunks have been loaded. Are you ready?"

Laura glanced around. "I'd like to say good-bye to Kathleen and tell her we're praying for her."

Ewan feared they might miss their train if they delayed any longer, so Rose offered to extend Laura's message and hurried away to do so. Laura kissed her mother's cheek, and then she and Ewan were whisked away by the well-wishers toward the carriage. Two gallant white horses snorted and pawed at the earth, eager to depart.

Ewan assisted her inside, then climbed in and settled himself beside her. "Ready to start our life together?"

"Absolutely."

"Zeke, how fast can you get us to the station?"

Zeke lifted the reins. "I'll get you there on time. You can be sure."

"Wait!" Rose raced toward the carriage. She pressed her hand to her midsection and looked knowingly at her brother. "You can't leave. It's *time.*"

"Now?" His voice hitched.

She nodded.

Laura dug her fingers into his arm. "But it's too soon."

"God's taken care of us every step of the

way, Laura. It's going to be all right. Have faith."

She met her husband's gaze, steady and sure. His belief was so strong. Could she ever feel as sure as he? As they walked back into the house and began the long wait, she thought of all God had blessed her with — three beautiful sisters, a mother who would do anything for her, a wonderful husband. He'd even delivered her from Winston.

Still, all that didn't take away the pain of loss. Her beloved father had been taken away. Her ability to bear a child was gone. Why? Would she lose this child, too? Had all her trials fulfilled a God-ordered purpose? Had they been fires to strengthen her like bricks in a kiln?

Kathleen's screams rent the air, and Laura stiffened. As if he sensed her fears, Ewan wrapped his arm around her shoulders and drew her against his side. "Our baby is about to enter the world."

Lord, please help my unbelief.

Tears coursed down her cheeks as Laura presented their newborn daughter to her husband. "She's perfect, Ewan."

He took the babe in his arms and stroked the back of his index finger against the infant's cheek. "Aye. That she is. I feel my heart is nearly bursting with love today. Very few men get a new wife and a new babe on the same day."

Laura sat down beside him. "God is so good."

"I'm glad you see that, my love." He glanced up. "And how is Kathleen?"

"Dr. Balch says she did very well. From the size of our daughter, he says he likely miscalculated the date she was to make her arrival." Laura dabbed at her tears. "Kathleen has given us a great gift."

Ewan pressed a kiss to the baby's forehead. "Aye, that she has."

Watching Ewan fall in love with their baby took Laura's breath away. Why had she ever doubted God? He'd not abandoned her. He'd taken every impossible situation and given her the family she'd always desired.

She was a wife.

And a sister.

And a mother.

Ten tiny fingers and ten tiny toes. Ewan had counted them twice already.

Everything was exactly as it should be.

ABOUT THE AUTHOR

Judith Miller is an award-winning author whose avid research and love for history are reflected in her bestselling novels. Judy makes her home in Topeka, Kansas.